The
Inheritance

ALSO BY CAUVERY MADHAVAN:

Paddy Indian (2001)
The Uncoupling (2002)
The Tainted (2020)

The Inheritance

Cauvery Madhavan

HopeRoad Publishing
c/o Peepal Tree Press
17 Kings Avenue
Leeds LS6 1QS

www.hoperoadpublishing.com
First published in Great Britain by HopeRoad in 2024

A CIP catalogue record for this book is available from the
British Library.

ISBN: 978-1-913109-33-2

eISBN: 978-1-913109-41-7

Supported using public funding by
ARTS COUNCIL
ENGLAND

10 9 8 7 6 5 4 3 2 1

For,
Beara and all who belong there

Ar scáth a chéile a mhaireann na daoine
It is in each other's shadow that people live

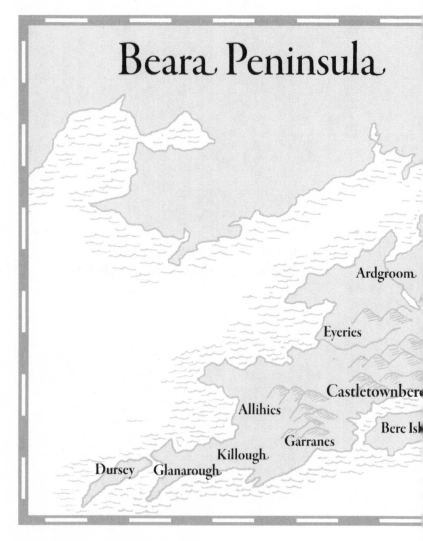

Beara Peninsula

Ardgroom

Eyeries

Castletownbere

Allihies

Bere Island

Garranes

Killough

Dursey Glanarough

Map data from OpenStreetMap
© OpenStreetMap
© JamesNunn

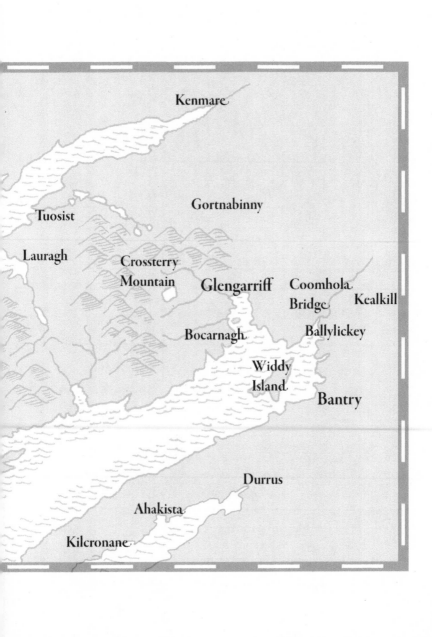

CHAPTER ONE

Glengarriff, Ireland, April 1986

It all began the day he found out that his sister was his mother. As the minibus hiccupped its way up the steep rutted road, Marlo repeated that to himself: *This journey started when I found out that Mary was my mam. And Mam was my nana.* The revelation had made his head spin for a good few days. In fact, his whole life was still spinning out of control, nearly. Maybe things would be better now that he was finally in Ireland – at least, that's what everyone had said repeatedly. It had taken him several weeks before he agreed that heading to the Beara peninsula, to the old cottage in Glengarriff, might be a move in the right direction. Perhaps.

'A chance to start afresh, son.'

'Don't fecking call me that, Mary. You'll never be me mam.'

She had teared up. 'Ah, Christ! Don't be like that, Marlo. It is what it is now, for God's sake.'

He looked at his sister and his mother facing him across the table in their new avatars as his mother and his grandmother. 'You keep telling me no one in Glengarriff knows – but are you sure?'

They both nodded. 'No one, not in Ireland and not even here, in London.' Mam reached out and took his hand in hers, squeezing it hard as Mary continued, 'Any other way and we'd have lost you. I'd have lost you.'

Mam wiped her eyes. 'Yes, Mary would've lost you, d'you understand?'

Four months later, at the airport, Mary had pressed a medallion into his palm and hugged him. 'Write every week and ring us when you can. Mam said there used to be a phone box by the Garda station in the village. Ring me at the surgery – I know Dr Khan won't mind.'

'I'll ring Mam when I can. Mrs Kelly won't mind giving her a shout across the landing.'

'OK, but call me too.'

Now, as he peered into the darkness outside the bus, he ran his finger around the smooth oval edge of the holy medal in his coat pocket. *St Jude! What the feck, Mary? I'm not a fecking lost cause.*

The bus came to a stop and the driver turned round to him. 'Right, lad, journey's end but it may as well be land's end. This here's your house, nobody lives past this cottage. The road rises up another mile and stops at the lake with nothing beyond except mountains, higher still, and heavy bog.' The man was smiling now. 'You're the image of your mam, d'you know? I was in school with Agnes right the way through from Low Infants. Ask her about me – Mossie Hanley. She'll remember me for sure. Meself and Agnes, we used to walk to school together.' He pointed into the dark with his chin. 'Just down that boreen there. Five minutes if we decided to race, ten if we walked. Below that gate and across the footbridge to Youngfields. A Dutch family bought the old schoolhouse a few years ago and, fair play to them, at least they've kept it standing. Put in a new-fangled sun room from Holland and all, they did. Tell Agnes, you tell her that our little school's still standing.'

Then he slapped his forehead. 'Ah, shite! I meant to show you as we passed by it in the village – the phone box is beside the gates at the Garda station. The coins jam it up sometimes and then you can blather on for ages for the cost of nothing. Tell Agnes when you ring, tell her I married Assumpta. But Jesus, would you look at the time, it's late and I'm back on the road to Cork early in the morning so I'd better be heading home meself. I drive five days a week and never let me customers down. All year round, bar Christmas Day. Assumpta wants that painted on the side of the bus.'

His hands made a wave with a flourish. 'The Beara Bus

Company. Allihies–Bantry–Cork. Monday to Friday. But I said to her it's a paint job or the new oven, and good woman that she is herself, she went with the oven. Right, lad, grab your bags, don't be keeping me now, I'd best be off. Be sure to tell your mam I asked after her.'

Marlo shuffled his large duffel bag down the steps of the bus. *Will I tell him Agnes is actually my nana?* 'You're good to have dropped me right to the house, Mossie. I'd never have found my way here from Glengarriff.'

'Ah, no worries, lad, sure aren't we your nearest neighbour? That was my house we passed there – before that last bad bend, when I stuck her into first gear to bring us up the mountain. I'd go the extra mile seeing as you are Agnes's lad, but sure, there wasn't even the extra mile in it, no there wasn't.'

With that he tooted the horn and began executing a deft three-point turn in the small cobbled yard. Another toot of the horn and he drove off, leaving Marlo in pitch dark.

Jesus. Mam had said it would be dark, but he couldn't even see his own hands. He fumbled for the small torch in the pocket of his backpack and sighed with relief when the thin beam of light came on. The key will be inside the house on the kitchen table, the solicitor had said over the phone. The back door is on a latch, just walk in and it's all yours.

And here I am, walking into what's all mine.

Marlo woke to a knocking. It was persistent, sharp. 'Bloody hell! I'm coming!' he yelled in the direction of the stairs as he pulled his jeans on and grabbed the jumper off the floor. He had crawled into bed last night, exhausted with the long journey from London, and having eaten a soggy egg sandwich, untouched since he had bought it in Gatwick, he had got into the sleeping bag that he had packed as an afterthought.

'Christ! Give me a moment! I'm coming!' he shouted down again as the knocking persisted. On top of the landing, he caught sight of himself in the bathroom mirror and, stopping for a moment, he smoothed down his hair.

He struggled with the front door and when he finally managed to yank it open there was no one there. The knocking hadn't stopped though and, stepping out, Marlo walked quickly around to the back of the house, past an empty lean-to woodshed built against the gable end of the cottage and rounded the corner to find himself in the rear yard where the bus had dropped him off last night. In the deep sill of the kitchen window a crow sat knocking on the pane of glass. Aware of Marlo, it turned around, cocked its head and did a short jig, hopping from one foot to the other.

'Well, what's with the knocking?'

The bird flapped off to a gnarled holly tree by the metal gate. Marlo eyed the bird and laughed. 'Morning, crow! That's a fine welcome. Better than being woken up by trains rattling the windows at the gaff back in Croydon. Or Mam snoring. Yeah, I'd be looking at me like that too, talking to a bloody crow.'

Dawn was just breaking. It might even get warm, thought Marlo as he dug his hands into his pockets and shivered. Then, turning around to head back in the front door was that moment that he would remember for ever. He let out a low whistle and stepped out towards the wooden fence instead, to gape at the vista. *Mam wasn't fecking wrong. She'd said it would take your breath away.*

'I can live with this, I think,' he said to the crow which had darted down from the holly tree and was preening itself on the far end of the fence. Marlo stood at the rail and looked down the near vertical slope, a crazy quilt of undulating green and ragged brown patches marked off by lichen-crusted stone walls. He realised why the bus had seemed to struggle its way up last night, needing every bit of the foot on the pedal from Mossie to power up the road. The cottage sat on a ledge high up the side of a range of mountains and the valley that stretched out below seemed to be many miles wide from north to south.

He could see white gable ends, a pink one too amidst distant trees. A few aging farmhouses, their smoking chimneys signalling their presence, dotted the mountains opposite – mountains that rose just as sharply from the floor of the valley as the steep drop at his feet. The rising sun bounced off a red corrugated roof, miles distant, wedged between craggy outcrops of rocks. *I'll walk up there one day, walk up that mountain and look at my house from the other side.* Below his feet the mountain fell sharply away from the yard. Meadow grasses were bent low with dew and clumps of gorse left bright blotchy patches in field after field, all the way down to dark green rushes that guarded the banks of a river far below. He was sure it was a river – it's steady gurgling could be heard even at this distance, and it had to be water that he could see glistening through an untidy curtain of leafless sally willows along what appeared to be a boggy edge.

Marlo watched the crow swoop down the valley and followed it till it disappeared into a patch of forestry. He shivered as he stepped back into the house; it seemed colder inside and was darker too. *This is the rest of my life now.* Where do I start? Coffee? Shower? Rereading the solicitors' letter? Or go through Mam's instructions, meticulous and detailed, taking up the first four pages of a 1986 page-a-day diary, a freebie given to Mary by a medical rep who regularly tried to chat her up at the reception desk, every time he called to Dr Khan's surgery.

Marlo stood inside the door and looked around carefully. The house was just as Mam had described it: 'A room with a large hearth on one end and on the other end a small kitchen extension, though God alone knows how they cut through that thick stone wall to add it on. The two bedrooms upstairs were added by Uncle Joseph the summer he came back from the missions. Uncle Patrick followed a year later but he had insisted, I saw the letter myself, with very precise instructions that a bathroom be added too. They were the talk of Glengarriff, they were. An upstairs bathroom! But they were priests and back from years of doing God's work in the Congo. Comfort was due and comforts they got. "The blessed brothers", they were called – Father Joseph and Father Patrick. Oh Lord, I remember how my back was broke and fingers stiff embroidering all those sheets with their initials entwined around crosses and shamrocks!'

Mam had then burst her side laughing. 'Would you believe, Uncle Patrick wanted serpents too! Me mam would have none of it, Marlo. She had prayed for them, she had prayed *to* them even, but when her brother asked for serpents on his pillowcase she told him off. "And you a priest, Father Pat! Our Lady bless and protect us!" She wouldn't stop crossing herself all morning.'

A beam of light worked its way past the front door which was still ajar and as Marlo turned around to shut it, the sun came up over the canopy of dense forest in the adjacent valley that could be seen from the front of the cottage, stretching all the way towards Glengarriff and its small harbour in the east. He walked over to the kitchen window from where he watched the fingers of sunlight reaching out through the old holly tree, moving over the damp cobbles in the yard, leaving their smooth edges shiny and glistening.

He opened the six presses, three under the counter and three above, but they were all empty bar the one under the sink which had the desiccated remains of something once delectable in a mousetrap that was still waiting, ready to be sprung. A large Stanley range, its chocolate brown enamel chipped in places, dominated the kitchen and a tired-looking refrigerator occupied the remaining space.

Marlo turned on the tap in the Belfast sink and suddenly the tiny cottage burst into life. A low moan filled the roof space, and the tap began to shudder violently. Under the sink, the pipes rattled against each other like they were possessed, and the ferocious vibration carried all the way behind the length of the presses and straight up the wall behind the fridge. As he reached out to close the tap, an explosion, that Marlo would later in a

6

phone call to Mary describe as the loudest watery fart he had ever heard, made him jump out of his skin. Dark red, grainy water coughed out in fits and starts, splattering the sink and the Formica counter with thick residue at every expectoration. He watched, paralyzed for a minute or so, and then looked around frantically for something to wipe up the mess. The tap had calmed down to a gurgle and the water in the sink went from red to brown. By the time he had mopped up the countertop with his hastily removed T-shirt, the only thing to hand, he knew that the first thing he'd have to do was to head into Glengarriff for supplies.

I'll have to get myself a cycle at the very least.

Marlo walked down the steep hill, carefully zigzagging every few steps to avoid losing his footing and being carried away by the mini avalanche of loose stones and bits of the road that were breaking free and rolling down ahead of him. A strip of coarse grass grew right down the centre, all the way down the slope and continued beyond where the road disappeared around a sharp bend. It was obvious the road to his cottage had seen very few cars in a long time and the grassy spine was all that was holding the tarmac together. He walked down past two ruined stone cottages, roofless and draped in ivy, stuffed with square bales of hay that had been loosely covered with a tarpaulin. The narrow road was made treacherous by deep ditches that ran on both sides and to the edges of which clung untidy fuchsia hedges and green straps of clumping crocosmia in their hundreds, camouflaging the danger completely. He made a mental note to always stay well clear of the edge of the road.

He had just rounded the sharp bend at the bottom of the hill when he was set upon by two collies, who leaped effortlessly across the cattle grid of an old farmhouse set right beside the road. They bounded right up to him and circled around, barking like their lives depended upon it. Marlo stood his ground and continued to walk, slower now as he quickly looked around

7

the hedges for a stick while shrugging his backpack off his shoulders, readying it in case he needed to wield it against the dogs. The collies went into a frenzy as he got closer to the house. He heard a door slam and the next thing the dogs stopped to look back.

'Come back here, you divils. You'll have that poor lad scared and all. Don't you be minding them now, Marlo O'Sullivan. Ye're welcome home to Glengarriff, you are.'

The dogs were unsure now, looking back at the house before turning their attention to Marlo again, their tails wagging tentatively as a tall and very thin woman walked out around from the back of the farmhouse and waited at the gatepost, wiping her hands on her striped apron, her bony face beaming as she looked Marlo up and down, making no attempt to hide her curiosity. One click of her fingers and both the dogs jumped back across the cattle grid to sit obediently at her feet.

'The black one is Blackie, and this here is Spot on account of his spots. Mother and son they are.'

Marlo hitched his backpack on again and, sitting down on his haunches, stretched out his hand, calling the dogs by their names.

'I might get a dog myself. I'm Marlo, but you already know that. This is Mossie's place, isn't it, and you're Assumpta?'

She nodded. 'They'll be as good as yours once they get to know you, the two eejits. Come visiting, they will. Making sheep eyes till they get a crumb of something. And yes, that's me, Assumpta. I've been keeping a lookout because I thought ye might be hungry, thirsty at least for a cup of tea. Mossie said you looked right shattered last night and he didn't think you'd any food brought along. How could the lad have brought milk and bread all the way from London? I said to him. But look, I've the kettle ready to go and sausages in the pan. Mind now, the grid is a bit loose, so step along the edge,' she added.

Marlo didn't hesitate, and minutes later he was sitting in

her kitchen, cradling a mug of hot tea and waiting for his breakfast to cook. Assumpta had insisted he have a fried egg, black pudding and rashers along with the sausages and Marlo's protest was polite but not sincere and as he sat with the two dogs nuzzling his hands, he confessed as much.

'I was headed to Glengarriff for supplies – there's nothing in the cottage so this is very kind of you.'

'Sure, it's no bother at all, Marlo, just being neighbourly, seeing as we're going to be neighbours. Marlo, it's a strange name they gave you. Did your mam pick it or your da? Wait, let me see, it was your mam, wasn't it? She would've picked that name. They say she had notions, but they'd say that about anyone who'd want to better themselves, they would. She was best off in London, you know what I mean? In the company of strangers with no one minding her affairs for her.'

Marlo had his mouth full and he nodded noncommittally. The dogs were on either side of the spindleback chair that he was sitting on, Blackie alert with expectation and Spot nudging his thigh gently. *I'm going to have to keep Assumpta on my side. Imagine if I told her Mary was my mother.*

'It's Marlon, actually, but no one ever calls me that.'

'Marlon? Agnes was a quare one all right. Don't get me wrong now, I liked her, your mam. She'd not know me really, don't think she'd remember me even, seeing as I was much younger. I was still in primary school down below in Youngfields, just across the river. Dutch family own the place now, Pieter and Ella, still foreign in their ways even after all these years. I was in Miss Casey's class, you know that time when your mam and Nealie— I mean, when she was found out and they had to marry. Sure, it's no secret so I don't mind telling you, and didn't it all end so well. Your sister Mary was baptised the same day as my younger brother. Agnes and Nealie took the boat soon after that and we never saw them since.'

'Mam might come now, she and Mary, now that I'm here. I need to get settled in first.'

'And she'd be very welcome too. So, what are you going to do with yerself? To settle in?'

'I might hitch a ride to Bantry from the village. See if I can get a few bits of furniture, sheets and towels, that sort of thing. Plus, I need to shop for supplies. I mean, for food and things, and buy a paper and I guess I'll need a radio, maybe rent a TV. I'd like to get sorted quickly. I plan to.'

'It's not often a man would get handed a house to call his own and at your age at that. The lad from the solicitors told Father Angelo, our parish priest, that the blessed brothers didn't leave you money, just the deeds to the house. So, what d'you plan to do to settle here? People are leaving the peninsula, you know. Very few coming back this direction.'

'I'm a writer.'

'For a paper like?'

'I'm going to write a book. But yes, I write for a newspaper too.'

Assumpta rolled her eyes as she put a knitted tea cosy over the teapot and sat down at the table across from him. 'Nothing ever happens in Beara, didn't your mam tell you that? If you were doing the death notices you'd likely get more work.'

'It won't be news really. I'm writing for an American paper. A weekly column for the *Montana Courier*. Just about life in Beara.'

'Well, wait till Mossie hears this when he gets back this evening! I told him that you'd only be coming here if you intended to keep the cottage and I was right, wasn't I? An American paper! Sure, why would you want to rent a TV when you could buy one with what they're paying you.'

Marlo laughed. *Jesus, she's going to be formidable.* 'It's only a short piece each time, a Saturday feature. They don't pay anywhere near top dollar, but it'll be steady money that'll keep me in bread and butter anyway.'

10

'The *Montana Courier*! Those Butte Irish never forgot where they came from and I'll tell you, lad, that's good for the likes of us. Mossie gets a few on the bus on and off every summer. Come looking for their roots, they do. He has to keep reminding them not to fall down those old copper mine shafts when they go poking around Allihies.'

Marlo laughed. 'They've done that?'

'The stories I could tell you about the returning Irish! But you wouldn't want to be putting any of that into your column. They might think you were taking the mick. They don't like that, they don't. Haven't much of a sense of humour, the Yanks – when it comes to the auld sod, they're all very earnest about their roots. Are you going to be writing about us then? Or about yourself and your new cottage? A bit of both will be nice but best not to mention any names. I'll tell you all I know – only if you want, mind. I wouldn't know anything about high falutin' newspaper columns though, you'll have to work that out for yourself.'

'I think you are going to be a goldmine of information, Assumpta.' *The mother lode, actually.*

'A hot drop?' she said, readying the teapot, a happy smile on her face.

'I should be heading off. Thank you for the breakfast, it'll keep me going for a while. I'll have to repay you for your hospitality once I've my place in order. What time does Mossie head off in the morning?'

'Oh, he's gone early, by six. He's a good man, my Mossie. He calls into the church and then to our son before heading off to Allihies. Our Thomas, the Lord bless and protect him, is buried in the graveyard as you come into the village. Mossie is with him every morning for a few minutes before heading to Allihies to start the bus run. I sometimes feel we should live in Allihies to save all the driving back and forth. See, he drives thirty miles down to the end of the peninsula to start the run only to come back through Glengarriff again to head to Cork. And the same thing on the way back. All the way past us here to Allihies at the tip and only then back home again. He's well knackered at the end of it all. Still, he has lots of regulars from Castletownbere, so he hasn't a choice, my poor Mossie. He's good man, he is.'

Marlo felt compelled to ask her the difficult question. 'Your son, what happened? I'm sorry to hear it.'

She crossed herself. 'Thomas, may he rest in peace, my poor lad. He got the measles – many did at that time, but he was the one the Lord took. Would have been twenty-five this year, about your age, I suppose.'

'I'm sorry Assumpta, so sorry to hear of your loss.'

'It's like he never left us though. With us all the time he is and a great comfort to me too. If I feel terrible on a day, sure I just tell him I miss him and you know something, Marlo, the black clouds pass. I'll take you to see him one day soon. Mossie has the grave beautiful and all.'

She gave him a fill of water in an old lemonade bottle as he left. 'It's a thirst-making walk, up and down the road, but once you are past Pooleen Wood it stays on the flat, well, nearly anyway. The best way to hitch a ride is to keep walking out of the village towards Bantry. You'll be picked up before the golf club if you're lucky.'

The dogs had followed him companionably for some distance, but at the crest of the next hillock Blackie stopped and let out a short sharp bark. Spot returned to his mother immediately and both dogs stayed, watching and wagging their tails till Marlo rounded the corner.

'Good dogs!' he shouted back and, smiling, set off at a steady pace.

Walls of rhododendron rose on either side of the narrow road, their magenta-tipped buds in the thousands holding promise of a great display later in the season. Through the dense hedgerows he could make out haphazard quilts of small fields on both sides, most of them full of rushes and a few larger

12

ones with what looked like poor grazing. But the clearings were few and the road cut its way through an impenetrable tangle of ancient oak, beech and holly, some growing in storybook style through cracked boulders the size of houses. The forest floor was forbidding, pocked with dark peaty pools and log-jammed with rotting branches entombed in ivy. Mosses and ferns in myriad green shades, jewel-like in their vividness, filled every wet crevice and he was certain he could hear a river rushing along somewhere to the right as he walked.

He had walked nearly a mile, stopping now and again to peer through the forest, wondering if it was possible at all to walk into it, to explore, even to camp in it overnight or if he would find himself sinking straight into its boggy heart. The sound of a car backfiring made him stop and wait by the side of the road. He could hear it approaching, gears crashing as it whined up the short steep hill that he had himself huffed over only a few minutes ago.

'Agnes's lad, are ye? Get in the back if ye like. Just push it all to the other end, lad, and make room for yerself there. What'd they call ye?'

Marlo bent down to look into the beat-up little car at the large swarthy woman who filled up the front of the vehicle. *How did you even fit in and how will you get out?*

'Thank you. If you leave me off in Glengarriff, it would be great. I'm Marlo O'Sullivan. How did you know? I mean, d'you know my mam?' As he got into the back of the car, he wondered about the missing passenger seat as he stretched out his legs into the empty space in front of him. Beside him the rest of the seat was full of old feed and fertiliser bags and empty catering-size mayonnaise buckets. He was sure the small dried pellets that he had flicked off the seat were sheep droppings, which would explain the smell that had hit him as soon as he closed the car door.

'You tell yer mam that Dolores picked you up and then tell me what she says.'

'I'll do that, Dolores.'

'Be sure now to tell me the first thing she says.'

Marlo laughed. 'You've me fired up to ring her now. A mystery on my first day here. I only got to Beara last night.'

'There's lots that's waiting to see ye, to see how ye turned out, like.'

'Really?'

'Country people are curious, but ye can't be blaming us. Ye'd need to know the measure of yer neighbours in these parts. Are ye good for help before the sun rises and are ye any use after closing? The helping hand or the big talker, we've both in this valley, by God. Are ye a drinking man, can ye be relied on or are ye both, the best of the best? I wouldn't trust a Pioneer meself, no I wouldn't. Did ye say Marlo, did ye? Now what kind of a name would that be?'

Take your pick, Marlo lad, valley of the squinting windows or the glen of the formidable women.

'I was christened Marlon. My drinking mates call me that sometimes but otherwise it's Marlo.'

'So, Marlo, ye like a few jars in yer spare time but what will occupy ye the rest of the day? I heard the blessed brothers, Lord have mercy on their souls, I hear yer mother's uncles didn't leave ye money, just the cottage.'

'The lad from the solicitors' has been talking, has he?'

'His mother is me cousin. Ye know him too?'

'I feel like I do already. He hasn't been slow broadcasting my affairs.'

She was watching him in her rear-view mirror. 'Who else knows? I thought it was confidential.'

Marlo laughed. 'You'd think it was. But apparently not.'

'Don't take it to heart, lad, 'tis what happens when ye come home. What's the harm in little bits about ye slipping out here and there. A heap of good might well come of it. Ye might get offered some work, a job even, seeing as ye have the house but no money. See, that might be the worst of it. Me da, Lord keep him, always said nobody cares for a secretive fellow.'

Is she reprimanding me? Marlo looked out the window and decided to change the subject. 'So, are we neighbours, Dolores? The only house I had passed when you picked me up was Mossie and Assumpta's.'

'As the crow flies, closer. I'm across the valley from ye, on the mountain opposite, ye can see the gable end of my house from yer yard.'

'The pink one?'

'What d'you think of it, the colour?'

'It stands out all right. I mean, it was the first house I spotted this morning when I was in the yard. A fecking crow of all things woke me, I might have slept on for much longer.'

'Ah, that crow. They have great memories, ye know, crows. The blessed brothers rescued one as a fledgling and he roosts up with a great big flock in the beech trees at the bottom of the valley from ye. That was at least ten years ago now and if he's ringed ye'll know it's the same lad. They live long, d'ye know that? They'd see out twenty summers if they were lucky and as well fed as yer grand-uncles kept him. He comes for the bacon, that's what they gave him every day, bacon scraps. Poor divil must have been knocking the windows around the house these few months since they died. Ye keep feeding him, it's the least ye could do seeing as they left ye the house.'

Marlo laughed. 'At the risk of never being able to have a lie-in I'll put bacon on my shopping list, Dolores.'

The car slowed down as they approached a main road. 'I'm heading into Kealkil myself, how far are ye headed? Or will I leave ye off in Glengarriff?'

'Is that Bantry direction? I was headed to Bantry.'

'Ah yes, Kealkil is more than halfways there. Come with me

as far as the Co-op. There's someone coming and going to and from Bantry all day long from the Co-op and I'll make sure ye get a lift.' She looked back at him and smiled. 'It's that accent, ye know. People outside of Glengarriff – they won't know ye're Agnes's son. The accent riles people up, so don't be shy telling them who ye are. Save yerself the trouble, and if ye plan to stay lose it as fast as ye can, lad.'

She doesn't hold back, this one. 'I'm here to stay all right. I can't change who I am though.'

Dolores laughed. 'There was no bending that Agnes either and she's reared ye no different, has yer mam. Still, I'd be careful, lad, careful outside the glen.'

As she drove through Glengarriff, she pointed out the Garda station with its phone box and rattled off the names of the owners of the few shops and pubs that lined the narrow street.

'In and out through the village before ye can say hallelujah – that's how small it is. We'll get to the Eccles Hotel as we round this bend and then we are past Glengarriff – a matter of minutes and ye'd have seen it all.'

The Eccles Hotel came into view as she had promised and laid out across the road from the wrought-iron porch of its art deco façade, like a picture postcard, was the beautiful harbour, dotted with tiny islands and several boats, forested hills rising all around and, in the far distance, the hazy outline of the Sheep's Head Peninsula framed the waters of Bantry Bay. Marlo craned his neck to take in the view, and in the driver's seat Dolores sighed and, with a crash of the gears, the car swerved to the right and stopped along the roadside, by a low stone wall that overlooked a concrete slipway.

'Makes yer heart sing, doesn't it, but the first time ye see this view is not how 'twill be the next time or the next or the next even. The light, the wind, the feckin' rain and the state of yer mind make the permutations endless. That's Garnish Island there, the one with the Martello tower. Ye can go over on the ferry at the Blue Pool, takes a few minutes, that's all. Unless there's kids on board – then sometimes Dinny might linger where the seals bask on those rocks.'

She had her window rolled down and shaded her eyes as she pointed out the landmarks. 'Dinny runs a ferry across to Garnish in the summer months. He's a distant cousin of yer mam's. Would have made something of himself if he wasn't near deaf.'

As they drove off again, Marlo leaned forward in the seat. 'Thanks for stopping, Dolores, it's just as lovely as I had thought it would be.'

'Oh, did she keep it then? Did yer mam keep the framed photo of the view from the Eccles Hotel? We did a collection for them both and bought it for their wedding present because we just knew they wouldn't stay on. Ye know they both worked at the Eccles, don't ye? Agnes cleaned and yer father, Nealie, he helped in the kitchens, and both waited at the tables if it got busy. But then, ah listen ye are a grown lad, so you know the story no doubt. They had to marry because of Mary and then Mary arrived and they took the boat over soon after. It ended well for them and for yer sister. Until your father passed that is. Poor Nealie, he didn't know ye at all, did he, Lord have mercy on him. We thought Agnes might've come back then, ye know, when he was killed. What a terrible accident. But she didn't and who can blame her. After fifteen years in London, who'd want to be smothered all over again. She did well to hold her own, I'll give her that.'

'She still has the picture. Mary had it reframed for her recently.'

'A John Hinde. An actual photo, not a postcard like the ones in the tourist shops.'

'Yes, she reminds us of that often.'

Dolores turned around to look at him. 'Ye need to mind the good stuff. Not everything old is shite bric-a-brac. I see Americans carting off things like that all the time.' She put on a

Yank accent. *'Gee, honey, look what I found! Just darlin', isn't it?'* She shook her head 'They're stripping the country bare and we're letting them.'

The car slowed down again, and Dolores pointed to a sign on the right. 'The Golf Club. Herself's a great supporter. They aren't all bad, the Yanks.'

'Who's Herself?'

'Maureen, she's the pride of Glengarriff, she is. Maureen, ye know, our Maureen, Maureen O'Hara.'

'From the movies?'

'The one and only.'

That's my first column written. They'll love this in Butte, Montana. 'When did she come? I mean, has she lived here long?'

His question remained unanswered as Dolores was peering ahead. 'Ahh, would you look at him up ahead? That's Donal – the old fella's made it all the way to the bad bend at Dromgarriff without a lift. His lucky day so, that we're on the road.' She beeped on the horn as she slowed down. 'Push up there, lad, and make room for a good neighbour.'

After a lot of shuffling and shifting, the plastic bags and mayonnaise buckets were deposited in front, where the passenger seat should have been, around Marlo's outstretched feet. The old man eased himself into the car and from his seat behind Dolores he tapped her shoulder. 'You were slow coming. Nothing but breeze went past this last half hour out of the village.'

'Donal, why didn't ye just wait at the village? Easier than walking and wondering. Someday I'll find ye outside Bantry town, I will.'

'In my time, girl, there was no other way of getting to town except on your God-given two feet.'

In the rear-view mirror Marlo could see Dolores rolling her eyes. 'But then the same Lord himself gave us Mr Henry Ford, didn't he? But wait till I tell ye now, Donal, this here's Agnes and Nealie's lad.'

The old man pushed back the peak of his flat cap and examined Marlo. 'They were two fine men, the blessed brothers. Must have left the house to you for a reason. A higher purpose as they say.'

'What are ye blathering about, Donal? Sure, who else could they leave it to? They hadn't anyone else bar their sister's daughter. And this lad here being her only son, it's only natural like.'

Marlo looked at the old man. 'You knew my grand-uncles then?'

'Donal lives in Rossnagreena way up above me and when his fire is lit, Marlo, ye can see the smoke rise from between the trees, in the highest part of the mountains to the north of ye. Mind, it's a good ways across from yer house.'

'Will ye give an old fella a chance to speak or the lad might think me simple.' The old man turned to Marlo and smiled. 'Me and the blessed brothers. We liked each other, even though they was taken away to be proper schooled and all, ye know up in Cork city, in preparation for the seminary. Hand-picked by the Bishop is what the schoolmaster used to tell us every day. We were to look at them as shining examples and most of the lads hated them for it – but not me. Not once they told me what they were fed. Three times a day, better even than the pig me own mother fattened. I wanted to be like them, I did. They came home soon after being ordained and came to the school with a few oranges for us all, even showed us how to peel them! My first orange.' He stopped and clicked out his dentures in a noisy fashion, drooling a bit as he pushed them back in with a finger. 'What'd they call you then, lad?'

'Marlo.'

'Marlo. Fierce peculiar altogether.'

Here we go again. 'You're not the first to say so.'

'There was never an O'Sullivan in all of Beara called that, so you are a trendsetter boy – isn't that what they are called these days? Trendsetters.'

Dolores laughed. 'So yer Aisling is after sending ye more of her magazines then, Donal? Making ye trendy and all? It's a trendsetter ye are yourself.' She turned to Marlo. 'A cleverer girl in the valley ye wouldn't find than Donal's granddaughter. She's made it big in New York no less. Says the boss is a right bitch, but she'd never quit the high falutin' fashion magazine she works for. A breath of fresh air she is when she comes home. They did a shoot, that's what she called it, a few years ago in the glen, would ye believe it? In wedding dresses, the models draped on fallen trees in the forest and laying down on sheep shite in the turf bog up at Barley Lake. That's up the road, past your place, Marlo. They posed them all over my old tractor too, all the models together, dressed as bridesmaids, and they wanted to paint my house pink to match the headpieces, but I held off till the art director, that's what they called the fella, agreed to pay for the inside of the house to be given a lick too. Called me his Irish location manager and all, the big talker that he was, full of guff. Still, I took those Yanks places even Aisling wouldn't have known. They came in droves for a few years after, was good for business in Glengarriff and 'twas all because of her. She brought them here, didn't she, Donal?'

The old man nodded and was about to speak when his dentures came loose again. Her eye on the rear-view mirror, Dolores tutted and shook her head. 'Would ye ever listen to the community nurse and use the Poligrip, Donal? She said ye'd likely choke if ye'd food in yer mouth.'

'Can't stand the feckin' metallic taste of that yoke.'

'Ye'll get used to it, for God's sake.'

'How's about ye get—'

She didn't let him finish. 'Ye're a hard fella to keep an eye on, ye are.'

'I thank ye for it, keeping an eye on me, but yer nose, sure that's a different matter altogether'

'Sure, if it wasn't for me nose how would me eyes know what to look for, Donal?'

Marlo listened to the back and forth between the two neighbours. *I could make myself at home, I could give myself up to this life entirely, but I'd have to hand my life to them on a platter first.* But then he stopped listening, for the road had burst through the dense overhang of trees and enormous clumps of rhododendron, and without any warning the vast expanse of Bantry Bay came into view below them. He hadn't realised how much the road had climbed steadily from the harbour at Glengarriff and now, from high up at Derrycreha, two peninsulas could be seen outstretched for miles towards the distant Atlantic, their long rugged bodies cradling between them a calm, glassy bay streaked by the mid-morning sun. Three large oil tankers, anchored peacefully in the deep channel, looked like abandoned pieces of Lego and from the direction of the harbour in Glengarriff, a small fishing boat was chugging out towards mussel lines that streaked the water's surface.

Donal tapped his arm. 'It isn't always like this. Weather in these parts is a right moody bitch.'

'A stubborn bastard more like. Keeps coming back, unchanged.'

'She's a good one for the . . . what's it called now, Dolores?'

'Repartee, Donal. Re-part-tee.'

Donal gave a toothy grin as he imitated her. 'Reparteeee,' he drawled, rolling out his Rs. 'It always sounds better in them foreign accents.'

Marlo laughed. 'I'm not taking sides. But what's that island there with those huge silos, Dolores?'

'That's Whiddy, with the oil tanks. Put us on the map a few years ago, it did.'

'Where the oil terminal blew up? I remember watching that on the news in London.'

Dolores shook her head. "Twas the ship that blew up, an oil tanker, the *Betelgeuse*.'

'But the terminal is still in use?'

'They had it back and running an all in a matter of weeks. The country would've ground to a halt without that supply of oil coming in. Ye can take the ferry across if ye fancy a nice day out.'

'Not much to see there that ye can't see around us in the glen.'

'Don't be putting the lad off now, Donal. How's he to feel at home unless he sees all of it?'

'Oh, I plan to for sure. As soon as I've my cottage in order. I was thinking I'd work my way up from the foot of the peninsula in Allihies.'

'If you want to do it right, start in Dursey, boy.'

Dolores nodded. 'Yes, Donal's right. Dursey's where it all ended for the O'Sullivans. Looks like ye'll need a car soon. Put the word out for ye if you want. No point in giving some blackguards of a dealer a cut of hard-earned money. Sure, they're all plain thieves they are, the lot of them.'

'Don't go for the looks now, lad. Something strong, sturdy, with room for a ewe to be put into in a hurry. Or you'll be modifying your fancy drive like Dolores here.' Donal pointed to the empty space at Marlo's feet and started laughing.

'The lad's no farmer, Donal. Look at him! A young fella needs a young fella's car. Just make sure ye get something with a hitch,' said Dolores. 'It's easy enough to borrow a trailer off one of us in the glen.'

The two neighbours discussed what would be the ideal vehicle for him, and without warning the debate moved on to Jim O'Reilly's ugly yoke of a Renault 4. It didn't befit the Garda to be driving his mother's hand-me-down and it mattered not that she had left it to him on her deathbed. They rambled on seamlessly, touching on the size of her funeral and then despairing about Jim's father who had, to everyone's surprise, taken to drinking at home – after all, he was known to have given his wife a right good clather many a time. Marlo paid scant attention, nodding non-committedly now and again for he was lost in the loveliness of the landscape that each twist and turn in the road revealed.

They were following the coast quite closely now, the road dropping steadily to sea level. The tide was coming in filling up the rocky coves, pushing up gently against the mouths of rivers, creating eddies that swirled silently and, in the crystal-clear waters of the shallows, fields of seaweed swayed, slapping the rocks to the rhythm of the current. All along to the left as they drove, a few houses, some new and proudly sporting green-fronted lawns, dotted the lush lower hills that were abundant with trees and wide untidy hedgerows that hid deep ditches. On the slopes above them, the contrast was stark. Ancient stone walling rose vertically up the mountains behind derelict farmhouses that were shrouded by gorse left unfettered. And even higher still, the mountains were treeless, with meagre layers of grassy soil smeared in the nooks of fantastical limestone folds. They drove past villages that were signposted but not to be seen, and as they rounded the tiny cove at Coomhola he was surprised to see a small flock of swans bobbing in the sea.

Dolores smiled. 'There's a good more than swan around here that'll have ye wondering. It's a different world altogether is Beara.'

Marlo nodded. 'And d'you know what, Dolores? I think I'm going to love it.'

CHAPTER TWO

Am I gone completely soft in the head? Marlo was chopping up pieces of bacon and bread before adding in some of the scrambled egg that he had set aside from his own plate, for the morning treat he was preparing for Crow, who waited impatiently, tapping at the window and hopping around on the sill. He lifted the sash up just a few inches, gently, and slowly slid the white and blue enamel plate towards the bird who set to eating with gusto. Crow cocked his head this way and that between morsels, while Marlo took in for the umpteenth time the sheer beauty of his iridescent plumage. Up close, the overlapping layers were anything but black. A purple-green sheen ran through his feathers, turning metallic when the sun caught it, fluid, like the surface of an oil slick. He and the bird had established a routine these last few weeks but Crow was still wary and any sudden movements would send him flapping from the windowsill, hovering a few feet away in an ungainly fashion before the crumbs drew him back to the sill again.

Sometimes when the food was all gone the bird would tap at the window expectantly, his eyes watchful, and Marlo waited for this, never failing to marvel at his intelligence and the way his wings seemed to quiver with every harsh chirrup of anticipation when the sash was lifted and the plate replenished with crumbs that Marlo had held back for this very purpose. Minutes later Crow flew away without any fuss, beating his wings to rise high in the yard and then sweeping down in a graceful glide down the valley to the nests in the beech trees.

Marlo opened the kitchen door and stepped into the yard. The cobblestones were still wet from the night's rain and, as he leaned on the fence, he could see the smoke curling up from Dolores's chimney. The slopes on the mountain across the valley seemed to heave as small waves of tiny white dots moved in fits and starts, diagonally across the mountain. Marlo squinted, trying to locate the two dogs he knew were corralling the sheep towards the dipping tank that he had helped Mossie empty and clean out, just the previous evening. Faint whistles carried across the valley and in the distance he could make out Mossie's tiny figure sprinting towards a breakaway pair of ewes. Assumpta would have your arse for that, thought Marlo, smiling. She was inclined to mind her man carefully, but nearly to distraction as Mossie had told him once. 'Sometimes I think I married me mother, for feck's sake!'

Higher up to the west in Rougham, he spotted Enda Crowley loading his tractor while his hungry herd lowed two fields away, gathered in readiness around their trough. He had met Enda a couple of times and was grateful for the lifts that had been offered without hesitation to and from Glengarriff and Bantry.

But the conversation on the journeys had been confined almost exclusively to questions about life in London. Was it easy to get on with jobs, how about a room to rent and where in London could one play Gaelic? He had heard that Irish were just as welcome there as blacks and dogs. He had wanted to know how that had happened. 'Jaysus, imagine us the same as blacks – there's no accounting for anything, sure there isn't, no more.'

Marlo had quickly gathered that the Crowleys had a reputation, for what he wasn't yet quite sure. In the pub a week ago Dolores, who had knocked back a fair few pints at that stage, snorted when the name was mentioned, and the next day when Marlo said this to Assumpta she had sighed several times and then headed to put the kettle on. It was a sure sign she had plenty to say but she had barely sat down with the biscuit tin in front of her when Father Angelo's car spluttered into the concrete farmyard. As the priest parked up at the back door with a hefty pull of the handbrake, Marlo made his excuses and fled via the front door before the old padre could corner him. Now as he watched Enda ride his tractor full tilt down the narrow boreen he wondered again about the Crowleys. No doubt Assumpta would fill him in once she had put the nervous anxiety of next month's Stations past her.

That thought brought him straight back to the task that lay ahead of him that morning. A strange compulsion had driven him to volunteer to paint the Hanleys' modest bungalow in preparation for the big day. It was probably the tetchy conversation between Mossie and Father Angelo or even the look on Assumpta's face, a few days later, when Mossie had flung his keys down on the kitchen table, collapsing into the fireside chair with a huge sigh. Marlo had been dallying in their kitchen and Assumpta had persuaded him, with no great difficulty he had to admit, to stay for the dinner that she had begun to plate as soon she heard the distant groans of the minibus as it struggled up the hill on the final stretch home.

He had the fork and knife hovering over the bacon and cabbage when he declared, 'Leave the whitewashing to me, Mossie. Now don't be saying no, sure it'll be no bother at all.'

If they were both surprised, they didn't show it, but Assumpta was well pleased and had broadcast his intent to everyone from the stone steps of the church, after mass the very next morning. All week long, wherever Marlo went in the village, he was accosted with pats to the back and the occasional vigorous handshake. He was told he was a good lad, a credit to his mother and all the while warnings of every sort were thrown at him.

'The trick is to prepare them walls well, lad. No good ever came from being in a hurry, mind.'

'A good wash down with sugar soap before you go anywhere near a tin of paint.'

There were plenty of offers of help, even though the ones who volunteered were never forthcoming with their names. The weather had been shocking and in the week since he had started with the heavy steel-wired brush he had only just managed to get the patches of green mould scraped off the outside walls, and now the house looked quite horrible, a patchwork of brush marks and dirt. Progress was held up when he discovered the gutters were full of the winter's soggy detritus and a morning on a wooden ladder, scooping the soggy mess into an old bucket that he had lashed onto his waist, had done his back in. But the sun was out this morning and the forecast was for a dry day or two, and as he watched Enda's tractor disappear around the bend in the distant boreen on the hillside across the valley, he bent down to stretch, tipping his toes and then reaching out to the sky above one arm at a time. Satisfied that there were no twinges from his back, he walked towards the little wooden gate and looked down the slope, towards the bungalow that awaited its whitewash. He had his work cut out and not much more than three weeks to finish the job, dodging the weather all the while.

Later on in the evening, Assumpta came out to him and balanced on the cattle grid as she handed him a mug of tea. Marlo had decided to go all in – repairing and painting the post and rail fencing that enclosed the front garden and the wooden gate which was now sandpapered and ready to be painted.

'Stop for a minute, lad, won't ye? Wait till Mossie sets his eyes on this – he'll be well pleased, he will. These past two summers he just ran out of time and energy. I wanted to have it done last April – my brothers said they'd have the job done and all between them – but Mossie wouldn't want to be obliged to my lot. By God, he's stubborn as a bull about things like that, ye know.' She ran her hand over the gate and smiled at Marlo. 'He took to you quick, didn't he? Seeing as you are Agnes's lad, I suppose. He does go all sentimental about his childhood. I wouldn't blame him, 'twas a happy time, a time before our Thomas died. But it isn't just Mossie. We all think, meself included, that you are a credit to them, to your mam and your da, may the Lord bless and protect his soul.' She finished crossing herself before asking, 'Will you stay for your dinner when you are done for the day?'

Marlo grinned. 'John Bosco said you'd bought pork chops yesterday.'

'That fella ought to know to mind his business about my business. So he got ye playing the football on Wednesday evenings then? Some of those lads are wasters, Marlo, just be careful the company you keep. That John Bosco's a decent enough lad, I'll give him that, but ye'd imagine he'd have better things to be telling you than details of my weekly shop.'

'He knows I'm at your table regularly. I think he was just giving me a head start, Assumpta – you know, in case you asked me to stay and I didn't know it was pork chops that you were going to fry. I could've make an unlucky choice but now that I know – by God, I'm staying.'

Assumpta's eyes brightened. 'So much flattery got you nowhere and everywhere, Marlo! I'm putting on the spuds in an hour or so. Mossie should be home by then.' As she walked back to the house shepherding the dogs ahead of her, Marlo ran the bristles of the paintbrush up and down his palm and wondered, not for the first time, how he had managed to settle so easily into life in the isolated glen. He had met John Bosco the first time barely a few weeks ago, while being served at the counter at O'Sullivan's Butchers.

'I heard we'd a potential player come new to the village and here you are yourself. Marlo, isn't it?' John Bosco was weighing the steak mince as he spoke. 'We train on Wednesdays at the pitch up at Reenmeen and then back to the village for a few pints. Come along this evening if ye've got nothing planned, they're a nice bunch of lads, always up for the craic. We're a few players short since the great exodus, with more leaving each week. You, me lad, ye did the reverse, coming back to the glen. Sure it's no wonder everyone wants a piece of you – you're our boy wonder, ye are.' He lobbed the plastic bag with the mince across the counter and it slid to a stop exactly where Marlo stood.

Is this butcher lad fecking taking the mick? Marlo looked back at him, unsure, and John Bosco laughed. 'I'm serious, boi – even me sisters, right wagons the three of them, are looking for the old introduction. The women are sick of dancing around their handbags in the nightclub.' He washed his hands at the tiny sink and then grabbed a towel before holding his hand out. 'It's John Bosco, JB to ye. This is me da's butchers.' He lowered his voice. 'I'll be gone soon enough meself. I'm following a girl to Oz. She headed off a month ago but I'll have to let me ma down gently. Will break her heart but it's hers or mine, you see what I mean?'

It was a lot to take in, but Marlo had nodded in sympathy as they shook hands. He had turned up at the pitch the following week, and despite taking a battering to his ego, his Wednesday evenings were now set aside for JB and the rest of the lads.

Marlo watched as Assumpta headed back to the house and as he dipped the brush into the tin of glossy black paint he shook his head in disbelief. It was barely three months since he had arrived, and already and inexplicably it felt like he'd never lived anywhere else, ever. *I may have been led to the water kicking and screaming but look at me slurping it all up in one mighty gulp.* There was a rhythm to his life now that was so utterly different from the pace in London; this was not the frenetic tap dance he had learned to tolerate, this was a slow waltz that he loved.

As he painted in steady strokes, his mind drifted to next week's column for the *Montana Courier* and that thought brought him to the urgent matter of getting himself a car of some sort, just to get him around the peninsula and to Bantry every week to fax the copy to the editor. He needed a hundred and forty pounds which would be enough to get his hands on a fairly clean-looking Ford Escort, a Mk2 that might still be at the second-hand garage in Bantry. He'd been kicking tyres around the collection of old bangers there every Friday for the last four weeks and it was John Bosco who had given him a heads-up on the Mk2.

'It's one to gun for, Marlo. Used to belong to a bachelor farmer. He wouldn't leave it to one of his own, he wouldn't. Willed everything to the donkey sanctuary in Ballydehob. Can you imagine that? Every fecking thing to the fecking heehaws! The house, car, the orthopaedic bed he died in, even his Sunday suit, it was all to be disposed off at auction. Even the auctioneer was embarrassed for the old fella like, dead and all though he was. None of the locals would buy any of the lots out of respect for the family, and didn't his eight sisters all turn up on the day to see if anyone would make a show of themselves buying what should have been theirs. Drama all the way! So it's been idling there for two years – long enough now for nobody to grudge you making a bid for it.'

It had become quite obvious very quickly that he would need a proper paying job in the long term. It wasn't just a car and the petrol it would need; even small comforts weren't got for nothing – books and newspapers each week, utilities every month and then the obligations: rounds of drink to be bought after the Wednesday game, and on Sunday he liked to join a few of the neighbours after mass for a quick jar. They shuffled out of the church and walked past the grotto to the pub where he usually bought Mossie a pint or two and Assumpta her preferred mineral. John Bosco was sympathetic and had offered to keep an eye and an ear out for a suitable job, though Marlo wasn't too confident – the Beara peninsula wasn't haemorrhaging young people for no reason. *Still, I might turn lucky.* But for now, this evening, after another coat of paint on the gate, he had Assumpta's pork chops to look forward to.

CHAPTER THREE

A week later Dolores called to the cottage; her car could be heard nearly a mile away as it coughed up the steep slope. Marlo winced as she heaved up the handbrake and shuddered to a stop. That little banger was an enduring miracle. *Ought to have a whole shrine to itself.*

'I've a job for ye, Marlo, fairly regular like, if ye want it. It's with the Headley-Stokes, they're English, fair decent though. They've a rambling estate down by the waterside in Bocarnagh, about twenty-two acres, I think, could be more even, nearly all in forest except around the house. They've a problem like the rest of us with the damned rhodos, especially around the water's edge – I think they want to get at it before they have a total infestation. They buy a lamb off me two or three times a year for their freezer and not a bit tight when it comes to the price. I suppose ye could call them the arty sort but mind, they're not yer hippie type – both retired here ten years ago with more than a bob or two, but age catches up, ye know, and the place is slowly getting out of hand for the two of them. Bumped into them at the post office yesterday and they said they were looking for a handyman, mostly gardening, plus a few bits around the boat-house and sheds and some occasional repairs inside the residence itself. And didn't I tell them I knew just the lad?'

Marlo could see himself motoring around in the Mk2. 'Jesus, your timing is perfect, Dolores. Any chance of a lift to Bocarnagh?'

She took him as far as Glengarriff and he had walked the remaining mile and a half to Bocarnagh, catching glimpses of Glengarriff harbour through gaps in the trees. The air was thick with midges and he wondered if he broke into a jog if they'd spare him. He pulled up the hood of his sweatshirt and swore at them instead. *Mam never said a word about these fecking tiny monsters.* Dense walls of rhododendron and enormous clumps of very high laurel and orange-barked myrtle overhung the worn gravel driveway and the land on either side was completely obscured by tangled vegetation. Hoary oaks, their limbs cloaked in moss, embraced neighbouring beeches and glossy holly shone wherever the light of the mid-morning sun managed to penetrate the green canopy. Halfway down, the driveway had begun to resemble a tunnel and the light at the end of it was dazzling. He was quite sure the glare was the sun bouncing off the waters of the bay and he wasn't far wrong; he could hear waves lapping as he neared.

His jaw dropped entirely as he emerged from the dark – the house was perched on a bare rocky promontory, clinging to the very edge, built of steel and glass. He stood for a moment marvelling at the architect's vision and the engineering that would allow a house to remain standing securely in such a precarious position.

Must be fecking loaded, these double-barrelled retirees. He looked for a doorbell but he had been spotted through the sheets of glass and a tall, thin woman in a kaftan wafted towards the door and opened it with a flourish.

She was all smiles. 'You must be the lad Dolores told us about. Marlo O'Sullivan, isn't it? We're delighted to see you. Come in, Edward's in his study and we'll have coffee with him and chat in there, shall we? I was about to go for a swim in the cove, but it can wait – the world can wait now since you come so highly recommended. I'm Tiggy, by the way. Is coffee OK?'

Marlo nodded. 'Yes, coffee is fine. Thank you, Mrs Headley-Stokes. I'm blown away by your home. It's quite amazing.'

'It's Tiggy, Marlo, call me Tiggy. We don't stand on the old formalities. Give me a moment now,' she said as she opened a door and popped her head in. 'Fresh coffee for us please, Kitty, in Edward's study if you wouldn't mind, and some of those nice biscuits as well.'

He followed her as she continued to breeze her way through

the vast open-plan space, her arms doing something strangely balletic as she moved. The walls held large brooding seascapes but he stopped in his tracks at the sight of a near life-size ceramic yawl, complete with canvas sails that rose all the way to the double-height ceiling. He could hardly tear himself away from the sculpture that cleverly divided the huge room into two manageable spaces. How in hell's name had it been brought into the house?

'A wonderful piece, isn't she? Our home was designed around her, the *Beara Belle*.' Tiggy was on a low landing, a few steps up, and she pushed open a door. 'Come on here now and meet Edward.'

A silver-haired man scraped his chair back from the desk he was sitting at and rose to shake Marlo's hand firmly. 'You might as well have been the Messiah, that's how eagerly we have been waiting for you. I'm Edward.'

Marlo laughed. 'I know what you mean, Mr Headley-Stokes, sir. I can see the grounds need strong hands and a reliable chain-saw. I'm happy for the work, to be honest. My writing doesn't keep me in anything but breakfast every alternate day.'

Edward smiled. 'Please, it's Edward. Tiggy and Edward. So, a writer, eh? In dire straits like the rest of them? Well, well, well! But we understand. We were both architects before we retired and came to live full-time in Beara. It allowed Tigs to paint and she in turn leaves me to sculpt.'

'So, the *Beara Belle* is your work? It's an incredible piece!'

'Our first collaborative piece. Tigs had been dreaming about it for years. Recreating a boat she spent her childhood family summers on, in and around the waters at Schull. She did all the initial sketching and plans and we went from there.'

Tiggy wrapped her arms around her husband's shoulders and smiled. 'Our home is just a boathouse for a dream.'

'Oh, I like that. Every dream needs a safe harbour.'

'So, what's yours, Marlo?'

'Don't want to be too greedy, sir, as I've only recently come into an inheritance. A dream enough to start with.'

Tiggy nodded. 'Ah yes, that lovely cottage up the road to Barley Lake.'

Edward leaned back into his chair. 'Good to temper your expectations from life, young man, but ongoing dreams, you've just got to have them.'

'Yes, but Edward, chasing them can be so exhausting,' said Tiggy as she sat down.

'Don't I know that, you did lead me a merry chase, Tigs.'

'As you can see, Marlo, my husband can hold a grudge a very long time. We will be fifty years married later this year.'

Marlo smiled as they both looked at each other and laughed.

'Yes, a big party is in the works for family, close friends and a few of our old clients too – so the whole place, house, gardens, grounds and our sculpture trail through the forest – we need it all shipshape.'

Marlo nodded. 'A golden anniversary is reason enough. Congratulations to you both.'

Tiggy plumped up a cushion. 'Thank you, but come on, sit down for a few minutes and tell us about yourself. Then we'll have a walk in the grounds after coffee and run through the list of things that need to be done. Some urgent and some can be prioritised. I wonder, should I have asked for sandwiches? Are you hungry, Marlo?'

He was about to answer when the door inched open and a young woman nudged her way in with a very large tray. She was quite petite and the apron tied around her waist accentuated her slim figure. She had scanned the room in seconds, her pretty brown eyes resting directly on Marlo.

He jumped up to hold the door open fully and she exhaled a quiet thank you as she put the tray down.

'I cut some sandwiches while I was at it. And not forgetting the biscuits. Would you like me to pour, Tiggy ma'am?'

'Kitty, I'm convinced you're a mind-reader. Thank you, but I'll manage. This is Marlo O'Sullivan, by the way. He's going to get the grounds or should I call it "our wilderness" back in order. Kitty helps me keep the house running, Marlo. I'd have no time to paint if not for her.'

Kitty wiped her hands on her apron and tucked her hair behind her ears before putting her hand out. 'So, this here is the saviour.' She held his hand firmly and looked at him quite frankly. 'You are nothing like what I thought you'd be.'

Before he could think of something to say back, she turned and stepped out of the study, shutting the door quietly behind her.

Tiggy sighed. 'Newcomers are always the talk of the peninsula. But we've only heard good things about you.'

Marlo tried hard not to crane his neck too obviously as he watched Kitty through the glass walls, walking past the *Beara Belle* in the direction of what he assumed was the kitchen.

Half an hour later, as they walked out of the house, he found himself hoping to catch a glimpse of her again, but she was nowhere to be seen. The chicken sandwiches, heavily laced with mustard, had been very good and he would have told her that. *And she would have spotted the eejit with the more than useless chat-up line. Marlo lad, just three months in the sticks and you've lost the touch.*

Tiggy and Edward were just ahead of him now, leading the way down an untidy gravel path heavy with encroaching chickweed. Waiting for a moment at the top of a flight of the stone steps, they walked hand in hand, quite carefully, down to the small wooden jetty and turned back to look up at Marlo.

'Perhaps you could start here, Marlo, and work your way back to the areas around the house and boathouse. The steps have become really lethal and these boards here need to be scrubbed clean.' Edward pressed down heavily with his foot and a few boards rose up in protest at the other end. 'Any carpentry skills that you might have will come in handy. The boathouse roof has a few slates missing and we'd like it painted. I'm not comfortable going up ladders anymore. At my age, it's a one-way ticket if I break a hip. Tiggy has the paint picked already – it must be in the shed. Dolores said you did a fine job at the Hanleys' with their fencing.'

'They're getting their house ready for the Stations next week and Assumpta's finally happy because the sacristan was on Mossie's bus yesterday and he had overheard Father Angelo tell old Father Aloysius that the house didn't look half as bad any more.'

'They need to get their own house in order, those men of the cloth. Terribly judgemental and that old padre Aloysius – still going, is he?'

Tiggy tut-tutted. 'Oh, Edward! Marlo doesn't need to hear any of that.'

Marlo took the hint and steered the conversation back to the business at hand. 'Dolores said you wanted a lot of the rhododendrons cut back – I'll need a chainsaw; it will be so much quicker and cleaner too. Makes very good firewood. Burns longer and hotter. I could chop and stack the thicker trunks and save the thinner branches for kindling if you have a woodshed.'

'We've no woodshed on its own, Marlo, but we have a large agri shed, well camouflaged behind that rock, away to the right of the house, with plenty of room for everything. We use a corner for wood and yes, please chop whatever you think can be used. You'll find everything you need in there. Chainsaws, tools and more.'

Marlo looked across the narrow inlet. 'That's some monster of a rock, you could hide a whole jumbo jet behind it!'

'The Lump we call it – a signature piece from the Ice Age, this peninsula is littered with them. When we finish showing you the bits and pieces we want done in the forest, we'll end up on that side of the property and I'll show you around the shed. This way now, young man – you'll see you've your work cut out for the next few months.' Edward led the way, heading towards a roughly hewn pair of stone balls that marked the start of a gravel trail.

Tiggy walked beside Marlo. 'We cut this walking trail though the forest, that first year after we moved. I can hardly believe that we did it ourselves, most of it except shifting the tons of gravel that needed Batty Mor and his mini-digger. We went where the ground would allow us – off the path it's very boggy underfoot, not unlike anywhere else on Beara. It winds about a mile, doesn't it, Edward? Inland at first and then you'll see it turns towards the coast, hugging our three tiny little coves, following the shore before finishing at the house back at the foot of The Lump. Edward's sculptures went in a few years later.'

'Not all mine though, Marlo, Tiggy's given pride of place to two giant metal bees that our grandson fashioned for a school art project and we've some works by artist friends from right here on the peninsula. Plus a few pieces we bought years ago in India and Cambodia too. You'll get to know them all and we'll give you a few months to tell us which are your favourites – some pieces take a while to grow on you.'

'Ben's work is rather clever and ingenious and that's not just the grandmother in me speaking. Our first grandchild has an imagination and an eye that just fills my heart with joy.'

'And his mother's with trepidation.' Edward had turned around and was laughing.

'I don't deny that. Marlo, you'll meet him later in the year. Ben has a whole plan mapped out for our anniversary party – he's just turned eighteen and is styling it like a festival! We'll need to be fighting fit for everything that he has in mind. But to the matter in hand now – Edward, do you want to start, or will I go on?'

And with that she began to point out the walls of rhododendrons crowding either side of the trail. 'A pure menace really. The pink blooms just trick you every year with their display. And all the while they choke everything in sight.

We need to really get a handle on them.'

They stooped now as they walked through a dense tunnel of the invasive species. The sunlight barely filtered through and the lack of light meant nothing else stood a chance of growing.

'So, I take it you'd like it cut back quite hard? Do you want to kill the ones that are encroaching on the trail itself?'

'Yes, a hard cutback. And a good clearance around the trail. We planted so much along the margins, you know, Marlo, and none of it stands absolutely any chance because of this intense shade and the toxic leaching from the fallen leaves.'

The trail itself had a springy feel to it and in many places water oozed up through the gravel as they walked. The path wound its way steadily upwards, skirting ancient sessile oaks that wind and time had fashioned into fantastical shapes and past huge beech trees that seemed to have erupted implausibly out of thin fissures in the enormous rocks that littered the sodden earth. Ferns, moss and liverwort, glossy green with damp, clung to every surface from the dark peaty quagmires on the forest floor to the high treetops where light shafted in. Everywhere he looked Marlo could see worlds within worlds, wondrous microcosms growing in each other's embrace, multiplying their dependence on each other, living trees offering their trunks to cling to, their hollows to fill, while fallen giants gave themselves up to be cannibalised only to be reincarnated in a multitude of life forms. A symbiotic energy filled the air and he stopped to take it all in like he had done countless number of times since he had arrived in the glen.

Tiggy put an arm on his shoulder. 'I see you can feel it too, Marlo – it's quite overwhelming, isn't it? There truly is not a spare spot left – so if there has to be living, there has to be some dying: living and dying – the cycle never stops.'

Edward turned around and laughed. 'You'll scare the young fellow, Tiggy, with your Hag of Beara impersonation.'

'But I do know what you mean, Mrs Headley Stokes – I mean, Tiggy ma'am. The glen has an effect on me that I'm trying to put down on paper. The trees, plants and every living creature, it's almost like a human community, don't you think. The highborn and the plebs, the workers and the wasters, the honest folks and the parasites, the strong and the weak – all held together by the survival instinct. The plant world is nearly like us, wouldn't you say?' Marlo was looking up at a large cleft in the leafy canopy through which sunshine was streaming through.

'Nearly, but thank God not completely. It's the lack of malice that sets that kingdom apart.'

Marlo nodded. Malice. Oh yes, malice! One man's malice was what had driven him away from London. His hellish experience seemed a lifetime away now and it was hard to believe that his life had been turned upside down only for it to be righted in the best way possible over these last few months.

They continued walking and both Tiggy and Edward pointed out things they wanted done, stopping now and again at a sculpture, explaining its provenance and sometimes arguing over the meaning of a piece or how they had acquired it. The steady climb brought them to a steep flight of stone steps that led to a treeless outcrop. The view made him gasp and the Headley-Stokes laughed in delight.

'It never fails to charm, Marlo, even after all these years. We've a better view than the one from Lady Bantry's lookout, don't you think? Our beloved harbour and its little islands – lovely in any season.'

Marlo shaded his eyes with one hand as he pointed across with the other. 'Is that Garnish there?'

'Yes, the Martello tower at one end marks it out clearly.'

They lingered there for a few minutes while Tiggy and Edward both took turns pointing out landmarks near and distant. By the time they had wandered back to the house via The Lump, Marlo knew that the work ahead was going to be laborious and back-breaking but he had taken an instant liking to both of them and the prospect of finally getting his own set of wheels, laying his hands on the Mk2 languishing at the dealer in Bantry, made his heart leap.

Edward stroked his chin. 'Let's agree on a sum for the first part of the job, Marlo – clearing from the jetty round the house and boathouse – then whether you take two weeks or twenty to finish it, that will be up to you. If we're all happy, we can sort out further work after that. That's fair on both sides, don't you think?'

Marlo lad, here's your chance – it's now or never.

'I've an eye on a second-hand car, an Mk2, so it's the cost of the car I'll be hoping to be paid. A hundred and fifty pounds, Edward sir. If I could have fifty in advance it would be handy as I could put down a deposit on it.'

Tiggy nodded at her husband and put her hand out. 'Let's shake on it then.'

Marlo shook her hand vigorously. 'It'll be a job well done, Tiggy ma'am.'

Edward laughed. 'You'll be answerable to Dolores, young man. That alone should keep you on the straight and narrow. Hold on here while I write out a cheque for the fifty pounds.'

As he headed for the front door, Kitty emerged from along the side of the house wheeling a cycle. Her hair was tied back with a scarf and she flicked down a pair of sunglasses from her forehead before mounting the cycle, wobbling for a few seconds, then steadying herself as she approached them.

'See you tomorrow, Kitty, and do take care on the main road.'

Kitty smiled and with a little wave she pedalled away.

'Kitty will sort lunch for you the days you are working here, Marlo. Gardening is hungry work, so just let her know when you want something.'

'That's very kind of you, Tiggy ma'am. I won't be shy asking.'

Not if it's Kitty I have to ask, no I won't, by God.

CHAPTER FOUR

Looking out of his kitchen window, it seemed to Marlo that it was a cruel god for whom all the arrangements had been made over these last few months. In the past week, the Hanleys' house had been shaken inside out, as Assumpta worked her way systematically down from the attic all the way to the two rooms at the front of the bungalow and out to the front door, which Marlo and Mossie had manged to heave open with great difficulty, as it hadn't been opened since the winter past. That done, she switched to an even more intense deep clean, taking in the bedrooms and the kitchen, tackling the small utility with a vengeance she normally saved for the dogs when they had rolled in fox shite. The narrow strip of carpet off-cut that she had bought at the Friday market in Bantry had been rolled out in the hallway and held down with double-sided tape. Assumpta was nearly ready.

'There'll be more eyes scrutinising the state of this place than will be on the rosary beads, I promise you, Marlo, so just be a good lad now and wipe down Our Lord above the back door. He's just beyond my reach.'

Mossie snorted and Assumpta whipped her tea towel at his head. 'I'll thank you not to be difficult! A fine example for Marlo you are.'

She stormed out of the room and Mossie grinned, his finger to his lips. 'Not a peep out of you, lad, if she catches us laughing – it'll be me own funeral mass you'll be attending, not the Stations. Ah, but why do women get like this? One of the actual mysteries of the Faith, if you ask me.'

Marlo was examining the picture of the Sacred Heart in his hand. Jesus had his chest rent open and the ring of thorns around the blood-red sacred heart seemed to pulsate all of a sudden.

'Jesus!'

41

'To be sure it's him, lad.'

'No, Mossie! For feck's sake – look, it's a whole load of tiny spiders under the glass!'

'Christ, would you ever just give that to me lad, quick like, before she comes back. The backing on the old frame must have come loose. Here, pass me a knife from the drawer there, good lad.'

Mossie prised open the one tiny black metal clasp that remained of the original six that held the backing and the cardboard fell away in shreds. A large spider scurried away, its offspring running helter-skelter across the glass and onto the kitchen table. Marlo scooped up as many as he could and released them on the sill of the open kitchen window.

Mossie put the frame back together using an old issue of *The Catholic* and sticky tape 'She hates spiders, don't you know. To think the feckers were sheltering in the bosom of our Lord. She'd see that as an omen of sorts for sure, so don't be saying anything to her now. Here, hang it back up before she cops on – her interpretation of omens are known to go either way.'

Marlo's shoulders were still shaking when Assumpta walked back in. 'It's just the cattle grid left for you to sort now, Mossie. I'll bury the Child of Prague myself tomorrow. I don't want to get too ahead.'

'You'd want to be ahead, marking your place in the queue, Assumpta. The whole parish is looking for favours to be granted.'

'D'you see him there, Marlo – brave because you're here. It's a sin to tease your wife.' She sat down at the table beside Mossie with a huge sigh. 'What if it rains?'

They had clutched each other's hands and groaned collectively.

Today, as he stood at his kitchen sink looking out at the storm, Marlo could hear that groan. Sheets of rain moved sideways, whipping across the valley, the wind howling unmercifully, slamming into the gable ends of the homes, buffeting the chimney tops and threatening to lift corrugated sheeting off sheds, sending cattle feeders rolling down the fields, upending troughs and water drums. The trees in the wooded area below his cottage looked crazed, the branches swirling wildly, and every few minutes even stronger gusts would leave them nearly doubling over. Crow hadn't made his morning appearance and Marlo wondered if the bird would brave the storm. He found himself waiting for Crow each morning, worrying until he heard the familiar impatient knock on the sash window.

He decided he would walk down to Mossie and Assumpta's to see if they needed any last-minute help. They must be disgusted with the day they had woken up to. Assumpta would surely be up to the nineties and driving Mossie in the same direction no doubt. He was surprised to see them quite relaxed at the kitchen table, a big pot of tea in front of them, the Kimberleys arranged on a small plate and a dog beside each of them, on the alert for crumbs.

She pushed the plate towards him. 'The way I'm looking at it, Marlo, they'll be less of that disrespectful behaviour with the usual bunch of wasters – showing face only to sit on the back walls and hang by the sheds, smoking and gossiping. This weather will bring them indoors, to actually pray, and Father Angelo always says there is power in numbers when it comes to the Rosary. The Lord will hear us better still. Will you have a drop, Marlo?'

'I won't right now. I just came to see if you needed anything done before everyone arrives.'

'Marlo, you aren't planning to— I mean, you are going to come, aren't you? Everyone knows how much you've helped, and Father Angelo was going to call you out by name, he told me so himself. He's so impressed, in fact, I think he wants you on the fund-raising committee that he is forming for the church roof.'

Ah, feck! Not a fecking chance, no fecking way.

'That's just his way of getting me to go to mass regularly, Assumpta.'

'And what's wrong with that?' Assumpta looked shocked.

Marlo looked at both of them and began to laugh. 'Ah no, you can't be serious. Father Angelo is as cute as they get and more still. But don't be worrying – I should be back here by five this evening. I was planning on going into Bantry to put down the next instalment on that car, but I'm not sure now. Do you think it might die down, Mossie? The wind, I mean?'

Mossie gave him a big wink. 'It might if you prayed regular, like.'

Assumpta ignored the jibe and shuffled to her feet, reaching out for the empty cups which she dumped in the sink. 'I know for a fact that Dolores is taking a calf to the knackery this morning, come rain or shine, so if you start walking at a quarter past eight you'll have your lift before you get to the main road.'

The rain had stopped and Marlo had just the wind to battle against as he walked through the glen, straining to hear the welcome whine and crash of the gears on Dolores's car.

She pulled up in her usual style, yanking the handbrake with a massive sigh. 'Jaysus, where would ye heading to in this feckin weather? What couldn't wait?'

'Well, the rain's stopped, maybe the wind will too, Dolores. Assumpta said you were heading to the knackery in Drimoleague. I'll come with you as far as Bantry if it suits.'

'It suits all right. Something urgent in Bantry? I thought you faxed yer weekly piece to Montana on Mondays. How're they liking your account of life here, the Butte Irish? Will we have droves of them heading to the peninsula on your say-so? I've two rooms to rent if ye hear of anyone looking for accommodation. One has the top half of an old pine dresser and the other one a cast-iron fireplace – the Yanks love that sort of thing. And I meant to ask how're ye getting on with the

Headley-Stokes? Are ye done with clearing that trail of theirs? Treating ye well, are they, lad?'

Our Lady of Eternal Questions, grant me some breathing room.

'I've been down to Bocarnagh nearly every day the last two weeks, and to be honest I still haven't broken the back of it fully. My fecking arms are sore as hell at this stage what with all the cutting and hacking. The chainsaw went bust a couple of times so things slowed down a bit. They got me a new one anyways, said it would be cheaper than the constant repairs. Plus, I have the second week's pay now – so I'm heading to the Ford garage.'

'A house, a job and now a car. We just need to get ye a wife and then ye'll be well set up, like. Listen, I can bring ye home too. Just have to pick up a calf now, from my grazing in Pooleen, drop it off to the knackery and I'll be back through Bantry in no time. Wait at the square and I'll collect ye. We'll be back and scrubbed up in time for the Stations.'

They had gone a quarter of a mile past Pooleen when she slowed down and pulled into a tiny layby beside a field gate.

'Give us a hand here, lad. You stay with the calf while I distract its mother.' She heaved at the trailer door and lowered the ramp and Marlo, not for the first time, couldn't help wonder at the sheer strength of the woman.

She grabbed the bucket of feed from the trailer and threw Marlo a length of rope with an old leather belt tied to it.

'Just as well I met you, lad – an extra pair of hands is what I needed like! I'll get her to the far end of the field and ye wait till her head's well in the bucket before ye throw that over the calf and walk it out. Just nudge it along and it'll move as it's told. Took me ten days before I realised it was born blind as a bat so I've no choice but give it a quick end at the knackery. They feed the hounds at the hunt with animals like that. You know, the useless ones.'

'Blind! Ahh, no! The poor creature! But it's only blind, Dolores, that surely doesn't make it useless.'

45

'Not just useless – Jaysus, it'll be more trouble to me than ye'll ever imagine.'

With that she slipped past the gate and began to rattle the bucket as she walked briskly towards the far end of the field. The cow didn't hesitate and followed Dolores nearly at a gallop. The tiny calf, sensing it was alone, was suddenly alert. Its skin quivered in a wave that travelled right down to its hindquarters and two apprehensive snorts were as good as a question about what might lie ahead. Marlo was regretting the lift even as he eased the belt over the tiny neck. Wet lips nuzzled the palm of his hands and the calf leaned into him, trying to suckle Marlo's fingers. The rough tongue nearly took his skin off and he yanked his hand away in pain.

From the far end of the field, Dolores was signalling frantically. 'Walk it out, lad, quick and into the trailer. Its mother here's going to fecking cop on in a second.'

Marlo hesitated for a moment and then scooped the calf up in his arms and manoeuvring his way out of the damp field, he kicked the spring-loaded gate shut behind him. The calf was now struggling to get free and when Marlo set it down, it sprinted straight into the back wall of the trailer, slamming its head hard against the thick metal bars of the frame. It staggered for a minute in shock before collapsing, lowing quietly like it was ready to die even before getting to the knacker's yard. Marlo secured the ramp and then, crouching in front of the calf, rubbed its head gently. 'You poor little fecker, that was some blow to your head.'

The calf's eyes were vacant, but its breath was full of fear. It tried to get to its feet, legs trembling and kicking in every direction. Marlo held it down with both hands, trying to soothe it by stroking it from head to tail. The flailing stopped and the calf nuzzled his fingers.

'For feck's sake, Marlo.' Dolores had her hands on her hip. 'The sooner I get that one to Drimoleague, the less agony for us all. Hop into the car now, and let's go before herself there goes demented.' She threw a look back to the agitated cow, calling and searching in the field.

'How much for the calf, Dolores? I'll buy him off you. How much?'

'Are ye fecking gone soft in the head, Marlo? What would ye do with a bull calf? And a blind one at that? Jaysus.'

'I'll pay you.'

'Stop. In the name of God – are ye gone mad, like? He's best off dispatched, no use to ye or to anyone else.'

'Dolores, let me take him.'

'No, I will let ye do nothing of the bloody sort. I don't see any udders hanging off yer chest.'

'I've seen Enda Crowley feed his calves milk from buckets.'

'Marlo, this is different – the animal is fucking blind. The poor cratur's got everything stacked against him – every danger is real and present. I'm doing him a kindness. The calf can't see a thing. I'm beginning to think ye can't as well.'

'An animal can be trained. Look, I once read of an octopus that could spell.'

'It wasn't blind though, was it?' She slapped her forehead. 'I didn't actually say that, did I? Right so, lad, ye hop out of my trailer smartly now and make yer own way to Bantry. I've got to get to Drimoleague before noon. Sweet Mother of God, would ye stop patting his head. He's not a fecking dog!'

Marlo stood up. 'Dolores, listen to me. Let me buy him. If I can't cope, if he can't cope – I'll have him put down. He can go to the hounds then.'

'The whole village, the neighbours and all, will think I tricked ye into buying him off me. I'll not stand to be called a cute hoor.'

'I can enlighten everyone myself. Today. Today, at the Station.'

'Jesus, Mary and Joseph, ye are mad, like. Fecking mad altogether.'

'Drive us back up to my place and I'll put him in the old woodshed for the moment. He'll be warm and dry till I rig up fencing around the upper field by the house. It'll be ready for him in a few days. It will be small and compact, and he can't come to any harm there. I can watch him from the kitchen.'

'And then what, Marlo?'

'And then life will go on, Dolores.'

An hour later they were in his kitchen washing their hands. Marlo opened the press and took out two glasses and a bottle of Middleton.

'It's been the strangest morning in many a year. Ah sure, go on then, Marlo. I'll drink to yer difficulties – may they be few and may the Lord and His Saints turn a blind eye to yer foolishness.'

'A blind eye!'

'It's the only time there will be a funny side to this story. Pour me that drink so.'

Marlo headed down to the Hanleys' half an hour before Father Angelo was to arrive. Mossie had asked him to supervise the parking and Assumpta added that she wanted the space beside the back door left free for the priest's car. The wind had almost died down, though the evening air remained heavy and damp and the hedgerows were still dripping from the earlier downpours while the mountainside was streaked with the remains of vertical rivulets that only hours ago had been thundering waterfalls, swollen by the rain. A great swarm of midges followed him down the slope, having a go at his earlobes every time he stopped swatting them away. He could see that some of the neighbours had begun to arrive, and he hurried down, picking up pace. Assumpta, who must have seen him coming down from the cottage, was waiting at the front door with a fluorescent bib. 'Here, put this on, Marlo, and no one will argue with you when you tell them where to park. Makes you look official like, if you know what I mean.' With that, she ushered Pieter and Ella in with a big smile, taking a large tray of neatly cut egg sandwiches from them. 'Ah, you are both so good! And I'll save this tray for Father Angelo – he likes his sandwiches like this, cut thin with the crusts off.'

An hour later, after Marlo had helped the last of the late arrivals reverse into impossibly small spaces, he stepped into the house, untying the bib and looking for a spot to hang it on.

'So, the man of many talents is traffic warden today?'

'Kitty! I didn't expect you to be here. You know the Hanleys then?'

'Mossie is my godfather. I had to show face. And you?'

'Assumpta's my fairy godmother. I had to show face too. I live just a bit further up above. I didn't see you coming in.'

'Oh, I've been here since three.' Her eyes rolled as she whispered, 'Cutting crusts off sandwiches, if you want to know.'

'Father Angelo?'

She giggled. 'So, you are in the know, Marlo – I'm impressed. But look, I think you're wanted. Assumpta's trying to catch your attention.'

'Be back in a minute,' he said, before shuffling his way past murmuring parishioners, bent over their rosary beads. The house was thrumming with incantations and there was a mesmerising quality to the collective drawing-in of breaths and the exhaling at the end of each decade as it was said. Assumpta caught his eye and beckoned him close. Marlo leaned over her shoulder.

'Be a good lad there now, Marlo, and have a look at Father Angelo's tyres, would you? The poor man thinks he has a puncture. And Marlo, get that Crowley lad to help you before he finishes everything there is to eat.'

With that she closed her eyes, the rapture returning as she turned her face to the pulsating Sacred Heart plugged into the socket in the good room.

When he returned to the kitchen, Kitty was nowhere to be seen and he found Enda Crowley in the utility, having a go at the biscuits, cupcakes and sandwiches that had been kept there in reserve.

'I'll be out to help ye in a minute there now, Marlo, ye go on ahead. I'm right behind ye, but this is some spread here, not seen nor eaten the likes of this in a while, I haven't.'

The priest's car did have a puncture and Marlo gave the tyre a good kick.

Just when I had a chance to talk to Kitty.

He set to work quickly, taking out the stepney and the tool kit. As he jacked the car up, he looked around wondering where Kitty had disappeared to. In the last few weeks, while working in Bocarnagh at the Headley-Stokes', he had tried his best to get a chance to talk to her, lingering close to the house at every opportunity in the hope that he might bump into her. But she was elusive and, though he sometimes caught glimpses of her moving through the glass-fronted rooms, she seemed always busy, carrying armfuls of ironed linen and clothes, sometimes hoovering or mopping the floors, taking trays of food to Edward and Tiggy where they worked over their books, drawings and canvases. Two weeks ago, coming out of the shed as he rounded the corner at The Lump, he saw her cleaning the tall windows of the room that faced the harbour.

He called out to her, 'That's a lot of glass to clean, do you want a hand reaching the higher bits?'

She jumped on hearing him and laughed as she steadied herself. 'Didn't see you come up, Marlo, you gave me a right scare there. How's it going up the trail?'

'Another few weeks and I'll be done, then I'll start around the boathouse and jetty. How are you going to clean the top of those windows? Will I get a ladder and do it for you?'

'Thanks, but it's fine really. The pole is an extending one.'

Marlo was disappointed, but he put down the wheelbarrow

that he was using to ferry wood and decided it was now or never.

'I haven't had a chance to chat properly or thank you for all the lunches you've left for me on the kitchen table. I thought my mother made the only apple sponge worth eating, but yours was the best I've ever had.' He wanted to kick himself immediately but spoke his mind instead. 'Jesus, that was a bit cheesy altogether, wasn't it?'

They could both hear the phone ringing inside the house. She pulled off her gloves and wiped her hands on her apron, laughing as she did. 'I'll give you an F for chat-up lines but an A for self-awareness, Marlo. But look, I must answer that call now – Tiggy asked not to be disturbed.'

He fretted the rest of the week about that conversation but hadn't seen her since. The weather had been dreadful and the work at Bocarnagh had come to a near stop. If only Enda Crowley would come out and give him a hand with the spare tyre, he might be able to get back into the house quicker and have another go at asking her out.

There was shuffling behind him – it was Enda still eating, pushing half a sandwich into his mouth.

'Those were for the priest. The ones without the crusts. Assumpta will have your guts if there's not at least a whole tray left untouched.'

'Fuck the priest.'

'I wouldn't go that far.'

'But he would, by God, he would. And further – so never ye mind the priest.'

Taken aback, Marlo stood up, the punctured tyre resting against his knee. Enda shrugged and rolled it away to the boot. They replaced the tyre in silence, lifting the spare onto the wheel hub, Enda grunting as he turned the spanner to tighten the nuts.

Marlo was about to thank Enda when a muffled lowing filled the evening air. It got louder and clearer, a lament that drifted down the slope, the wind holding still as if to let it through.

Enda spat into the grass by the car. 'That's yer blind one,' he said as he flung the spanner and jack into the boot. 'Drop down to me for more milk for him in the morning. He's going to be more trouble than ye think.'

'Thanks, Enda, I will and listen, I appreciate your help.'

Enda nodded and kicked the car before walking back to the house. Marlo lingered for a second before walking to the gate and looking up the slope in the direction of his cottage and the melancholic calling.

It's what Mam and Mary said was my greatest weakness. Impulsiveness.

He walked back to the house and popped his head into the good room. Assumpta looked up immediately from the beads in her hand and he gave her a discreet thumbs up. 'Fixed,' he mouthed, and then headed off to look for Kitty.

Pieter and Ella, who were in the kitchen rinsing out cups at the sink, smiled as he walked in. Pieter picked up a dishcloth and started drying. 'Ahh, Marlo – JB said to tell you he'll see you on Wednesday as usual at the pitch. He had to give Kitty a lift home. We hear you've adopted a calf. Blind and deaf, I believe. Fair play to you as they'd say here. Fair play to you.'

'Just blind, Pieter, just blind.'

Ella was shaking her head slowly and Marlo was sure she was tut-tutting under her breath. He could feel his own irritation rise. 'Would you like to see him for yourself, Ella? Call in tomorrow?' he challenged.

To his surprise, she nodded enthusiastically. 'Oh yes, can I bring something?'

Pieter rolled his eyes. 'A white cane?'

Ella switched to Dutch. '*Je denkt dat je zo grappig bent, Pieter!*' Then she turned to Marlo. 'I've two bales of straw that I could spare, Marlo. You could use it for bedding perhaps?'

'I won't say no, Ella. That's very kind. I'll replace it as soon as I can. I know the Crowleys up above have plenty. I'm buying milk off them as well for the moment. Till he, you know, is weaned – is that what it's called?'

Pieter stroked his beard. 'Well, technically speaking he's kind of weaned already, isn't he – as he's separated from his mother.'

'Anyway, he's warm and dry at the moment.'

'But obviously frightened,' said Pieter, glancing at the open window. The calf's distress echoed around the valley, his agonised lowing wafting down with every break in the wind.

'I was planning to stay till this was over, but I guess I better head up and see what's the matter. Tell Assumpta I'll come back later if I can, will you, Ella?'

Then, with a nod in Pieter's direction, Marlo stepped out of the house. The calf sounded as if he was being murdered and he resisted the urge to run down the Hanleys' drive, leap over the cattle grid and run up the slope. There were plenty of holy joes who had taken position at the windows of the good room, merely going through the motions in the presence of the priest and neighbours, while their sly eyes scanned the goings-on in the yard. He knew the word was already out about him being a right soft eejit, but it wouldn't do for anyone to see him sprinting to the calf.

Hours later, piteous moans kept Marlo tossing in his bed and, cursing loudly, he took his old sleeping bag out to the wood-shed. Nudging the calf down onto the straw till his spindly legs buckled under, he sat up close, right beside him, gradually making himself comfortable as he stroked his head and face, talking nonsense to the animal in what he though was his best hypnotic voice, till the calf calmed down and went silent.

He suddenly wondered where he had put the medal of St Jude that Mary had given him at the airport five months ago. *Here's a lost cause you can help with, Jude lad.* Tomorrow, I'll hook that medal to the old belt around the animal's neck. *And why bloody not?* he reasoned with himself, as he pulled the sleeping bag close around him. Wasn't faith all about clutching at straws?

CHAPTER FIVE

Mossie called to the house a week later. 'This is for you,' he said, unwrapping a bottle of brandy. 'It's from the both of us. Assumpta was wired for weeks, but with no small thanks to you, lad, everything went off without a hitch on the day. No one made a show of themselves, and Father Angelo was in good form. He overstayed his welcome if you ask me – ate everything in sight. He did ask about you after mass this morning.'

Marlo put down his biro and picked up the bottle. 'I've been struggling with this week's column – it's only half written and has to be faxed tomorrow. But thanks for the bottle, Mossie, there was no need at all, you know. Seriously, I can't repay you both enough as it is.'

'Ah, stop, lad. Come here now, where is he, the talk of the town? The voice that rings across the valley – they've christened him Stevie Wonder, d'you know that?'

Marlo laughed out. 'As good a name as I'd have thought of! Let's wet the head, will we, Mossie? He's bedded in the old woodshed but the paddock is ready – I finished fencing it yesterday. Would you cast your eye over it?'

They walked around the small three-sided field beside the house, and with Mossie satisfied, they headed into the shed.

Mossie leaned over the half door of the shed. 'How're you getting on with the feeding?'

'He gets two litres twice a day. Knows my voice and where to head to for the bucket as soon he hears the clank. He had a go at the grass today, picking all around him where I had him tethered outside for a few hours.'

'Careful now, don't make a pet of him like. You'll just be making fierce trouble for yourself. Right so, lad, I'll be off down to herself and leave you to your column. It's dinner and early to bed for me. Where did the weekend go? she said to me. Where did the half the year go? I said back to her. Anyway, here we are

– back to work tomorrow and I've a full bus of the regulars plus two Yanks and a German to be collected on the way.'

Marlo pulled out the brandy from his jacket pocket. 'Hold on there, Mossie, let's not forget!' Marlo sprinkled a few drops of the brandy onto his fingers before making the sign of the cross on the calf's wide forehead. 'Stevie, you're going to be the wonder calf.'

Grinning, he turned to Mossie, offering him a capful of the brandy and when Mossie had thrown his head back and downed it, Marlo did the same himself. 'Jesus, I need that since a week ago. A bloody lot has happened since then.'

Mossie slapped him on his back. 'They're waiting for you around every corner, lad. Curved balls in every size.' He smiled and then dropped his knees and feinted from side to side. 'Duck and dive, duck and dive. It'll be the makings of you.'

The rest of the day flew by and as Marlo finished typing up his piece he heard a distant wail. He was certain it wasn't the calf but still, he slid the typewriter to one side of the dining table and put away the sheet of copy into a plastic folder. He walked into the yard when the sound drifted up the glen again, closer now, and he felt a shiver run through his body. *Surely that's an ambulance*, he thought and stood still for a moment, waiting and wondering. He walked to the gate to get a better view down the slope and saw Assumpta rush out from her house and wait at the cattle grid, the dogs behind her barking. He raced down towards her and when she saw him coming, she looked again towards the road below her house before collapsing to her knees, her head in her hand.

'He's taken, Marlo, he's taken and, God help us, I think we're too late.'

Marlo sprinted into the house and pushed open the door to the kitchen. Mossie looked like he was having a nap. He had his arms crossed over a copy of the *Southern Star* on his chest and his eyes were closed.

'Jesus, Mossie. Mossie. Mossie. Wake up, man, come on! Mossie, you've got to be joking.'

Flashes of red light bounced off the kitchen walls as the ambulance drove into the yard.

The paramedics took over. 'Can you step outside quickly please, sir. Can you stay with the wife? Are you the son? Could you leave the room, take her with you. We need to clear space around him, you understand?'

He stayed with Assumpta outside on the kitchen steps, hugging her as she sat, twisting her fingers and cracking her knuckles. 'I cleared away the dinner and then did the washing up. I thought he was asleep on that armchair all that while or he would have helped dry. He knows I like the kitchen clean when we come down in the mornings, especially Monday mornings. Lord knows he might've tried to call out to me, but I had my back to him all the while at the sink, now he's gone, oh Jesus, he too is taken from me.'

She wept inconsolably then, her shoulders heaving under Marlo's arm as he held her close. She squeezed Marlo's hand. 'He won't be alone, sure he won't, they'll have each other now, him and Thomas.'

Faith has its uses, he thought, as he hugged her and tried at the same time to look past her shoulder into the kitchen. They were bent over Mossie's body laid out on the floor, the electric pads attached to his chest. The body rose and fell with each attempt, and in the end the paramedics hung their heads in despair, before one of them came out to Assumpta.

She nodded her head wordlessly and huge big sobs burst out of her.

Marlo looked towards the kitchen in disbelief. *Just a few hours ago we wet the calf's head and now this. Jesus, Mossie.*

Some of the neighbours from across the valley had begun to arrive, alerted by the siren and flashing lights. Marlo held onto Assumpta tightly as Finbar Cronin and Batty Mor gave him a quick nod before they headed into the kitchen, thinking they could help. Nan Murphy just stood beside Marlo, shifting from one foot to the other, dabbing her face with a crumpled handkerchief. The Crowleys and the Harringtons lingered respectfully in a small group near the back wall, waiting for Finbar to emerge with some news from the kitchen. And when he didn't appear as they had expected, they proceeded to resurrect every other sudden death that had occurred in the valley, embellishing the details, delving deep into their collective memories to reveal some forgotten detail that astonished them all and had them shaking their heads and kicking small stones at their feet to accompany each sharp intake of breath.

Dolores was not far behind them, her hands to her forehead and then to her mouth, as she got out of her car.

'It's Mossie, is it?'

Marlo nodded.

'Ahh, no. Are they taking him to the hospital?'

Marlo shook his head.

'Ahh, lad! Jesus. Ahh, no!' She knelt down and cradled Assumpta's head in her hands. 'Ahh no, the poor man. The poor man.'

The two friends wept in each other's arms.

Inside the kitchen, Finbar was at the phone on the wall. His lips were pursed as he dialled the priest first and the doctor immediately after, constantly wiping his forehead with his sleeve as he spoke. When he put the receiver back on the cradle, he rested his head against the wall beside the phone and cried quietly. Batty stood beside him, crossing himself several times with heavily calloused hands and even as his own strong builder's shoulders slumped, he patted Finbar on his back. The two of them and Mossie had known each other from their first day in the little school at Youngfields. They went back a long way as had their fathers and grandfathers before them – many generations bound by friendships and enmities and everything that fell in between. The paramedics signalled to Marlo to come into the kitchen.

'Are you the son? Oh? Not even next of kin? OK, anyway, maybe you could tell the wife – we'll have to take him, the body to the hospital. For the post-mortem. Sorry, but it's the standard procedure. Of course, she will have a little time while we wait for the doctor to come to certify the death. It's Dr Feeley on this weekend and we asked that neighbour there to ring him. Will you let his wife know?'

Assumpta rose up slowly, pushing away Dolores's hand.

'I heard you. Mossie will need his jumper on and shoes too. I'm not sending him to Bantry in those slippers. The dogs have had a right go chewing at them.'

Dolores was quick to follow her into the bedroom. 'Assumpta, you can't – they won't let us. Remember when me brother passed at home, it was the same. Not till the post-mortem was over were we allowed to dress him. He went a whole two days in his old dressing gown. Ahh, Assumpta, come here now, love, the lads will cover him and keep him warm under blankets for the journey. I'll make sure of that. Come here now. Father Angelo will be here any minute, I'm sure.'

Nan Murphy put the kettle on for the paramedics while the gurney was got from the ambulance. They drank their tea quietly outside the kitchen door as Marlo went to the neighbours gathered outside and filled them in.

Joe Herlihy stepped up to Marlo and held him by the shoulders. 'Don't be worrying, lad, it'll all fall into place once the doctor and the priest arrive. They've this down to a fine art. Living and dying – between them they know nearly everything about it.'

At that very moment they heard Father Angelo's car, and everyone stood up straight as he swept into the yard. The doctor followed right behind and was out of his jeep even before the priest stepped out of his car. The two men shook hands, acknowledged the neighbours in the yard with brief nods and stepped into the house, the doctor giving way to the priest at the door. The neighbours had hardly gotten over the arrival of the two men when Jim O'Reilly's squad car spluttered into the yard. The young Garda took his cap off as he walked briskly up the steps to the kitchen, with just a tip of the chin in their direction before he disappeared into the house as well.

The Harrington lad, who Marlo had met on the pitch a couple of times, let out a sigh of relief. "Tis the Holy trinity no less. Things will be sorted now.'

Enda Crowley spat into the ground. 'What are ye on about? The man's dead like. What's to sort?'

Everyone pitched in, their voices high and their nerves shot.

'Too right, it's the one thing the three of them can't do.'

'Stop blathering, the lot of ye. Spare a though for herself left alone.'

'Ah, Assumpta, the poor divil. First Thomas and now her Mossie.'

'I'd say it was his bad heart.'

'His da and uncle went the same. Must run in the family.'

'Like delusion runs in yours – since when did ye become a doctor?'

'And since when are ye policing my thoughts, ye eejit?'

'Shut yer faces, ye both, or get on home and stay there.'

The sparring halted when the ambulance crew emerged with Mossie on the gurney. Everyone crossed themselves hurriedly and shuffled closer in a semi-circle around the ambulance, only to step away, nearly falling backwards over themselves in shock as the siren and lights came on before the vehicle drove away across the cattle grid and down the mountain road out of the glen.

Marlo looked towards the kitchen door. They must be comforting her in the good room, he thought. He hesitated and then gave in to a sudden urge to run behind the ambulance as it made its way down the valley. Five hundred yards later, he stopped, panting loudly as it disappeared around the corner at the old stone bridge and then, catching his breath, he wiped the tears that were freefalling down his face. The dogs had followed and now they stood close to him, unsure of themselves, looking up at him, licking his salty fingers gently, trying as they always did to judge the mood of the moment.

'He's gone, Blackie, Spot. He was a good man, a really good man and he's gone.' Marlo patted the mother and son and waited at the bridge for his tears to abate. When he got back to the house the neighbours were gathered in the kitchen and Nan Murphy immediately put the kettle on once again.

'You'll be needing a drop now, Marlo lad.'

He nodded.

'She's in the front room and holding herself up.'

Joe Herlihy sighed. 'It's the shock that does it.'

Garda O'Reilly popped his head into the kitchen. 'Ah, Marlo, Father Angelo wants a word with ye – in the front room.'

Nan Murphy pushed a cup into Marlo's hand. 'Let him bring his tea in with him, Jim, God knows he needs it.'

Assumpta was sitting on the couch, her eyes closed, with Dolores beside her. The doctor and priest were both standing at the window.

The priest looked worn. 'Marlo, you're going to be a true godsend. It's what Mossie would have wanted and Assumpta, as well, feels it should be you that takes on the job.'

Marlo looked at Assumpta. 'I hated the thought of him going alone but they wouldn't let anyone else in the ambulance, Assumpta.'

Her eyes welled up, but before she could speak the priest came forward and took both of Marlo's hands in his. 'There is the immediate matter of the bus that we have to deal with right now. Mossie's regulars plus the tourists who have to be picked up tomorrow. Not everyone can be informed and the regulars have to get to work, the tourists have planes and ferries to catch once they get to Cork. We've discussed it between us – we think you'll be the best to take over the run for the next few days, Marlo.'

'Me? You mean, you want me to drive Mossie's bus?'

Assumpta stifled her sob. 'It's what Mossie would have wanted. I know it.'

Marlo knelt in front of her. 'Assumpta, look at me, it's not going to be a problem. I'll do it. I know he'd trust me to.'

'Bernard Causkey is the first on – at the post office in Allihies. He'll show you every stop on the way.'

Dolores nodded. 'Mossie's regulars could drive that bus blindfolded. He used to say that so himself.'

Marlo could see Garda Jim signalling him to come into the kitchen. The doctor put a hand on Marlo's shoulders as he headed for the door. 'Good man, that's one less worry for Assumpta and a huge one at that.' He leaned in closer and lowered his voice. 'The weeks and months ahead are going to be hard on her, poor woman.'

Garda Jim had taken out his little book and was poised with a pen. 'I'll sort the insurance issues with my cousin. He's a broker across in Skibbereen. I take it you've a full English licence? I'll need a few details for him – your age and date of birth, that sort of thing. I'll have you totally legit to drive the bus by tomorrow morning.'

CHAPTER SIX

Bernard Causkey boarded the bus with a huge big sigh, his belly preceding him, his large hands gripping the rail along the steps of the bus. 'Ahh, lad, I heard 'twas going to be a young fella driving. Marlo, it's yourself, is it? The missus had a call from her sister in Glengarriff last night. We were up till the early hours this morning talking about it. Shocking sad business altogether. Father Angelo called soon after and said I was to show you all the stops. Said I was to make sure ye missed no one. Father, I says to him, I'd do that with me eyes closed I would. Bernard is me name.'

Marlo shook the huge hand that was thrust out at him. 'I'll do my best, Bernard. Mossie would hate to let his regulars down.'

'You can motor on now, lad, we've no one now to board the bus till Castletownbere. On Thursdays we pick up one of the Hare Krishnas from the crossroads for Dursey, but not today. Then we take on two fellas outside the bank on the main street and Mrs O'Connor just outside the town opposite the Island View Bed and Breakfast. Mossie will have the tourists in his book. They usually book directly on the phone with Assumpta. Did she give it to you?'

Marlo pulled it out of the glove compartment. 'I have it here. Three Yanks from Adrigole at the church and a German fella from Ballylickey at the petrol station. I'm sure I'll have the hang of the route in a few days.'

Bernard nodded. 'Ahh, you will. You will, for sure.'

They drove quietly for a while, Marlo concentrating on avoiding the huge potholes on the road while Bernard shifted in his seat, constantly bracing for the bumps with dramatic intakes of breaths.

Marlo wasn't in a mood for small talk. The enormity of what had happened was overwhelming and before the run down the peninsula to Allihies he had stopped at the phone box in

Glengarriff and rung Mrs Kelly in Croydon. He fed in the coins as he pictured Mam and Mary dropping everything and rushing across the landing to their neighbour's good room, where the phone sat on a small shelf that was adorned with a crocheted pelmet, leaving no doubt of the instrument's special status in the household. Marlo knew that they had the receiver cradled between their heads, an ear each pressed to either side of the black Bakelite, while Mrs Kelly lingered not too far away, smiling benignly as she deciphered the gist of the news from overheard snatches.

Mary had hogged most of the conversation as his mam had been shocked into silence for a moment.

'I'm going to drive the minibus for Assumpta, will you tell Mam that?'

'Jesus, will you be able for it, Marlo?'

'For feck's sake, Mary, would you ever stop with that. I was driving a bread van in Croydon right through three years of college if you care to remember, and anyway the roads are near empty here. It's the Beara peninsula, not Trafalgar Square, for God's sake.'

Mam had intervened. 'Will you tell Assumpta I asked after her, Marlo? I'll send her a mass card, will you not forget to tell her that, Marlo. I'll ring her after the funeral. Do you know what the arrangements are?'

'There's the post-mortem first so we'll know in a few days, Mam, and I'll ring you about it.'

'What about the English couple? Aren't you working for them?'

'I've the weekends for that, Mary. The money is too good to stop. Anyway, this bus driving will only be for a few weeks till Assumpta decides what to do with the business. I must go now, I've my first pickup in an hour from Allihies.'

Their goodbyes were subdued and he hung up quickly. Now, as he drove towards Castletownbere, he regretted being so short with Mary. *I've said worse things to her over the years, and she my mother all that time.* He gripped the steering wheel. *Deal with it, Marlo — they both did and you agreed it was the best outcome for everyone.*

At the back of the bus, Bernard had got up from his seat and was walking up to the front. He blew his nose into a large checked handkerchief before sitting down right behind Marlo.

'Mossie Hanley had a bad heart, sure we all knew it. If ye ask me 'twas never right since they lost Thomas. God love him, a little bit of him died every time he thought of his child. I never paid much heed to him going on about how his memories of Thomas kept him going. That kind of heartache just chips away at your very being. There's no escaping it.'

Marlo looked at the large swarthy man filling up his rear-view mirror.

'Were you friends long?'

'We knew each other very well for a very short while and then years later we picked up again where we had left it, no bother. I think I must've been nineteen and himself a year younger when we first met, loaded into the back of an old lorry at the town square in Bantry, no better than bullocks for the mart. Dropped off in pairs we were, along the many miles of roads in the peninsula, with just a shovel each, to dig holes to put in the electric poles. I bet ye can't imagine life without the electric now but, men like us, young ones then, we dug them holes, 'twas us brought the power into people's homes. Was fierce hard going, it was. Water seeped in once ye went below a foot or two, flooded yer boots, and then we'd be digging in pure muck and sinking deeper into shite with every shovelful that we took out. Pure hardship it was, lad, and to think a flick of a switch is all it takes now.'

He stopped to blow his nose again before he continued. 'We spent a summer paired up, our feet totally shredded with the cold and wet till we both got infections and he lost a toe. The surgeon fella in Bantry said Mossie was lucky he didn't lose his foot entirely. That sure put the fear of God in me mother and she begged me father not to send me working for the Electricity Board no more. It was twenty-five years later that we met again when I stepped onto his bus heading for my first day at a new job in the factory in Ballincollig. We picked up where we left, he was great craic, a good man. Kind. Patient. The regulars are going to be shocked, lad, shocked when they see you and realise why.'

Marlo nodded. 'Yes, it's going to be a difficult journey.'

'Leave it to me. I'll break it to each of them. I told Father Angelo I would.'

'Thanks. Might be best coming from you, Bernard.'

'I'll leave you to keep your eyes on the road.'

And what a road it is too, by God.

The lonely and remote tip of Beara on the very south-westerly edge of Europe, with its mountains of folded rock reminiscent of a slab of Vienetta and towering sea cliffs hunched over Bantry Bay, was the kind of place that could revive your soul, its flower-strewn lanes bursting with oxeye daisies, foxgloves, montbretia and wild garlic, and its untidy hedgerows crammed with whitethorn, fuchsia, gorse and holly. But even Marlo, a blow-in freshly arrived, knew that it could just as easily turn on you – here, rain howled and wind thundered; the elements were a savage law unto themselves.

The two lads at the bank got on board the bus, their faces sombre, and giving Marlo quick nods they immediately took their seats behind Bernard. They had heard the news already and wasted no time looking for details.

Bernard folded his handkerchief. 'Will ye wait till Mrs O'Connor gets on? Save me repeating meself. This here is Marlo O'Sullivan – he'll be driving us for a few days at least.'

'Good lad, Marlo. I'm Fionn. I get off at Cork. And this is Connie.'

Connie raised his hand and gave a little wave. 'I'm with ye till

Bandon. 'Tis hard to get our heads around the terrible news. Would ye believe I'd managed to get a ticket to give Mossie, Lord keep him, for the match on Friday night. Are ye from 'round here then, seeing as ye're driving the bus?'

Bernard interrupted. 'Coming up ahead there, Marlo, that lady with the striped bag. We need to stop for her and don't be shy about telling her to sit down first. Mags O'Connor has a tendency to linger on the first step till she gets to hear all she wants to know.'

By the time they got to Rossmackowen, the sun had vanished and a sodden mist completely shrouded the view of Hungry Hill. Dan O'Driscoll was waiting at his roadside cottage, and he waved as Marlo slowed down and then raised his eyebrow at Bernard as he boarded.

'Sit down properly now, Dan, before I tell ye the news.'

Mags O'Connor couldn't wait. Her tears began to fall in anticipation of Bernard's words, and on seeing Dan's absolute shock she crossed herself and kissed the rosary beads tightly clasped in the palm of her hand.

Marlo was grateful that Bernard had taken his promise to Father Angelo so seriously. By the time the bus skirted the little bay in Adrigole and pulled up at the church, the scene of the tragedy in the Hanley house was as real to everyone as if they had been there themselves. Marlo resisted the urge to correct the details. What matter, now that Mossie was gone.

Bernard half stood up at his seat. 'Right, we won't be gloomy from here on now. Mossie was particular about showing his best face to tourists. We've Yanks ahead, so let's do his job for him, may the Lord bless and protect him.'

Marlo took his cue and hopped out of the bus, shook the hands of the middle-aged couple and loaded their bags into the small hold. They were from Detroit and were heading to Wales in search of his family roots. Hers were firmly in Adrigole, and she had just laid flowers at the family grave and said her goodbyes. There were smiles all around and Dan O'Driscoll immediately set about trying to see if he was related to the American lady.

'Two generations of O'Driscolls went to America and never came back. My father's people are the ones who stayed, we think because they couldn't afford the passage.'

'Or wanted to hold onto the land, more likely.'

'That too, Bernard, that too. Who'd want to give up a side of Hungry Hill if they could save it for themselves.'

All thoughts of Mossie Hanley were set aside while the Americans were entertained. *I bet Mossie never put on such a show as this lot are doing in his memory.* Marlo caught Bernard's eye in the rear-view mirror and smiled, joining in by asking them about their onward journey. The connections and the conversation moved back and forth, about this and that, the Yanks never guessing for a moment that a collective effort was being made to keep up a dead man's tradition.

The mist dissipated as the bus approached Zetland and Marlo put his foot on the pedal to crest the high hill past the old national school. The Yanks gasped at the view that unfolded from the vantage point, and then, as the bus snaked its way downhill, Bernard pointed out the landmarks at Seal Harbour, Whiddy and beyond.

A mile or so later as they went around a sharp bend, Bernard tapped Marlo on his shoulder. 'We've a stop coming up just at Shrone, around the corner here. I'll tell you when to stop.'

Marlo nodded.

'Up ahead there, Marlo, the lad's just coming out from the house, you can pull up at the green gate. That's our Sully. I'll get the door, he can't reach the handle yet.'

A young child waved to an unseen person at the window inside the small roadside bungalow, before boarding the bus. He stood on the step and gave Marlo a long look before unhitching his backpack and sitting down on the single seat. The regulars all called out to him.

'Sully, ye champ, how's things?'

'Fine new cap there, Sully, did your mam get you that?'

'Strap up, Sully, we don't want you falling out now, boy.'

'Bernard, introduce him to our driver.'

Bernard gave the child a big wink. 'Now, Sully lad, this here's Marlo and he's driving the bus for Mossie for a while.'

Marlo gave him a wave. Father Angelo had never said anything about a child on the bus. No one had. He couldn't be more than five or six years old. Why on earth wasn't he on a school bus?

Sully looked straight ahead, and Marlo put the bus into gear.

Mrs O'Connor stifled a sob as she leaned forward towards Connie and Fionn in the seat ahead of her. 'D'you think he knows? Will he have been told?'

Bernard hissed under his breath. 'For God's sake, Mags! He isn't deaf as well and it's not our business to tell him what his mother might or might not want to tell him.'

With that Bernard shuffled up to Marlo at the front of the bus and lowered his voice before asking, 'Did Father Angelo, or Assumpta even, say anything to ye about the young fella?'

Marlo shook his head.

'Ahh, feck. See here, Marlo, I suppose with the shock of everything that's happened in the last twelve hours – I'm not surprised that it didn't cross their minds. The child's not going to be a bother to ye at all – I can tell you that much. He'll sit quietly on the bus all the way to Cork and ye just need to drop him off to the house on the way back.'

'What d'you mean, Bernard – I mean, where's he going to, where does he get off?'

'He doesn't. I mean he doesn't get off. He's not going anywhere.'

'I don't understand. Why is he on the bus then?'

'OK. I'll put it like this, Marlo – he's just on it for the ride, see? He gets on, sits in the bus all the way to Cork and the all the way back. His mam will be waiting at home for him when you drop him off. Look, I shouldn't be standing while you drive so I'll fill ye in when you stop at the Eccles for Daragh Keohane. He has his work kit to load and it's a chance to step off the bus for a minute. I wouldn't want the little lad to hear me talk about him. Ye know what I mean?'

At the car park of the Eccles Hotel, Daragh introduced himself as Marlo opened the hold for him. 'I heard about Mossie this morning, Lord save him. You're the neighbour, yeah? Good on ye. I'd be drowning in shite or worse if I didn't turn up to work.'

Bernard stepped off the bus and steered Marlo out of earshot. 'The little fellow doesn't speak. Ye know what I mean, he's mute like. So, he just gets on for the ride, he's not a bother at all.'

'Mute? As in he can't speak at all?'

'Never a sound out of him. A sad situation, but Mossie taking him on made a huge difference. The mother works while he's on the bus and she sort of home schools him the best she can the rest of the time. The school won't have him. Tough going for her and an even tougher road ahead for him, poor sod.'

'So, the bus is a creche for this child. Jesus!'

'He's never a bother and we all know him. He has a ham sandwich and two chocolate bourbons in his bag, which he'll eat when you are waiting in Cork for the return passengers. He has two bottles with Mi Wadi – the blackcurrant is for the journey to Cork and the orange he drinks on the way back. He's very particular, our Sully. Always the same routine and never a bother to anyone.'

'But I'm responsible for him? Christ, I don't know what to say actually.'

'Have a word with Assumpta this evening when you get back. She'll explain the arrangement to you. Mossie was very fond of this little fellow.'

'Jesus, no! I'm not going to trouble Assumpta – I mean, I really couldn't. She's the wake to organise and Mossie not even brought home as yet. The post-mortem could be a few days. But what do I do if he, I mean if the child, wants something?'

Bernard shrugged. 'He never does. He can't speak so he never wants anything.'

'That's just terrible. What kind of parents would let a helpless child get on a bus full of strangers?'

'Ahh, now lad, you're rushing to judgement. That's too harsh like! He has no father, he hasn't. Just his mother. Mossie was no stranger, as are none of us. Sure, the lad knows everyone. Anyways, he sits looking out the window all the way there and all the way back. As I said, not a bother. I suppose we better get on before that lot in the bus wonder what the feck we are doing dossing here by the side of the road.'

Marlo shook his head. 'I'll do it for Mossie but sure as fecking hell don't ask me to understand it.'

The road rose steadily to Derrycreha and despite the day that was in it, Marlo prepared himself for the view that never failed to fill him with a sense of wonder. To his right, on the other side of the road below the untidy fields bursting with purple loosestrife and gorse, Bantry Bay lay roiling between the two peninsulas, reflecting the mood on the bus. The distant horizon was blurred at the edges with ominous high banks of cumulo-nimbus clouds readying themselves to scud across the bay and saturate everything that lay underneath.

Marlo glanced over his shoulder quickly at Sully. The child had his nose pressed to the window, his legs swinging to a slow rhythm under him. He had a head of dark curls, big eyes and seemed content with his lot.

'You OK there, Sully?'

The child looked at Marlo briefly and then looked back out of the window. They were driving over the bridge at Coomhola and Marlo turned his attention back to the road, slowing down as he took the hairpin bend. The mouth of the river was being sucked out by the receding tide and the little cove was now a large shingle beach with three intertwined rivulets rushing towards the sea. Fronds of seaweed lay limp across the pebbles exactly as the tide had left them, while oyster catchers strutted, scouring the shallows.

At the petrol station in Ballylickey the German passenger got on without any fuss, cradling a fuchsia sapling in his hand.

'For my Oma,' he said, overcome with a need to explain.

Bernard gave him a little clap. 'Add a bottle of Irish whiskey and she'll be striking everyone else off her will.'

The German looked confused and for the rest of the journey to Bantry, Connie and Fionn took turns miming the death of a grandmother.

They were driving into Bantry before Bernard asked them to shut up. 'Would you ever let the fella alone, lads, his head's spinning with the panto you've put on for him. Marlo, the next pick-up is at the town square, pull up outside Biggs Hardware there.'

In his rear-view mirror, Marlo could see Mags rolling her eyes to heaven. 'Lord be praised, the two sisters are on time.'

'Never did it when Mossie was alive, had to wait till he was gone, the eejits.' Bernard was swearing under his breath.

Two middle-aged women and one young man got on, each one of them crossing themselves on the first step as they boarded.

The stouter of the two women stopped in front of Bernard. 'What happened?'

The woman behind nudged her with an elbow. 'Move on and sit down first, Nancy, my feet are killing me as it is.'

'Jesus, would you have some respect for the departed, Nuala. I was only asking after Mossie, for God's sake.'

'Nuala, sit in here beside me so.' Mags lowered her voice before she continued, 'Mind, we've a few visitors on the bus so let's keep it calm like.'

'I'd be happy to, Mags, thanks, seeing as herself is going to be like that. How's the little lad today? How are ye, Sully? It's

Monday so have ye been counting all the red cars, have you?'

As she sat beside Mags, Nuala covered her mouth with her hand. 'Does the boy know? About Mossie, I mean – we just heard about it an hour ago as we were getting ready.'

Bernard stood up and let the young man slide into the window seat beside him and then shuffled towards the women, leaned over and put a hand to his lips. 'We've no idea what he knows so we'll just leave it be for the moment.'

He went back into his seat. 'How's things today, Liam?'

'Nuala and Nancy are just after telling me about Mossie. I hadn't a clue till five minutes ago. Shook is what I am. Well shook. Who'd have thought when I stepped off the bus on Friday I'd not see him again. He was good to me, he was. There's no telling what lies ahead, sure there isn't. Life's some bitch.'

Bernard patted him on his leg. 'Marlo's taking over the bus for a few days till Assumpta decides what to do.'

Nuala gave Marlo a small wave. 'You'll be careful at the bends as we get into Bandon. Me and my sister here can get very sick if ye go braking too much. The young lad too, we think. He doesn't say anything, though.' She turned to Mags beside her and whispered. 'Does this new driver know that Sully can't speak?'

Nancy shushed her immediately. 'We don't know if he can't speak. We know that he doesn't speak and hasn't ever. But we also do know he isn't deaf like!'

Marlo had been taking it all in. 'I'll be very careful, no worries.'

The bus was full now with just one vacant seat. The Yanks had long fallen off to sleep, leaning on each other, snoring gently. As they drove out of Bantry past the graveyard by the shore, Marlo suddenly thought of Mossie lying in the mortuary. *I hope they've kept you warm.* I hope they left the slippers on, even if they were the ones the dogs had chewed. Poor dogs, they'll be lost without you. He felt his eyes fill up, but his thoughts were interrupted by Bernard leaning forward. 'Have you been on this road, lad, beyond Bantry – driven down this way to Cork city like?'

'Just once – when Mossie picked me up from Cork airport a few months ago. But it was late and completely dark by the time we got to Crostera.'

'Ahh, sometimes he switched timings with Eamon and did the evening run. Sure, it's a fairly straightforward drive. Stay on the R586 all the way through Drimoleague, Dunmanway and Enniskeane, then you're at Bandon. A few get off there and then you head on for the airport before crossing the city to Kent Station and stop at the newsagents opposite. It's where most of us get off. The newsagent has the list of the returnees – could be ten or sometimes no one at all. You wait about thirty minutes till half eleven and then leave.'

'So, how do you all, the regulars on the bus, get back?'

'Eamon O'Reilly from Eyeries does the second run and his bus leaves the city in the evening at six. He and Mossie dove-tailed nicely – sometimes they switched times if needed. They had a good partnership, and it means a lot to us regulars. Jobs are hard to come by on Beara. Mossie knew the bus was a lifeline for most of us.' Bernard sat back into his seat and sighed loudly and having muttered something about not having slept a wink the previous night he nodded off, his head lolling from side to side.

Marlo glanced back at Sully. The boy had opened his backpack and was drinking out of a small bottle, his nose still pressed to the window. His was the only seat with a makeshift seatbelt fashioned from a bungee cord and hook, and a good thing it was too for the road surface was atrocious in parts – several mile-long stretches were just a continuous patchwork of tar and hardcore, where potholes had been filled temporarily and then forgotten for ever. The bus heaved over the bad sections and Marlo drove slowly, aware of the sudden responsibility that rested with him for the lives on board. *And the child to top it.*

The landscape inland was not as dramatic as the coast – the fields lay flatter and the hills were low and rounded.

Whitewashed farmhouses, each surrounded by a collection of corrugated roofed sheds and barns and enclosed within galvanised farm gates, were like tiny little kingdoms, set in the midst of rich grazing.

Everyone in the bus had gone silent, most were asleep, and as Marlo scanned the group in his rear-view mirror, he wondered about them.

You never ever really know what's happening in anyone's life. Wasn't that Mam's mantra? But he knew now that all along, every time she said that in admonishment if he was being uncharitable, or as an explanation when she was faced with unreasonable behaviour or more often than not in empathy, all along it was their own lives she was referring to as well. Mam, her Mary and their Marlo. She might have been referring to Mrs Kelly's dodgy hips or to Princess Diana's marriage but every time she repeated it, it had been the three of them that she was empathising with, the three of them she was praising – a pat on the back again for being together still, for having managed to keep him against all odds.

He had relived that conversation with Mam and Mary countless times, remembering the way the two of them had held each other's hands tightly, pushing a box of tissues between them as they shed tears, and each time that memory had chipped away at the confusion he had first felt. His new relationship with his mam he could handle – mother to grandmother was not such a huge leap, staying loving wasn't hard. But Mary – she could only ever remain his sister. Marlo realised that she was expecting and hoping for more and was eager for him to be filial, but it was too hard just as yet – she was going to be disappointed. He couldn't remember a time he hadn't fought with her, most of the time viciously, refusing to be disciplined by a sibling, older though she was. Mam usually intervened and played peacemaker but Marlo could see now that all those years Mary just couldn't help herself, deny herself the role that she had given up for his sake.

He had asked them who his father was. 'You owe it to me, Mary. You can't land me with news like this and not tell me the whole story.'

'He's nobody.'

'Bullshit. He can't be a nobody if he's my father.'

'Fathered you, that's all.'

'What the feck difference does that make?'

Mam had her face in her hands. 'She hasn't told me either.'

'Jesus. What are you both like!' Marlo had stormed out of the room, and hours later when he had returned well jarred, with a chicken tikka masala from the curry house down the road, they were sitting at the table exactly as he had left them.

Mary had taken out a plate and fork from the kitchen press and put it on the table. 'There was no point in walking out like that. How can that be helpful? And Mam was worried sick too. Marlo, are you even listening?'

'Seriously, Mary, you have to have your head examined. *I'm* being unhelpful?'

He hadn't spoken to her for several days after, holed up in his room after work, studiously avoiding her at all cost. It was Mam who had accosted him four days later.

'One day you'll understand or maybe you never will, Marlo. But have the grace to be civil till then. You were the only thing that mattered to her then and nothing's changed.'

'Why even tell me? Things were OK as we were and you can tell her I'm not interested in half a story for sure.'

'Telling you the truth was hard and she'll tell you – and me – the rest when she's ready.'

Now, as he drove the bus along the road to Bandon, the thought struck him that Mam could go just as suddenly as Mossie. A morbid thought, but not outside the realms of possibility. Mary and me left squabbling for ever unless, unless maybe I rang Mary at Dr Khan's. It would make Mam happy – all she had wanted these past few months was for him to forgive Mary or, as she had put it, just put yourself in her shoes, Marlo. *That's what I'll do, ring Mary and take it from there.*

As Marlo slowed the bus down to a near halt, to take the turn onto Kilbroggan Hill in Bandon town, Dan O'Driscoll and Fionn shuffled up to the front.

Dan ruffled Sully's mop of curls. 'See you tomorrow, champ. Just here'll do mighty, Marlo. Me and Fionn are for as far as Bandon.'

'Sees ye tomorrow and may he rest in peace, our Mossie.' Fionn crossed himself as he stepped out of the bus.

The Yanks had to be woken up as they approached the airport, and soon after Bernard guided Marlo as he drove across the city and over the Lee to Kent Station, where he pulled up at the small layby right in front of the newsagents. The bus emptied quickly and no one lingered beyond saying elaborate goodbyes to Sully in turn. He ignored them, his attention on the two dogs tied up outside the shop.

Mags tapped Marlo on his shoulder. 'I'll bring the little fellow back in a minute.'

Bernard was helping the child with his backpack. ' It's OK, Marlo. It's the routine once we get here. Mags takes him to the toilet and brings him straight back, before she heads off herself. There was always a coffee for Mossie in the shop once he got here. Or tea if you want, lad, but I'll go in and let them know the situation. Follow me and I'll introduce you. They'll have the return list for you if anyone has booked in. All ye have to do is to just wait here till everyone is on board and then it's all the way back just the way you came. It's just you to look after the lad, but his mother is always there when you get to the house.'

Marlo had a head full of questions, but before he could ask Bernard patted him on his back. 'The little lad will not ask for anything, and the return lot will tell you where they want to get off and sure I'll see ye tomorrow bright and early like. You did well filling in today. Mossie will be well pleased. God bless and protect his poor soul.'

To Marlo's relief there were no return passengers and he was nursing a welcome cup of coffee when Mags came back with Sully. She waited till Marlo had the bungee cord strapped around the child before turning abruptly and leaving.

'OK, Sully, looks like it's just me and you today, all the way home. Will we turn on the radio? I wouldn't mind some music for the way back. Seeing as there's no one else on the bus. OK, I'll take that as a yes. My mam always did that when I didn't answer, you know, when I was a kid. Took it as a yes.'

Sully looked at him for a moment before readying his second bottle of drink from out of the backpack. Then with his cheek resting against his window, he kept his eyes on the windscreen and the road beyond.

The journey back was slow, the soft drizzle of morning having turned into driving rain which drummed loudly on the roof of the bus. Now and again, they slowed down behind a tractor and in his rear-view mirror Marlo could see the little boy sit up straight to get a better view as they overtook.

Marlo smiled. A perfectly normal little boy then. 'It's a Massey Ferguson, that one. D'you know, Mossie had a red one and it's always really shiny too. Mossie used to wash it every weekend. D'you know that, Sully?' Marlo turned around to him. 'I'll keep chatting to you if you don't mind, Sully. Just this and that, you know, or it would feel a bit strange sitting in complete silence here. You don't have to even nod or shake your head or roll your eyes.'

Marlo laughed to himself. *Like I used to when Mary would start at me.* Roll my eyes at her and drive her mental. Or give her the silent treatment when she asked questions about his day at school, his friends, the teachers. Or worse still, dip into a repertoire of sulky replies: I'm saving it to tell Mam. What's it to you, Mary. Nosy parker, Mary. Curiosity killed the cat, Mary. Mary, Mary, quite contrary. *God, I was a brat.*

Once past Bantry the road was more familiar and Marlo put his foot on the pedal whenever the road allowed him to. They were driving through Glengarriff when Marlo wondered what he was to do if the child's mother wasn't there to meet the bus. Lucky there weren't any other passengers, no one to take to the far end of the peninsula, so he supposed he could just wait in the bus at his house till the someone came for him. They drove past Casey's Hotel and then the road twisted its way towards Ellen's Rock, hugging the waterfront close. The tide had begun to rise, and waves sloshed against the rocks that lined the seafront. Sully was now looking straight ahead, his little legs swinging vigorously, and his face twitched now and again, his body charged with a nervous energy.

'Nearly there now, Sully. I'll turn around at your gate as I've to head back to Crostera – you know, to leave the bus off at Mossie's house. Keep sitting now, good lad, till I take off your belt.'

As he swung the bus around, he could see the front door open, and he breathed a sigh of relief. He stood up and stepped over the gearbox and no sooner had he unhooked the bungee cord than the little boy had shot out of his seat, ducking under Marlo's arm.

Marlo put his hand out. 'Whoa there, lad, watch yourself now – don't fall down those stairs!'

But Sully had jumped off the top step and, to Marlo's absolute surprise, it was right into Kitty's waiting arms.

'Kitty! Jesus, I didn't expect to see you. What're you doing here?'

'Collecting this little babba here, my son.' She gave Sully another hug and kiss. 'I wanted to say thank you too, Marlo. I only heard about poor Mossie about half an hour after you had collected Sully. It's been a crazy morning – I sent him off with no clue that anything had happened or that it was you that was driving the bus.' Her voice broke and she wiped her tears on Sully's shoulders. 'John Bosco called to the house here with the news – I was floored, as is everyone in the glen, I imagine. It was such a relief when I heard it was you at the wheel. Bernard and Mags must have looked after him, they always do. I'd be lost without their help. Was he OK coming back alone with you? Were you a good boy, Sully? Were you good for Marlo here?'

'I never knew you had a son.' *Why the feck did I go making that sound like an accusation?* 'I mean, it makes sense now, Kitty, you know, why you never lingered after you hung up your apron at work.' *And there was me always hoping you would.*

She pushed her hair back from her eyes. 'I guess I don't know much about you either, Marlo.' Then she touched him on his arm briefly. 'What I do know is that you'd become good friends with Mossie – you must've had a very difficult day as well. I just can't believe he's gone. He was the kindest man, a gentle soul. I might've lost Sully, you know. If it wasn't for him.'

Her eyes were filling up. 'I had to leave Bocarnagh early today. I just wasn't up for any work, you know. Tiggy was good about it though – soon after I got there she insisted I take the day off and got Edward to load my cycle into his station wagon and drive me home. They knew Mossie was my godfather and that he took Sully on the bus with him. Anyway, I'm going up to Assumpta's in a while – just have to give this young man his dinner first.' She hugged Sully tightly. 'Are you hungry, my little pet? Will you eat like a whale or a dinosaur? It's rooster chips and fish fingers, your favourite.'

Sully kicked his feet which were wrapped around her waist and hugged her back and she laughed. 'Is that a fish finger hug? Where's my rooster chip hug, you little monkey?'

Sully hugged her again and then squirmed his way out of her arms and ran to the front door.

'I'll wait for you if you like, Kitty. It will save you the cycle up with him. Looks like rain might get heavier still.'

She hesitated and then nodded. 'I think I will, thanks, Marlo. There'll be good few calling in to Assumpta, the poor thing, this evening, and I can always get a lift back when Sully gets tired. He can be a handful as soon as that happens. Come in till then, I won't be too long.'

'I won't get in your way – I'm happy to wait in the bus and you can get on with what you need to do for the lad. Carry on, Kitty.'

'Ah no, I couldn't leave you out on the road. Just come on in. I'll make you a cup of coffee while you wait. Come in, please.'

He followed her into the tiny bungalow. The glass-fronted porch was a geranium jungle and two black cats lay curled up between the terracotta pots and the cleaved leaves of a shiny monstera. The porch opened into a room that was as close to a schoolroom as could have been possible. The sofa and two armchairs in the corner nearly felt out of place amongst the bookshelves stacked with small plastic trays of crayons and craft materials and books by the dozens, a large blackboard on a home-made easel and laminated posters of animals, birds and trees on the wall. A big globe took up all the space on the deep windowsill and an old-fashioned wooden desk with its built-in seat and an inkwell, packed full of colouring pencils, sat opposite the blackboard. Beside it, sitting in one of the armchairs was a giant teddy bear lounging with its feet crossed and head leaning back on a cushion.

'Say hello to O'Sullivan Bear, Marlo, while I get you a coffee.' She laughed as she and Sully disappeared into what he guessed was the kitchen. He could hear her chatting to Sully. Asking him to wash his hands and bring his empty juice bottles out from his backpack.

'Up at the table now for your dinner and I want you to eat all on your own like a big boy. Milk and one sugar as always, Marlo?'

'Yes, thanks.' He was looking at a collection of pencil sketches, some blu-tacked to the wall over the mantlepiece and some resting on its narrow cast-iron shelf. They had a childish simplicity to them; nearly all were of horses and horse heads. Some of the horses were being groomed, some were of a single horse grazing, others were studies of the head with elaborate head collars. The sinuous lines in pencil were anatomically true, the trees and background foliage rendered with a deft touch.

'Are these yours, Kitty?' he asked, as she walked in with a mug of coffee. 'Have you shown them to Tiggy?'

'Oh, those aren't mine. They're Sully's. He's mad about horses. He draws them all the time. There's a riding school in the valley across from you at Rossnagreena, up near where old Donal lives. They have permission to go hacking in the reserve, so we see them around in the glen a good bit and some-times they even swim in the cove at Coomhola. But my lad is obsessed. Not just with horses and the trees but with everything in the forest reserve. I take him rambling there several times a week, he just loves it.' She pointed to the mini gallery over the mantle. 'He comes back with his head brimming with pictures to translate onto paper. I've boxes and boxes of his drawings under the bed – I can't bear to throw them away, plus he'd have an actual blue fit if I did.'

'Do you take him riding then? I mean, for lessons?'

'I might next year if he, you know, you can just guess – the riding school were hesitant, like. For safety reasons they said, since he doesn't speak.'

'As yet.'

She gave him a long look. 'Yes, as yet. There's nothing that he doesn't understand, you know, Marlo.'

'He's gifted, Kitty – imagine having an eye for such detail at his age. But here, look at me telling you what you already know for sure.'

'D'you want to come into the kitchen? We can talk while Sully's eating.'

He followed her through glass double doors into a small kitch-en with a solid fuel stove. A round table and four spindleback chairs took up most of the space and the fish fingers were being demolished at speed.

'He'll tackle the chips after – it's the one issue I've never had with him. He's a good eater.'

Marlo sat down at the chair she pulled out for him. 'Have you lived here long, Kitty? It looks like a very old cottage – much like my own.'

'Not surprising, Marlo. Neighbours often helped build each other's homes and sometimes two or three would be built back-to-back over one summer. Ours was built in 1830, we think, but of course has been chopped and changed since. My mother had the little porch built for my father to sit in. He had a stroke when he was fifty-five and lived his life out on his chair looking at the waters in the cove across the road. He could tell when the tide was going to turn the second before it did.'

'Must have been tough on your mother.'

'She got on with it. She hadn't a choice.'

'Does she live with you?'

'Oh no, she died two weeks after my father.'

'I'm sorry, Kitty. That must have been very hard, to lose both your parents.'

She nodded. 'It was and I couldn't have coped without Mossie. I was expecting Sully and he kept me sane. He and my dad were first cousins, but as good as brothers, as close.'

She tapped the table in front of Sully. 'Come on pet, ten chips to go. Will I do a countdown?' He nodded his head and picked up a chip in each hand. 'No stuffing your mouth, Sully, that's not what I meant. Sorry, Marlo, I know we are keeping you, another few minutes and we can head.'

Marlo waved away her apology. He would have been happy to sit here at her table for as long as it took for him to figure out what it was about Kitty that he had found so intriguing from the moment he had first met her at the house in Bocarnagh. She seemed so without guile, totally unself-conscious and there was an assuredness in her manner with her son. The severe ponytail that she wore to work was gone and her hair, a mass of auburn waves, framed her face. Her maroon wraparound skirt was topped off with a cream blouse and she had leather brogues, the same ones that she wore to work. She was wiping Sully's face with the dampened edge of a dishcloth and Marlo was immediately transported to the kitchen in London, to the times when Mary would hold his head in a vicelike grip and clean his face as he twisted and turned, protesting loudly to Mam that Mary was being bossy yet again. Mam never took sides, and there was nothing more than a smile and a 'go easy on the lad' from her. He must have been shaking his head at that sudden memory because Kitty was looking at him, the dishcloth poised mid-wipe. 'It has to be done, you know. I'm not hurting him even though he would give you the impression he's being murdered.'

Sully had managed to slip out of the chair as soon as his mother had turned to talk, and Marlo clapped as the escapee ran out of the room.

'Oh God, don't encourage him,' she said. 'All the glen will be there at Assumpta's and I don't want him looking untidy. Right so, Marlo, I'll just get our jackets and we can go now.'

As the minibus left the Kenmare road and turned into the forest, the reality of what faced them at Assumpta's house was brought to the fore and they stayed silent, except when Kitty pointed out a heron to Sully as the bus crossed the stone bridge under which the swollen river was bouncing over the rocks. The little boy became animated, nearly agitated, as the road wound its way deeper into the woods, shifting seats constantly, pressing his nose flat against one window and then another, until a plea from his mother had him back beside her, up front where he had started.

From about a quarter of a mile before the Hanley house, a line of parked cars clung to the edge of the narrow mountain road, all hugging one side of the road to allow for others to pass.

Outside the house, neighbours and friends stood in subdued little groups, men flicking cigarette ash to the ground and acknowledging old acquaintances that they hadn't met since the last funeral in the valley. Imperceptible lifts of the chin and little sideways twitches of the head meant everything when the men had nothing left to say. It could have been any one of them dead on the kitchen floor, taken too soon from their families – there was nothing to it but shake their heads in disbelief and stop to wonder about what the fates had in store for each of them.

The women on the other hand were all talking at the same time. They recounted, each of them with their own version, the last time Assumpta had told them how Mossie never knew when to stop. Lord, they said, crossing themselves, Lord have mercy on him, pronounced dead on the floor and she, now left alone in the same kitchen. In between speculating about the fate of the armchair, for surely the poor divil would not be able for it to remain in her kitchen, they took turns making tea and sandwiches, filling kettles, washing the cups and drying them off, tut-tutting at the ignorant lads who were lashing spoons, wet from stirring tea, directly into the sugar, all the while taking a good look around the house but keeping to themselves what they thought about the homemaking skills of their newly widowed neighbour, because everyone knew there was time and place for judgement.

Father Angelo's car was parked right up at the back door. The priest bloody well not be looking for his sandwich crusts to be cut today, thought Marlo as he pulled up the handbrake with a heavy heart. He could hear the muffled barks of the dogs.

'I'll come in a minute, Kitty, you carry on. I want to check if Blackie and Spot are OK.'

She nodded, and holding Sully's hand firmly walked to the back steps.

People standing around the shed made room for Marlo as he strode towards the door, whistling twice, short and sharp, like he remembered Mossie used to. The dogs went silent in anticipation and when he opened the door they lunged at him in delight, barking and whining in turns, happy to see a familiar face. He knelt down on the rough cement floor and let them have their fill of him. 'You poor lads, how long have they had you locked up here?'

And then the tears came out of nowhere as he hugged them both. The dogs licked his face and Spot pawed him over and over again. *Tears for a man I had known for a just a few months or is this something more?* Tears for the father I've never known? Will Mary ever tell me who he was. I'm owed that at least. He choked up and slumped against the wheels of the Massey Ferguson, his head between his knees. Blackie stood beside him whimpering and wagged her tail tentatively when he looked up. 'The world will never be the same for you two. But we'll make the best of it, OK?' He patted both their heads and wiped his face with the back of his sleeve. 'You're going to have to stay in for a little longer though, lads. I'd better head in now and see what's to be done.'

Inside the house, Assumpta was sitting on a kitchen chair with Father Angelo beside her. Batty Mor and Finbar directed the steady traffic of neighbours and friends who shuffled slowly towards her, offering their condolences, shaking hands and some bending over to hug her before heading into the kitchen for a tea and a biscuit. She saw him across the room, stood up and said something to the priest and then beckoned him over to the bedroom.

Marlo made his way to the bedroom picking up the threads of many an opinion being proffered like some sort of wordy balm to sooth everyone's agitated minds.

'She's in an awful shock, a fierce awful shock.' Nan Murphy had made that declaration several times, ringing her hands and reaching for her rosary beads.

'Shock and all, 'tis unnatural to sit there without a tear in her eye.'

'But that's what I mean – 'tis the shock that does it. Dries the system of all tears.'

'It can turn your hair white, ye know, overnight like.'

'Like in an instant?'

'How would I know. Jesus. What do you take me for?'

'My mam didn't shed a tear till the month's mind came around.'

'Bottling those tears did no one no good. It's terrible heavy on the heart.'

'Yes, fluid around the heart – people die from it, like.'

'Mother of God, man. Where d'you get yer theories from?'

And on and on it went, everyone had something to say. What a load of shite, thought Marlo, but he sensed that they all knew it too, recognised the palliative talk for what it was – helpful nonsense and nothing more.

In the room, Assumpta took Marlo's hands in hers, and he could feel her fingers trembling as she spoke. 'Thank you, Marlo, what ye did today was more than anyone would've done. Not my brothers or their lads, though Mossie would've stopped me even asking them. He hated being obliged, you know. But never to you, you he had taken to so quickly. And to land the little lad on you without warning! Lord forgive me, I had completely forgotten about Sully till Father Angelo said it to me.'

Marlo gave her a hug. 'No matter, Assumpta, the child was no problem at all. He stayed quiet all the while. I didn't know he was Kitty's son. I know her, you know – from the Headley-Stokes' in Bocarnagh.'

Assumpta sighed. 'Kitty. She's a law unto herself. Mossie was her godfather and I'll leave it at that, not a word more for Mossie's sake. So many things I'll have to do now and for ever for Mossie's sake. D'you see them all there, Marlo? Wondering where my tears are. I want to tell them I have a lifetime ahead to cry and I'll do it in my own time – no need to shed them all in the one week. For now, I think how nice it is my lads are together at last. Himself and Thomas. And they'll be waiting for me. I have no fear now. I'll be ready when the Lord thinks I am. Till then I'll do what Mossie would have wanted.'

'I'll keep the bus going, Assumpta. For the next little while anyway, you know, till things settle.'

'Are you sure now, lad? I'll pay you, of course. What about your writing? Will you have the time for it all?'

'I'll manage. In a day or two I'll know the routine and then the daily drive to Cork will be my thinking time. It's more useful than you can know.'

'Dolores will help with the sheep – she's been up to them already. I'll think more about all of that after the funeral.'

Marlo hesitated and then asked, 'The post-mortem is over then?'

'Dr Feeley rang to say they will give Mossie back to us tomorrow. We'll wake him at home. It is what he would have wanted.'

Marlo could feel the tears well up again and he turned away from her.

She clutched at his sleeve. 'Now, lad, it will be a tough few days, but it has never been anything less since Thomas died. I'm well used to the heartache.'

The door opened and Dolores popped her head in. 'Is everything OK here, Assumpta? There's many waiting – though ye don't have to come out if ye don't want to.'

'I'll do what I have to do, Dolores.'

'Good woman, I want ye to have some tea now and I'm not taking no for an answer. And Marlo, would ye check on yer singing sensation up at your place? He's just started an awful dirge.'

Marlo nodded. He could hear Stevie's lowing come rolling down the hill.

On his way out of the kitchen door he spotted Kitty in the utility talking to John Bosco. Her eyes were red, and she was wiping her nose. Sully was fidgeting with the dial on the washing machine and she swatted his hand away.

'Sully, I'm going to have to go straight home now if you don't stop messing with that.'

'Would he like to come up with me to see my calf?'

John Bosco poked him in the shoulder and laughed. 'The blind one? You're some glutton for it, boy. Taking on a blind calf.'

'He's a lovely animal, JB.'

'You can't be telling a butcher that, Marlo. To me that only means one thing.' He smacked his lips.

Kitty rolled her eyes and knelt down in front of Sully, her hands on his shoulders. 'Do you want to walk up to Marlo's yard pet? He has a little calf he says that you might like to see.'

'You could draw him and give me a signed copy.'

Kitty smiled. 'Oh God, he would too.' She took her son's hand and headed out into the yard. 'Thanks, Marlo – this is no place for him with everyone so upset. We'll head up there slowly. I was well winded the last time I tackled that slope! But you'll wait for me, JB, don't go off without us, right?'

As Marlo rummaged for his jacket that seemed to have disappeared under several others hooked on the back door, he watched John Bosco looking at her walking away, holding Sully's hand as he jumped down the three steps, one at a time.

The minute she was out of earshot, John Bosco turned to Marlo and looked him straight in the eye. 'She doesn't suffer fools, our Kitty. I'm the lad's uncle, by the way. His father's brother.'

'Are you telling me something?'

'Just that she's still only barely coping. It's been a hard few years.'

'I'm hardly the bogeyman, JB.'

'Jesus, you are hardly that.'

'So, then?'

'Nothing. I never said a word. Go now before that bellowing wakes the dead. Christ Almighty, the good Lord took his sight but gave him a fine fecking voice in return.'

Was he warning me off? Marlo wondered as he strode up the slope as fast as he could. He could see Kitty and Sully up ahead, rounding the acute bend. By the time he got to the cottage they were standing at the edge of his triangular field, Sully on his tiptoes on the fence, his hand out to the animal willing it closer. The calf had sensed their presence and his head was held high, his nose and ears twitching nervously.

'Watch this,' Marlo whispered to Kitty and Sully before clicking his tongue. 'Up here to me, Stevie. Come on, good lad. Up here to me, up here to me, lad.'

The calf snorted in delight, shook his head and made a short leap in the air. Then he started walking slowly in the direction of Marlo's voice.

'I've to keep the chant going. You see, he follows my voice,' he said, looking at Kitty. 'Up here to me, lad, come on now, Stevie, up here to me, up here to me now.'

The calf gathered speed and a few seconds later was nuzzling Marlo's hands. 'You can stroke him now, Sully. On his head or he'll take your little fingers off. His tongue is like sandpaper, and he only ever wants to suckle anything he can feel.'

Kitty smiled. 'I know why everyone thinks you're soft in the head.'

Marlo laughed as he slipped into a pair of rubber boots at the back door, turned on the outside tap and brought out a small bucket of calf nuts from the woodshed. He swung his legs over the fence and, taking hold of the collar around the calf, led him towards the galvanised water trough. 'I'll be putting him in for the night, but I'll have to let him have a small feed here. Plenty of water still,' he called out. 'Ella and Pieter must have come by as they said they would. Ella's completely taken with him. She's going to check on him during the day while I'm doing the bus for Mossie.'

'For Assumpta, you mean.' Kitty's voice broke and the tears

came pouring down her face. She wiped them away, turning her face away from Sully. 'He was a huge part of my life, my godfather. More so after my father, and then my mam, died and then when Sully was born.'

'I never knew my father.' *Why the hell did I volunteer that?*

'Neither did Sully.'

The stood beside each other then, on either side of the fence, for what seemed like ages, not saying a word, Marlo nearly afraid to breathe for fear of breaking whatever spell seemed to have been cast by the creeping dusk. Stevie had walked back up to Marlo, and Sully leaned over, tracing the outline of the calf's opaque eyes, feeling the silky ears between his fingers. The rain had stopped, and a cacophony of cawing had begun to fill the air. Many hundred crows were all returning home to roost, and they flew around, circling in great waves, then settled into their perches only to rise again like they had heard a starter's gun, starting the ritual all over again, swirling like winged dervishes, around and around, before sinking back into the branches. Marlo hadn't seen Crow at all that morning before he had left on the bus, though the pieces of egg and bacon he had left scattered on the sill were all gone. He scanned the valley below to see if the bird was flying across towards the cottage. He knew that sometimes the yank and scrape of the sash window and clank of the metal plate anytime of the day was enough for the bird to wing his way to the sill.

On second thoughts, maybe not today, Crow, maybe not today. I don't want her thinking I'm some kind of a weird Pied Piper, gathering waifs and strays as I go. One creature at a time; Stevie will do for today.

He cast a look at mother and son beside him and then turned towards Rougham Mountain, lit up from beyond in the west by the setting sun. A halo of pink, red and orange lingered over the mountain range and the crows had finally begun to settle into their perches. The wind had died to almost nothing and the river could be heard, the day's rain still finding its way down the boggy mountain, and near invisible midges readied themselves for their unrelenting assault. Up at Rossnagreena wispy smoke rose from distant chimneys, and in Rougham lights flickered on at windows for a brief while, before curtains were drawn and houses disappeared entirely into the gloom of the dusk. The sheep could no longer be seen on the mountain. It was only a few days ago that he had watched Mossie herd his flock into the dipping tank. Some curved ball you threw me there, Mossie. *I'm ducking and diving and catching whatever's going to come my way. Just like you said.*

CHAPTER SEVEN

Cloichin's Story, Glengarriff, 1602

The boy Sully was in the forest today but didn't come down my way like he usually does. I can always feel his presence in the woods; it doesn't take long – you see, my senses are finely honed. All except one. Oh yes, I'm a child too, mute just like him, only no one ever calls him a dumb ass. How do I know that? you might ask. It's because I see him, I watch him; he's here often, walking the paths in the forest with his mother, and when I look at him, he's happy most of the time. He smiles as soon as he spots me and waves back sometimes. That's when his mother starts with the questions. 'Who are you waving at, Sully? Who do you see, Sully? Is it an animal, Sully?' And on and on till she sighs and gives him a hug like he was some poor fool.

In my time, I never smiled at no one nor dare wave; you wouldn't, would you, if people called you a dumb ass. Even asses have their ass language. Me – I couldn't even bray, so smile I definitely didn't. It would get me beaten up – they'd say I was up to no good and that I'd been communing with the Devil – for why could an unfortunate like me have cause to smile. So along would come a sharp slap across the back of my head or a whip to my arse.

Everyone calls me Cloichin, for that's what I am – a little stone, as silent as one, and I'm not allowed to forget it.

Most of the time I stayed out of everyone's way, laying low for a while under an overhanging rock or high up in the crook of an old oak. I had my hidey holes – places even the Devil himself would've found it hard to find.

I knew small kindnesses in tiny doses, that I'll admit. When he first came to be with us in the forest, Friar Felipe, the Spanish priest, had told them to be charitable to a poor mute like me. He soon changed his tune when he fell off the ass he was riding and bloodied his forehead. All fingers pointed to me for I had prepared the animal for the padre, putting on the saddlecloth, harness and reins, but to my luck, bad as it nearly always was, hadn't someone spotted me smiling to myself a few moments before the ass bucked him off. The padre was to go to bless the creaght, hidden in a valley a mile away in Coomerkane. Instead, he lay on his back like a fat beetle upturned, unable to move while they tried not to laugh and so pointed their fingers at me.

On that occasion, even my own father, who had come to fetch the friar, agreed that I was saved from a hiding, a good and proper hiding, by none other than that English shit himself, General Sir Charles Wilmot. He and a dozen of his men were spotted riding up from Kenmare in the direction of Bonane, and one of the McCarthys rode hard and fast into our camp to tell us so. Imagine my luck – just as the padre got to his feet and readied his thick belt to drive the Devil from me, the news of the approaching danger meant the leathering I was to get was put off and I was forgotten, my punishment reserved till the next time blame needed a villain.

So, I hardly smile. But wait, forgive me – all the terrible memories I hold have a habit of snuffing the few joys I've known. The Devil take me if I should forget my lord, Donal Cam O'Sullivan Beare, my good lord of Beara and Bantry. He did give me reason to smile sometimes. Ask me where his greatness lay and I can tell you it wasn't in his legendary march from these forests in Glengarriff to Leitrim 400 miles away in the north; no, it lay entirely in his kindness to the cursed mute boy, to me, Cloichin.

Often times he'd wink as he threw me a bone for his dogs with bits of meat still on it, or leave buttermilk half a finger deep in his drinking cup and none but me, who was tasked to refill it, knew. I would quaff the wholesome liquid back in an instant, rip the few shreds of flesh off with my teeth, suck up the marrow before throwing the bones to his dogs. Ah, I loved them, the three great big wolfhounds – they were like kin to me, the brothers I lost.

Hunger made everyone sheltering in the forest canny and they'd notice the small favours bestowed on me and, when my lord O'Sullivan Beare was not about, they would torment me with their words. Sticks and stones broke not my bones but their taunts did shrivel my soul. And what of my father, ye may ask. He could be a father only when he was around and never was he around, the truth be told. His duty was to the creaght – and a great honour it was too, to be amongst the handful of the bravest, picked to guard our wealth. They were our everything – while they lived, they gave us food, when they died food again, and cloaks to keep us warm, shoes to keep feet dry.

Our creaght numbered three thousand cattle and two thousand sheep, secreted away in the valley at Coomerkane, herds that we had captured during our raids all across Beara before that other English devil, Lord Carew, drove us from Dunboy into this stronghold in the forest. Dunboy, where we suffered a great defeat, from whence we retreated to Dursey, that saddest of islands, where hundreds of our kin, my mother too, were thrown off the cliffs. No mercy shown as she was tied to her children, my brothers and my sweet sister just a babe, all bound together with strips of her own skirt, only to be rolled over the hill and flung into the foaming sea far below. They perished on those cruel jagged rocks, their heads smashed open, the tide dragging away their remains, later returning a few limbs and shredded entrails to the shore for the gulls to feast on.

We survivors took comfort in the sure knowledge that their souls rose straight to heaven, though it is said their screams can still be heard echoing around the cliffs anytime the sea is still and the wind a mere whisper. Friar Felipe recounted the tragedy of the massacre over and over each night, as we gathered around the fires. Different families and their particular losses were eulogised till we all wept at the savage barbarity of their end.

'Gorrane McSwiney,' he said, looking at my father, 'find your courage, man, rejoice in the knowledge that when your time comes, you will surely meet your kindly wife and innocent children seated by the side of our Lord in Heaven, for that is where they went directly.'

And then each time the priest would finish with a fist in the air declaring that the devil English, every one of them, would rot for ever in Hell. Whenever I heard this I couldn't help but wonder what manner of place was Hell – would it really be any worse than where we were? For surely this forest, oozing deadly damp at every step and in every direction, would properly rot us from feet up before the English even got to the gates of Hell. Roused by Friar Felipe, the gallowglasses, bonnachts and kernes would rise up and swear revenge and my father would join in, as did the rest of the kinsmen. And on cue my lord O'Sullivan Beare, who often wept unashamedly at the memory of the massacre, would turn to the priest. 'Lead us in prayer, Friar, that we may overcome Elisabeth, that wicked English Queen and her army of evil sinners.' Then the whole lot of us would drop to our knees and mournful murmuring filled the air as the priest led the congregation through the prayers for the dead and, also for those of us barely living, in case we succumbed before dawn.

We waked them thus, night after night – our mothers and fathers, wives and husbands, our brothers and sisters lost in such a brutal manner. The defeat at Dunboy and the slaughter at Dursey was what led the remainder of us to hide here in this fastness, so thickly wooded and wet underfoot that nearly all of it was impassable to anyone except on foot. For six months we only barely survived, scrounging for food, desperate to keep dry, trying every minute of every hour to shake the cold from our bones. Captain Tyrell and William Burke divided us into small camps, the locations carefully chosen, so that we could be approached from one side alone. We made our beds on bracken and branches but there wasn't any shelter worth its name from the ravages of wind, rain and snow, snow which I saw for the first time in my life. The damp crept into our every bone and nothing would assuage it. We picked on berries while they lasted, chewed on sorrel leaves and made do with weak broths that the women cooked from bones. A dab of cheese and a sup of sour whey – all rationed carefully for the stores had to last us through this winter siege. We had to wait our turn as the warriors had to be fed first for it would not have done for them to be weak from hunger. It's not a wonder that we fell like starving dogs on anything we found in the forest.

I would hope every day that my father would return to our camp, for when he did, he sometimes brought me a small scoop of milk in his drinking horn. When I had drunk from it he would rinse it in the stream, shake it dry and wipe it down with a corner of his mantle. He minded that stag's horn with more care than he had looked after me most times, for my mother had brought it with her, from her father's home, on her wedding day. Its pointy end was silver-tipped and around its rim was a thin band of silver again into which both their names, entwined, had been engraved. It was my father's dearest possession, always securely slung across his chest with a leather lanyard that she had braided herself. That horn is long lost, cut away from him, his hands hacked off as he clung to it, the day we both died. But I am rushing ahead of myself for there is more to my story and I'll tell it to you, should you wish to listen.

I'll tell you my story, the story of my kin, while I wait for the boy Sully. I know we could be such friends, the two of us.

CHAPTER EIGHT

How's things working out for you, Marlo? I mean, with the bus – are you going to be driving it for much longer?' Tiggy had walked out to The Lump near where Marlo was cutting up wood, readying it to be stacked.

If I had a pound for every time I was asked that question this last week alone, I could bloody well retire.

Mam and Mary had been asking him that very question, since the funeral and every time after when he had rung them.

'I don't know,' he said to them the first time.

'It's too soon to ask Assumpta,' he had explained a week later.

'I hope she doesn't think you are going to do it indefinitely.' Mary was indignant and Marlo felt his hackles rise.

'You aren't here, Mary, to understand the situation, so would you ever just leave it, will you?'

'So, what is the "situation"?' Mary, true to form, wasn't going to back off till she got what she wanted. These past few weeks he had been trying his best to restore things, clear the air between them but with Mary it was always one step forward and two large ones back.

Mam had intervened before they got at each other's throats. 'Marlo, tell her I pray for them, for her and for poor Mossie and their Thomas – Lord have mercy on their souls.'

He could picture her crossing herself with sincere intent. Mary tut-tutted in the background and Mam admonished her. 'He was my childhood friend, Mary! You need to respect the dead.'

'For God's sake, Mam, this phone is eating coins. Can you and Mary slug it out later?' Marlo was in no mood to talk and hadn't called them for a whole week since then.

It hadn't been any different, a few days later, when Dolores had called to his cottage early on a Saturday morning to castrate Stevie. Marlo hadn't slept the night thinking about the poor calf and what was to be inflicted on him and had confessed as much to Dolores.

'What sort of a soft eejit are ye, lad? But why am I even asking – I should know the answer to that, I should. It's the reason that animal's living the life of Reilly here with ye.'

She laughed when Marlo had winced at the sight of the Burdizzo. 'Ye need to forget about yer blind fella and his precious goolies and concentrate entirely on what I'm telling ye or it won't go according to plan. Then he might hurt more than he should.' She elbowed him playfully. 'Be a man, lad!'

When it was all over and calf had stopped bellowing, they headed back to her car.

'I'm going to call in to Assumpta. The poor divil – has she said anything to ye as yet, I mean about the bus? I know Mossie had taken out life insurance but I'm sure not enough to last for ever. She might need for the bus to remain a going concern, ye know. So she can continue to have a few bob to live decently. Ye know what I mean. He would hate it, absolutely fecking hate it, if she became dependent on her brothers. The man would turn in his grave.'

Marlo shut the door of the car and leaned in towards the open window. 'I'll wait till she decides what she wants. I'm in no hurry and she's insisting on paying me wages while I drive. Mossie was good to me, Dolores. I won't let him down.'

'Good man ye are,' she said over her shoulder as she released the handbrake and slowly rolled down the slope towards the Hanleys' bungalow. She had a notion she saved a good bit of petrol if she managed to free roll down any slope she had to drive.

The talk had been the exact same last Wednesday when he met John Bosco and the lads at the pitch.

'Fair play to you, Marlo, giving Assumpta a dig out with Mossie's bus. It's been two months now nearly, isn't it? Has she decided what to do with it?'

'Not sure really,' said Marlo, pushing his chair back and heading to the bar to buy his round. When they were only the two of them left, John Bosco emptied his glass and tapped the table. 'What's the story now, Marlo? Ye can tell me.'

'No story, JB. No story at all. The woman's been widowed barely eight weeks. She's got those awful brothers of hers giving her advice she doesn't need or want. So, I'll hold my peace for a while and go with the flow – whatever it brings.'

John Bosco looked like he was about to say something, and Marlo waited, but the young butcher just toyed with his empty glass and then tipped the dregs back into his lips, smacking them with a flourish. They walked out of Casey's a few minutes later and parted with a quiet shake of hands.

'Till next Wednesday, boi.'

'Sure thing – see you at the pitch, JB.'

It felt like the whole world wanted to know what was to happen to the bus run and now, here he was in Bocarnagh at the Headley-Stokes', chainsaw at the ready and Tiggy waiting for an answer to the very same question. She had her new camera in hand and had spent the Sunday morning taking photographs of the bay from vantage points on the property.

'I'm sure people have been asking you this for the past few weeks.' She had the lens to her eye as she spoke. 'Edward and I have been wondering too.'

He found himself weary all of a sudden and put the chainsaw down. 'I never thought I'd end up thinking about the regulars. They'd be in trouble, Tiggy ma'am, if the bus were to stop. Eamon O'Reilly can't do both the morning and the afternoon runs – it just wouldn't work. There are lads who need to get to work and back, plus Mags and the two sisters in Bantry couldn't afford anything more than the fare that Mossie was charging them. They'd have to pay nearly twice as much if they changed to the CIE service.'

And I have to think about Sully. He needs the bus more than anyone else.

Tiggy must have read his mind. 'I hope Assumpta will think

carefully before she hires someone permanent to drive it for her. If she keeps the business, that is. No one else will be willing to take a child on a bus back and forth every day, to be responsible in effect, especially for a child like him.'

'He's just a child like any other.'

She shook her head. 'Yes and no, Marlo. He needs to be in school, a school that can cater to his very special needs. Life is going to be tough for him as he grows older, and he needs every chance he can get to deal with the challenges. Kitty is fighting – working and saving to make that happen and her godfather Mossie was helping her buy time.' She concentrated on putting back the lens cover on the camera before looking up and smiling. 'Will you come in for some coffee before you leave, Marlo? Edward wanted to show you some sketches he's made for the next piece he's working on. He thinks you might be interested in seeing it evolve from conception.'

'Definitely. I'll come in once I'm done for the afternoon.'

Marlo watched her walk back to the house, her windblown silk scarf leading the way like some crazed maître de. He turned to the work at hand and decided to stack the pile of wood that he had already chopped. As he filled up the wheelbarrow and headed to the shed his thoughts turned to Sully.

On Friday morning, eight weeks after he had first started driving Mossie's bus, the little boy had given him a small rolled-up piece of paper as he boarded the steps and passed the driver's seat.

'I'll have a look once we get to Cork, right, Sully? We are running a little late and I don't want to keep Nancy and Nuala waiting in Bantry.' He gave him a big wink. 'They'll give out to me and that won't be good for any of us, will it?'

Sully's little legs had swung even faster in the seat under him, but his face was turned, as always, to the window. Bernard Causkey reached over and patted the child on his head. 'Marlo's fierce lucky to have one of your masterpieces, Sully. Fierce lucky.'

All the regulars on the bus nodded sagely and the Hare Krishna began to sway as he started a chant below his breath.

Mags O'Connor turned around to look at him. 'Is that one of those mantra things then? I saw a fella do that in *The Pink Panther*. Did you watch the filum last weekend, Bernard? It was on television before the *Late Late Show*. Talking of which, I personally thought Gay looked tired. Tired after the carry-on from the last show. Did you watch the last show, Bernard? The one before this last one?'

In the rear-view mirror Marlo could see Bernard rolling his eyes. 'I leave Gay to herself, Mags. She watches and tells me all about it the next day. I get the post-mortem over me weekend morning fry. It suits me to eat and nod. Or even nod off, sometimes.'

Mags wasn't amused and blew her nose into her handkerchief. The Hare Krishna was now clicking his fingers in rhythm to his incantation.

Mags looked back at the saffron-robed devotee who had his eyes closed. 'Is he disturbing you, Marlo?'

'Not really, Mags.'

'Well, just drive carefully then, will you?'

'You can be sure, Mags. Nothing will distract me.'

Marlo studiously avoided looking in the rear-view mirror. He knew Fionn and Dan O'Driscoll were having a good laugh, and Bernard's shoulders were more than likely heaving.

When they got to Kent station, Marlo picked up the drawing and waved it in the air at Sully. 'I'll wait till Mags bring you back from the toilets, champ. I'll check for my return passengers in the meanwhile.'

They had to wait a short while for three passengers off the ferry from Wales. Marlo released the rubber band and unrolled the paper. The sketch was of a high stepping horse, decked out in a richly caparisoned saddlecloth and a decorated bridle.

'My God, Sully, this is just beautiful. How long did it take you to do this? Looks like it was a fancy dress parade at the riding school. Did you go there recently with your mam?'

Marlo knew not to expect a reply of any sort but still, he waited for a change in the child's expression or in his eyes, but Sully was unconcerned, his face to the window, his nose pressed to the glass.

Marlo had turned to the sketch in his hand. He found it was impossible to understand how a child so young could have this sort of skill, put in this depth of detail into a drawing. The horse head was beautiful in its proportions and the bridle, like miniature bunting, seemed animated, fluttering in some unseen breeze. The saddlecloth had been rendered quiltlike, embossed with tiny swirls and circles. Marlo wondered if maybe Kitty had bought her son illustrated books that he was copying the details from. Where else could he have seen such an elaborate saddlecloth?

He turned to the little boy. 'I wish I could draw like you. Thank you, Sully.'

Later that day, as Kitty collected Sully off the bus, Marlo unrolled the sketch and marvelled at the details again. 'What an imagination he has, Kitty.'

'Oh! I didn't even know this was being drawn for you, Marlo. Consider yourself special.'

'I do. I've thanked him already, but you might say it to him again that I loved it.'

He watched her walk back to the house, carrying the boy in her arms and him kicking his legs in excitement, his hands wrapped around her neck.

Did Mary ever carry me like that when I was a kid? He was taken aback at his thoughts. *Jesus, where did that come from?* On the way home, he was overcome with an impulse to stop at the phone in the village and ring Mary, but Mrs Kelly across the hallway wasn't at home and the phone rang out each time.

He had been so busy thinking about Sully's extraordinary

artistic abilities that he surprised himself at how quickly he had manged to move and stack the logs that he had spent the morning splitting. He pulled off his wellingtons and stepped out of the blue overalls that had saved his clothes from the muck and dust. In the house, Edward was standing at his desk looking at a series of fairly large sketches; they were studies, he said, for a large sculpture of a wooded island that he had been visualizing for a while.

'Well, what do you think, young man?'

'Technically challenging is what comes to mind, Edward sir. Will you sculpt it in sections and put them together? Where will you fire it?'

'Ah, I knew you'd spot the troubles ahead. But let me fill you in with the background first. I'm working from memories and a collection of photos from our trip to Japan nearly twenty years ago. Tiggy and I were both fascinated by the art of bonsai and the way trees were miniaturised, sculpted in effect, to mimic what they looked like in the wild. We saw whole forests raised this way, some of them many hundreds of years old, growing in containers barely as large as this tea tray. I've always wanted to replicate those living miniatures. D'you know what I mean? In clay and three-dimensional, of course. I was hoping to sculpt a view of Garnish Island in the style of a Japanese bonsai. There will be a Martello tower too. What do you think?'

'I guess translating these studies into clay will be pretty demanding. I know nothing of the technical aspects, but I think you've captured the windswept angles of the trees perfectly.'

'It's the first thing my eyes see when I look out across the bay – the stigmata of the prevailing wind. Nature is the master and I'm only mirroring what she fashions. Proportions will be everything, Marlo, but I'm at an impasse of sorts – thinking about the overall size, its feasibility. I might need to build a kiln maybe, here on the property.'

'Where will it sit in the house?'

'Yes, that's where Tigs says I should start too.'

It was a stimulating afternoon and they told him about their travels in the Far East and asked about his life in London. He was quite shocked at how distant that life felt, another life altogether, as he told them about growing up in Croydon, living his teenage years in the local library, reading everything that he could lay his hands on and then driving a bread van at four every morning, during his college years, studying for a degree in journalism.

He jumped out of the sofa when he realised it was nearly three o'clock. 'Jesus. That flew by, Tiggy ma'am. I've to head right away, Edward sir, thanks for the coffee!' And with that he was out off the house and seated in his pride and joy, his new Mk2, driving out of Bocarnagh. He had a date with Kitty and Sully. *Of course, I must be the only man in the world who needs to feed a blind calf before a first date.*

He collected them at four o'clock and they drove the short distance to the car park in the nature reserve.

Last week, when he had asked her out, she had smiled and declined. 'You know, I haven't anyone I can just leave Sully with Marlo, so I'm sorry I can't.'

He didn't hesitate. 'Why don't we do something with him?'

'If you are sure of that? He doesn't like to go anywhere other than the forest.'

'Right then, the forest it is.'

Now, as they pulled up at the car park in the nature reserve, he stayed sitting in the car for a second after she got down, wondering how things would pan out. She tied her rain jacket around her waist before hitching on her knapsack and helping Sully with his. Marlo watched them as they headed off a few steps ahead of him.

She stopped at the wooden bridge and turned around. 'Come on, slow coach, you've got to keep up with us, right,

Sully?' But Sully had just scampered on ahead, his hands in the pockets of his blue jeans.

Marlo laughed. 'He's only just a bit bigger than that bag on his back, Kitty.'

'Mossie got him that backpack the day he started on the bus two years ago and he won't go anywhere without it. There's never anything in it other than stuff to eat.'

'The famous ham sandwich and the bourbon biscuits!'

'I packed some for us too. We could stop once we are past the Big Meadow. Have you been down that way before, Marlo?'

'No, I've only ever done the shorter loop, but lead me wherever you want, I'll follow.'

She had stopped to put her hair into a ponytail and she looked back at him smiling. 'It'll be mainly Sully doing the leading, Marlo. I hope you don't mind. He has places that he absolutely has to stop at – I'd swear you'd think he was an old woman doing the obligatory Stations. You'll see for yourself, he'll linger at certain rocks, then spend time poking a stick into small peaty pools and insist on climbing a hoary ancient oak, wait till you see the size of it – it's seriously big. So you've been warned about our route – it's almost always the same each time, but he's so happy and tired when we leave, I just let him at it. You know what I mean, Marlo? He sleeps like a log the days we walk here.'

'A little boy's paradise. I had nothing like it growing up in Croydon. But, d'you know how many adventure stories I read growing up, that were set in forests exactly like this? Trees to climb, rivers to raft down and swimming holes to jump into. I could easily become a little boy again, just to get to know this glen, its valley and everything it has to offer.'

'It's not exactly paradise. Depends on where you are looking in from.' She gritted her teeth and skimmed a stone across the river. It skipped four times before hopping onto the opposite bank. She looked back at him in delight. 'Did you see that, Marlo? Sully, did you see what I did? Four skips! My best ever in a long while.'

To their left the river ran swift but silent, the shallow, crystal clear waters swirling here and there in small eddies at confluences where tributaries tumbled in from the boggy surrounds or where the river wrapped itself around tiny islands midstream. Some of the islets were mere raised pebble beds and some had whole trees growing on them.

'So I need five skips to beat you,' he said, as he began to look around the river bed for flat stones. He gave up after a couple of tries as stone after stone sank on impact. 'I'm no good when I have an audience. That's my excuse anyway.'

Kitty was laughing as she walked on ahead to where Sully had just turned the corner. 'Come on, Marlo, we're now going to count the ant hills in the Big Meadow.'

When he caught up she was kneeling, tying Sully's boot laces, asking him to stay still for a moment. Marlo was overcome with a sense of déjà vu. He must have been the same age as Sully and it was Mary who was on her knees, getting him to stand still. 'Would you just let me tie your laces, you brat.'

Instead he had kicked out at her face. Mary had yelped in pain and Mam had spanked him across his butt without hesitation, right there in the shops, in front of everyone. *I was a brat.*

'You are patient,' he said to Kitty as the little boy ran off down the path.

She shrugged. 'I'm his mother and he's all I have. We both have our moments, Marlo – there'll be no saints to canonise between the two of us.'

'Can I ask? What happened to his father?'

'Whiddy. John Paul died in the Whiddy Island disaster.'

'I'm sorry. I shouldn't have pried.'

'You're grand, Marlo.'

They walked a while in silence.

I'm going to have to hold my tongue. Let her tell me what she wants, and in her own time.

They were quite deep in the forest now, and every surface of the ancient oceanic woodland was slick and wet from the morning's rain. Ferns, lichens and moss-cloaked tree trunks and rocks, creating fantastical shapes as they clung to the tiniest of moist crevices, strangling and splitting their hosts over time. A good few foot on either side of the river bank, swathes of long grass and montbretia fronds lay near flattened to the ground by the last flood. The rivers and streams swelled and receded along with the rain as it fell and abated, the rising waters coming an hour or so after heavy precipitation over the Caha mountains that ringed Glengarriff. Flash flooding was a common occurrence, but the raging torrents receded just as quickly, returning the river to its placid state, for the water didn't linger but rushed down to the sea, roaring into the harbour at the Blue Pool behind Casey's Hotel. The high water mark from the morning's flood could be seen very clearly; the debris of sticks and leaves that had been washed downstream remained in untidy but distinct lines where they had washed up.

'There isn't the remotest possibility of leaving the path and just walking into the forest, is there?'

Kitty stopped in her tracks. 'Just look at it, Marlo, you'd be floundering knee deep in the ooze and that's within a few feet of stepping off this track. I don't think there are many truly dry spots, unless you picked an actual rock.'

They crossed the river over an iron footbridge, stopping to look down at the water.

Marlo scrutinised the riverbed carefully. Every grain of the gravelly sand could be seen clearly and the smooth white-veined river stones in shades of slate, ochre and black shone glossy in the water as the sun reached in through gaps in the leafy canopy. 'I read somewhere that the waters here are home to freshwater pearl mussels. It's so crystal clear – just imagine if we spotted one.'

'Oh, I have one of them. John Paul found it years ago and – well, I still have it.'

Marlo waited. Her voice had trailed away as she spoke and she bent double over the rusty bars of the bridge, like as if reaching out to something below.

'He was saving to buy me a ring when he found the pearl by pure chance. It's a one in a million find, so why wait he said and he asked me to marry him that same day. He told me I could have it set when he had the money gathered and all. I was the happiest I've ever been those two months of November and December. He died in January. It's nearly seven years now. I never did anything with it, though. My mother said it was the unluckiest thing she'd ever set her eyes on.'

'Mothers can say the cruellest things sometimes.'

'She never thought him good enough.'

'If he was anything like his brother, he must have been real sound.'

'Sound he was. All three of them – John Paul, John Bosco and John Joseph, in that order. The Three Johnnies they were called in school, all sound as pennies. John Joe is on the oil rigs in Alaska and John Bosco off to Oz soon, I'm sure you know. They are just running away from having to see Whiddy across the bay every day – it's an inescapable reminder of what happened to their John Paul. But that's not me. I look across the bay and all I can see is beauty. And I know he's there somewhere.' She sighed and looked up. 'Sorry, Marlo, that was a lot to take in and you just asking about freshwater mussels.'

'Does Sully ask about his father?'

She stared at him and then burst out laughing.

Marlo slapped his forehead. 'Jesus, I'm one thoughtless eejit – I'm feckin' sorry, Kitty. Of course he doesn't.'

She stepped off the bridge and was smiling as she signalled him to follow. 'Come on, Marlo, I need to keep Sully in sight.'

'Kitty—'

But she cut him short. 'You don't need to apologise again, Marlo. I know malice when it's a mile away and that was just you being curious without intent.'

'Impulsiveness is my downfall.'

'I'd say it's what makes you likable.'

'You think?'

'I think you're fishing.'

'Oh no, Kitty, I was just . . .'

'Ah stop, Marlo, I'm teasing.'

He laughed aloud. 'I'm relieved, I'll keep my mouth zipped now.'

'Only until you see the Big Meadow, I can bet on that.'

'Tell me about it.'

'You'll see for yourself why it is special. It's never been ploughed or worked on in living memory. The ground untainted by human activity, left to be what it wants to be. Full of wildflowers in summer and more ant hills than you'd be able to count. Plus, it has one of the largest oaks in the forest. One of Sully's obligatory stops. I sometime feel he thinks there are imaginary children there.'

'Does he know other children, Kitty? I mean, with being home schooled and all it must be hard to make friends.'

'Oh God, it is, and it's not because he's not yet in school. It's almost like people think what he has might be contagious – that their precious sons might catch it and stop talking if they mix with him. No friends as yet, but that means nothing. He's only just six and I'll get him into a special school soon. Not giving up on that.'

'You should talk to Father Angelo. The priest can move mountains apparently.'

'That man? I won't be asking him.'

'You aren't the only one that doesn't care for him. Enda Crowley said the strangest thing to me – insinuated stuff, you know.'

'I've no time for that priest but I wouldn't believe everything that Enda says. That fella can hold grudges like no other man in the peninsula and that's saying a lot when you are from Beara.'

Marlo laughed. 'I picked that up driving the bus these last few weeks. Not about Enda. No, just in general. That there are some serious grudge matches being played out over generations all over the glen and beyond.'

Kitty nodded. 'Nothing as succulent as an aging old wound that's kept well salted. It becomes meaty, the stuff of legends, don't you know? Wait till you've spent one winter here and when nothing else is happening other than five types of rain and four sorts of drizzle – you'll see the need to revive old resentments.'

'You think it's boredom? Ah, surely not, Kitty.'

'Don't tell me I didn't warn you.'

Sully had walked back to them, and he grabbed his mother's hand and dragged her towards a very large rocky outcrop that overhung the path. It had a holly tree growing through a fissure and he stood at the base and waited.

'OK, Sully. Turn around and I'll hoist you up. Wait, maybe if you'll let Marlo do it, he'll be able to get you higher? What d'you think? Will I ask Marlo?'

Sully left his mother's side and walked up to Marlo and waited.

'Hitch you up onto the rock? Sure, champ. If I put you on my shoulders and then you can step onto that ledge, what do you say?'

Once on the ledge, the child clambered higher still, on his fours, to the very top of the rock. He held onto the trunk of the holly and looked down at his mother before scanning the view around him. Then Marlo saw him lift his hand and wave tentatively.

'There must be somebody up there, Kitty, higher up on the hill. Sully's waving to someone. Yes, there he is doing it again.'

'He imagines it, Marlo, he does it all the time and I've never seen anyone. The same places too.'

'What d'you mean? Like an imaginary friend?'

'I guess you could call it that. It used to bother me at first but he never seems fearful or afraid so I reckon it's something he's conjured up for himself.'

'Well, if his drawings are anything to go by – he does have a vivid imagination.'

'Yes, I got a book from the library in Bantry written by an American psychologist fellow. He thinks it's not unusual for a child like him to create his own world.'

'And does this expert says it should be encouraged? Wouldn't that make him introverted?'

She bit her lip. 'It's hard trying to figure it out on your own. But cope I must.'

Marlo was looking up at the child who was at the highest point of the outcrop. 'Do you want to come down now, Sully?'

Sully gave a small wave in the direction of the hill before slowly slithering down to the ledge.

Marlo held out his arms and asked him to jump.

The boy was light as a feather and wriggled out of Marlo's arms immediately, running off along the riverine path.

As they followed Sully, Marlo stayed quiet, sensing Kitty wanted to say something. Her voice was emotionless, as if she had steeled herself before she spoke. 'People judge me, you know. For having him, for keeping him and for the way we live. Him on the bus, while I'm at the Headley-Stokes.'

Marlo kicked a pine cone out of the way. 'People are like that. It makes them feel better to measure their good fortune against the troubles of others.'

She looked at him. 'Tell me about yourself Marlo. Our mystery philosopher from Croydon. Who are you and what brought you here to the glen?'

He held his breath for a moment. *Oh Jesus, will I tell her?*

'It's a long story, Kitty.'

'It's a long walk, Marlo.'

In the end it didn't take all that while for him to tell her.

She put her hand on his arm. 'Yours is a good news story. You do know how lucky you are, don't you? Most children like you ended up badly.'

'I was loved, I am loved, I know. But I swear, Mary is a hard nut to deal with. And I wish she'd just tell me who my da was.'

'But the pain was hers, Marlo, to have been forced to remain a sibling when her instinct was to mother you.'

'It didn't stop her, I can tell you.'

'Now that you know, what did you expect?'

He thought about what Kitty said and his mind drifted to Mary and Mam. He decided to call them later before heading home. He knew he had to make an effort with Mary – if only he knew how to move beyond the predictable confrontation as soon as they said the first hello.

'I was just speaking my mind, Marlo. I wasn't lecturing. And sure, Mary's secret is safe with me. Don't I know how tongues can lash around here. I hope I haven't offended you.'

'Oh no, Kitty, no offence taken. You just made me think, that's all. I'm going to ring her later this evening on my way home.'

Sully stopped as they turned a corner and jumped up and down.

'The Big Meadow's up ahead, Marlo. Shall we race, Sully? Last there is a silly monkey!'

With that, they set off and Marlo followed, collapsing beside them at the foot of a huge oak that seemed to have multiple trunks.

'Is this one tree, Kitty?'

'No one really knows. Might have evolved from the one trunk that cleaved hundreds of years ago. Incredible, isn't it?'

Sully had opened his backpack and the ham and cheese sandwich was demolished in no time. He drank his Mi Wadi noisily, exaggerating the sounds each time Kitty admonished him. Then he headed off to climb the lower branches.

'He's so good on the bus, you know, Kitty. Never a bother

– exactly what Bernard Causkey told me that first time I drove the bus.'

'I was terribly ill with flu about two years ago and Uncle Mossie had called to drop off my script from the chemist. When he saw the awful state I was in, he said he'd take Sully with him on the bus the next day. Just to help, you know. That's how it started. He did it for three days and then volunteered to do it for longer, till Sully started school – to allow me to me get a few hours work.'

'He was a good man. The kindest.'

'Yes.'

'The regulars are so good with Sully.'

'Strangers tend to be less judgemental, you know. It's your own who pick the first stone.'

'What's Sully got to be blamed for?'

She waited a moment before matching his own earlier candour. 'We weren't married, his father and I. We were engaged but my John Paul – he died before we were married. His family, and mine, had to cope with his death and then a few months later a fate worse than death – I was pregnant and, worse still, I wasn't going to take the boat or part with my baby.'

'Were you pressured to give him up?'

'Oh, I held my ground. There were a few that backed me up on the quiet, though. John Bosco and John Joseph. Uncle Mossie.'

'Assumpta?'

'She was disapproving of me from the start, even when I was in school. Thought I had notions. She was never unkind but – you know how formidable she can be. Also, for her there was the matter of not getting on the wrong side of Father Angelo. She likes to be teacher's pet.'

'That's the power of blind faith – makes you blind.'

Kitty nodded. 'I had my own home, so I was saved from complete shame because I'm not dependent on anyone – though

I think that very fact incensed the mudslingers.'

'But you've survived, both of you.'

'It's a blur, but I did – you see us, we're happy.'

'Like my mam and Mary did, but they had each other.'

'Yes, they were lucky. I think I broke my parents' hearts. But I've no regrets, how could I?' She looked towards her son balancing in the crook of two branches, peering intently into a hole in the trunk.

'Sully's planning to climb higher, I think.'

She stood up. 'I just hope there are no wasps nesting in that hole.' Then, brushing away bits of grass from her jeans, she walked towards her son, coaxing him to come down lower. He, in turn, was signalling her to climb up to where he was.

'Oh, Sully, not that hole again, pet. It's packed full of abandoned bird nests and a whole load of creepy crawlies. And we're definitely not taking home any spiders today. No beetles either.'

He stamped his foot, insisting.

But she held firm. 'Well, if you won't listen, Sully, we won't be going to the dragonfly lake. It will be straight home in Marlo's car.'

'Sure, go ahead and make me the bad guy, Kitty.'

He rolled up his rain jacket and placing it under his head he lay down in the grass and looked up at the sky. The Big Meadow was probably the only part of the forest that had such an expansive, clear view of the sky, which was streaked with contrails as aircraft crossed the Atlantic. He wondered where those souls were headed, heartbroken or happy, on the way to their destinations.

What about me – where am I headed? And will she come with me? He lifted his head and shoulders to see where they were. Kitty was bent over the grass with her son by her side. She had coaxed him down and they were examining something on the ground at close quarters. She was talking to Sully, as she stroked his hair.

He had over the last few weeks wondered about what life

would be like with her. With her and the lad. The attraction he felt for Kitty was so strong despite the fact he didn't really know her properly but what he did know was that he hadn't felt like this about any other woman before. I'm not going to rush this or put her off in any way; I'll just take it as it comes. He closed his eyes and thought about the possibilities, knowing in his heart that he was jumping the gun. He drifted off into a dream space until he felt something crawl over his neck and cheek. As he brushed it away he heard muffled giggles. Kitty and Sully, armed with feathery-ended long grasses, were tracing patterns across his face.

'What kind of man asks a girl out and then falls asleep?'

'I was dreaming.'

'Is that so? Well, we're going to break the spell, Cinders.'

He sat up and stretched as he looked at Sully. 'What's next, champ?'

Kitty pointed in the direction of the path. 'We are headed to the lake. Come on!'

Sully had run off ahead and they followed not far behind. Marlo was struck with the freedom she gave the child, keeping him in sight but not holding him back on a tight rein. Not like Mam and Mary who had always insisted on holding his hand – no wonder I rebelled, kicking and screaming from the moment I could.

'What were you dreaming of, Marlo, you looked happy asleep.'

'I'm happy awake too, walking here.'

She looked at him amused. 'There's an energy in this forest that cannot be quantified. But believe me it's real, very powerful and can lift your spirits like nothing else can. I mean, it has a really calming influence, you know, on Sully. I know he gets hyperactive when he gets here but it's the anticipation of the new and different things he's going to see and hear. All of it is just so good for his soul, mine too.'

'Fresh air.'

'No, not just fresh air and the outdoors, sure I can get that in my own garden or at Ellen's Rock. No, Marlo, this is special. I feel it each time I walk here with Sully.'

'Oh, I don't doubt you. Every time I step out into my back yard, I'm entranced. The way the mountains ring the valley, it's like being embraced. D'you know what I mean? And then there is Crow, an old soul. I find myself talking to the bird sometimes and he seems to know exactly what I'm on about. When he cocks his head at an impossibly acute angle, I know he's questioning my sanity. As you are probably doing now.'

She shook her head. 'You've come back to where you belong, that's all.'

'Shall we do this again?'

'I'd love that.'

He thought she might have heard his heart thump. 'What about Sully? Will he mind me taking up your time? You probably do stuff with him when you come walking here. You mustn't let me stop you both doing what you want.'

'Sully has a mind of his own when we come to the forest and I give him a free rein, I must admit. But it's nice, really nice, to have you with us, Marlo.'

Later that evening, when he dropped them back home, Kitty made Sully shake hands to say thank you and Marlo was taken aback at the firm little grip from the child.

'See you on the bus tomorrow, Sully. Red cars Monday it is.'

Kitty stood waiting in the sunroom till he drove off, waving back as he tooted the horn.

He headed for the phone in the village, pulling the car up just beyond the Garda station. To his surprise John Bosco emerged from the booth.

'The line down at home, JB?'

'Was ringing herself in Melbourne because you know what it's like with my three sisters and mother – it's like surround sound in reverse. They can earwig through solid walls, the wagons.'

Marlo nodded. 'Oh, I know all about that.'

John Bosco continued, 'By the way, I forgot to tell ye – they were sorely disappointed, my sisters, when I told them that you were off the market.'

'You told them what?'

'I told them you were concentrating on our Kitty. Not wrong, am I?'

Marlo was taken aback. 'Jesus, I didn't think it was that obvious.'

'You'll have your work cut out for you, Marlo.'

'Tell me about it. I played the waiting game.'

'You mean she's agreed to go out with you? You jammy dodger. What about Sully?'

'We took him with us. I'm just after dropping them back home.'

'You're taking the mick, aren't you? She's been out with you already? And Sully went as well?'

'Yes. We walked in the forest. I loved every minute of it.'

John Bosco stared at him for a long few seconds. 'I knew there'd be someone who'd come along and be absolutely mad for her. I'm glad it's you, Marlo. And fair play to you, boi.'

'Why the heck wouldn't there be?'

'Ahh, now lad. I see you jump to her defence but it's a fecking long story.'

'She gave me the gist and it wasn't that long really. Blame and shame – the usual Catholic shite.'

'Too right you are.'

The two men looked at each other. Marlo put out his hand.

'I'm glad you stood by her.'

John Bosco turned away and stared down the empty street. His eyes were full when he looked back at Marlo and shook his hand. 'He was my brother. He was crazy about her, you know. John Joe and I, we do what we can.'

'Yes, she told me that too.'

'I'm working on my mam – trying to get her to come around. My da will if my mam does. Look, that's Batty Mor heading this way and I bet he's for the phone. You'd better get in before he does.'

A few minutes later, as the phone rang at Mrs Kelly's, Marlo jingled the coins in his pocket. He was hoping Mary would be at home.

'Marlo, I was hoping you would call today. Mam's been sick worrying. She got it into her head that something was going to happen to you.'

It did, Mary, and she's called Kitty.

'Is she OK though? Not actually sick?'

'You know yourself.'

Marlo took a deep breath. 'And you, Mary? You OK?'

'Christ, Marlo, what's happened?'

'Nothing. I was just wondering how you were. I hadn't called in a while and so was just wondering.'

'Oh. It's just that you never ask. You know, about me.'

'Yes, I know. So, I'm asking now.'

'Are you?'

'Yes, Mary.'

'Dr Khan's been driving me mad so that's nothing new. Mam has a bit of a chesty thing, so that's not new either.'

'So, what's new then?'

'Nothing. Do you have anything new to tell me?'

Marlo decided to take the plunge. 'Tell me what I was like as a baby, Mary.'

'Oh. Marlo. You came into the world kicking and screaming, and when the midwife gave you to me you just stopped immediately. 'Twas like you knew me, you wrapped your fingers around my thumb, and they couldn't prise them open for a long time.'

They didn't speak for a while, both of them silent, till Mary began to cry quietly.

'I didn't mean to upset you, Mary.'

'I'm not upset.'

'Well, don't cry then.'

'I can't help it.'

'Tell me more, instead.'

And she did and Marlo took it all in, not interrupting except the times when she stopped to ask if he was still on the line.

'I am, Mary, I'm listening.'

She was tearful again as she told him how ill he had been with pneumonia just before his first birthday. 'You were on a drip in the hospital and Mam wasn't allowed to even hold you, and me – I wasn't even permitted onto the ward! I knew then that I had to forever cope with the sadness of being just your sister. It's been the hardest part.'

Marlo sighed. 'You'll never be just my sister, Mary, not any more.'

He leaned against the grimy panes of glass and listened to her sob.

After a minute, he asked the question he knew would make her stop and gather herself. 'Is Mrs Kelly not around?'

'Oh, Jesus and the state of me face. You know how she hates missing anything. She'll be back any minute for sure – she just went across the hallway with some rock buns for Mam.'

They both laughed in unison. 'Rocks!'

Marlo heard Mary sniff away the tears and he could picture her wiping her face with her sleeve.

'Batty Mor's stepped out of the pub for second time, Mary, and he's looking this way. I've got to let him have the phone. Tell Mam I called and that I was asking after her, will you.'

Mary sighed. 'Call me again like this, Marlo, even though I'm not the better for it.'

As Marlo got into his car, Batty Mor knocked on the passenger side window. 'I didn't mean to hurry ye on there, lad.' He winked and twitched his head to the right. 'I would just as easily have stepped in for another pint.'

'I'd run out of coins, Batty – it's all yours.'

'Calling yer mam, were ye? Is Agnes going to come home for a visit now that you are well settled in? Your sister should too.'

'They will, I'm sure.'

'Are you heading back home? Come here to me now, lad, and I'm asking from concern, d'ye understand. Is herself up at Mossie's doing OK, d'you think? It's hard for me to call in and check because she does put on a brave face and all.'

'She's finding it hard, Batty, but I think she'll cope. She knows you're all there for her.'

Batty was stroking his chin. 'And going to daily mass helps her.'

'I'm sure.'

'Don't see you there too often, lad.'

Marlo put the car into gear and looked up. 'I don't fully buy into it, Batty.'

Batty sighed. 'Neither do I, lad, and isn't that just the whole problem. I turn up hoping my faith will help me see past the carry on.'

As he drove home though the glen, Marlo was struck by that unexpected confession. It wasn't hypocrisy, but a pure dread of being singled out that coloured everyone's public persona. Memories were long and tongues longer still. Things were never forgotten nor allowed to be forgotten. But the reckoning applied to everything. No slight was put aside, no kindness let slip and the balance sheet of your reputation was a public record that anyone could add or subtract from.

As he approached the bad bend near Pooleen, dusk had given way to the dark and he slowed as he crested the slope. Dolores's car was pulled into the small layby a hundred yards ahead and he stopped behind it, wondering where she was.

A flashlight waved up and down in the field to the left and he heard her call out. 'I'm grand, lad, just got a bit late checking her water. I think this one's in calf again, I might give her some extra nuts.'

She appeared out of the darkness and swung the gate open.

'You don't need to stop, Marlo. I'm going to leave the nuts just inside the gates. Or do you need something? How's Stevie? His voice broken after the chop?' She doubled over, laughing at her own joke.

'Saw your car, Dolores, and was just making sure. You know, just checking. I'm going to call into Assumpta's before heading home to that bullock of mine. And seeing as you are asking, he's healing nicely, thanks.'

'Was heading to the Hanleys' meself. Tell her I said to get the kettle on.'

Twenty minutes later they were both sitting at the kitchen table, on either side of Assumpta, as she poured out the tea. A plate of ham sandwiches was passed around between them and they ate in companionable silence.

'Father Angelo isn't coming tonight, I see.'

'What are ye on about, lad?'

Marlo pointed to the crusts.

Dolores grinned. 'Ye're an awful messer, you know.'

'He is particular though, isn't he?'

Assumpta was not entirely amused. 'The crusts give the man awful heartburn, 'tis no sin to not want to eat them.'

Marlo changed the subject. 'The bus needs a service, Assumpta. I feel there's something not right with the clutch, it's a bit sticky.'

Assumpta put her cup down. 'Marlo, I've come to a decision and you're going to have to make one yourself.'

Dolores sighed and pulled her chair closer. 'A hot drop, lad?'

'Sure, go on, Dolores.' But his attention was on Assumpta who was wiping her hands on her apron.

'I've decided to keep the bus and the business going, Marlo.

122

Will you drive for me? Permanently, like? I'll pay you as I do at the moment and give you a quarter of the profits. To make it worth your while.'

Dolores drummed her fingers on the table. 'Fair play, Assumpta. A good plan if I may say so.'

Assumpta was looking at him directly, her hands balled up tightly. 'See, I thought you liked doing the bus and you know the regulars and they like ye. You'd be Mossie's first choice too,' she said, throwing a glance at a photo of her husband freshly hung on the wall below the Sacred Heart. 'We'll go to the solicitors and make it official and all. Would be a relief to me if you said yes and to know that it would be something you'd want too.'

Marlo nodded. 'Yes, very much. I was hoping that's what you had in mind.' He got up to shake her hand, but she hugged him before he could say a word. 'You were God sent, ye know, God sent.'

Dolores slapped him on his shoulders. 'No better man, just keep motoring and steady as you go.'

CHAPTER NINE

I've always been a watcher. What else could you be if you couldn't speak? You can only watch and whether you want to or not, you end up learning more than you ever want or need to and that's what happened to me. I watched and the things I saw and learned I wish I had never seen or known.

Some said I didn't speak because of the horror and the cruelties I witnessed as a babe. Of course, it was the kinder ones who said that. Some were convinced that the Devil held my tongue on the prongs of his fork, others declared it was the Lord himself who had denied me a voice. Fingers were pointed at my mother too – it's what she deserved, her tongue would make do for two, they said. They relented a little, after she was killed in Dursey, afraid of speaking ill of the dead, but all of them agreed that it was a cruel fate that had left my father bereft of all his able sons but burdened with me, mute Cloichin, silent as a little stone.

I watched and listened, as they passed judgement on me, and knew very quickly the few I could count on for a little kindness, a place by a fire and somewhere half-dry to lay down my head. How I yearned for my mother's lap, her fingers running through my hair each night as she murmured her nightly promises, of a day in the future when I would be able to speak. She told me over and again that she loved me best of all and those whispered words consoled me, soothed my soul like a balm.

Hunger and cold should have killed us all but, perversely, it was the incessant gnawing in our stomachs and the uncontrollable shivering that kept us alive for longer. I might have been six years old, I think, when we fled to the forest in Glengarriff after the defeat of my lord O'Sullivan's forces in Dunboy and the massacre of over three hundred of our kin – women and children, the elderly and infirm – on the island of Dursey.

To prevent the resurgence of O'Sullivan and his people, Sir George Carew, the Lord President of Munster, decreed that the whole of the Beara peninsula be laid to waste entirely. Farms and crops were burnt, herds seized, and every rebel captured met his death, but not before being tortured into revealing the whereabouts of others.

Within days, our numbers in the ancient oak fastness swelled to over two thousand, as terrified and defeated people straggled into the relative safety of the dense forest, having made the perilous journey from all across the hinterland. They came from every corner of Beara and from further afield too. Some had slunk in, evading the Crown forces entirely, while others had seen their families set upon with devilish glee, their babies skewered alive on pikes and the heads of their men strung on ropes, trophies bouncing off the bloodied saddlecloths of the English steeds.

I arrived, weak with hunger, carried on my father's shoulders for close to three days and nights, while he served duty scouting a safe passage for the remainder of the sept. It was the only time he repeatedly thanked God I was dumb, silent and unable to make any sound that would alert our cunning enemy who were scouring the countryside for us. He guided the remaining O'Sullivans and McSwineys, along with the Caseys, Cronins, O'Keefes, Carrs, Quigleys and O'Driscolls along the coast and then over the mountains to find refuge here in the impenetrable fastness of the rugged glen, amongst the ancient oaks, beeches and holly. Our creaght, the cattle and sheep captured in many lightning raids across the peninsula in the months before the fall of Dunboy, had been gathered and driven to the safety of the remote, secret valley in Coomerkane, which was surrounded on all sides by towering mountain cliffs. Here, my lord O'Sullivan hoped the animals would be safely overwintered in small pastures that were completely hidden from the spies that General Wilmot tried to set to work in the forest.

There was a job waiting for everyone as they arrived. If you could stand you were set to work; if you wanted to eat and live you did as you were told. My lord O'Sullivan had been fostered in my father's house, fed at the breast of my grandmother, even as she nursed my father himself. They had shared a childhood, dangerous and happy in good measure, and had grown into young men together, learned soldiering from my grandfather and uncles and now, as seasoned warriors, they continued to remain close.

My father was a trusted foster brother, a man who had proved his loyalty to my lord O'Sullivan and it was no surprise he was picked to protect our creaght. The lord's own uncle, old Dermot of Dursey and his lady wife Joanna promised my father that they would keep me safe. The widows who made themselves useful cooking for the lord O'Sullivan and his lieutenants, said I reminded Joanna of Dursey of her own son, Phillip. I had heard of him too – the eleven-year-old who had been sent away, the year before, to the Spanish court, along with five-year-old Donal, my lord O'Sullivan's firstborn, as hostages to the King of Spain, in return for arms, gold and soldiers. I saw my father barely a few times a week but knew he was on the way through the forest to our camp by the unseasonal bird calls he made, alerting the sentries as he approached. He wasn't around all the time to keep me from being tormented on the sly, so I was happy to remind Lady Joanna of her son if it meant I was not constantly harassed for being the only dumb ass on two feet.

How very different is life for that other dumb lad in the forest. I followed the boy Sully yesterday, and on seeing me he waved back from atop the high rock. I've never seen him get so high up, but he stayed safe, holding onto the holly tree that grows through the cleft. I was afraid he might fall into the gap but reminded myself that it has filled up with roots from the holly and the debris of many an autumn past. We share an affliction, but that's all we share, for his time in the glen is nothing like

126

mine was – a constant matter of life and death. Life and death, I am never sure which one we wished for in those desperate months and why we even constantly switched between longing for one over the other. There was only one thing that kept us from just laying our heads down to die. It was a terrible hunger, so intense, like hot embers on your skin, only you couldn't brush it off. So, we did as we were told most of the time.

We children were sent foraging every waking hour for any edible morsel we could lay our hands on – to return empty-handed meant you had eaten what you had found, drawing the wrath of the women, who spent the day trying to prepare the woefully meagre meal that we ate, huddled around the small fires. They gripped our chins roughly and prised opened our jaws looking for evidence – our tongues stained by berries or our breath smelling lemony from chewing sorrel. Once I bit a widow, chopping down on her big snout as she sniffed right inside my mouth, convinced I had eaten the wild garlic leaves I was sent to pick. In return she nearly took my own nose off, pinching it tight and twisting it from side to side to teach me a lesson. It was Lady Ellen who saved me that time. She scolded the widow severely and then, in that inexplicable way that the women in the forest seem to be wont, they looked at each other and collapsed into each other's arms weeping. The other women gathered around, morose and silent, as the wife of our lord O'Sullivan and the widow of a dead bonnacht consoled each other. Despair was everywhere that autumn, ripening like a cankerous sore and it oozed its poison every now and again.

I slunk away, took the opportunity to remove myself from the scene before the sharp little stones came flying in my direction. Cloichin! Take this, Cloichin! I can hear the taunts still.

Could you blame me for preferring the company of animals any day? The shaggy wolfhounds that lay beside my lord O'Sullivan were as good bedfellows as you could find. If I was lucky, I might have found myself lying in the midst of them, my feet, so puckered with the damp, pushed well in under one of their warm hairy bellies. Some nights, as the fires died out, one of them might get up for a slow stretch and then circle over and over again before settling half on top of me with a sigh – in which case I would remain absolutely still for as long as I could, for to move under them was to risk unsettling all three and then it would be some other cold and frozen child that might have the comfort of those warm creatures by their side.

But it was a horse that changed my fortunes, a horse that elevated me, despite me being dumb. The first time I saw An Cearc he had thrown his young groom off and was snorting wildly, trying to rear up again. It took two others to calm him down and lead him, skittish as he still was, to the small make-shift stable fashioned from loosely woven willows and covered over with old goat skins. The horse was living in luxury that the rest of us could only dream of. But, of course, everyone knew that An Cearc was no ordinary horse. He was beloved of my lord O'Sullivan, not only because he was a elegant creature, but because he was a gift, a gift from the great legend that was Red Hugh O'Neill himself, an acknowledgement of the bravery and courage that my lord had shown at the Battle of Kinsale.

I heard a child ask why a horse would be called An Cearc – The Hen? Wait till you see it walk, the child was told, and so I too waited all evening and then I understood. His high stepping gait was so hen-like I thought he might even start clucking. When I saw An Cearc's nostrils flare ever so slightly, neighing softly at the sight of his master, nuzzling him with the sweetest of affection, I knew not to be afraid. That night I left the cold rock I was shelter-ing under and crept into the makeshift willow stable. I stretched out my hand out like my lord had and An Cearc blew his hot breath into my palms. The shock of that heat made me braver still and I stepped forward slowly and felt An Cearc exhale down my shoulder. Closer and closer I went till I rested my head against his legs, allowing his animal warmth to envelop me.

The next day my lord O'Sullivan himself told my incredulous father that they found me that morning sleeping in the crook of An Cearc's neck as he lay on his bed of pine needles. From then on, I was sent for as soon as my lord returned to camp on An Cearc; my presence, they said, was enough to calm the highly strung horse, though no one knew why. Within a few days I took to sleeping beside the horse, pushing my body as far into the space between his head and chest as I could. If I closed my eyes, it was almost like being with my dear mother again.

CHAPTER TEN

September brought the weather that everyone had predicted. Now that the summer holidays were over and children had returned to start the new school year, the weather played its yearly joke. Dry and sunny days followed, blue skies dominated the peninsula and the balmy breeze wafting across the bay put everyone in a good mood. No conversation opened without reference to the perverse timing of the sunshine.

'Every feckin year,' said Dolores, flicking a maggot off her overalls. Marlo was helping dip her sheep. 'Every feckin year the sun comes out a few weeks too late. But we'll take what the Lord dishes out.'

Marlo nodded as he hauled in an escapee by its hindquarters. Late August had been a complete washout and on the bus that had meant grumpy regulars complaining about the smallest of things.

Mags spent several of those miserable days going on about the fogged-up windows. 'There's nothing to see the whole way. Plus, it's disorienting. Makes me nauseous, it does.'

'Leave the lad alone, Mags, he can't be blamed for the weather.' Bernard often jumped to Marlo's defence.

Nuala, who was sitting behind Mags, tapped her on her shoulder. 'You'd never have made an astronaut. They do the return journey with flames licking the windows and blocking their view, imagine that.'

Mags didn't bother turning around. 'Stop, will you, Nuala.'

'What? Ye don't believe me? Well, I saw it on BBC, I'll have ye know.'

'It's Cork I'm going to, not the moon.'

'I wouldn't trust those BBC English feckers for a minute,' Enda Crowley muttered as he shifted his holdall from his knees to his feet.

Nuala gave him a dirty look. 'Is that why ye are on your way to

London for work? Happy to take the shilling, you are.'

'Oh, I have my reasons to go and I've no need to blast them about here.'

A heavy silence filled the bus and everyone's thoughts remained lingering on the tips of their tongues.

Nuala broke the spell with a sigh. 'They sent a dog up first. Laika. Imagine that.'

Mags turned around in her seat. 'Sweet mother of God, what are ye on about, Nuala?'

'You can watch it on the telly yourself. It's to be repeated on the weekend.'

Bernard brought an end to it all. 'Cross purposes, ladies, ye are talking at cross purposes as always.'

Mags wasn't pleased, and when she brought Sully back from the toilets at the newsagents, she made her feelings known. 'D'you sometimes think that Bernard fancies he's the boss on this bus? You should keep him in check, Marlo.'

He waited till she stepped off the bus and was well down the road before he rolled his eyes.

A protesting ewe at his feet brought him back to the present. Marlo didn't realise he was smiling – not till Dolores nudged him. 'Something funny, lad?'

'I'll give you a laugh, Dolores,' and he told her what had happened on the bus that week in August.

She clung to the galvanised gate, her entire body shaking in mirth.

Later, when the last of the sheep had shot out of the dip, she stood with her hand on her hip and looked him in the eye. 'Are ye happy out? With the bus, I mean? Is it working for ye?'

He nodded.

'Yes? Nothing to add?'

He was taken aback.

She didn't wait for a reply. 'You didn't inherit the cottage to become a bus driver, did you? The blessed brothers had a grander plan than that, I'm sure. Assumpta worries about it. OK, ye needn't look at me like that – sure, but first let me tell you what we both think.'

He braced himself. 'I thought it was what Assumpta wanted and you were just as pleased if I remember that evening at her kitchen table. Have the regulars complained or something?'

'Jesus lad, why would they?'

'So, what's the problem?'

'Well, how'll I put this, Marlo?'

'Straight to my face, Dolores. It's the best way.'

'OK, lad, it's just that we both think the boy, ye know Sully, well your interest in his mother is obvious and we're worried.'

'Why so?'

'Well, you are young, unattached.'

'So is she.'

'There's a lot of baggage.'

'She has a son. No baggage.'

'See, ye're taking offence when we only mean well. D'you mean to, ye know . . . are ye, I mean – what are your intentions?'

'They're good.'

'Sure, you're honest if nothing.' She let go of the young ewe that she had in a neck lock. 'They're a package, ye know. The mother and son.'

'Spit it out, Dolores. I shouldn't fancy her because of him? Well, it's too late now.'

'Have you said anything to her?'

'No, but I think she might have guessed.'

'Yes, all those walks in the forest.'

He laughed. 'I didn't know you and Assumpta were counting. If you want to know we're going to Dursey tomorrow.'

'Jesus, why?'

'It's for a piece I'm writing for the *Montana Courier*. About the massacre of the O'Sullivans at Dursey. She said she'd show

132

me a few places around the island. I wanted to eyeball the graveyard where the vault is – the O'Sullivan family vault.'

'And you think researching a massacre will impress a girl?' She began to belly laugh again. 'I tell you what, Marlo O'Sullivan, you are as quare as they ever come. But fair play to ye if that's what ye think will float her boat.'

He grinned back. 'She's not your ordinary woman.'

Dolores didn't reply but hollered at the sheep instead and Marlo joined her, driving the flock uphill towards the commonage. He stopped to catch his breath at the crest of the last hairpin bend and looked across the wide expanse of forest, farms and bare mountain, towards the Kenmare road in the far distance as it disappeared into the first of the Turner's Rock tunnels, on the very edge of the Cork border, re-emerging on the other side of the mountain in County Kerry.

Half an hour later, after thanking him for his help, she stopped for a moment before opening the door of her car. 'You've got to like the lad as well, you know. And everything that goes with him.'

He shook his head. 'No, Dolores. The question is – does Sully, does the little lad like me?'

He didn't know what to make of her reply – a hearty thump on his back delivered before easing her large frame into the small car. Marlo watched as she released the handbrake and cruised down the steep slope, swerving sharply at Assumpta's gate, rolling to a slow stop a few feet from the back door without so much as having turned the key in the engine.

Marlo walked around to the back of the cottage. Stevie had heard his voice and was walking to the fence, his nose sniffing the air. The young bullock was growing at an alarming rate and yet had the demeanour of a lazy and affectionate dog. He loved having his shoulders and the back of his ears scratched and would search for Marlo's hands with his wet nose, nudging them if he didn't get the attention. Of late, Crow had taken to flying into the shed in the evening to see if any morsels could be had at feed time. Perched patiently on the half door, he would wait till the bucket of nuts was placed in the holder on the inside of the door. Once Stevie started eating, Crow would hop around under him, flitting silently around and in between the heavy bovine hooves, picking up the bits of semi-masticated softened feed that dropped on the ground.

Marlo felt sorry for Stevie, could understand how the bird messed with the bullock's senses. Sometimes the animal would stop eating, lift his head out of the bucket, his ears on alert, confusion written across his face at the phantom presence so close to him. When this happened, Crow, as if sensing his unease, would stay stock-still till the bullock turned his attention back to the bucket, after which the bird would then get busy again eating every last fallen morsel.

Marlo scratched Stevie behind his ears and the animal stretched his neck first to the left and then to the right, every sinew exuding undiluted satisfaction. Marlo was smiling as he headed to the kitchen door. *Jesus. Whatever became of me. Here I am – slave to a bird and a bullock!*

He headed for the shower and readied himself to head into Glengarriff. He was to meet up with John Bosco and a few other lads at Casey's for the legendary Saturday special – steak and home-made chunky chips washed down with a few jars. He wanted to ring Mary before heading into the pub.

She sounded chirpy. 'You're not a minute too early, Marlo. I was hoping you'd call before I left. Mam's just down at the shops, she'll be back in the next few minutes. I've left the door open, so she'll know I'm here talking to you. Plus, Mrs Kelly's keeping a lookout for her.'

Marlo could just picture the scene. Old Mrs Kelly would be alternating between patrolling the landing, hanging out of her window overlooking the street below and walking slowly past the phone in her hall, hoping to pick up some little thread with which she could start a probing conversation with Mary and Mam the next time they walked to the bingo together.

'Where're you headed?'

Mary hesitated long enough for Marlo to wonder what exactly she was going to say.

'This is worse than telling Mam.'

'What is?'

'Telling you where I'm going.'

'Mary, for feck's sake.'

OK, it's a date, sort of a date anyway. I can't say anything more.'

Marlo was taken aback. A date. Mary, who had sworn nearly every day as far as Marlo could remember, that she had neither the time nor patience time for any man, was going on a date.

'I had my hair done this afternoon.'

'At the hairdressers?'

'Of course, you eejit. Where else? Mam was pleased. And Dr Khan gave me the afternoon off.'

'Are you going to tell me more?

'We're going to see *Phantom*. In the West End.'

'It's not where or what, Mary. It's with who?'

She burst out laughing. 'After all these years you're throwing my own words back at me!'

'I am.'

He waited, and heard her wheeze slightly as she replied. 'Maybe I shouldn't go. It'll all be wasted on me – the tickets and the dinner and all the foosthering and fuss. I could get Mam to ring and say I'm not well.'

'Jesus, Mary, don't make a whole drama of it. Waste of a hairdo as well.'

'It's Raymond.'

'The undertaker?'

'Yes. He used to take you tobogganing when you were small, d'you remember that?'

'What's that got to do with anything?'

'Nothing. I just thought I'd remind you.'

Raymond McCarthy was probably the same age as Mary and had lived all his life down the road with his parents, in their home above their funeral parlour. 'He took his time asking.'

'Well, I wasn't interested all along.'

'And now you are?'

'Dr Khan said I should give him a chance. Oh, feck it, Marlo – maybe not . . .' Her voice trailed off.

'Mary, you've known him all your life.'

'So why is he asking me now? Maybe this isn't such a good idea.'

'He had to muster up the courage obviously. You're hardly Miss Sunshine.'

'Dr Khan's patients love me.'

'Well, they are sick and desperate.'

'Would you ever just shut your face, Marlo?'

'Mary, just go!'

'D'you think?'

'I'm saying. Go.'

'Jesus, here's Mam now – I must be late so. Ring me soon, will ye?'

'Tell Raymond I said hello.'

'Really?'

'You're reading a lot into a hello, Mary.'

'And you're some feckin' cheeky pup.'

Mam was on the phone immediately. 'Mary had her hair done.'

'She told me that, Mam.'

'Raymond's sound. We'll see Phantom next time you are home. If Mary likes it, she might come again. Raymond too.'

Later, in Casey's, Marlo was left pondering over where home was any more. John Bosco was at the bar getting the pints and the steak at the neighbouring tables had him salivating even before their orders were taken. A small crowd had gathered around a corner table by the stove. He strained his neck to see what was happening when John Bosco returned with glasses of the black stuff, their creamy heads waiting to be slurped.

''Tis Herself,' he said, setting the pints down carefully.

'Ahh. I was wondering.'

'Have you met her ever? No? We'll remedy that the minute those Yanks leave her alone. Our Miss O'Hara, Maureen, she loves meeting people, especially if you are from Glengarriff.'

'D'you think, John Bosco – if you loved life in Australia it could ever replace here, you know and become home?'

John Bosco didn't stop to think. 'Never. Nothing could replace here. Sure, I'm only going to Oz to fetch her back, you know, Marlo. My mam was consoled by that thought. I plan to head there in time for Christmas and we'll be back together to celebrate the next one back here at home.'

'Will you get hitched once you're home?'

'She's some notions of getting married on a beach in Bali on the way home, just the two of us. Wait till she sees how I react to insect bites. Nothing romantic about being a giant red blotch.'

'How long have you known her?'

'Since Low Babies in school and we've been together since her sixteenth birthday.'

'That's handy.'

'Handy? What's handy about it?'

'That you knew her well enough before. You know, you didn't have to wonder if she was the right person.'

'Jesus, that's some heavy stuff out of you tonight, Marlo, boi.'

Marlo twirled the pint glass, held it high and examined it up close.

'The oracle isn't there sitting in the glass, you know.' John Bosco put his fist to his heart. 'Just follow the old ticker.'

'I've been doing just that,' said Marlo as he cut into his steak.

Driving to Dursey the next day, he looked across at Kitty as she pulled her hair into a ponytail. She hadn't quite succeeded in taming her curls – tendrils emerged one after the other, teased out by the strong breeze from the open window. It was a warm day, only a bit overcast but the forecast wasn't great. He peered through the windscreen at the clouds overhead.

'It could be entirely different on Dursey,' she said. 'It could be lashing, or it could be sunny.'

'Typical,' he replied, laughing. 'A weather report to cover every eventuality. I'd hate to be a weather man in Ireland, trying to predict the unpredictable.'

'On the other hand, you'd never be too far off the mark,' she said, sticking on her dark glasses. 'The glare gives me a head-ache.'

'Mary suffers the same.'

'Have you been talking to her?'

'Yes, I have. We aren't biting each other's head off. Not as much as before anyway. She went on a date yesterday. To see *Phantom of the Opera* in the West End.'

'Nice.'

'She was dithering though, but she did go in the end. I can't remember her ever going out with any man. And when she does, it's with an undertaker – I hope she enjoyed it. She told me she'd had her hair done so she must have wanted to make an effort for Raymond.'

'Oh, he's someone you know?'

'I've known him all my life. Nice guy, shy – I remember him being quiet and kind. His parents were good friends of Mam. They gave great send-offs to more Croydon Irish than you can imagine. Was a mighty turnout when they were buried themselves. Waked in their own funeral parlour and the church was packed the next day. Was a fine affair, as my mother said almost enviously. Like she was giving notice of what was expected of me and Mary when her time's up.'

'They died together? Raymond's parents, I mean.'

'Yeah, it was quite bizarre. They were run over by their own hearse. Something about the handbrakes failing on Hill Street. You are allowed to laugh, Kitty – everyone does the first time they hear it.'

She giggled with her hand to her mouth. 'Oh, I really shouldn't!'

'Heck, I forgot Sully – I hope he didn't hear that.' Marlo was half whispering.

She turned around to look at her son. 'He's fallen asleep. Would have gone over his head anyway.'

'Or maybe not, Kitty. He's smarter than his years.'

She nodded. 'It's the constant listening – I think he takes in a lot. People forget that he can hear.'

They were at Adrigole and the road rose uphill, closely skirting the huge church set on the right by the road. Further on, past a hazardous hairpin bend, the road fell away to the coast very quickly, hugging the fringe of an exquisite half-moon bay where seals basked on small rocky outcrops dotting the shallow waters.

'I never tire of the views, not even after these months of driving this route five times a week.'

'Uncle Mossie used to say the very same thing. He loved it, loved the fact that it was different each time. God, I miss him.'

Marlo hesitated before touching her shoulder lightly. 'I know how you feel, Kitty. I knew him just a few months and both alive and dead he's made such a mark on me.'

She closed her eyes and smiled. 'It's a great way to be remembered, sure it is.'

'How'd you like to be remembered, d'you think?'

'As a mother who never gave up trying.'

Marlo took a deep breath in. 'You've a tough battle ahead. Both of you.'

She choked up a little before regaining her composure. 'The first years never prepared me, you know. I was on my own, but he was the easiest of children and in most respects not unlike many other babies. He cried if he wanted something and even though his crying was different and I did wonder about it sometimes, I never worried. When he was about twenty months old the public health nurse felt there was something not quite right, and for a long time I felt he was just a late developer. Well, I haven't lost hope, you know. All the reading I did, the visits to the GP and the early childhood clinics, the books I ordered convinced me that he would speak, as long as he was well stimulated. So, we've been walking, drawing, painting and reading like our lives depend on it. And I guess it does. I held out hope, you know what I mean, that he would start speaking once he went to play school.'

'And did he? Go to school?'

'For a few months when he was about four. But they couldn't cope – they'd never had a child who couldn't speak and didn't know what to do with him. And then when he was ready to go to primary school, he was refused a place.'

'Can they do that?'

'They dithered at first, then said yes, then backtracked saying the school wasn't geared for him. I've given up, Marlo – you know, knocking on the doors which will never be open for a child like him. I'm just going to do it on my own.'

'That's just terrible, Kitty.'

'No, what was really terrible was a man of the cloth, with a red biretta on his head, sagely telling me that Sully couldn't speak because he was conceived in unspeakable sin.'

Marlo pulled the car up to the side of the road. Kitty was looking straight ahead.

'A bishop told you that?'

'To my face.'

'This is some bloody country.'

'Yeah. Let's drive on. If he sleeps all the way, he'll definitely be up for everything that Dursey has to offer.'

They drove in silence for a while before she spoke. 'Thank you, Marlo.'

'For what?'

'Just for listening.'

'Kitty, for feck's sake, it's nothing.'

'I've never told anyone about being judged like that. He's a beautiful child, made of love – from love. His father would have adored him.'

Marlo looked at her and nodded quietly. He thought about Mary, who was still being stubborn as hell, refusing to have the conversation that he had tried many times to initiate. Despite his better judgement, he had tried to catch her unawares a few weeks ago.

'Should I be ashamed, Mary? Is that why you won't tell me?'

She had got so upset that Mam had snatched the phone out of Mary's hand and given out to him. 'Can we leave all of this till you are home next, Marlo? She's gone off crying now anyway. It isn't something to badger her on the phone now, is it? Mary will come around. I've never known what she's holding so close to her chest, but she'll tell us both in her own time.'

'Don't you want to know, Mam?'

'I'm afraid I won't be able to unhear it.'

He was thinking of what his mam had said to him when Kitty tapped him on his forearm. 'Sorry, Marlo. I managed to gather a lot of dark clouds and us still only in the car.'

'Oh no, Kitty, don't apologise – I was just thinking about Mary and my own father. I wonder if I'll ever know who he was.'

She stayed silent in her own thoughts and as they came up to Castletownbere he slowed the car down at the newsagents in the town square. 'It's ice cream time – we need cheering up. Are you awake, champ?'

Kitty looked delighted. 'A Loop de Loop for me please, Marlo. Sully,' she said, turning around to him. 'Ice cream, yeah?'

He smiled a sleepy smile.

'Get him the same, Marlo.'

'Better still let him choose for himself. Kitty, you mind the motor. Come on, Sully. Buying ice cream is man's work.'

When they returned, Marlo laughed at Kitty's sharp intake of breath.

'A ninety-nine was what he pointed to, and a ninety-nine with a flake is what he got. He's well able for it.'

'Jesus, Marlo – he and your car are both going to be a right mess.'

'Nothing a bit of water and a wipe won't sort. Can I lift you onto the bonnet, Sully? We'll finish the messy bits before driving off.'

Sully stood in front of Marlo and waited till he was scooped up onto the bonnet. He pulled his little legs up and resting his hands on his knees, he tackled the chocolate flake carefully before licking the soft scoops.

Marlo leaned against the car, his Cornetto in hand and laughed at mother and son as their ice creams began to drip uncontrollably.

'Christ, Marlo, we can't get into the car like this. Give me a few minutes – I'll take him into Murphy's Bar and give us both a quick clean.' Kitty walked briskly into the famous establishment across the road, Sully on her hips.

Half an hour later, when they finally got to Killough and the turn-off for Dursey, Marlo found himself falling into a quiet anticipation. This happened to him often – his thoughts went on hold when he knew a vista, glorious and unpredictable, was about to reveal itself as he drove around a sharp corner or crested a hill. It didn't matter if he had seen the views several times all week and month long, the sight of the mountains squashed into fantastical folds that rose up high, only to abruptly fall away into the sea, sweeping panoramic skies which looked like they had been painted by brush strokes of changing light or the ocean – benign wherever it came into the many hundreds of inlets and coves, but formidable as it rolled out from Bantry Bay towards the vast Atlantic – all of it was breathtaking each time, every time. Peaks could be shrouded in swirling mist one moment and the next minute seemed ablaze as sunbeams bounced off the shards of glistening slate. Beara was never shy about revealing its spectacular delights and all the times on the bus when he'd forewarn tourists to gear up for a Beara special, it was himself he was setting up for a moment of jaw-dropping beauty, like the view before him now as they drove downhill towards the tiny cable car station nestled into the hillside.

Dursey lay stretched out to the left, nearly all of its length and breadth visible across the roiling waters of the narrow channel. Waves crashed over the rocks below and sea spray whipped up by brisk winds blew a salty tang all around the tiny car park.

'Mother of God, is that it?' Marlo looked up at a small pale green box moving slowly along steel cables suspended two hundred and fifty feet over the treacherous, foaming waters of Dursey Sound.

'What did you expect, Marlo? It's hardly a ski resort! It can only take six at a time.'

Sully, now fully animated and with his head looking skywards, tracked under the cable car running as fast as he could, to where it was heading to dock beside the ticket office. Kitty sprinted behind him and grabbed his hand. 'We have to wait our turn, Sully. People have to get off before we get on.'

But instead of people, it was four sheep that emerged first, cajoled by an old farmer who shepherded them straight up the ramp of a waiting trailer but not before he tipped his chin to Kitty as he walked past. 'Mind where you step in there, gurl. Two of the ewes have the scour fierce bad. I'll throw in a bucket of water over it now in a minute so.'

Despite that, the cable car stank to high heaven and Sully wrinkled his nose in disgust.

Marlo was looking at the worn, slatted floor when Kitty poked him in the ribs. 'No chance of you falling through, Marlo – the gaps are in case the animals have weak bladders.'

The tiny space was made even smaller by two wooden benches, along either side of the cable car, facing each other. The two other passengers, an elderly couple who looked like they might be islanders, took charge of bolting the doors behind them, giving a thumbs up to the operator who a few minutes ago had doubled up as ticket seller.

The man looked at Marlo. 'Yer first time on?'

Marlo nodded as the little cabin began creaking loudly, lurching in fits and starts towards the pylons from whereon it jerked its way further up and finally began to move slowly over the foaming sea. Sully had climbed onto one of the benches and was on his tiptoes trying to peer out of the narrow windows, high on the cabin walls.

'And my first time back in eight years,' said Kitty, almost to herself. 'My father used to bring me out here once a year for Cemetery Sunday.'

The woman's eyes lit up and she nudged her husband. 'Did ye hear that, Paudie?' She ruffled Sully's hair and then turned to Kitty. 'Who are your people?'

'I'm a McSwiney.'

'Ahh, sure there's plenty of yours that have lain here for centuries. The poor souls. My daughter-in-law was a McSwiney, you wouldn't be anything to her, I wonder now? Are ye of the McSwiney Mors?'

The man was quick of the mark. 'More a McSwiney Iolair – ye all have the trademark hair.

Kitty laughed. 'Yes, Iolair. The curls are a giveaway for sure. My grandparents came from Cahermore.'

'By the old forge?'

'Yes.'

'I knew it! Can ye not see the resemblance there, Paudie? Remember, Mrs McSwiney who took us in fifth and sixth class in National School? Oh, she put manners on us all. I used to help clean for her when she got very old. Imagine that, just imagine that now, Paudie – all these years later her granddaughter right here. There's a mighty resemblance all right.'

'I never knew them, my father's parents; they died years before I was born.'

'Lord have mercy on their souls.' They both crossed themselves before looking pointedly at Marlo, who had lifted Sully up off the bench so he could see better.

Kitty smiled as she gave in to their curiosity. 'My son Sully and a friend, Marlo O'Sullivan.'

'An O'Sullivan and a McSwiney on the cable car to Dursey! Is this a pilgrimage so?'

Before Kitty could answer the woman, the man rubbed his chin and said, 'Not the Marlo who drives Mossie Hanley's bus for the widow?'

Marlo tore himself away from the view. 'The very same.'

'A strange name, not one I'd forget. 'Twas Bernard Causkey that was telling us about you a few nights ago in Cronin's. All good, of course.'

The woman was looking directly at Marlo as well. 'Was your mam a fan of Marlon Brando? I remember some girls being wild for him, you know. Father Peter used to say it was a sin the way they carried on – pinning up his pictures in their bedrooms, over their beds even.'

Paudie started laughing. 'Sure, weren't the lads the same with Marilyn Monroe? But me and me brothers were never allowed anything more than the Sacred Heart on our bedroom wall.' Having said that, he was suddenly full of remorse and crossed himself hurriedly. 'Lord have mercy on my poor mam – she was a reasonable woman in every other respect.'

A few minutes later, having failed to establish any other tenuous connections between the four of them, they all fell quiet much to Marlo's relief. As the cable car crossed the halfway point, the dramatic geology of the island, and the mainland that it had calved from, was laid out for their eyes to feast on. Marlo knew that this was one of those scenes best observed in silence, so that every detail could imprint on his mind's eye. Suspended in slow motion over the turbulent sea, in what felt like a rickety garden shed, Marlo's senses were electrified by the panoramas stretching out in every direction.

The crystal clear waters of Dursey Sound below them were a startling bluey green, except along the shore, where waves pounded jagged rocks and crashed furiously against sheer cliffs, creating white foaming eddies that seemed to boil with frenetic energy. The body of water was well known for its treacherous currents and a vicious tidal race that made ferry crossings dangerous and near impossible even in the best of weathers. To compound matters, the narrow channel also had a submerged rocky reef lurking across the middle – an ever-present danger at high tide.

A few feet from where Marlo stood, a small blue-capped clear plastic bottle labelled Holy Water dangled from a piece of twine and began swaying in ever-increasing arcs. A sheet of paper encased in a tattered plastic slip case was pinned to the wall beside the bottle. The instructions left nothing to doubt: *'Psalm 91 – Read Every Day For Protection.'*

Paudie saw Marlo looking at it closely. 'A powerful psalm. When the winds pick up it's not just the animals that shite themselves.'

His wife's hand flew to her mouth. 'Paudie!'

'Well, it's the truth, by God it is. More people have returned to Our Lord's bosom riding this cable car than ever did sitting on a church pew.'

'Ah, would you ever stop, Paudie! Enough with scaring the young folk. Sure, it's a grand day and they've nothing to be afraid of.'

Even on a calm day, the crossing wasn't for the faint-hearted with overactive imaginations. But the reward for parking all doubts along with the cars at the ticket office, was the thrill of witnessing nature's fury and beauty merge into one, to realise that the soul could find sanctuary in the very spot where there was also the danger of losing life and limb itself. Gannets and gulls swirled around, escorting the cable car through the pylons on the island.

The elderly couple were all smiles as they parted company at the docking station on Dursey. They pointed to their small cottage in the distance. 'Call in if you have the time. The kettle's always going, it is. The little fella might fancy a Wagon Wheel.'

A few minutes later, while Kitty buttoned up Sully's jacket and helped him to hitch on his backpack, Marlo consulted the sheet map that he had picked up at the ticket station.

'Any thoughts on the route, since you've been here before, Kitty? What will Sully be able for?'

'We should stick to the main loop road – I think off road is almost certainly very boggy. The ruins of St Mary's Abbey and the graveyard, you know the one was I telling you about, are just down the road from here.'

'Where the O'Sullivan family vault is? Yeah, that'd be a good place to start all right.'

Marlo looked all around him. The entire island was treeless, which wasn't a surprise as surely nothing could possibly withstand the ferocious, destructive winds that gathered strength as they tore across the vast oceanic expanse of the Atlantic. There was no shelter from the elements, but the ancient stone walls and hedgerows together created a haphazard living quilt of fields that lay draped over the island, in some places hanging nearly over the edges, fringing in green the jagged and deeply indented black cliffs that were continually being re-sculpted by the ocean.

'We should probably aim to make our way to the old signal tower, Marlo. It dates from the Napoleonic era. I know Sully will make it there, no problem.'

'I can hitch him on my shoulders if he tires.'

She nodded. 'I can too, but let's see. He's great stamina. Don't you, pet?'

Sully waited till she double knotted both his shoelaces and then turned on his heels, running on ahead, his empty backpack flip-flapping against his back.

'That old backpack!' said Kitty, laughing. 'If it goes missing or, God forbid, gets lost, I'm done for!'

'Tell him Santa Claus wants it for one of his elves this Christmas coming.'

Her eyes widened.

Marlo continued. 'You know, let him give it up himself to save you the trauma if it should get lost.'

'And you're suggesting Santa be part of this subterfuge?'

'Sure, why not? Say he asked for it – in exchange for the gifts that'll come down the chimney.'

'There's a method in your madness, Marlo, I must admit.'

'It's how Mary and Mam got me to give up my grimy old Paddington Bear. It went to the elf that sewed buttons for Mrs Claus.'

'What'd you get in exchange?'

'A Meccano set. But Santa was in such a hurry that he left it wedged well up the chimney. The box was in tatters by the time we levered it out with the coal poker, and, even though I blamed Santa entirely, Mam wouldn't talk to Mary till after the Queen's Speech was over and only because the gravy boat was out of her reach.'

'Oh my God, Marlo.' Kitty was doubled over laughing. 'Please stop.'

He grinned. 'OK, I will. Tell me though, what was that in the cable car about McSwineys and O'Sullivans on pilgrimage in Dursey? And you mentioned another surname. Iolair?'

'Oh, that. Iolair is just a nickname for our branch of the McSwineys. We go back many centuries, us McSwineys and you O'Sullivans, and were very closely linked, you know. My father was big into the history of both our peoples. Apparently, we migrated from the Scottish Isles to serve as gallowglass to the O'Sullivans, this was in the tenth century or close to that time if I remember right. And then, a few centuries later, as the O'Sullivans were pushed south and fought successfully to make West Cork their stronghold, the McSwineys and their O'Sullivan overlords became more than just paid mercenaries – many of them were kinsfolk by marriage. My father fully believed the family lore – that, as a child before he took on the Lordship of Beara, Donal Cam O'Sullivan was fostered by a McSwiney family.'

'Was he an orphan?'

'Oh no – it was a custom of the time. Sons of the leading and important families were fostered by trusted lieutenants in their homes, away from plots and intrigues. It was safer, you see, Marlo, and in the security of their foster homes they were educated – learning their fighting skills, like archery, horsemanship, musketry and hunting and, of course, knowledge of the old Irish Brehon laws. They got life lessons from men who were professional soldiers – till they came of age. Often, the foster mother would have wet-nursed the child in infancy, so you can imagine how very tight the bonds were. Milk kinship, it was called. Of course, it was a very particular honour to be picked to be a foster family. It came with many privileges and the all-important protection of the overlords.'

'So, O'Sullivan Beare grew up with McSwineys?'

'Well, my father was convinced that he did. Legend has it that when O'Sullivan Beare fled Glengarriff for Leitrim, he left behind his wife Lady Ellen and their baby Dermot in the care of his foster brother Gorrane McSwiney, who was charged with keeping them hidden in the forest.'

'And did he? Keep them safe, I mean?'

'He must have because historical records have documented

that two years later O'Sullivan Beare and his family were reunited in Spain.'

'And what of Gorrane?'

She sighed. 'A mystery really, as there is no solid proof he even existed – just stories. But my father always insisted Gorrane McSwiney was more than a just a figment of a fertile romantic imagination because he reasoned that we couldn't be labelled McSwiney Iolairs if Gorrane hadn't done what he did.'

'Done what he did? Come on, Kitty, no riddles, tell me the story in the right order.'

She laughed. 'But that's exactly what history is in these parts, Marlo – one big riddle. Folklore says he hid Lady Ellen and their baby Dermot in a cleft in the high cliffs above Coomerkane where they remained undetected by the marauding English.'

Marlo interrupted her. 'The cliffs at Coomerkane? You mean at Eagle's Nest?'

'Yes. So apparently we, the descendants of the survivors of that branch, were called McSwiney Iolair ever since – quite separate from all the other McSwineys.'

'McSwineys of the eagle's nest?'

She burst out laughing. 'No *Iolair* is the Irish for eagle so we are the McSwiney Eagles if you are translating.'

'This legend, I want to believe – that you're descended from the family of this hero, this Gorrane McSwiney.'

'Can't be proved or disproved, but here we are – we remain the McSwiney Iolairs with our trademark curly hair.'

Sully had come running back to them with something held enclosed between the palms of his hand.

'Be prepared now, Marlo, it could be anything.' Kitty's eyebrows were raised high as she waited for the surprise to be revealed.

The three of them examined a small egg, intact but cracked, that Sully had placed gently on the ground.

Kitty turned it around with the tip of her finger. 'Poor little bird – it never hatched. Must have been stolen from its nest, by a gull probably, and dropped. A miracle it didn't break fully.'

Sully opened his backpack but Kitty was quick to pick up the egg before he did. 'It's smelly, Sully, and will stink up everything. Shall we bury it instead?'

The little boy thought for a moment and then knelt down to pull at some sprigs of heather at his feet.

'Great idea, pet. We'll wrap it first.' Kitty turned to Marlo and winked. 'Marlo, will you get digging the grave?'

Marlo dug a fist-sized hole using his car key and the egg was buried with a sprigs of pink purple heather to mark the spot.

As they dusted off their hands and walked on, the ruined abbey came into sight. Marlo held his arms out wide. 'Imagine living out your life here – so wonderfully bleak and so terribly beautiful.'

'You'd have to be very self-contained, don't you think, Marlo? It's not for everyone – not for most really. The island emptied out very quickly in the last few decades. People didn't want to choose hardship as a way of life.'

Marlo looked at her. 'Depends what you want from life, I suppose.'

She pushed a strand of hair away from her face. 'D'you ever miss London, Marlo? You know, get lonely for the big city?'

'No. I thought I would. But no, I can't think of anything I'd hate more than having to go back to living in Croydon.'

She opened the iron gate into the ancient graveyard. 'Why'd you leave? I mean, you could've sold your inheritance or rented it out even. Most people in the valley thought you'd sell. They were surprised when you turned up. I know Uncle Mossie was.'

'I just got very fortunate. I punched my boss across his jaw, dislocated it, lost my job and was told I'd be blackballed and never work again as a journalist in London. He was a malicious bugger. So here I am, never having sold or rented the cottage – lucky or what?'

She raised her eyebrows. 'I know you said you were impulsive, but it couldn't have been without reason. I mean, punching your boss – why?'

'He called me an Irish bastard. It was the day after I found out I actually was one.'

Kitty shook her head. 'It's a particularly cruel word. I should know.'

He stopped in his tracks, but Kitty waved away his apologetic look. 'Carry on, Marlo. What happened then?'

'I was lucky no charges were pressed. I wallowed for a while, jobless and aggrieved, and I remember wanting Mary to suffer, and Mam too. Jesus, I was one awful fecker of a fellow those weeks after. Then, when the solicitors' letter arrived, Mary and Mam persuaded me – it took them a few days convincing me that the cottage would be a fresh start. But it's turned out more than that. I inherited whole new possibilities.'

She was about to say something when they saw Sully trying to climb an old stone wall, looking for a foothold to get up the crumbling gable end of the ruined abbey. She hurried towards him and grabbed his ankle before he got any higher.

'You've got to listen now, Sully. These stones are all so loose and dangerous. See if this one comes loose the next one will too and the next one after that and then whole wall could come tumbling down. I've told you this before – you could crack your head open. Plus we could be in huge trouble, all three of us, if we caused any damage.'

She had lifted him clear off and put him down on the grass, but he continued to look up and Marlo saw him wave in the direction of the windowless opening in the gable wall.

'He keeps me fit,' said Kitty, laughing as she dusted off bits of dried moss on her jeans.

'He's brought his imaginary friends with him. I love the way he conjures them up.'

'Oh, that's Sully as always.' Then she looked at him, smiling.

'That was some coming home story, Marlo. It's almost fitting we came to Dursey really – if you wander around amongst the headstones and the vault over there, you're amongst your ancestral people.'

'And many of yours too?'

'Yes, many.'

She then turned to point east, across the ruins, to where the grassy fields fell sharply away to the sea. 'That tiny little island, Oiléan Beag, used to have a fortified castle on it. It belonged to Dermot of Dursey – he was O'Sullivan Beare's uncle and remained loyal till the very end.'

The sun had broken through the clouds and Marlo shaded his eyes with the palm of his hand. 'There doesn't seem to be anything left of it on the island though, Kitty, nothing that can be seen from here anyway.'

'It was razed by Elizabeth's forces, Carew and his gang, the same time as the fall of Dunboy Castle. I think the foundations are evident if you actually went onto the island. The cliffs themselves made up three sides of the castle, the walls rising directly from them. Must have been impregnable from the sea. Once, when I was here with my father, he told me that, as a child, when the tide was very low, he and his brothers used to scramble over that short and narrow strip of jagged rocks and across onto the island. They got a good leathering every time they were found out but stopped only when one of their cousins was washed away by a big wave.'

'Your father grew up here?'

'Oh no, he grew up in Cahermore on the mainland. His great-grandparents were cottagers here on Dursey – it was the home place, as they'd say. It went to my father's grand-uncle and, when he migrated to America with his family, there were no more McSwineys left on Dursey. I'll show you the ruins once we're past Kilmicheal. A single gable wall is all that's left. Oh, I just remembered something else you could write about in your

153

column, Marlo – not far from the house there's a giant of a boulder resting against the cliff, creating a very tiny passage of sorts. It's called *Cro na Snathaid*. In the old days, islanders believed that if a newly-wed woman managed to go through "The Needle's Eye" from east to west three times, she would not die in childbirth. The islanders were always so superstitious.'

'I get the impression many of the older people in Beara still are.'

'Oh, you mean in the glen?'

'Yes. Dolores, for example. She wouldn't pass a magpie without saluting it.'

'Jesus, Marlo, neither would I.'

Marlo wasn't sure if she was pulling his leg, but she must have been deadly serious because she looked embarrassed at her confession and turned away to look at the little island again.

Marlo followed her gaze. 'I'm sure you could kick a football over, it's that close.'

She laughed. 'You sound like John Bosco. Actually, it used to be connected to Oileán Baoi, I mean Dursey, with a drawbridge – in its time, those four centuries ago.'

She let go of Sully's hand to point in the opposite direction, to a field on the hillside above the graveyard. 'And up there, that's Pairc an Air, the massacre field. Where Carew's men killed all of the women, children, the elderly and infirm that had been sent here to the island for safety. When they tired of murdering them with their swords and bludgeoning them with axes the English soldiers just bound the remaining wretches together and pushed them over that cliff.'

Marlo looked at the field, a pretty picture with vast swathes of fragrant chamomile tumbling downhill like a river in bloom. It was hard to imagine the horror that Kitty was describing. He scanned the island from west to east again and heaven seemed to meet earth in every direction. The view across the width of Bantry Bay was jaw-dropping. In the distance, the Sheep's Head peninsula lay stretched out from end to end, framing the waters of the bay and, further back on the horizon, the dark outline of Mizen Head rimmed the glorious seascape.

He stood for a while letting it soak in then walked to the very large ancient vault, circling it several times, examining the monumental stones placed on top of each other before wandering around the fallen tombs, running his fingers across the weathered slabs, the names and dates ravaged and erased over many centuries. He wondered if he was directly descended from any of the people buried here. Do I have their eyes and their nose, is my hair like any of theirs, are there under these cold stone slabs second, third or fourth cousins here, many dozen times removed, and did some of them, like me, not know their fathers? *Did any of them fall in love with a McSwiney woman like I think I have?* A small shiver went up his spine as he looked towards Kitty who was kneeling beside a cluster of tombstones closer to the ruins.

She was rummaging in her bag. 'My father always lit a candle here and I felt I needed to do it for him today.'

Sully had followed her and, squatting on his haunches next to his mother, watched as she wedged the candle between two stones and tried to light it. 'I see why he used his cigarette lighter – I don't stand a chance with matches in this breeze.'

'Hold on, Kitty, let's try this,' said Marlo, kneeling down beside Sully and cupping his hands around the wick as she struck a match again. The flame danced unsteadily, and Marlo put an arm each around Sully's and Kitty's shoulders and drew them in close around the candle. They watched over the flickering light until a gust of wind finally got the better of it. Sully wriggled away and Kitty sighed. 'Thanks, Marlo. I'm happy I did that for my father.'

A few minutes later, as they walked on together towards the remains of the long-abandoned cottages of Ballynacallagh, he couldn't help reaching out for her hand. 'It's going to be a special day, Kitty, I can feel it.'

She leaned into him, not taking her hand away, and for a long while he held his breath, not wanting anything to change.

CHAPTER ELEVEN

Cloichín's Story, Glengarriff, 1602

It's a wretched island, Oileán Baoi – they call it Dursey or somesuch these days. Nothing would have dragged me there to that place where I last saw my mother, where a bare handful of us managed to survive, to bear witness to the beginning of the end. But then I never thought the boy Sully would set foot on it, so I returned.

He wasn't surprised at all when he saw me atop the gable of the ruined abbey. I had brought nothing with me to the island to show him as I would have done in the forests of the glen or by the big meadow. No shaggy wolfhounds, no gentle donkeys or long-horned cows to entice him with. I hadn't An Cearc by my side, showing his mettle, snorting and tossing his head, pawing the ground, his ears alert and his eyes curious, ready with his gold-embroidered saddlecloth and caparisoned bridle befitting a horse that my lord O'Sullivan would ride. All I had with me that day on Oileán Baoi was my fear, wrapped around me like a cloak of ice.

Could you blame me? For it was here on that terrible day in the summer of this year that Carew's men caught us off guard, landing on a side of the island we did not think they would dare attempt, but they did and the Devil brought them ashore with utmost care at the same time as God abandoned us to their unmerciful savagery.

So it was that from the castle in Oileán Beag our beaten warriors emerged, crossing the drawbridge, knowing they were defeated, tricked into surrendering, thinking all their lives would be spared – only to be killed, every one of them. And when they were slain it was the turn of the remaining wretches: women begging for mercy, pleading for their children to be spared. But it was to no avail – Carew's men took to their weapons, tossing bloodied children from spear tip to spear tip, bludgeoning mothers, beheading old crones and bringing their battle axes down on aging old men. Cornered in a quivering pile against a rocky outcrop in the field above the abbey, we began to fall atop each other, a huge mound of dead and mortally wounded. My mother's fingers slipped through mine and as I fell to my knees in the crush, bodies fell over and around me. Carew's men stomped up and down that hillock of dead souls looking for any movement or cry from the bloodied heap, their spears at the ready, prodding and thrusting into the flesh at their feet, thirsting to despatch any signs of life.

Mute as I was, I lay rigid with fear, the blood of many of the dead above and around me seeping into the very folds of my skin, leaving me slick like the seals that played around the rocks of the bay.

When Carew's men had exhausted themselves and when their weapons had become unwieldy, slippery with blood, they lashed together the remaining few dozens and threw them over the cliff. I imagine often that terror must have taken my mother's tongue and that even as my brothers clung to her skirts and my sister to her breast, she uttered not a cry as they were roughly bound to each other and rolled over the precipice – I know in my heart that her last thoughts were of me, only of me, her helpless child left behind.

Many hours later, when darkness fell and a deathly quiet descended over the island, I crawled out from under the pile of stiffening bodies with their oozing entrails and continued on my belly, getting as far as I could from the horror of it all. Now the blood was my own, seeping from scraped knees and elbows, as I kept going in the dark till I suddenly sensed I had crawled onto a smooth stone. I felt around with my fingers and, by the size and shape of it, I knew immediately it was the large slab that capped the souterrain in the field that belonged to my uncle, my father's brother. I raised myself to my hands and knees and found the small opening and made my way in, sliding down on my belly till

I slipped into the small underground chamber. I lay there for a while unmoving, exhausted. A sound made my heart stop and fear convulsed through me once again.

Then a hand reached out and fingers felt my face and ran through the curls of my hair for a moment before wrapping me in an embrace. 'My son! Sweet Christ be praised! God saved you, God saved you!'

With that, I found myself safe in my father's arms. He wept quietly for hours, his tears wetting my face, inconsolable and grateful in good measure as he rocked back and forth till day broke. We stayed four days and nights in the chamber, my father rationing the cheese that he had with him packed into his silver-tipped horn and making me wet my lips on the moist rocks that lined the souterrain. He cradled me for most of those days and he told me of his own fortuitous escape. 'God saved us, my son, for some great reason and we will know it soon enough. When I was picked to leave the castle to scout the shore it was God's doing – for why else was I spared? God surely has a purpose for me and you, for us.'

A few days later, digging into his memory and using every bit of his knowledge of the shores, rivers and mountains of our peninsula, and his skills as a scout, he led us few survivors to the safety of that impenetrable fastness known only to the O'Sullivan and their kin – the ancient oak forests of Glengarriff.

We were seven weary souls when we left Oileán Baoi, but along the way our numbers grew. Carew's men were on a rampage across the peninsula – looting, burning homes and putting to death anything that moved. Terrorised families and survivors of the wanton butchery hitched their faith to my father's determination and we made our way slowly under cover of darkness, sometimes skirting the coast, sometimes creeping inland, all the while managing to evade the Crown forces till, to our great relief, we passed our own sentries and were finally safe in the forest camps.

I know it was my father's belief, that he and I had been saved for a reason, that kept him going, bringing with us a great many people to safety.

You can see why I hold Oiléan Baoi in such dread. But I don't grudge the boy Sully his time there. He'll be back soon to the forest on the familiar boreens that we both know so well. But till he comes again, I must tell you the rest of my story. I must tell you how I came to still be here lingering, waiting and hoping. I have waited so long, an eternity really, not knowing when and who would come by to help me leave. I must tell you why I approach this boy who is so like me and yet nothing like me, who suffers from the same affliction as me and yet seems not to suffer at all. Do I envy him? you may ask, and I know not what to say, for my heart is heavy with envy, but of what use would that be, where would that get me with what I want him to do for me?

Let me now tell you what happened to us, what became of us, many hundreds holed up in the depths of this forest, in miserable encampments under the watchful eye of the gallowglass and bonnachts that served my lord O'Sullivan. We were all a wretched lot in the summer as more and more stragglers, with nowhere else to go, made their way to the sanctuary that the Lord of Beara and Bantry could afford them. My father guessed that we might have numbered about two thousand seeking refuge in the glen. If you could move a limb you were put to work, gathering and concealing our stores of food under the watchful eyes of the bonnachts, searching for fodder for the creaght, making fortifications and traps. When the women hadn't sent us foraging for meagre pickings of fruits and berries, children like me were tasked with helping with the plashing, for our nimble fingers found it easier to interweave the slim branches of the undergrowth, creating natural-looking pathways in an otherwise impenetrable forest, tempting the enemy to explore further in and leading them into deadly ambushes where they were hacked to death.

But as autumn approached, our bleak future began to look entirely hopeless with each leaf that fluttered down to the boggy forest floor. As the foliage thinned, the curtain that shielded us was slowly drawn back, leaving us at the mercy of Carew's spies. And the word was that he had set a cunning man to find and finish us – General Sir Charles Wilmot. 'The Bastard Wilmot' is the only way my lord O'Sullivan spoke of him, and outwitting the Englishman was proving increasingly difficult. With every skirmish came death and terrible injuries and the fate of any Irish taken prisoner was so chilling that fear overtook any sense of duty, and courage gave way to pure terror. And so, barely a few months after all the fighting talk and oaths of allegiance, there began the slow leaching of fighting men who started weighing their chances of survival and just slunk away in groups, hoping to inveigle and rehabilitate themselves back into favour with the invaders. When Captain Tyrell and his men rode off and abandoned us, many other ditherers followed, scuttling away, traitors all, deciding to make their own luck away from that of my lord O'Sullivan.

With the trees now bare, the fires the women cooked at, around which we huddled for warmth, were now harder to conceal and so we had to do without. As the weather worsened, my father came more often, leaving other bonnachts guarding the creaght in Coomerkane, seeking me out only to give me a sup of fresh milk carried carefully in my mother's silver horn. He hurried away quickly each time, but not before holding me close, running his fingers through my curls and telling me as he had done countless times since the massacre on Oileán Baoi that we had been saved for a reason. Those nights when he had been and gone and the gnawing in my belly had eased somewhat, I didn't stop to wonder what he meant, all I could think of was getting as close to An Cearc's warm neck and belly as he would allow me. My lord O'Sullivan would come to see his horse each night and his laugh woke me every time. 'The dumb creatures have each found their kin,' he would say, stroking his horse and tousling my curls.

But when he lay down himself, it must have been a hellish sleep for he knew time was running out for him, for all of us. Late autumn had become decidedly wintery and even Dermot of Dursey, who would have been the oldest man amongst us, said he hadn't seen a November as cold. My father spoke nearly every day to my lord O'Sullivan directly, telling him each time that the creaght were increasingly poorly without enough fodder or fresh pickings. When our animals died there was great sorrow for the future and then a short-lived joy in the immediate that we might have fresh meat. I still remember how the wolfhounds, all skin and bone and completely listless, came to life when the meat was carried into the camps. They paced slowly around the women preparing the broths and slunk off into the bushes with the tiniest piece of gristle thrown in their direction. The cows that were in calf were no longer milking and stores of our cheese and buttermilk began to dwindle.

Each night the gallowglass gave an account to my lord O'Sullivan and his captains, and the news worsened as the weeks passed. By mid-December there were daily skirmishes with Wilmot's men who had begun to make deadly forays, descending each time over the mountains from Kerry. It was on Christmas Day that our scouts came with news that a small army of Wilmot's men had been sighted making their way over the Caha ridge and past Rossnagreena. They were encamped in a particularly wet and boggy patch of ground at Gortnakilla, near Youngfields. Though the forest that separated us from Wilmot's men was near impossible to penetrate, the enemy was nevertheless barely a few miles away and fear engulfed us like never before – we were afraid to leave the vicinity of the camps and the women were like flies jumping at the merest wisp of a sound. Our efforts at plashing were now discernible – the bare branches exposed our handiwork and didn't tempt the enemy as

162

before, and fewer of them died while our losses just from the icy cold ran into dozens each day.

Friar Felipe led mass every morning but the responses to the prayers grew weaker with each passing day till his was the only voice, coughing out desperate supplications to our God above. Each morning revealed the night's attrition, the young and old who had simply perished as they slept, frozen to death – their last breaths seemed to be captured in icicles trapped around their mouths and eyelashes. Some of the older children who had tormented me ceaselessly, teasing me with sharp stones thrown with such malice, had perished too. I couldn't help think God had finally punished them, for they lay in their ragged shrouds in cold, wet ground while I had managed to stay above, helping gather stones to place over their graves.

On the last day of that year, my lord O'Sullivan sat in council with O'Connor Kerry, Owen Burke, Turlough O'Driscoll and the gallowglass around a small fire after darkness had fallen, planning their course of defensive action for the next day, but God had other plans and it was in one fell swoop that my lord O'Sullivan's decisions were made for him.

I was curled up under the hounds with my feet to the fire when I heard my father's distinct bird call.

A cuckoo in winter, to alert the sentries as he approached the camp. A few minutes later he rushed into the clearing, panting and bloodied, and all the warriors jumped to their feet, their hands to their weapons. He was almost unrecognizable, but for the horn slung across his shoulders, its silver tip glistening through the red cloak of blood that dripped off him. His eyes were wild-looking and he buckled to his knees. 'My lord, we have lost the animals. Every single head. We've lost the creaght, slaughtered along with those who guarded them.'

'What are you talking, man? McSwiney, to your feet, brother! Here, drink this!' A cup was thrust in my father's mouth and he drank, half choking, before he turned to look at the four other bonnachts who had stumbled into the clearing behind him, all wounded and just as bloodied as my father.

My lord O'Sullivan roared, 'For God's sake, Gorrane, what has come to pass, man? Spit it out!'

I left the hounds and crawled to my father's side but he didn't even so much as lower his glance at me, but yet held me close as he described the fierce battle that had been fought and lost. The few stragglers who followed my father into the camp, grown men and fine warriors all, stood weeping inconsolably as they listened.

'It's a field of blood, my lord, just a field of blood. They crept up, must have come through the valley in Coomerkane, descended upon us and took us by surprise.'

My father choked as he described the carnage that followed. 'Every head of cattle and every sheep slaughtered. The ponies too. The bonnachts fought to the very end – they died drowned in an oak field of blood, my lord.'

My lord O'Sullivan was quick with his instructions. 'Attend to these men, Friar, we will need every soul for what this night might bring.' He then turned to some of the kerne standing stunned beside him, all shaken to their core. 'Make haste, lads, and send word to all our people in other camps. Ask them to gather here without a moment to waste. Our lives will depend on the next few hours.'

The urgency was palpable as he signalled his Uncle Dermot of Dursey and other trusted commanders to walk with him a short distance away, to a large overhanging rock, out of earshot.

As for the rest, we stood open-mouthed, a terrible hush descending over us on hearing of our great, irretrievable loss. Everyone knew immediately that a fearsome fate was to befall us – for to lose the creaght was to lose all means of survival, to lose all hope, and that devastating news was relayed from camp to camp.

In that moment, however, all could I think of was how my

mother tended to my wounds when cruel stones cut into my skin. I left my father's lap and, fashioning a pouch out of my ragged cloak, began gathering all the moss that I could find, pulling it away from boulders and bark till my belly bulged like a woman with child. I squatted beside my father and began to wipe the blood from his face with a handful of soft moss. He closed his eyes and allowed me to sponge off the sticky gore till I had worked my way across his arms and legs by which time his breathing slowed and he stopped trembling, and he reached out to hold my shoulder. 'My son, we must make ourselves ready for I feel the time has come when our purpose will be revealed. The reason we were saved, why God spared us in Oiléan Baoi.'

He reached out and took some of the remaining moss in his own hands and began wiping clean the silver-tipped horn slung across his shoulder, all the while looking anxiously in the direction of the overhanging rock where my lord O'Sullivan paced up and down as he took counsel. Some of the warriors were arguing, gesticulating wildly. O'Connor Kerry and Turlough O'Driscoll walked away from the group only to turn on their heels and go back again. Owen Burke held his face in his hands and all the gallowglass looked tense.

Whatever was being planned – there seemed to be little agreement about it between any of them, until my lord O'Sullivan raised his voice. 'It is a matter of life or death, and by God I choose to live and give every wretched one of us a chance too.'

A minute later, nodding briefly at each other, the group dispersed abruptly, and my lord O'Sullivan strode purposefully towards us.

Even as my father rose to his feet, my lord fell to his, kneeling before my father. 'I haven't a moment to lose, Gorrane, and understand, brother, that this is not a decision that I make in haste but one I take from having no choice. If we're to live we must leave and make our way to safety in the north. The O'Rourkes in Leitrim will give us their protection. To stay now will mean certain death for all. Wilmot will have gauged our position – he'll know our situation without the creaght is hopeless and he'll be back looking for us in a few hours when dawn breaks.'

He then took my father's hands in his. 'I ask this of you, my milk kin. Keep my good wife Lady Ellen and our son from harm's way as if you would your own.' He lowered his voice and whispered, 'Make haste now with them to the cliffs at Nead na Fhiolar. I feared this moment would come and I am glad you prepared for it. You remember, Gorrane, as young lads how we hid there for a jape all those summers ago.'

A small smile crossed my father's face. 'Ah! We soared with the eagles, and when we were found days later, it was only because we showed ourselves.'

My lord O'Sullivan hung his head low for a second before standing up, his hand on the hilt of his sword. 'I entrust you with their lives, brother, and so, should I perish the future of the O'Sullivans is in your hands.'

My father stood up immediately, rising to his full height. 'My lord, brother, no honour could be greater. I will guard them with my life.' He hesitated then, nearly fearful to ask his question. 'But what of the rest of our people in the forest? How many fighting men are to remain with us?'

My lord Sullivan's reply stunned everyone into silence. 'None. Every fighting man leaves. None will be left behind, Gorrane. It matters not how many warriors stay back – we are done for now and to remain here is certain death. If we leave now, immediately, we might have a head start of half a day and that will give us some small chance of survival. I've sent word with my commanders for every able-bodied man, woman and child to join us this instant. We will make our way to St Gobnait's shrine tonight and then surely the Saint will stay with us the rest of the way to Leitrim.' He turned to look around at the people gathered around, aghast at the plan being thrust on them.

'Anyone who is too ill to walk with us – God have mercy on your souls. Make the best of what you can in our beloved glen, this the oak forest that has been our sanctuary these months. I ask you pray for us as I will pray every minute that you who remain stay safe and, should the end come, that it be quick.'

Then he turned to my father again. 'My boy would not survive this winter journey and Lady Ellen must stay too. I command you with the burden of looking after him, Gorrane. Keep them both safe till I send for them. God willing, we will be reunited before long.'

With that he walked briskly towards the gallowglass who had begun to ready their steeds for the journey; some of them were already mounted and trying to rein in their skittish horses whose heightened senses could sense unknown danger. The bonnachts and kernes on foot looked shocked as their wailing women and children clung to them not knowing whether to flee into the unknown or stay and face certain death. My lord O'Sullivan rushed around giving instructions for the vanguard of fighting men to start moving towards the edge of the forest in the direction of Carrignass, urging the unarmed men, women and children to gather as quickly as possible behind them. The toughest warriors were picked to make up the rearguard and no sooner had the advance party begun to move briskly out of the camps, cautiously making their way out of the forest, than the captains of the rear began shepherding the many hundreds of the unarmed to follow close behind on foot. My lord O'Sullivan walked up and down the lines, his voice steady as he hurried the wretched remains of his people. 'For God's sake, let us be quick. We must use this night, use the darkness as a cover, for Wilmot would never dream that we plan on walking to Leitrim at a moment's notice.'

Dermot of Dursey was put in charge of the twenty thousand ducats of gold that had been sent by the Spanish King at the time of the fall of Dunboy. Along with the gold, our remaining supplies of gunpowder – miraculously still dry – were placed on a dozen ponies. It was very clear that the journey to Leitrim was going to be either fought for or paid for.

When I think back on that dramatic day as our people fled, a pitiful human caravan of about a thousand souls cowering in fear with barely a few hundred armed men to fend off attacks to the front and rear of the column, I know that the cleverest thing that my lord O'Sullivan did was to give instructions for fires to be lit wherever people still remained. 'Let that bastard Wilmot think that we still linger here in the forest, for he will be slower to come in. I wish for all of us to be away in the next half hour.' No one spoke for the sobbing and crying as the elderly and infirm were abandoned. Some tried to make a go of it, limping and hobbling, trying to keep up, thinking there would be safety in numbers, but they collapsed only a few hundred steps from the camps. Prayers for their quick deaths were muttered by the rest as they trudged past in the snow, crossing themselves, wondering how long before the same fate might befall them.

My father meanwhile wasted no time and grabbed my hand. 'Come, lad, we must make preparations.'

I made as if to follow him but when his back was turned, I slipped away to the rough willow shelter where An Cearc stood restless, snorting softly when I called his name. I wrapped my arms around his legs and pressed my cheeks to his soft chest and wondered who would keep me warm at night. Minutes later my father found me and dragged me away from the beautiful creature. I knew in my heart I would never see An Cearc again and I began to weep, my tears freezing on my cheeks even as they fell.

My father stopped and, stooping to look me in the eye, he shook my shoulders. 'This is where you have to show your mettle, my son, you will be more than just a Cloichin, a dumb little stone of a boy. We were saved in Oiléan Baoi for this purpose – we are the guardians of the future generation, you and I. You heard the lord. We are entrusted to do his bidding, do you understand?'

I nodded feebly and stumbled after him to the small hidden boolie where Lady Ellen and her baby had sheltered these last months. Dermot of Dursey's wife, Joanna, was kneeling over the baby boy, wrapping him in a wolfskin before binding him securely to Lady Ellen's back. She covered mother and child with a thick cloak, and they held each other close, both weeping quietly. My father stood aside as my lord O'Sullivan strode in, and we looked away as he embraced his wife, holding her very close for while.

When she began to sob, he pushed her away gently and turned to my father. 'Go now, Gorrane, make haste for there is not a moment to lose. If you follow the river along up the standing stones and past the crooked ridge, it will lead you to the lake below the cliffs, and to our sanctuary.'

My father nodded – he didn't need to be given directions – the forest had been his playground growing up and there wasn't a part of it that wasn't etched into memory. He had also been there recently, making preparations should this sad day come upon us. The snow had begun to fall thick and fast, and as Lady Ellen followed after my father, she held out a hand to me and we stumbled away from our people into the dark, not knowing if we would ever see them again.

CHAPTER TWELVE

Marlo drove past the line of cars parked up along the road in front of the church where the faithful from the furthest reaches of the parish were gathered for Sunday Mass. He could see that it had started, for the heavy and creaky front doors of the church were closed, ensuring a very public shaming for latecomers. He carried on till he got to the grotto, which was nestled high in a gigantic rock, and then turned right heading for Bocarnagh. Marlo tried to tune the scratchy car radio, searching for a station that might reflect his buoyant mood. *Forgive me, Lord, I'll be worshipping at another altar.*

He was still smiling a few minutes later as he swung the car through the gates of the Headley-Stokes' estate. He stopped several times to inspect his own handiwork on either side of the gravel, rolling down the window of the car, well satisfied at the way the forest had already begun to show small signs of recovery. The many weeks of hacking and digging away the rhododendron infestation had paid off and the long driveway was no longer shrouded in near darkness during the day. Sunshine filtered through and in the dappled light, the strips of forest on either side were no longer being choked to death. He pulled up outside the house, marvelling, as he did every time, at the bold architectural statement of the steel and glass structure – it was as elegant as it was daring.

Tiggy and Edward were standing on the narrow jetty looking out towards Garnish Island. She waved at him. 'Morning, Marlo! Come on down here and just see how lovely this is.'

As he stepped down onto the jetty and walked towards them, he tested the planks that he had replaced, bouncing lightly to see if there was any movement.

'It's holding firm,' said Tiggy, bouncing at her end as well. 'You did a good job.'

'I was thinking of one more coat of the sealant, Tiggy ma'am, before the weather turns.'

Edward patted him on the shoulder. 'And turn it will. We'll bring the boat into the shed next week. Next Sunday, if you are free, Marlo? I'll need a hand.'

Marlo nodded. 'That shouldn't be a problem.'

Tiggy had walked to the end of the jetty, and she stood with her arms out wide, her face to the sun. Edward watched her, with an expression so intense and tender all at once that Marlo felt he was intruding on a private moment, and he looked away only for Tiggy to call out to him. 'Look at it, Marlo – could there ever be a more beautiful sight?'

Marlo knew what she meant. The woodlands that framed the hilly shoreline and the dense thickets that clung to the fantastical rocky outcrops that dotted the little cove were now coloured in shades of crimson and yellow, tinged with flashes of orange, amber and gold. The myriad autumnal shades seemed to float gently on the still surface of the cove and as a pair of swans rounded the tiny headland, a gentle wash rippled the reflections till land and sea seemed to wobble.

'Oh, Edward, did you see that?'

Edward nodded as they stood with their arms around each other. Tiggy looked over her shoulder at Marlo. 'Every year I think it will never be matched again but autumn never disappoints.'

'I should get going for the morning. I want to bring in the rest of the wood from the far end of the trail.'

Tiggy nodded. 'Come in for some lunch before you head off, Marlo, though I can't promise you anything as good as Kitty can rustle up.'

Edward laughed. 'She's left some really lovely parsnip soup in the fridge. We could work around that, I'm sure.'

Marlo grinned. 'I'm actually heading to Kitty's for lunch. I want to see those caves at Eagle's Nest and we're going to do that this afternoon with Sully. I hope the rain stays away.'

Marlo caught the briefest of glances fly between Tiggy and Edward.

But when Edward spoke it was very matter of fact. 'They're actually vertical clefts strewn across that steep cliff face, Marlo, not quite caves as you'd imagine it. Very hard to spot them even close up.'

Marlo nodded. 'Yes, Kitty did say that.'

Tiggy, however, couldn't contain herself as well as her husband. 'I think she likes you, Marlo. She's never had time or the inclination for anyone till recently, till you came to us here.'

Edward looked embarrassed. 'You needn't pay any need to Tiggy's notions, Marlo.'

'What's the point in watching them skirt around each other, Edward? Life's too short to play those games. You don't mind, do you, Marlo?

'That you spoke your mind? No, ma'am.' Marlo looked across the small cove towards Garnish, outlined by a golden glow of early sunshine. 'It's a work in progress. I don't want to put her off by even remotely suggesting she should forget the love of her life.' He shook his head, sighing as he added, 'It's doubly difficult when that's exactly what I want her to do.'

Edward ran his fingers through his silver hair. 'Young John Paul was a gentleman, I remember him well. He was very well liked. Sound, as they'd say in these parts.'

'That's not being helpful, Edward.'

'Yes of course, Tiggy, you are right. Sorry, Marlo, I was just reminiscing . He used to help me on the boat sometimes.'

Tiggy looked thoughtful. 'She doesn't have to forget him though, does she, Marlo? That's not what you want – you want her to see that she has another chance, one just as good. For her and Sully.'

'Yes, for her and Sully.'

'You're very good to him. She's told me that.'

'He's a good kid, a very clever one too. His artistic ability borders on genius. You've seen his work, Tiggy ma'am – what d'you make of his imagination?'

'Extraordinary really, the child is gifted.'

The three of them stood quietly for a minute on the jetty before Edward spoke. 'So, what's stopping you?'

Marlo smiled at them as he walked away, down the jetty towards the shed. He turned around and called out, 'Nothing, now that I think of it, nothing at all.'

He put on a pair of overalls and set to work bringing in as many large logs on the wheelbarrow as he could each time. As he stacked the logs inside the shed ready for him to chop later, he thought of Kitty and the look on her face as she'd handed him a pink plastic bag when he had dropped Sully off the bus on Friday.

'I was in Bantry with Tiggy today, she was at the bank, and I did the weekly shop for her. I got this for you at the market. I couldn't resist – it had your name all over it. I'm sorry, though, that I hadn't the time to buy any wrapping paper.'

He must have looked surprised as he held it in in his hand because she began to laugh. 'It's a gift, Marlo, it won't bite you.'

'For me? Really?' he said, as he opened the bag and pulled out what looked like a sweater.

'Open it out, Marlo – no, the other way!'

When he did, it was his turn to laugh. 'Oh, I absolutely love it!'

He traced the raised outline of a crow, its head cocked to one side, embroidered in white across the front of the navy lambswool. He winked at Sully. 'Wait till Crow sees this!'

'It's from Sully and me – just to say thank you for minding him on the bus.'

Marlo slipped it on and tried looking at himself in the rear-view mirror. 'Can't see much in this mirror, how does it look?'

'Are you rushing? Come in for some coffee and you can model it for us inside. I can take it back to the stall next Friday – you know, if it doesn't fit.'

Half an hour as he left, still wearing the jumper, he gave her a quick hug, thanking her again. Her hair had smelled of chamomile and as he drove back home in the bus, he breathed in deeply, wanting to drown himself in the traces of fragrance that lingered on his new sweater.

That was two days ago and now, as he loaded and unloaded the wheelbarrow, he thought of how she had very casually adjusted the shoulders of the sweater, removing a bit of loose lint before standing back in satisfaction. She looked happy.

Marlo had posed with an exaggerated swagger. 'I take it the lady approves?'

She'd looked at him and laughed. 'You need my approval?'

'Always.'

'Only if you tone it down a bit. The last time I saw someone pose like that was when those models descended on Glengarriff from New York. Did Dolores ever tell you that story?'

There was a moment there, a moment before she had replied that he should have grabbed, but instead he'd taken off the jumper, folded it and said he'd have more milk in his coffee before having her in stitches as he recounted Dolores's version of the tale of the models from New York.

He came back to the present when he realised the pile of logs in the shed had grown substantially and as he put the wheelbarrow away, he thought about what Tiggy had said earlier on the jetty – her powers of observation obviously extended beyond the artistic. But she was only half right because he wasn't the sort who'd skirt around anything; Mary often said that his directness was the undoing of him. *I'm doing exactly the opposite, Tiggy – I'm just minding my chances.*

He looked at his watch. He had planned on ringing Mary and Mam from Glengarriff before heading to Kitty's. It was nearly noon, and the crowds would have thinned in the village after mass. As he slipped off the overalls and headed back to his car, he saw Tiggy inside the house and gave her a big wave, pointing to his watch. She nodded and waved back, mouthing something and then miming with her hands, she shooed him on his way.

The village had emptied out, mass-goers having headed home to their Sunday dinners and, other than a few cars parked at Casey's, there wasn't anybody about. Marlo waited in the booth while the phone rang at Mrs Kelly's. He was just about to hang up when she picked up the receiver, slightly breathless. 'Ah, Marlo, sure, I knew it would be yourself. I'll go and call your mam, but let me tell you now, Mary might have some news for you. But it's not my place to share it, sure she'd want to tell you herself.' With that he could hear the phone being placed down carefully on the crocheted doily and he waited, wondering what Mary's news was. Maybe Dr Khan had given her a raise or maybe the practice manager who had been a twenty-year thorn in Mary's side had finally decided to retire. But it was Mam who came to the phone, and it sounded like she was alone.

'Were you at mass then, Marlo? I thought you might have been, seeing as it's so late in the day.'

'Ah, not that again, Mam.'

'There's not much use in me praying for you here, if you haven't been to confession in weeks.'

He tried to change the subject. 'Where's Mary?'

But Mam was in a one of her holy moods. 'It's a help, you know, Marlo, going to church. Not everything about it is bad.'

'I never said it was, Mam. It's just not for me at the moment.'

'You can't pick and choose your moment. It's not a kebab menu.' She paused then, before delivering the real reason for her peevishness. 'I met that Philomena Crowley at the drop-in centre. Turns out her nephew is Enda from up Rossnagreena way, and isn't he staying with her, filling her in with everyone's business.'

'Enda Crowley? He was on my bus to Cork a few weeks ago, on his way to London, never said he was heading to Croydon.'

'They were a strange lot, the Crowleys, and his Aunt Philomena's no better. I had to hear it from her that you're doing a line with a widow, you never said anything to us.'

'How the feck did she even know?'

'Did you even listen to me? It was Enda that told her.'

'How would he know?'

'How should I know, Marlo? You ask yourself. He must know enough to have told Philomena and I've to live with her now telling the rest of Croydon at the bingo. You may as well know that Mary is demented with worry.'

'I would've told you both when and if there was something to tell. I'm not doing a line, she's not a widow and it's none of his business anyway,' said Marlo, annoyed that Mam had to hear about Kitty from someone else.

Mam suddenly whispered, 'Mary's here.'

'I'm not afraid.'

'Don't say anything to her you'll regret now, Marlo.'

Marlon gritted his teeth 'It's her that you need to say that to.'

But Mam had passed over the phone to Mary.

'So Mam told you what we heard.'

'I'm twenty-nine years old, Mary.'

She seemed silenced by that. He heard her sighing. 'Tell me about her. I hear she has a child.'

'Yeah, a boy called Sully. Sullivan McSwiney'

'Who calls their child Sullivan? For God's sake.'

'You called me Marlo.'

'I watched his films when I was pregnant. And I couldn't call you Brando, could I?

'Kitty must have her reasons too.'

'Ah Mam, look,' said Mary loudly, as if calling out to her mother. 'Look, we have a name.'

'Stop playing the eejit, Mary. As if I don't know Mam's beside you, her ear pressed to the other side of this feckin' phone. What are you both like, for God's sake.'

Mary was a bit conciliatory then. 'Jesus, Marlo, it was hard for us to hear it from that Crowley woman.'

'Yeah, I feel for you, Mary.'

'Well, are you going to tell us more or what?'

'There's nothing to tell, Mary. She works at the Headley-Stokes' and her little fella rides the bus every day with me to Cork and back.'

'Is he in a posh private school up in the city, like?'

He took a deep breath and they listened to him in silence as he told them about Sully and the arrangement that Mossie had made to keep him on the bus.

Mam tut-tutted. 'Ah, the poor lad.'

Mary didn't let up. 'And you fancy the mother?'

'You could say that, Mary. You'd probably like her too.'

'A woman with a child like that. She's probably all over you like a rash.'

Marlo could hear Mam's sharp intake of breath. But he got in before she could say anything. 'Don't judge her, Mary. She didn't lie to her son. She stood up to the world.'

'And you think I didn't?'

'It's not about you, Mary, and don't go fecking making it about you. I'm just asking you not to judge her.'

'Well, it's the truth. Which woman with a child like that wouldn't want what you can offer. There's not many men that would go for someone like her.'

'I could just hang up on you, Mary, but I won't because I have to tell you that it's quite the opposite. It's me going for her and I'm not sure she'll have me.'

There was silence from both the women on the other end of the phone. Mam spoke first. 'Why in heaven's name would she not want you? A nice lad like you?'

'Sully comes first and last.'

'That's understandable,' said Mary.

None of them spoke for a while as they just listened to each other breathe.

Suddenly weary, Marlo decided to end the conversation and salvage what was left of his earlier happy mood. 'I'm going to meet her for lunch now. We are walking to Coomerkane along with Sully later so I'd better be off.'

'Lunch and a walk. You don't do lunch and a walk unless you fancy someone, she'll know that.

'You were at a lunch and a walk yesterday, Mary, so does that mean—'

Mary cut her mother off abruptly. 'It's for me to tell him, Mam, not you.'

'Jesus, Mrs Kelly did say that you had something to tell me, some news. So, what's your lunch and walk about, Mary?'

Mam was quick off the mark. 'I'll go now, Marlo – if I don't put on the spuds now, I'll never make it to bingo in time. I can't hear too well if the seats in front are gone.'

Marlo shook his head and smiled. Mam, forever the diplomat. But Mary still hadn't said anything.

'The coins are being eaten up here, Mary.'

'Raymond asked me out again.'

'For a lunch and a walk? Are you telling me he fancies you?'

'There's nothing wrong with me.'

'For feck's sake, Mary, that's not what I meant. It was just a question – are you telling me he fancies you?'

'I think he does.'

'So, what happens next?'

'I don't know, Marlo. I'm going to be forty-five next month.'

'I know that, Mary. That shouldn't stop you now – if you feel the same, why should that stop you?

'He'll be forty-five too, a few weeks later.'

'He's obviously no speedy Gonzalez – he took his time

178

asking you out. I mean, you lived just down the road, what was he doing all these years?'

'Actually . . .' she said but her voice faded away mid-sentence.

Marlo waited, sensing her hesitation before asking, 'Actually what, Mary? We never spoke to him except when we were at funerals and even then it might have been to ask where the afters were.'

'He took you tobogganing. Twice.'

'Me and nine others from the Youth Club.'

'He's nice, Marlo, quiet till you get to know him, but nice.'

'If you say so, Mary. I'm not going to judge.'

She grunted. 'There's no need to get smart.'

'Just saying.'

'So, is she making lunch for you? Sunday dinner like?'

'Don't read too much into that, Mary. It's Sunday dinner because it's the only free day. I'm driving and she works the rest of the week. Plus, she teaches Sully, you know home schools him in the evenings.'

'I'm going to Ray's later. For Sunday dinner.'

'Scandalous altogether.'

'Shut up, you pup. He asked Mam as well, but she wouldn't give up the early bingo.'

He laughed. 'OK, I've to go now. Tell me more about your affair on Wednesday. I'll ring you in the evening after the football.'

'It's not an affair and would you just stop. You're making it sound seedy.'

Marlo was contrite. 'Sorry now, Mary, I was only messing.'

As he drove out through the village, he ran through the conversation in his head. Mary had called him Ray, which was a whole lot different from 'Raymond, the undertaker'. Curiously he found himself glad for Mary as he pictured her heading off for lunch. She was pretty and had always taken care of her looks, dressing well, never leaving the house in anything less than the clothes she might want to be laid out in. But that tongue of hers. Jesus, she could give anyone a lashing that even the Holy Cross nuns could never match. As he pulled up at Kitty's, Marlo realised that Philomema Crowley had done him a huge favour. 'The Lord bless and protect every nosy bone in your body, you saved me from having to tell them myself,' he said aloud as he shut the door of his car.

'Were you talking to yourself, Marlo?' Kitty asked, as she let him in. 'I thought you were.'

'Just this reflexive tic I get every time I have a skirmish with Mary. She's a wagon.'

'Ah, go easy on her.'

'I will if she went easy on me. But listen, we were OK today, in the end.'

'How are they both?'

'Well, Raymond is now Ray.'

She raised her eyebrows.

'You know, Raymond the undertaker. Mary's seeing him, I think, like going out with him.'

'Well, good for her.'

'Yes, I'm happy.'

Sully was in the sitting room writing in his copy.

'He didn't do a jot of work yesterday, Marlo, so he's writing his alphabet for me. Or we aren't going to Coomerkane, right, Marlo?'

'I'm not going to be part of your carrot and stick agenda, Kitty.'

Marlo stood beside Sully and looked over the copy book. The handwriting was neat and steady. 'Sure, it's nothing for you, champ, is it? What's an a, b or c when you can draw a whole horse?'

'Marlo, he has to learn.'

'Oh, I'm not disputing that. Just giving him some moral support. Mothers can be right wagons.'

Kitty laughed. 'Don't be putting ideas into his head. He needs no encouragement, it seems nowadays.'

'The regulars on the bus wouldn't say that. He's as good as gold.'

She glanced at her watch and headed for the kitchen. 'I better check on the lasagne in the oven. I followed a new Darina Allen recipe in this week's *Southern Star*. It's just that, chips and a mixed salad, Marlo.'

'You should have told me – I'd have gone to Assumpta's. She'd have the full works going. A plump, stuffed chicken with mash *and* roast. It's the way Mossie liked it – all of it drowned in gravy.'

Kitty walked back into the room where Marlo had eased himself into sofa beside the giant O'Sullivan Bear on the armchair.

'I'm messing.' He grinned. 'I love lasagne.'

'How is she, Marlo? I was thinking of calling into her, but it's always been a bit awkward. I know what Assumpta thinks of me, and the problem is she knows that I know.'

'I'd say she'd be glad for a visit. She asks about you.'

'She does? About what, like?'

'Oh, this and that. About Sully too.'

'Oh, OK. I never thought she would.'

'I should help you, shouldn't I? Will I put out the plates, Kitty?'

She nodded and pointed to the press by the window. 'The glasses are in the same place. And bowls for dessert too. I made jelly and custard on account of you know who,' she said, looking at Sully. He held up his open copy to his mother.

'Bring it here to me, pet, and let me see if it is neat.'

She looked over his work, patted his head and pulled out a numbers copy from the shelf beside the blackboard. 'Right so, just a page of numbers for me, Sully, and then you are done for today.'

His shoulders dropped dramatically and he carried the copy to the desk, as if it weighed a ton. Marlo couldn't help laughing. Kitty put her finger to her lips as she slipped back into the kitchen.

Sully traced his pencil over the dotted shapes, his head turned to one side, his cheek resting flat out on the desk, boredom writ across his face.

Marlo was immediately transported to the kitchen in Croydon – with him back from school, doing his homework on the kitchen table. Mary would give him extra lines if she found him sitting in any fashion other than upright.

'*You're just a bully, Mary. No, you're a big fat bully.*' It was his refrain and depending on her mood she would either laugh, ignore him entirely or stand with her hands on her hips and give him a look that meant business. It usually ended badly for him.

Marlo headed into the kitchen to lay the table. 'Homework is what came between me and Mary. That's how it began, it's how I remember it anyway. She used to collect me from school and we'd bicker over everything – washing my hands, eating with my mouth closed, finishing my dinner, sitting with my back straight and the damn homework – we fought till Mam came home. Then she'd let Mam cope with my unchanging complaint: "Why do I have to listen to Mary?"'

Kitty laughed. 'But look how you turned out, Marlo.'

He put the glasses down and poured out the water. 'Do you know what used to really drive me mad? The answer to everything was just one word – "because" – nothing before or after that. That was supposed to satisfy me!'

Kitty fiddled with the oven controls. 'Oh, I had my red rag words too. That shite mantra about not making a show.' She slapped the counter with her oven mitts. 'And then, guess what – didn't I show them all, didn't I make a right holy show of myself?'

They looked at each other, shocked at how those memories had resurfaced without warning and then both of them laughed nervously.

'Jesus, talk about buried traumas!'

'What're we like – angsty teenagers in a flash,' she said.

Marlo shrugged. 'Anyway, it's only us. We can be whatever we want.'

She had the lasagne in her hands. 'Marlo, get that chopping board down on the table, will you please, quickly!'

And when she had placed the hot dish down, she slipped off the mitts and turned to him. 'Yes, we can – you know, be whatever we want to be. I was never one for pretence.'

After lunch, Kitty was business-like. 'It's a long enough walk, Marlo, and if you want to have some time exploring near those caves we need to get going straightaway. I'll get him to the toilet and then we'll be ready to head off.'

Marlo dried the dishes while he waited, struck by how much he enjoyed the simple domesticity of his afternoon with her, with them both.

'D'you want me to drive us halfway?' Marlo asked. 'The evenings are definitely drawing in.'

She looked at her watch, 'Ah no, the joy will be gone from it. We've plenty of time, Marlo, unless our man here decides to climb every rock and tree on the way. He loves going to Coomerkane, don't you, Sully?'

Once they had walked past the cluster of houses in the tiny townland of Shrone, on the outskirts of Glengarriff, the poorly surfaced and very narrow rural back road wound its way uphill, cutting through dense forest on either side. Marlo was taken aback at how successfully rhododendrons had invaded the forest floor. They were everywhere as far as the eye could see, many dense thickets the size of a small house and burgeoning all around were smaller clumps of the toxic plant.

'Edward was right, you know; in a short few decades it will have choked this ancient forest to death.'

'The tourists just love it. The spring season in Beara is all about the rhodos, though we can't compete with Kerry. It's wall-to-wall pink there.'

'Kitty, I've spent months now trying to undo the damage in Bocarnagh, and even then there is no guarantee that Edward and Tiggy are actually rid of most of it. The neighbouring lands are infested so they'll have to keep on top of it – for ever really. It's such a prolific spreader. Dolores was telling me that the only way to get rid of it is to poison it. Put a herbicide into deep cuts in the trunks.'

'Some farmers are beginning to cop on, but they need to be obsessive about it – like they are with ragwort.'

Kitty suddenly stood stock-still, pointing to something in the forest. She grabbed Sully, knelt down beside him and directed his gaze, whispering. 'Look, Sully, look, it's that old goat. Remember, we saw him last year?'

Marlo squinted into the undergrowth, a tangled mess of living and fallen trees – oaks, elder, ash, birch, holly and hazel rose from sodden ground, their branches tattooed with lichen and draped in moss and brilliant green ferns that colonised every moist crevice. The forest fell away very sharply to the right of the small road, and they could hear the sounds of a river tumbling over rocks below. The late afternoon sun penetrated only in thin shafts here and there and much of the forest around them was shrouded in a shady green light which made it difficult to spot anything more than fifty yards away. Marlo squatted beside Sully, to see what Kitty was so excited about. They could clearly hear distinct crunchy sounds as twigs snapped and fallen leaves rustled and then all of a sudden out of a thicket emerged a huge, hoary old goat, his coat dirty brown and shaggy around his belly, with enormous horns that curled twice over. They held their breath as the ram picked away at shoots on the forest floor. He was as big as a small calf and his huge heavy horns, like a helmet around his head, must have caused him great difficulty but despite his size he was agile, his cloven hooves enabling him to clamber onto fallen trunks and over giant boulders with total ease. They tracked him as he grazed, in and out of the undergrowth, sometimes barely discernible only his horns giving him away. Suddenly, he stood as stock-still as them before turning to look into the deeper forest. He bolted then without warning, crashing through the fallen branches and was gone before they knew it.

'I wonder what scared him,' said Marlo, standing up.

'He might have just sensed us,' said Kitty. 'Wasn't that just fantastic, Sully, to see him again? He's a magnificent animal. Have you ever seen the herd, Marlo? They are completely feral.'

He shook his head. 'No, but I've heard Dolores mention them.'

'They descend from some long-escaped domestic ones that must have made a bolt for freedom. They're very shy, but if you're lucky you can spot them around Dereenboy and on the rocky escarpments in the commonage around Coomerkane and up your way too, Marlo, at Barley Lake.'

They continued walking for half a mile or so, when Sully un-hitched his backpack and dug out his drink, sucking at it noisily.

Kitty muttered under her breath. 'Just ignore that noise he's making, Marlo, because I am not going to pay him the slightest attention. I think he does it just to test me.'

Marlo turned his face away from Sully, laughing quietly. 'There is something universal about little boys knowing how to press the right wrong buttons, if you know what I mean.'

But Kitty's attention was on a little boreen that went uphill to their left. The narrow stony path, deeply furrowed by rainwater running downhill, was constricted even further by brambles spilling from out of overgrown ditches that ran on either side. A rusty farm gate and a wooden stile could be seen a couple of hundred yards away. Her eyes widened. 'Would you look at those blackberries! We should come up in a week or so with baskets – in your car, if you can, Marlo? Tiggy will be happy for some too. It must be the heat we've had this year – it makes for plump extra sweet berries.'

'I need no persuading.'

'You know, Marlo, it's interesting to be here after our trip to

Dursey. O'Sullivan Beare made his final stand, lost his creaght to the English here.'

'You mean right here?'

'I think the actual spot is further up, past that gate. The pasture up there is very sheltered and well hidden. Two thousand cows and a thousand sheep were massacred on one day, so many that the place is said to have flowed with blood for days. We are in Derrynafulla – the oak field of blood.'

'It's very hard to even conjure up something as gory, just look at how peaceful it is here.'

A few minutes later they crossed an old stone bridge and Marlo stopped, leaning over the wall to look down at the river rushing below. 'Just listen to that birdsong. You'd forget any worries at all that you had.'

'Do you worry, Marlo?'

Marlo was taken aback at her question. 'To be honest, I guess I do sometimes. Yeah, I do, I worry.'

'About what?'

'Oh, ducking those curved balls, other normal stuff. Don't you?'

'Sully's my only worry at the moment.'

They looked at the little boy who had clambered over a huge boulder and was lying flat on top of it peering into the fissures.

'I can't home school him for ever, you know, Marlo. I'm going to have to teach him to sign which means I'm going to have to learn it myself. I've been talking to the community nurse but it's very hard to get any proper help – you know, a structured plan that we both can work to.'

'What can I do, Kitty, I mean there must be something I can help with?'

She held his forearm for a second and nodded a very quiet thank you. 'If John Paul were alive there would be more empathy. It's like I'm being punished for having defied everyone, for having carried him for nine months and then for having kept him. I've slowly come to grips with the fact that it's not just about me and him. It's what lies ahead – you know, it's him and the rest of the world. And I have to ready him for it.'

Marlo put his hand on her shoulder and turned her around. 'You just have to tell me what's needed.'

'Yes, I know that, Marlo. Tiggy and Edward have offered to help as well. But nothing's straightforward. I can't afford to give up my job with them just as yet, which means he will have to stay on the bus for a little while longer while I figure it out.'

'We'll figure it out,' said Marlo firmly.

Sully was standing on the boulder now, looking in the direction of a gnarled old holly dominating an enormous craggy outcrop of limestone that floated like an island in the patch of wet heath. He had drawn himself tall, one hand on his hip and the other shading his eyes. He seemed rapt in attention, motionless.

'That's an explorer in the making if there ever was one.'

Kitty shook her head. 'Gives me the palpitations sometimes.'

'But he's like a mountain goat – I've seen how he manages to find the tiniest of footholds. I'll put money on him summitting Everest.'

Kitty laughed. 'As long as I don't have to watch! Come on now, Sully, you need to come down carefully. Here, give me your hand, pet. Come on, we're heading to Eagle's Nest, remember?'

Sully climbed down immediately and led the way, striding ahead on the fractured tarmac. The lonely country road, which wound its way through the narrow gap in the hills, was in a state of utter disrepair. It seemed to be held together by the power of clover and chamomile that had rooted in every fissure and crack while a haze of purple and pink heather hid the crumbling edges of the asphalt. All around them, boulders the size of houses laid strewn across the several hundred acres of the valley floor.

'They must have tumbled down from those mountains at some stage as the glaciers melted and moved,' said Marlo.

'Imagine if these stones could talk – they have stood here for tens of millions of years, silent witnesses to everything that's happened since.'

'That massacre of the creaght, I might focus on that for my next piece for the *Montana Courier*. You know, write about what happened here in Derrynafulla and Coomerkane.'

'The library in Bantry will have a lot of information, Marlo, my father badgered them constantly.'

As the road crested the small hill, they could see a reed-filled lake ahead. Bulrushes and yellow flagstaff ringed one side and a dozen or more ducks were preening themselves along the banks that were choked with water mint and horsetail.

Marlo took a deep breath. 'Beara's best kept secret, isn't it? I love this place and I've only been here once before.'

'Did Uncle Mossie bring you here?'

'No, it was actually Dolores.'

'Ah, Dolores, I like her – she's some woman, isn't she?'

'I've often wondered about her. Did she have a family, like I mean, does she have children?'

'Don't tell me Assumpta hasn't yet told you her story.'

'No, she hasn't actually. You have me curious now, Kitty.'

'Lord forgive me, Marlo, I'm gossiping, but it's no secret – she was the youngest in her family and the only girl. Apparently, the father looked at the size of her and knew there would never be a man in the valley taller or stronger, who'd see fit to marry her. So she was deemed perfect for the convent and that's where she was packed off to when she was about fifteen, to become a novice.'

'And did she want to? Become a nun, I mean.'

'This was the early forties, Marlo. Her father's words were law. She went anyway and came back less than a year later. She nearly killed a priest and was proud of it.'

'Jesus, she didn't!'

'They put her to work in the piggery in the abbey, given how strong she was. Then a priest made a grab for her one evening, came up behind her, and she wasn't having any of it. She just took him by the scruff of his neck and held his head down in the pig's trough. He nearly died, so my mother said anyway. She was sent packing right back, you know.'

'Yeah, that's Dolores all right. I can just see her doing it, and good on her. What happened after?'

'Well, tragedy followed and her behaviour was blamed for all the bad luck. The rest of the family were all buried one after the other within a few years. Her father and two of her brothers died from TB. One brother drowned working the mussel beds in the bay and the last one was so afraid of his fate my father said he fulfilled his own prophecy and drank himself dead. And our Dolores, who made her own luck, was left with her mother and the entire farm when she was just twenty-one. She looked after her mother well till the end and the farm even better.'

'What a woman! I like her even more now. I can see her with the Burdizzo in her hand, emasculating men with just her look.'

'It's funny you say that, Marlo. Even the sanest of men in the glen are afraid of her "evil eye" and none of her generation would dare to cross her. But not Uncle Mossie – he helped her out on the farm right from the start in the early days. She repaid all that kindness when Thomas died. They were the dearest of friends.'

'Well, I can tell you, Assumpta would be lost without her.'

'That's Dolores. That's why I like her – she's just so sound.'

As they walked towards the lake, Marlo pointed to a thatched farmhouse ahead, painted in a startling red. 'That's where we went the day I came with Dolores. She rents grazing off the family that lives on that farm. I think she has a couple of dozen cows in there at the moment.'

'Ah, the O'Sullivans.'

Marlo started laughing 'Everyone's an O'Sullivan here!'

'They're the Sullivan Bawns, your kin actually. I think your mother was a Sullivan Bawn, on her father's side.'

'Jesus, how would you even know that?'

'Batty Mor told me that when I was waiting behind him at the post office.'

'Did he add anything else?'

She laughed. 'Marlo, you should know by now. People need to know these things. It places you correctly in the big jigsaw of Beara life.'

'I don't know if I'll ever get used to it.'

The road diverged on either side of the lake, splitting into two smaller tracks that looked like they might have once been tarred.

'We need to continue on the right, Marlo. The caves are in those cliffs behind the O'Sullivan Bawns' farm.'

'Have you brought Sully to the caves before, Kitty? He seems to know where we are heading.'

'Oh, he's been a good few times. It's his second favourite place after the Big Meadow. But it isn't easy getting close to the caves themselves. Last summer we had a good long dry spell, not unlike what we've had this year, and the ground at the base of the cliffs was approachable instead of being a pure bog, so we came a few times. That farm there, beside the O'Sullivan Bawns, had a sow that had littered, so that was an added attraction. Fourteen bonhams and we got to carry each little piggy, didn't we, Sully?'

Marlo scanned the whiteish cliff face, which was sheer vertical in the main, with a few slim ridges on the diagonal. Vegetation clung onto any smudge of soil, shaped and twisted by the prevailing winds.

Kitty opened the gate and Sully climbed onto the rungs as it swung open. 'It's hard to make out even one cave from here but there are definitely a few along the base of the cliff – some are merely small slits in the rock face and some deep enough for one or two people to stand in out of the rain, that's all. But just a little higher up, you can just about make out the openings in the limestone, and those are a little larger. I know John Paul had climbed up to one of them with John Bosco when they were schoolboys – they just followed the lines of those ridges.'

'I thought they were inaccessible.'

'The ones higher up, yes. They'd be near impossible to get to, all right. You'd nearly be wanting to rappel down from the top. Of course, at that height, it's impossible to know how many caves there even are.'

They were now on a barely discernible path in a grove of hazel and willow, walking straight towards the cliffs.

'Are we going onto private property?'

'Yes, but I know them and sure, you're kin, Marlo.' She poked him in the ribs and laughed.

The peaty ground was springy underfoot and he could imagine how a few days of steady rain could quickly transform the approach to the cliff into sludgy peat soup. As he walked ahead, Kitty called out to him, asking him to look up to where she was pointing.

'Can you see that, Marlo? I know it's hard to make out at first but look – see that white stone beside the twisted dead tree? Just look directly above that and you can see there's a slit, a long vertical opening in the rock.'

'Oh, I see it. I might clamber up to it – go on to that low ledge with the gorse and then head sideways up the ridge – what d'you think?'

'Normally we wouldn't be able to even walk up to where we are now, so I'd say today's the day if you wanted to make a go of it.'

It took him a few minutes to reach the ridge about twenty feet above and he shuffled sideways towards the opening. Sully was watching him open-mouthed and Kitty, sensing the child's eagerness to join Marlo, grabbed hold of his hand.

'It's way too high, pet – when you're little older, maybe next summer.'

Marlo called down to them. 'It's barely wide enough to

squeeze past and I'll have to pull away at this curtain of ivy growing across it first.'

To his surprise the creeper came away from the rock with just a few sharp tugs, and it hung to one side like an open door.

'Are you going in, Marlo?'

He looked down at them. 'I will, if I can squeeze in.'

His cheek was jammed against the cold rock as he manoeuvred himself in, twisting his body from side to side. All of a sudden, he was free of any constriction and he held his hands out feeling his way around him, peering into the darkness. 'I wish I had a torch, Kitty,' he shouted over his shoulder.

An eerie echo filled the space, and he felt a cold rush of air wrap around him. He stood still for a moment and then slowly backed out towards the gash in the cliff wall, the icy limestone against his cheek once again as he squeezed out.

He squinted, his eyes adjusting to daylight again before he looked down. Sully was stamping his feet and Kitty was bent over him.

Marlo laughed and called down, 'I'll bring you up here next time, Sully. It's absolutely no use today without a torch. You won't be able to see even your nose in there, champ.'

A few minutes later, Kitty was brushing away bits of dirt from his jacket. 'There's stuff all over your head too, Marlo. Was it hard getting in?'

He bent over, shaking his head and running his hands through his hair a few times. 'Let's put it this way – if I'd had Assumpta's Sunday lunch I wouldn't have made it. We should come back, Kitty, with torches though and see what it's like. There must be other openings because I felt an icy draught blow around my face.'

'It could be bats, Marlo,' she said as Sully tugged at her hand.

Marlo tousled his hair. 'I don't think so – bat caves have a particular smell. Cheer up, Sully, we'll come back to Coomerkane, only next time we'll do it properly equipped.

It'll be soon, champ, I promise.'

Sully was looking back at the cliff where the unhinged ivy swung in the breeze, flapping like a door against the cleft in the cliff. He lifted his hand and waved slowly in the direction of the cave, before walking back to hold his mother's hand.

CHAPTER THIRTEEN

Marlo was putting his football gear into the boot of his car when John Bosco called out to him from across the car park at the pitch.

'See you at Casey's, Marlo. For a few jars as per usual.'

'I need to make a phone call before I come into the pub, JB. It might get too late for Mrs Kelly if I leave it till after. She's my mam's neighbour.'

'Work away, boy, me and the lads will keep your seat warm for you.'

Marlo was well ready for a pint. They had played most of the game in a fine drizzle and he was quite cold despite having dried and changed. His stamina had improved over the months and he was no longer the butt of all the friendly digs in the post-game banter in the pub. He honked at the others as he left the pitch and smiled as a litany of short sharp honks came back in reply. See you, lads, he thought, looking in his rear-view mirror.

Two young teenagers were hanging out of the phone booth, with two more inside when Marlo arrived. He parked up beside them and stood outside the car, leaning against the door, hoping that they would get the message. After a few minutes of whooping and shouting the boys left, backslapping each other, delighted with whatever mischief they had been up to.

Mrs Kelly was slow to fetch Mary when Marlo rang. 'Your mam's been at her rosary beads since yesterday. Mary's taking a whole two weeks off work. That girl never took more than a day or two off. Now your mam tells me she's taking two weeks off and won't tell her why.'

For a moment Marlo forgot who he was talking to. 'Really? Mary's taking two weeks off?'

'Maybe she'll tell you why. Let me go call her.'

Mary got to the point immediately. 'Jesus, Marlo, what stories has she been telling you? She said you were surprised I'd arranged a few days off. Mrs Kelly's an awful gossip.'

'Nothing's changed. Mrs Kelly will always be Mrs Kelly.'

'I would've told you.'

Marlo contained himself. 'You don't have to tell me anything, Mary – it's your business.'

'I did it on a whim, Marlo. But I don't think it's worth it. I've had to put in double the amount of work trying to organise things at the surgery for when I'm away.'

'Nobody's indispensable, Mary, they'll figure it out without you.'

'They might, but I'll have to pick up the pieces when I come back, and it wouldn't have been worth taking time off in the first place. You know the patients are used to me plus I know the ones that are genuine, there's an awful lot of time-wasters that turn up.'

'Well, don't go away then.'

'But I've told Ray and now he's taking holidays too.'

'And what happens to the dead?'

'Don't be an eejit, Marlo. He's hardly going to close down the funeral parlour. Sure, he has a young lad that he's been training for a few years. You might remember him, the Murphy lad, with the head like a turnip, who hung around outside the bookies. His father came to Ray a few years ago, after the mother was buried, and asked if Ray would take him on. Turns out he's a proper flair for makeup, the young fella. Brings the deceased back to life, says Ray.'

'Where're you heading, Mary?'

'What do you mean?'

'You're taking holidays and going where, Mary?'

'Oh, I haven't thought that far, we haven't made any plans. We might go to Kew for the day. And if it rains, we can wander around in the glasshouses.

'You are forty-five years old, Mary – you haven't the time left to waste in glasshouses in Kew.'

'Oh Jesus, Marlo, I don't even know why I took the holidays. It's not like as if I can go away with him, can I?'

'Who's to say not?'

'Well, I haven't told Mam and Mrs Kelly will be shocked.'

'Feck Mrs Kelly.'

'Ray said we could call into Thomas Cook. Imagine me in Lanzarote.' She giggled. 'Me in Lanzarote on a beach.'

'You'll need some of those fancy sunglasses, to remain in-cognito.'

'I've fancied the thought, you know, Marlo. So many patients send us postcards in the practice with "Wish you were here" or "Sun, sea and sand" and I've always fancied it myself. With a straw hat and a matching straw bag. With a scarf tied around the handles.'

'What use would that be?'

'Princess Di does that. Ties scarves around her beach bag.'

Marlo was suddenly overcome. 'You never did have a proper go at life, Mary. And it was because of me.'

'Sure, you were my life, Marlo. You are still our life – mine and Mam's.'

'And he escaped scot-free of all responsibility?'

'Who?'

'The man who was my father, that's who. Why did you let him away with it, Mary? Did he ever give you a penny towards me?'

Marlo could hear her catch her breath before she blurted, 'He never knew.'

It took Marlo a few minutes to get his head around Mary's confession. 'You mean, you never told him? So you never gave him a chance, you never gave me a bloody chance. Jesus, that's an awful thing to do. I wish I'd never asked.'

'I wish I hadn't told you that.'

'I can't unhear it, can I?'

She was crying now, and Marlo's anger turned to exasperation.

'Just stop, Mary, you can't cry your way out of this one, for God's sake.'

'I know.'

'So are you going to tell me.'

'I will.'

He held his breath.

'I need some time to get my head around things.'

'You've had a long time, Mary.'

'I know.'

'Don't leave it too long more. You more than owe me.'

John Bosco signalled, whistling at Marlo as he walked into Casey's. JB was at the bar, waiting for his pint to be pulled. 'The rest of the lads are in the corner there. It's my round, what'll you have?'

'Jesus, man, I need a drink.'

'Bad news?'

'I don't know.'

'Christ, that's some cryptic shite from you this evening.'

Marlo held his glass, looked at the creamy head for a moment before taking a long drink from it. 'The bloody curved balls are coming faster than I can duck or dive,' he said, as he put the glass down on the table and wiped his lips.

John Bosco thumped him on his back. 'Mothers and sisters – we all have to suffer them in doses.'

'Yours giving you grief too?'

'They're a bit angsty what with me leaving next month. Mam's fussing so much and cries at the drop of a hat. I had to hide my passport when it arrived in the post yesterday. She'd have organised a wake for me over that alone! Drama – my life is full of it. So, how's it going with herself and yourself?'

'Kitty, you mean?'

'Sure, there isn't someone else, is there now, or I'll be cracking open that jaw of yours.'

Marlo grinned. 'No fear, JB.'

'You've nothing to add? Is that it?'

'I don't want to rush it, you know.'

'It's called dithering.'

'She talks of him a lot, you know. I mean, your brother. Her John Paul. I don't think she'll ever let him go.'

'Jesus, you are an eejit, don't you know. You can't be fighting ghosts, Marlo. Trust me on this, boi.'

'I couldn't share her.'

'She won't expect you to.'

'D'you know what I mean, though?'

'Feck it, Marlo, life's too short to be beating around the bush. Tell her how you feel. She'll say yes or she'll say no. And either way no one's going to die.'

Marlo looked at him and laughed. 'And tell me how you ended up a butcher?'

'Good lad. Sort it before I leave the country, will you? Now let's get these pints back to that lot.'

The next morning Marlo led Stevie into the field and shook a handful of calf nuts into the bucket. 'Eat up, lad, and look, here comes your mate.'

Crow had flown up from his roost on the beech trees below by the river and was waiting on the windowsill. Marlo scratched the bullock behind his ears and the animal, his mouth full, took a step forward, searching and then leaning in to rub his cheeks against Marlo's jacket.

Marlo looked into the unseeing eyes. 'You poor sod.'

Crow wasted no time, knocking on the pane, then turning to Marlo, cocking his head and hopping from one foot to the other. Marlo headed into the house; his morning routine had begun.

An hour and a half later, he was in Allihies, and as he drove down the hill, towards the deserted and sweeping white expanse of Ballydonegan beach, the sun danced off the waves that rolled in. It was a cool morning and as Bernard Causkey clambered onto the bus, his every huff and puff was visible.

'I feel better since I've started walking to the village to get on the bus – that episode last month was a wake-up call. I didn't tell you, lad, but I was fair breathless a week ago and herself had to get the doctor out. He put me on a diet and herself's been policing my every move.'

'You were lucky, Bernard.'

'Sure, I know that I could have easily gone like Mossie. But listen up, boy, wait till you see what I have to show you.' He pulled out a newspaper from his jacket pocket and unrolled it. 'It's the actual paper you write for – the *Montana Courier* itself – and look here at your piece about Dursey. A cousin of mine in Butte sent it in the post.'

Bernard sat down right behind Marlo and carried on. 'He's a travel agent and he says he's already booked two tours to Beara for next summer. Apparently, you've made us famous all over again, boy. He's planning a recce in March, he told me, to check out an itinerary he's putting together. He's never been to Dursey, so he wants me to show him around.' Bernard tapped the page. 'He says they love all that history that you have in your column.'

Marlo was tempted to stop the bus and have a look at the paper, but instead Mags read his words out aloud, pausing only to give her own commentary every few paragraphs.

'You're a fierce good writer, d'you know that, Marlo. This is powerful stuff about the massacre. Sure, the Americans love that kind of thing.'

When Sully got on the bus, she folded the paper into a neat rectangle and showed it to him, running her finger under Marlo's name. 'See that, Sully. That's our Marlo himself – he's famous in Montana.'

The paper was passed from person to person as the regulars boarded. Arriving in Bantry, Marlo double parked outside Biggs, hoping Nuala and Nancy were not going to be too late. Marlo was sorely tempted to honk when he saw them stroll around the corner. They bickered about who was responsible for the tardiness even as they boarded the bus.

Mags thrust the newspaper into Nuala's hands. 'Would you ever stop for a moment and read this – it's by our Marlo.'

All the way to Drimoleague the column was read aloud once again, Nuala modulating her voice every few sentences but not forgetting to give Nancy scathing looks between paragraphs. As she read it out slowly, sometimes going over sentences two or three times, clicking her tongue sharply in places, Marlo wondered what she was disagreeing with.

When she reached the end, she turned the page over, looking to see if the column continued.

'I see you haven't mentioned the cable car timings.'

Mags snorted. 'It's a commentary on life, Nuala, not a travel guide.'

Nuala looked straight ahead. 'A commentary? On life? Sure, what life is there on that Godforsaken island?'

Mags wasn't backing down. 'His column is for the historic minded.'

Bernard intervened. 'What Mags is trying to say—'

Nuala cut him short. 'Mags is always trying to say something.'

'Commenting on the commentary,' said Nancy, her lips pursed, and her hands folded neatly across her lap.

Nuala bestowed a smile on her sister and then called out to Marlo. 'I'll give you some history to think about. Could you blame Owen O'Sullivan for betraying the route, for guiding Carew's men through the treacherous waters of Dursey? The man was looking to free his wife – kidnapped and held on Dursey by none other than O'Sullivan Beare. Owen was only doing what a good husband would do.'

Marlo looked back at her. 'I didn't know that, Nuala.'

She sniffed. 'I didn't expect you to.'

'And did he get her back?'

'By God he did. We think we are descended from that line of the O'Sullivans.'

Mags was determined to prove her point. 'But to kill innocent women and children. They were thrown over the cliffs to their deaths, Nuala.'

Nancy spoke. 'O'Sullivan Beare did the same thing in Carriganass. Only they were burned alive.'

'The English,' said Bernard. 'They divided and ruled and here we are – still haunted by it all.'

'I'm not haunted, thank you, Bernard.' She pointed to Sully sitting in front. 'But you know who will be with this gory talk.'

No one spoke for a while with the silence punctuated only by Daragh Keohane's loud snoring. Finally, Bernard leaned across the aisle and took the paper out of Nuala's hands. He pushed it back into his pocket firmly and tapped Marlo on his shoulder. 'You can have it for yourself when we get to Cork.'

Later on in the day, when he was dropping Sully off back in Glengarriff, Kitty asked him in for coffee. At the kitchen table he pulled out the *Montana Courier* and showed it to her, telling her what Bernard had said. 'I didn't think I'd get such a kick out of seeing it in print.'

'This is great, Marlo,' she said, reading it. 'You've never shown me what you've been writing all these months.'

'I don't care for that photo beside my name, though. I look grumpy.'

She laughed. 'I agree. Why don't you send them another one?'

'I just might do that.'

Kitty got busy plating up Sully's dinner and coaxing him away from the desk where he had taken out his colouring pencils and sketchpad. Marlo watched her, his cup of coffee in hand, and wondered what it would be like to push the curls away from her face and kiss her. He thought about what John Bosco had said and, though he realised that the psychologist in butcher's clothing was right, he couldn't quite figure out how to go about telling Kitty how he felt about her. *Jesus, the state of me.*

When Sully finally came to the table and picked up his knife and fork, Kitty sat down beside Marlo. 'I met Assumpta at the butchers – JB was serving her when I walked in – and you'll never believe, but she's asked me to call in on Sunday. For dinner. What do you make of that?'

'That's nice. But why speculate, Kitty?'

'I was never in Uncle Mossie's house more than a few times and hardly ever since Sully was born.'

'Maybe she's trying to make up for it.'

'I'll hold judgement till after.'

'But you'll go, won't you?'

'Oh, I'll go all right, I told her I would. I'll do it for my uncle's sake, you know.'

Twenty minutes later, as he backed the bus up at the yard at Mossie's, Assumpta came to the kitchen door. 'Will you come in for a bite to eat?' she said. 'I'm doing pork chops. John Bosco pushed them under my nose, blathering away about how you loved the way I serve them. It's not just the pinch of the nutmeg in the apple sauce, I said to him, it's the soaking in milk. That got everyone waiting at the counter talking and they were still at it after I'd paid and left.'

Marlo laughed. 'That fella's always looking out for me, and I'll only be too happy to come for a bite to eat, Assumpta. Will I have time to go up and feed Stevie?'

She nodded and headed back into her kitchen, shooing Blackie and Spot out from under her feet.

The dogs followed him up to the cottage, their tails held high, their gait jaunty as he whistled to them. Stevie had got used to the dogs, who seemed to sense he was a bit different. Now the mother and son waited by the fence at the little field as Marlo called out to the bullock. 'It's only me, lad, your dinner's up in a minute.' Stevie bellowed in delight and when Marlo had the feed and water ready, he led the bullock into the cowshed. The forecast was for heavy rain overnight and Marlo wanted to bed the animal in. The dogs explored the shed, sniffing every corner like as if they'd never been in it before, their noses rifling deep through the layers of straw in the corner, convinced that there was something lurking underneath.

Marlo walked out into the yard and looked up and down the valley below, peering into the dusk, his ears listening for that slow and steady flapping as Crow approached, but there was no sign of the bird. He left the half door to the cowshed ajar just in case and headed inside. He freshened up, changed his boots for a pair of trainers and pulled on the jumper that Kitty had bought for him and headed down to Assumpta's. He had his hands in his pockets, and as he walked down the steep slope he whistled for the dogs, thinking of the dinner that awaited him.

Assumpta noted his new apparel. 'I see you've a new jumper on ye. Are you dedicating your life to that crow?'

Marlo laughed. 'Sometimes I think I already have. Kitty got me this, in the market, in Bantry.'

'Oh, did she – what for?'

'A thank you, for minding Sully. You know, on the bus.'

'She'd need to be giving you more than a jumper for that.'

'I'll tell her you said so.'

'You'll do none of that. Stirring up shite will only get you covered in it yourself.'

Marlo sat down at the table, laughing as he pushed the log-book and cash towards her. 'We had seven passengers other than the regulars today, Assumpta. One no-show in Cork and I waited long enough. The wipers need replacing but I'll sort that on Saturday.'

She nodded as she put his plate down in front of him. The pork chops glistened on a bed of mash, their pan juices running in little rivulets into the carrots and peas. Helping herself to the apple sauce, she then pushed the jug towards him.

'I met Kitty this afternoon outside the butchers, she was with the Headley-Stokes woman.'

Marlo could see Assumpta was trying to be as casual as she could – so he waited.

'She told me she had been planning to call in here to me, along with the young lad. So, I said sure why not come and have dinner on Sunday. Will you join us, Marlo, after you're done your morning's work in Bocarnagh?'

Marlo, his mouth full, nodded.

'She's not one of those new-fangled vegetarians, is she?'

'Who, Kitty? She's not. Whatever made you think that?'

Assumpta shrugged. 'She looks like one, d'you know – with that attitude. Thanks be to God she hasn't pierced her nose yet.'

Marlo burst out laughing. 'So, vegetarians pierce their noses?'

'I've seen them inside Only Organic.'

'The food place in Bantry?'

'Yes, I go there to get lavender oil. You'd never seen the like of it. Body piercings everywhere you turn. I can hardly bear to look.'

'She's no body piercings.'

Assumpta gave him a long look.

Marlo carried on. 'She's no attitude either. She just has her back up sometimes – d'you know, with the way people treat her.'

'It was of her own making.'

He put his cutlery down on the plate. 'No, it took two of them. They were to be married, Assumpta – it could have happened to anyone.'

'I see you're carrying the torch for her.'

'I am.'

'Does she know?'

'Jesus, Assumpta, you're not the first person to ask me that this week.'

'Does the whole valley know your business then?'

'I'm just trying to figure out the best way to tell her.'

'She's no fool, but she'd surely be one if she refused you.'

'She's got a lot more to consider than just herself, Assumpta. She's nicer than you'd imagine. It's why Mossie liked her, you know.'

'Well, I asked her for dinner, didn't I?'

'I am surprised, but don't get me wrong – I'm delighted.'

'I'm doing it for Mossie's sake.'

He nodded as he scraped the last bit of mash off the plate. *You and Kitty – that makes two of you in it then.*

When he pulled into the yard on Sunday, Kitty's cycle was leaning against the kitchen door. He walked in to find her on her own, on her haunches stoking the fire.

He hung up his jacket behind the kitchen door. 'Have you been abandoned? Where's Assumpta?'

'She's taken Sully to see the tractor.'

'Oh, he'll love that.'

'She told me that Mossie had once told her he wanted to leave the tractor to Sully.'

'Leave the tractor to Sully? He's barely six!'

'That's what I said to her. I am so glad you're here as well – she didn't have much to say. It could be an awkward evening.'

'She's never short on words, Kitty. Nothing would make her feel awkward, I can tell you. Should we go and see what they are up to?'

As they walked down the yard, Blackie and Spot pushed their way out of the shed and bounded up to Marlo, barking furiously, circling his feet in a crazed fashion, delighted to see him.

Spot placed his forelegs on him, trying to lick his face. 'They miss Mossie, you know. He talked to them all the time. Nothing like a natter with the dogs, isn't that right, Spot? All that listening and no judgement passed.'

Kitty was on her knees, Blackie's face in the palms of her hand. 'I remember the day Uncle Mossie brought you home. You took a pee on my lap, you bold thing, didn't you?' She looked up at Marlo. 'I cycled down with John Paul and John Bosco to see the new pup. He had bought her off a farmer in Kealkil. She was gorgeous then as she is now. Getting old, aren't you, pet?'

'There's plenty of life in her still.'

'I was sixteen then, the summer I started going out with John Paul. That makes her about twelve.'

Marlo had spoken his mind before he knew it. 'What was it like losing him, losing the love of your life?'

She stood up and dusted the dog hair off her jeans.

'I'm sorry, Kitty, that came out of nowhere.'

'Came out of somewhere though, Marlo. I don't mind. Talking about him has helped me to cope.'

'I'm listening.'

She pushed her curls away from her face. 'And I know that, Marlo, thank you.' He was surprised when she continued quietly, wrapping her cardigan tight around herself. 'My world fell apart, you know. And there was overwhelming sympathy, whichever direction I turned. People couldn't do enough for me, for my parents, and of course for John Paul's family – they had lost a beloved son. But five weeks later came the mighty land – when I found out that I was pregnant. All that sympathy went rushing out, sucked away like a receding tide. And when I insisted I was going to keep our baby, our flesh and blood, the only thing I had left of John Paul, any leftover compassion just dried up overnight. There were some few bits of pity all right, thrown at me from a safe distance, like as if what I had was contagious. I had to abandon all grief just so I could steel myself to fight an altogether different battle. They came at me from all sides, so I hadn't a choice really.'

Marlo put his arms around her shoulder and drew her close. 'Jesus, what are people like?'

She shuddered slightly. 'These past few years, I just put my head down, kept out of everyone's way and carried on the best I could. I never allowed myself grief, I felt it would take the joy out of rearing our son.'

Marlo shook his head slowly. 'Christ, you're some woman for one woman. You know that, don't you? You've done a great job of it. He's a wonderful little boy.'

'Do you think?' She was smiling at him.

Marlo squeezed her shoulder and then took her hand. 'He's a star. Come on, Kitty, let's see what this unlikely pair are up to in the shed – they've been there a while now.'

They both couldn't help but laugh when they walked into the huge shed. Sully was sitting on the tractor seat, his eyes shining with excitement, his little legs kicking away. His arms were stretched out to the maximum as he held onto the steering wheel.

'Doesn't he look well on it,' said Assumpta, who was standing on the kickboard leaning against the door of the cab. 'A farmer in the making.'

Kitty looked up at her son and waved. 'Did you drive it all the way to Coomerkane and back, Sully?'

The little boy pretended to swing the steering around sharply and nearly fell off the seat with the effort. Assumpta steadied him and then looked at her watch. 'I'd better be going in or sure there won't be any dinner for anyone. Will you stay with the lad, Marlo, and Kitty can come give me a hand?'

Kitty nodded and was about to say something when Assumpta carried on. 'If you do the spuds, I'll sort the roast. It's a nice bit of beef he gave me, that John Bosco. I hear he's heading off to Australia soon – his mother will be fit for nothing, another son gone and only her girls left. It's daughters that matter in the end though. I made it my business to tell her that in the sacristy as we cleaned the church the other day.' She looked at Kitty and smiled. 'Does the lad prefer mash or roast or both?'

As they walked away towards the house, Marlo watched them, wondering what was behind Assumpta's sudden change of heart. Or was it even that? Maybe she was pandering to her own curiosity, but whatever it was, Marlo couldn't quite get his head around it.

He turned his attention back to the child. 'Will we tell the regulars on the bus that you drove a tractor, a real tractor?'

Then, getting Sully to make some room on the seat, he started the tractor and showed him how to turn the lights on and off, revving the engine to the child's delight. A little later with the boy in tow, he popped his head into the kitchen. Kitty was making a cup of tea while Assumpta lined a baking tin with foil.

'We were just talking about you,' said Assumpta.

'Right so. Time for me to go then. I'm going to take Sully up to see Stevie – back in about ten minutes if that's OK with you and we're taking the dogs with us.'

He was helping Sully over the cattle grid when he heard the familiar sound of gears crashing. A few minutes later Dolores drove up and stopped by the gate.

'Did his mother not come with him?'

'Oh, Kitty's in the kitchen with Assumpta.'

'Thanks be to God. For a moment I thought – ah, never mind. Are you taking him up to see your four-legged tenor? I heard him yesterday – him and Donal's donkey across in Rossnagreena were having a fecking sing-off!' She started laughing.

'I won't be too long, Dolores. I'm just going to show the lad the tenor as you call him, and hopefully Crow will be down too. He's going to do me a drawing of Crow, aren't you, Sully?'

'Will it be long before dinner you think? Are they at it together?'

Marlo had his hand on his hips. 'Are you staying for dinner, Dolores?'

'It's not the dinner I'm interested in, boy. I just came to see if anything came of the seed that I'd sown.'

'You mean Kitty's here for dinner because of you?'

Dolores shrugged. 'Sure, somebody had to make her see sense. Assumpta, I mean.'

Sully had begun to wander up the slope, the dogs on either side, shepherding him like they would a lost lamb.

Dolores twitched her chin towards Sully. 'How long can you be minding that child on a bus and how long can that child remain on a bus?'

'It's none of my business, Dolores – that's for his mother to decide.'

'Can't you see what I'm trying to say, boy? Here's Assumpta on her own and there's a lad on a bus – do you see what I mean? Well, put your cap on it, and when you come back from the opera house above, you might see we've a solution under our noses.'

With that she beeped the horn and swung into the yard. Marlo watched her as she eased herself out of the tiny car and walked up the steps into the house, giving him a thumbs up before stepping in through the kitchen door.

Marlo followed Sully up the slope. 'Hang on there, champ, give me a minute to catch up.' He lifted Sully onto the fence and showed the boy where Stevie liked to be scratched. The child stood on the rungs of the fence and traced the animal's features, his fingers lingering around his unseeing eyes.

A little while later, as Sully threw sticks for the two dogs in turn, Marlo thought about Dolores and the deep well of kindness that was in her; and yet the woman's reputation had for decades now been wrapped in notoriety because she had near drowned a priest for trying it on with her.

According to Assumpta, it was the Angelus that saved him from death. 'Dolores let him go when she heard the bells ring. It's why she won't ever pass the grotto without stopping, Marlo. She believes Our Lady saved her from being a murderess.'

He mulled over what Dolores had said at Assumpta's gate,

wondering what Kitty would make of it. He watched the little boy put every ounce of his strength into throwing sticks as far as he could for the dogs. Sully had a stubborn determination that was admirable, and instead of frustration his lack of speech translated into fluid and exquisite expression on paper. His quiet tenaciousness was so extraordinary that Marlo found it hard to believe how very young he was.

He called out, 'We've one thing left to do, Sully.'

A minute later, they stood beside each other and took turns banging on Crow's enamel plate, scanning the valley to see if he would appear.

Marlo bent down and pointed out a distant black speck to Sully. 'There he is! Wait here now, Sully, and you can watch him fly towards us while I get a bit of fruit for him from the kitchen.

Crow was flapping on the windowsill, wary of the child, when Marlo returned with a banana. Then, loud throaty chirrups erupted as Sully peeled the fruit and broke it into pieces on the plate.

'Now steady as you go, Sully, just put it down – slide it along there on the windowsill and we'll stand back now and watch him eat. He's hungry, isn't he?'

Sully wouldn't take his eye off the bird and a few minutes later he ran after the crow, towards the fence around the yard, to watch it fly away, looping in ever-decreasing circles down to the trees at bottom of the valley.

Marlo patted Sully on his head. 'You'll see him again, champ. He knows you now – so he'll be happy to see you too. Next time we'll give him something different.'

Meanwhile, the dogs had wandered down to the river and were barking at something on the far side. Marlo squinted to see what had got them going.

'I can't see a thing, can you, Sully?'

When Marlo turned around, the little boy was also looking in the same direction, his arm raised, waving.

'Oh, I see, it's your friend! Let me call the dogs back up in that case.'

The dogs returned on the first whistle, Spot panting with the exertion of having run straight uphill while his mother zig-zagged up at her own pace. Marlo took Sully's hand. 'Come on, champ, time for us men to head back and see what the women are plotting.'

When he walked into the kitchen the three women stopped talking immediately, heads turning in near unison to look at him and then back at each other.

Marlo grinned. 'I have a feeling you were discussing me.' He pulled out one of the spindlebacked dining-table chairs and sat down. 'And I have a feeling my feeling was right.'

'We were comparing notes, you know,' said Kitty, getting up. She took Sully to the sink, and hitching him on her hip, she leaned over so he could wash his hands. When he had washed them twice over on her insistence, she sat back down again with him on her lap.

Assumpta leaned across the table and gathered the tea pot and empty mugs towards her. 'It wasn't all bad, you can rest easy, Marlo.'

Dolores stretched out her long legs and drummed her fingers on the table casually. 'We just agreed that you were a quare enough fellow, you know, a bit soft in the head given the carry-on with the bullock and the crow.'

'Would you ever look at your face, Marlo.' Kitty was laughing. 'So serious.'

'Jesus, would you blame me? It's like walking into a witch's coven,' he said, shaking his head. 'Sully, what do you think? Look at the three of them, around the table, cooking they say, but it looks more like they're plotting. We are going to be turned from two princes into frogs.' He croaked loudly and leaned forward, making his fingers hop across the table to the little boy.

Dolores patted him on his arm. 'Did your ears not burn up,

boy? It was full of praise we were. Never known a blow-in to settle in so fast.'

Assumpta was indignant. 'Go away out of that! His mother and father left but now he's back – sure that doesn't count as a blow-in.'

Dolores nodded sagely. 'True, true. I take me words back. There are people who've been here longer than the Hag of Beara and you couldn't rely on them.'

Marlo crossed his arms and leaned back into his chair. 'Keep going, please don't stop. I could wallow here in the praise for ever. Would you just give me a cert to show Mam and Mary?'

'Have you been talking to your mam?' Assumpta asked. She had got up and was taking out the plates.

'Let me do that, Assumpta, you keep sitting there,' said Kitty.

Assumpta turned to Dolores. 'You'll stay to eat, like you said? I've made enough to go around. It's the beef that you and Mossie always liked so much.'

'Oh, I came here with that very intention, Assumpta.'

Assumpta turned to Marlo. 'So, have you spoken to your mam recently?'

Dolores got in before he could reply. 'Garda Jim caught a lad from Adrigole taking a piss in that phone booth last night, would you believe it. Not outside, but fecking in it. Gave him a tongue lashing, then booked him.'

Kitty pulled a face. 'I heard it was that young Burke fella. Needs more than that to control the likes of him.'

Dolores cracked her knuckles. 'I'd knock plenty of sense into him if they give me a go.'

'Marlo, you haven't answered. Your mam, is she well?'

Marlo nodded. 'She's grand. Busy with the bingo, three times a week now because she won thirty pounds with a full house on her card last month. She's convinced she's going to be lucky again, the big monthly jackpot is five hundred pounds she said.'

'And Mary?

'I think she's seeing someone.'

Assumpta looked at him, her surprise barely concealed.

Now why in God's name did I volunteer that. I deserve everything that's coming.

Assumpta stood up. 'I have always wondered why she never married. It's not like your mam needed minding. Mary must be in her forties now, am I right?'

'People have their reasons,' said Dolores. 'And they have reasons not to give their reasons.'

Marlo caught Kitty's eye again before he spoke. 'It's a long story, but she has someone now and I think she really likes him.'

'Who is it?'

'Oh, it's somebody she's known, and I've known too, for a long time but I think he only plucked up the courage to ask her recently.'

'They must be both well past their prime like.'

Marlo faced the barrage as best as he could, aware that Kitty could barely hide her grin as she nuzzled her son in the neck.

'Better late than never,' said Dolores.

Assumpta wasn't giving up. 'Is it someone she met at her Pakistani doctor's surgery? A foreign sort?'

'No, he's someone she went to school with but never really had much to do with him since. He lived with his parents down the road, the other end of the main street from us. His father ran the funeral parlour there.'

Assumpta's eyebrows shot up. 'A funeral parlour in Croydon?'

Dolores began to flick imaginary notes through her fingers 'There's money there, so.'

Kitty fled to the toilet. 'I think Sully needs to go. I won't be a minute.'

Marlo conceded defeat and there was no holding him back. In for a penny, in for a pound. 'They lived in a large flat above the premises.'

Dolores nodded. 'The father must've had a good head for

business. No trade was ever missed living over the premises.'

Assumpta wasn't satisfied yet. 'He must be Irish?'

'Yes. And they did all the Irish funerals.'

'Your father's too?' Assumpta crossed herself quickly. 'God rest and keep him, the poor man.'

'Yes. Mam said they took a lot of trouble and had him looking better than he ever did.'

Dolores leaned towards Marlo. 'I'm not surprised. The English wouldn't have a fecking clue how to give the dead a proper send-off. You know, a wake that people would talk about for years, a solemn removal and everything else that goes with it, like.'

'A decent wake is the makings of a person,' said Assumpta.

Dolores laughed. 'After they're dead?'

'Sure, when else could a wake happen like? It puts a signature under someone's life, doesn't it?'

Dolores was apologetic. 'Too right you are, Assumpta. That was a legendary wake that we gave Mossie. A whole day and night in it. The valley won't see the likes of it in a long while.'

Kitty had come back into the kitchen. 'Uncle Mossie was so loved; he couldn't have had anything less.'

A huge big sob choked Assumpta. 'He was loved and he is still loved.'

'Oh, Assumpta, I didn't mean to upset you,' said Kitty, her hand on the older woman's shoulder.

'But you were exactly right there, Kitty. Don't mind me.' She wiped away the tears on her sleeve and then became business-like. 'Will the little fella eat with us, d'you think, or would you like to feed him ahead?'

'With us, Assumpta, if that's OK with you? I know Marlo has an early start and I wouldn't want to delay it for all of us.'

'We can stick your cycle in the boot, Kitty.' said Marlo. 'I'll drop you both back in my car.'

A few minutes later Dolores sliced the roast beef, and once

the gravy was poured there was little spoken for a while. But having caught a glimpse of Dolores's face, Marlo was quite certain he could hear the gears clicking in her head. He wasn't wrong, for she put down her knife and fork down before asking Kitty, 'How're you getting on with the home schooling?'

Kitty looked a bit taken aback but she had her mouth full and had time to think. 'I've a meeting with the community nurse. She said I must look into learning signing. To be honest, I don't think I can hold off any longer.' She took another mouthful, chewing thoughtfully, buying herself some time.

So, this is how you avoid saying things on impulse. You chew and make them wait.

Assumpta exchanged a fleeting look with Dolores before she spoke. 'Does he have to keep going on the bus every day?'

Kitty looked at her, surprised.

Assumpta was quick to explain herself. 'I don't mean that he's a problem on the bus, because he isn't. I was just wondering if it was the best thing for him?'

'I'd rather not discuss this, you know, right now like' said Kitty, looking pointedly at her son.

Sully was busy fashioning small mountains out of the mash and letting peas run down the buttery slopes. He seemed oblivious to the conversation around him.

But there was no stopping Assumpta, who lowered her voice, but carried on. 'What I was trying to say is – I could look after him. I could mind him at your house in the mornings when you head off – that way he won't have to be on the bus so early or on the bus at all.'

Dolores cleared her throat. 'You may not know this, Kitty, but Assumpta was a teacher, you know. She taught in Derrycreha, but had to stop when Thomas was born. You know what it was like in those days. Your boy will be in good hands, learning in the morning while you are at the Headley-Stokes'.'

Marlo felt sorry for Kitty – she had clearly been ambushed.

'I don't think it's something that Kitty can decide at the drop of a hat.'

Kitty took a sip of water before speaking. 'Actually, I think I can, Marlo.' She looked Assumpta in the eye. 'That's such a generous offer and I'd be a fool to say no, Assumpta. I just need to get my head around this, it's unexpected. I just need a little time to think over it?'

Marlo was taken aback at Kitty's receptive response. And yet it was exactly in keeping with her pragmatism.

Assumpta patted Kitty's hand. 'You take all the time you want, I'm not going anywhere, am I?'

Dolores had cleaned her plate, wiping up every last bit of gravy with a small piece of roast potato. She sat back, beaming. 'We didn't have to look far, the solution was under our noses.'

Kitty was subdued as they drove back to her house. She was sitting at the back, with Sully nearly asleep on her lap. Marlo looked over his shoulder. 'You don't have to do it, you know, if you're not comfortable.'

'I know it's the best immediate solution for him, for both of us, actually. But it did come a bit out of the blue, don't you think?'

'I think Dolores had something to do with it.'

'Dolores? Really?'

'Yeah, I think she was the one put the idea into Assumpta's head.'

'What do you make of it?'

'It makes a lot of sense, Kitty, she being a teacher and all. I know it's over twenty-five years since she was in a classroom but I don't think it's something you'd forget. I think I told you that Dolores bought all of Mossie's herd off her and now leases all the grazing from her as well. Plus, I'm driving the bus so she's really at a loose end with no one to mind except her own self and the two dogs. I think she's doing it as much for herself as she is for you, Kitty, so you never need to feel obligated.'

'We never talked about paying her, though – I couldn't let her do it for free.'

'Why don't you ask the Headley-Stokes for a raise?'

'D'you know, that's a good idea, Marlo. They are so kind, and they'd understand, especially if I said that it was to pay Assumpta.'

'Well, you won't know until you have asked them. Why don't you do a trial run – you know, let Assumpta spend time with Sully while you're there, in your house? It might just make it easier for Sully too.'

'Oh, I wouldn't just leave him without seeing if it would work between him and Assumpta. Bad enough that people think I abandoned him on the bus, you know.'

'You haven't cared about what other people have thought all this while so why go down that route now? The regulars on the bus and me, a good few others – Tiggy and Edward, Dolores, Mossie, everyone that matters, even Assumpta for all her abrasiveness – we all know the reasons.'

She nodded her head. 'That's true. I know I half said yes to her, but I'm going to have to think about it for the next few days. I'll give her a ring from the Headley-Stokes' when I have my mind made up – will you tell her that, Marlo?'

'I'll let her know when I'm taking the bus tomorrow.'

When they got to the house, Marlo lifted the sleeping child off Kitty's lap and, cradling Sully close in his arms, carried him into the house.

Kitty smiled. 'You know, he's very fond of you, Marlo, he can't say it, but I know. All those little drawings he does just for you – he never did any for Uncle Mossie.'

Marlo put him down on the bed gently and kissed him on his forehead. 'Sleep tight, champ. You're going to start a new adventure. And God help you since it's going to be with Assumpta.'

'She'll have to be ready for him as well, you know – he's not always as angelic as he looks.'

Marlo watched as Kitty pulled off his shoes and tucked him in. 'I wonder if my father, whoever he was, whether he might have wanted to come around to put me to bed.'

'Oh, Marlo, you can't do this to yourself with all the what ifs. And she will tell you. Most times silence is just a shield.'

'Maybe for her. It's a weapon as far as I'm concerned. There was so little point in Mary having opened up only to clam up when it came to the most important detail. And I do know I have to give her time, I know that. Just having a little rant here, if you don't mind.'

She laughed. 'Rant away. We can take it in turns.'

In the porch she gave him a hug. 'Thank you for bringing us home.' The two cats lifted their heads from their baskets under the trailing geraniums. Kitty picked up the smaller one. 'It was a lovely evening, Marlo, and to think I was anxious about what Assumpta'd be like.'

He lingered on the doorstep and then turned back to her. 'Putting the little fella to bed – we felt like a family, don't you think, just there for a moment?'

'You'll make a wonderful father, Marlo; I've seen the way you are with Sully.'

For a moment he didn't know how to respond. Was she trying to say the exact same thing he was trying to say to her – only he had sounded like a right eejit talking shite about families when what she needed to hear how he felt about her and her alone. *Feck, I made a right hames of it.*

It was just as well that the cat jumped out of her arms and slipped past him and out of the front door.

Kitty lunged after the cat. 'Ah no! I'm going to have to leave the window open for her or stay awake till she decides to come in. Neither of them a great choice, I'll admit.'

'Will she come back if you called? I can give you a hand.'

'Thanks, Marlo, but you carry on. I'll just leave this top window ajar, they both know the route in. I've placed that tall terracotta pot upside down on the windowsill just so they can reach up.'

He laughed. 'And you say that I spoil Stevie!' As he got into the car, he called out to her, 'Today was a good day.'

She waved back. 'And Sully will be ready for you bright and early tomorrow.'

CHAPTER FOURTEEN

Cloichin's Story, Glengarriff, 1603

There were times in those first few days, after my lord O'Sullivan had set off with twelve hundred or more souls – his loyal gallowglass, bonnachts, kern and able-bodied followers, on his hasty retreat to Leitrim, that I wished I had been born stone deaf as well, not just dumb. Exhausted after the desperate battle for the creaght, my father – who had been tasked with keeping Lady Ellen and her infant Dermot alive– sometimes could not muster enough strength to hold his hands close against my ears, and so I was forced to hear them, the screams that rent the cold air, terrifying death throes that carried through the leafless forest. Howling pleas were silenced by guttural cries, the sort that rose from deep within a man in the seconds before he wielded his weapon against a helpless body, bludgeoning, stabbing and decapitating mercilessly. It was a fearsome sound, heralding certain death with no mercy shown.

When we had first made our way to this well-concealed refuge, all had been eerily quiet. There was no trace in the air of the vicious battle for the creaght that had taken place only hours earlier, nor of the terrible horrors that were to come. Lady Ellen kept up with my father who slogged a few paces ahead in the snow, holding up his hand now and again, signalling her to stop, to stay still as he listened out. We trudged on for what seemed an eternity in the bitter cold, knowing full well that only moving would keep us from freezing to death. I walked for a while and then was lifted onto my father's broad shoulders, his hands firmly around my ankles, as he took us well off the usual tracks and paths, cutting instead through the boggiest and most dense sections of the forest.

When he saw Lady Ellen hesitate, he reassured her. 'Have no fear, my lady, the ground underfoot will hold the weight of a troop of horses – the bog pools are frozen solid, we'll be safe, and this will be quicker.'

When we finally arrived in Coomerkane, a low hanging full moon lit the snow-covered mountains that ringed the valley and the small lake shimmered, the ice-crusted reeds along its frozen shallow edges sparkling like clusters of magic wands.

My father pointed towards the cliffs outlined in the moonlight. 'Take heart, my lady, we're nearly there. It's the very spot your husband chose himself, many weeks ago. He trusted me and me alone to prepare it these past weeks.' He turned to her, shaking his head. 'When that cursed traitor Captain Tyrell abandoned us, the Devil take him, my lord O'Sullivan knew this day would come. So, he had me get it ready – we had many a summer adventure here as young lads, so it was only natural that he would remember this hidden place.'

Lady Ellen nodded her head. 'He thought of everything despite the heavy burden on his shoulders. Our Lady in Heaven keep and protect him.' She crossed herself and so did my father as he sat me down beside a large boulder and, putting his hand on my head, told me I wasn't to move. 'Not an inch because your life depends on it. All of our lives. So, I bid you not to wander off.'

I nodded and sat on my haunches, shivering uncontrollably as I watched him urge Lady Ellen to start climbing.

''Twill be best for you to crawl, and I'll follow right behind you, my lady. It isn't as hard as it looks and you'll thank me for it when you are up there, for 'tis dry as a bone.'

The baby Dermot hadn't uttered a sound since we had fled the camp and I looked at the bundle on her back and wondered if he had simply frozen to death like many dozens of children had when the weather turned against us so cruelly – their knees drawn up to their chests, fingers clenched into tight fists with mouths open, like life's breath had left them mid-scream. How could I ever forget? Never, never, not even in an eternity.

Lady Ellen hitched her robes and made her way slowly up towards the rocky ledge, the steep and narrow path treacherous with ice. My father was right behind, steadying and helping her back to her knees every few paces. She turned to look back at him several times, uncertain as to where she was meant to go, for it looked like she was heading straight into the stone face of the cliff, so well was the entrance hidden. Finally, when it looked like she could climb no further, my father crawled past her and pulled at a clump of scraw and an entire gorse bush hinged away from the mountain, revealing a narrow cleft. Lady Ellen nearly slipped again in shock. The rough door had been fashioned from living branches of gorse, growing out of the fissures in the rocks, that had been plashed and interlaced with sods so cleverly that it would have fooled the most clever of scouts. My father urged her in and then looked down to where I was waiting by the boulder. He put his finger to his lips and signalled to me that he was coming down, but I didn't wait. I raced towards him on my hands and knees, and a few minutes later he was able to grab me and push me past the gorse door, which he pulled back behind him, allowing it to hang back against the cliff. Holding me by my shoulders he turned me sideways. 'Go on now, child, through that gap, thank the merciful Lord, we are safe for now.'

I eased myself in, with my father right behind, grunting as he squeezed his large frame between the two walls of solid rock. I didn't quite realise then that we had for all purposes just disappeared into the bowels of the high mountain, into a narrow fissure that was more than fifty paces long, a secret chamber that would house us for a good few months.

The cave was entirely dark, and I stood there shivering, warm blood oozing from my badly scraped knees and palms. I felt Lady Ellen beside me and heard her robes rustle as she fell to her knees and began to pray. My father pushed me down on the ground beside her. 'Stay here beside my lady until I return.'

And all of a sudden he was gone. We could hear him move further and further away from us until his steps faded away entirely.

Lady Ellen searched for my hand. 'I am afraid too, but Gorrane has brought us to safety so we must trust him, as my husband bid me to. Is that blood on your palms, child? Here, take the hem of my robe and wipe it away.'

I did as I was told, even though the ragged hem was stiff with dirt and so rough it hurt me twice over. But I forgot all about the painful stinging when I heard her gasp. 'Your father brings us a light.'

Never was the rank smell of a tallow candle as welcome. The flame flickered, as my father walked towards us, his own shadow stretched out and looming over the sheer rocky walls that encased us. He beckoned silently for us to follow him, and we did, deeper into the cave till it widened a little into a tiny chamber.

'We'll have the comfort of the candle for but a short while, for there's no telling how long we'll have need to be here, my lady,' he said, turning round to her.

In one corner, a pile of sheepskins lined the floor and, pointing to the child, he said, 'Allow me, my lady.' Then he undid the binding that held the little boy close to his mother and laid him on the sheepskins. In the candlelight we could see that his lips had gone blue, and my father rubbed his hands together, before vigorously massaging the child from head to toe. The boy finally whimpered, and Lady Ellen gathered him up in her arms swaddling him again and then sat down with her back towards us and began to nurse him.

I followed my father a little further into the cave where he put down the tallow candle and held me close for a moment, before laying me down on a thick bed of well-dried bracken. 'This spot is for us,' he said, 'and I will be back with something that will please you.'

The shock of the soft dry bed made me reach out with my hands, searching for An Cearc, for I was certain the horse must be near. Surely this was the boolie where I bedded him down each night, where I slowly shuffled my way towards the heart of his animal warmth, where I lay my head on his chest, his hot breath blowing down my cold body. But no, it was my father's icy hand that I felt instead, handing me a piece of hard cheese and a sup of sour whey from the silver horn.

He shared the same with Lady Ellen, and when he returned it was with a small sheepskin that he threw over me. 'Just sleep now, child,' he said. 'We are safe for the moment.'

The candle was extinguished and he lay down beside me, groaning in exhaustion. A soft lullaby slowly filled the chamber as Lady Ellen hushed her baby, the very same one that my mother used to sing to me, soothing all the hurt I had endured during the day. I crawled towards my father, reaching for his chest, and as he held me close I cried myself to sleep, yearning for her and An Cearc, dreaming the saddest of dreams.

For the first three days my father wouldn't even approach the opening of the cave. Utter exhaustion meant that we just slept all the time, grateful for a dry and soft spot to lay our heads down. We woke only to eat small pieces of cheese and strips of dried beef that my father handed out to us with a small gulp of whey, sucking on a piece of cloth that he laid against rock that was damp from water seeping from some unseen source hundreds of feet above.

Lady Ellen was grateful each time. 'Thank you, Gorrane, my lord O'Sullivan chose you well to be my protector.'

The only other time we heard her was when she whispered a lullaby to Dermot. The child seemed weak and poorly, and though she fed him at her breast nearly all day long, he didn't seem to have the energy for more than a whimper. When the sun rose, we could see slivers of light dance at the opening of the cleft, but inside the cave we remained in darkness. My father would not allow a tallow to be lit except for a brief few minutes each day, when he headed to where the food was stored. On the third day he spent most of the day standing absolutely still behind the door that he had fashioned so cleverly. By midday, the blizzard had dissipated and a short while later he rushed back inside to us fairly agitated.

'Our people, they have fires lit in several places just like my lord O'Sullivan had ordered. I can see the smoke rise in several places in the forest and in the camps in the hills beyond. It's no wonder Wilmot and his men have stayed away. He must think my lord is still in the forest with his followers. Wilmot will not dare to make another incursion into the fastness as yet if he thinks we are waiting once again armed and ready. So many of his own perished at our hands when they raided the creaght – I killed close to twenty men with my own hands and mortally wounded just as many.'

In the dark we could hardly see my father's face, but I heard him console himself. 'Lord have mercy on my soul, they were my enemies and would have killed me given a chance.'

Lady Ellen clasped her hands and raised her eyes up. 'I pray to Our Blessed Lady that my husband has passed Gougane Barra, that he has found food and succour on the way. They left with no provisions, Gorrane. What use are those twenty thousand pieces of Spanish gold when there is nothing to be bought for love nor money?'

'An Cearc would have carried him safely, my lady. He has twenty warriors alongside, astride their own horses, and two hundred fighting men, men who want to live, just as he wishes to live another day to see you and the child. That desire alone will keep him alive.'

'Maybe Wilmot will not come at all,' said Lady Ellen.

I picked on the drying scabs on my knees and listened to my father tell Lady Ellen not to be deceived. 'No, my lady, we must remain here and be prepared for the worst. Wilmot and his men are just gathering themselves together. They will be back, and when he realises that his quarry has fled his anger will be beyond our comprehension. He will finish off anybody who remains in the forest.' On hearing this, she curled up into a ball, shuddering I knew not whether from cold or fear.

The fourth day came and we waited, listening, the dread growing with each passing hour.

Lady Ellen wrung her hands. 'What is the devil planning – I thought he would be back in the morning after he slaughtered our cattle.'

My father repeated his warnings from the day before. 'It's as I said, my lady. Wilmot's just licking his wounds. When they've gathered a few more men, arms and gunshot they will come back – but for the moment our campfires have succeeded well – have tricked them into waiting.'

She stared at the chink of light coming past the gorse door. 'My husband needn't have rushed – perhaps we could've gone with him.'

My father shook his head. 'Oh no, my lady, the chances of survival would have been very poor – there is little doubt you would have survived no more than a day or even that very night itself. I was with him the night we returned from the siege of the castle at Carriganass. The route home was treacherous in the summer, and in winter now would be fraught with danger at every step. There would be very little hope for the child and for you too for you, my lady, in this cursed weather, with the rivers swollen, the bogs like quicksand and Owen O'Sullivan's blackguards after our skins, wanting to prove their loyalty to the Crown, the traitorous bastards that they are. My lord wanted to buy time for you and the child – this here, for the moment is safety, believe me.'

She had her head in her hands as she nodded. 'I know, we spoke about every avenue of escape several times these past months in the forest. But how long will we survive, Gorrane – am I to ever see him again?'

She began to cry and that was when all propriety was lost. My father put his arms around her as she sobbed, and I watched as he held her close, stroking her cheek like I had seen him do with my mother sometimes. She stayed in his arms, and when her sobbing had subsided my father gently moved away and stood up.

'I have salted salmon and beef saved away the past few months, my lady. We have tallow candles and cheese. I gave my word to my lord, my foster brother, he who was my beloved childhood companion – I made him a solemn oath I would keep you alive and the child safe and I don't intend to break my promise.'

Later when darkness fell and Dermot was finally content in her arms, as we sat beside each other picking on a few hazelnuts, she turned to my father. 'Tell me about my husband when he was a child. It would give me great comfort to hear of it. He oft expressed a fondness for his childhood and wished his boys could have had the joys he had.'

I moved closer to her, leaning against her side, letting Dermot wrap his thin little fingers around mine like I used to with my own baby sister's. I remember how much she loved me and how she would smile and coo back when I pulled faces at her. Would she have been terrified that fateful day in Dursey or was she blessed, too young to know that as she dropped from the cliff, she was heading to her death? Dermot pulled my finger into his mouth and I let him chew it, his toothless gums squeaking as he did so. I was happy for this child to like me – it was a long while before he would know that I was dumb and call me Cloichin. As Dermot gnawed on my finger, I listened carefully to my father reminisce about his childhood with my lord O'Sullivan.

'My lady, I remember well our summers in Eyeries. For a while I was taller than him and stronger too. When I managed to get the better of him with the sword he wouldn't talk to me for a week and snuck away from lessons learning the languages and law. Instead, he begged my father to tutor him more in mastering every type of weapon – and that was the last time I ever beat him.'

My father smiled at the memory, polishing his drinking horn with the end of his linen shirt. 'I didn't mind as long as he continued to talk to me. The first time we were allowed on a cattle raid, we returned here to Coomerkane with our fathers – triumphant, blood pumping through our veins, we thought nothing would ever touch us, we were like the old Gods. We hid here for a lark and when the search parties thought we had been carried away ourselves or worse still drowned, we emerged and ungodly was the thrashing we got. They were good times, my lady, the years before his own father died and before his uncle claimed the leadership for himself.'

'That is a fine drinking horn you have, Gorrane. I see you mind it so carefully, a precious thing it is no doubt, worth more to you than the delicate silver that encases it.'

My father looked at the horn closely and kissed it tenderly. 'It's all I have left of Maeve. My wife gifted it to me on our wedding day. We drank our mead together from it and thought a life of happiness lay ahead.' He held it towards Lady Ellen. 'See, my lady, it has our names engraved, entwined with ivy. Yes, fidelity and loyalty – she was all of that and more, till the very end. And that wasn't all she brought with her – I was richer by twelve cows and twenty pieces of silver, and to think that now I consider myself lucky just to have my own head still on my shoulders. It was a marriage arranged by your husband, my lady.'

'May she rest in peace and the souls of your children too, Gorrane. Who were your wife's people?'

'She was an O'Driscoll, my lady, from Adrigole, and I loved her from the moment I set my eyes on her.' He looked at me, his voice trembled and then suddenly it was his turn to be tearful. 'I entrust my child to you, my lady, if something should happen to me.'

'Take you back those terrible words, Gorrane. There's not much I can do for him if something should happen to you – we will all perish without you.'

My father nodded, wiped his tears and straightened himself up. 'Forgive me. Nothing shall happen to me, my lady, I gave my word to my lord O'Sullivan.'

On the fifth day we began to hear sounds, faint at first – we could hear horses neighing and then louder shouts and cries and finally, the death throes of the unfortunates who had been left behind. 'Wilmot's fury will be unimaginable,' sighed my father. 'None will be spared.'

And he was right, for the English general's mood turned to fury and vengeance as he went from camp to camp unchallenged, only to realise that his quarry had escaped with a head start of four days. Days earlier he had ordered the slaughter of O'Sullivan Beare's creaght, and now he set his men upon the sick and maimed remains of my lord's kin – old or young, none were to survive.

That's when my father held his hand over my ears, trying to muffle the agonising sounds that drifted up towards us. 'Don't be too sorry,' he said. 'They are the lucky ones, my son. The Lord in Heaven has shown them His grace. It may be a terrible death, but it is mercifully quick.'

As the days wore on the cries got fewer and finally a deathly silence descended all around the forest.

It must have been more than a fortnight before my father made up his mind to venture out.

Lady Ellen was distraught. 'I beg you not to leave us, Gorrane. What if you should not return? What will become of us?'

'My lady, I must set forth to scout our surrounds, but I will not go further than the far side of the lake below, right here in Coomerkane.' When he pushed away the living gorse door on the cliff wall, a shaft of sunlight streamed in and we were drawn instantly to the warm light, taking in deep breaths of fresh air as we stood in its glow. But it was a momentary delight for the gorse fell back into place, and with that my father was gone.

Hours passed and Lady Ellen began to pace up and down in the dark with Dermot in her arms, rocking him to a crazed rhythm, her humming worming its way into my head, filling it with dread. I retreated further into the cave to my bed of bracken, so fearful of what would become of me if my father did not return. Lady Ellen was kind in fits and starts – when she remembered my presence –but most times she ignored me entirely, her attention devoted solely on the child.

I heard her approach, her voice trembling. 'Your father must have gone further than he said he would.'

She gasped as I suddenly stood up and rushed past her to wait at the gorse door, stiller than a heron, straining my ears, even closing my eyes in the vain hope I could hear better. I had guessed right; there was someone scrambling up the ledge, and a minute later to my utter relief my father lifted the door and stepped in. I flung myself against his legs, but he unpeeled me and without a word slumped to the floor.

'Not a single soul was spared. None.'

He did not speak any more than that for a few days, sitting by the wall unmoving, his legs drawn up to his chest, his head on his knees. When I got hungry myself, I brought out small bits of food for us, as he had done the days earlier. He allowed me to unsling his drinking horn from across his chest so I could fill it with the sour whey, offering the first sip to Lady Ellen as I had seen him do. What horrors had my father seen, more than what we had already witnessed, that could have broken him thus? We were never to know then, for he wouldn't speak of it despite Lady Ellen's gentle probing days later.

Then, one day when I woke, he was gone again. I crawled to the opening and squinted thorough the thorny branches of gorse, but there was nothing to be seen.

Lady Ellen whispered, 'Come back here, child, your father will return as he did before.'

I crawled back to her and heard the rustle of her clothes as she invited me into the crook of her arm. Her silken robe was in tatters and her cloak of wool smelled sour, the lingering odour of her milk and dribble from the baby, but she had made room for me and I shuffled in, my fingers reaching out to Dermot's, who was being cradled on her lap.

I tried then to remember the particular smells that wrapped around my mother, breathing in deeply in the hope that I might get even just a waft of her presence. Sometimes she had smelled of seaweed and salt, after hours of harvesting the green fronds at low tide. There were days in late summer she would have been sweetly fragrant, sticky all over from collecting honey, and then I followed her like a pup, for she would sometimes let me lick the nectar off her fingers. On cold evenings she smelled earthy – bent over the fire, her hair infused with a peaty aroma. There was also sweat and stink as she laboured at our births and stale odours as she worked to keep us alive – but her love and kindness crowned it all and kept her fragrant in my memory.

The baby's fingers closed around mine and he gurgled. I closed my eyes and remembered how An Cearc would snort softly when he saw me, his lips fluttering like as if he were speaking to me. I wondered how my four-legged friend was doing, how far he had gone with my lord O'Sullivan and whether his groom was being gentle, not leaving him to lie alone at night. Then, just as I was picturing him with his coat gleaming, prancing with his ears cocked and alert, the magnificent creature suddenly faded away in my mind's eye. I let the baby's fingers go as I sat upright, sensing that something terrible had happened to the stallion.

It was a few months later when my own life had left me, that I knew An Cearc had drowned near Ballingeary, his leg breaking as he tried to heave himself out of a quagmire of peat, in boggy ground by a waterfall. In the end, when no amount of effort could extricate him, it was my lord O'Sullivan who took a merciful spear to his heart. Now, as I tell you my story, it matters not, for he is beside me always, my beloved An Cearc, as much

my horse as he once was my lord's, by my side still, while my
business here is unfinished.

So it was that weeks passed, with no sight or sign of friend nor
foe. My father allowed a small fire to be lit, but only after night
fell, and never when the moon was out. He pointed to water that
seeped down the rocky walls in places. 'Smoke will find its way
up the same way water finds its way down'.

As the days began to stretch out a bit, he began to venture
out at dusk, waiting for the rain to turn heavy, in hopes that
it would cover any tracks. He would be gone sometimes for a
few hours, other times return almost immediately. Every time he
left; I stayed close to the opening, breathing in the fresh clean air
that came with the wind. Once when he wasn't there, Lady Ellen
lifted the curtain of gorse and scraw and stepped out onto the
ledge with the baby. I followed her and she held my hand and we
stood there awhile our faces turned to the sun till the baby's happy
cooing drove us back in. She looked guilty when my father
returned but knew that her secret was safe with dumb Cloichin.

Winter turned to spring and the days got longer and my
father became bolder. One day, unable to resist, I followed him
out, but when he turned around at the huge boulder and saw me
a few paces behind, he waited. 'Maybe it's time you came with
me, my son, you need to learn a few things should something
happen to me.'

I spent the next few weeks with him as he cautiously combed
the forest. He showed me how to move through the undergrowth undetected, where to cross the streams when rainwater
turned them into raging torrents and where to forage for roots
and leaves. He watched as I set traps the way he had showed me
to and caught small fish in baskets that he had woven from willow. We returned with rabbits and birds which we roasted over
the embers of a small fire that he would stamp out carefully
each morning before dawn broke.

The child had begun to gain strength and I was sometimes left to look after him while Lady Ellen rested and slept. I would play with him like I used to with my baby sister, the little games that my mother had taught me, which made him kick his feet and giggle in delight. Once as she watched me tickle his toes, she stroked my head. 'You poor wretch, Cloichin, you're but a babe yourself and yet what torment you have been through and what hell your eyes have seen. Who will tell your story?'

A few days later my father asked my lady if she wanted to bathe in the lake. 'I am certain the valley is deserted. Wilmot's soldiers have long withdrawn – perhaps they fight battles away from Beara altogether.'

She was shocked at the suggestion, but my father reassured her. 'I will keep a lookout, my lady. There is a place barely a few paces away from the big boulder below, hidden by the hazel grove where a small stream empties into the lake. You will be safe there.'

It was the first time she had ventured off the ledge outside the cave and she wept when we got to the big boulder. 'I never thought I would set foot below, Gorrane.'

We hurried to the hazel grove, and while my father kept a watch, she took a scoop of the softest sand on the banks of the stream and washed months of grease and grime off me and the baby. With the baby in her arms, she made an attempt to rinse the dirt off our ragged clothes in the crystal-clear waters, and when she thought she had done as much as she could, she sat the baby out on the sun-warmed stones beside me. 'I bid you keep a good hold on him. It's my turn now.'

I saw my father watch her from the corner of his eye as she stripped off her clothes and waded into the lake. She was no different from my mother, all skin and bone, her breasts weary from having to constantly feed her child. She went in neck deep first, then immersed herself completely, disappearing under the surface entirely a few times, before returning to the shore.

We were back safe in our hideout in the cliff when she unwrapped the corner of her cloak and shook out the sprigs of heather that she had plucked from around the boulder. She gathered them by their stems and took them carefully to the small altar that she had fashioned within days of our arriving in the cave. She had made a cross, tying together two thick sticks of holly, and placed it on a small flat rock that jutted out from the walls. Her green rosary beads carved from Connemara marble were draped across the wooden cross. Beside it on one side she had placed a relic of St Gobnait's given to her by her mother – a lock of the saint's own hair encased in a small silver locket shaped like a bee. On the other side, wrapped in a small velvet bag was a lock of her older son Donal's hair. He been sent away as hostage, at the age of five, to the court of the King of Spain to guarantee my lord O'Sullivan's loyalty to the Catholic King. Each day, she prayed for both her sons, the one she cradled and the one in a far and foreign land. Lady Ellen had also been marking the days with each sunrise, scratching out a line on the rock face, for each day as it passed.

'It will be Easter soon – Friar Felipe had told me it was to fall on the last day of March.' She counted out her marks on the wall. 'On the holy day, on the day of Christ's resurrection will come renewed hope for us – I am certain my prayers will not be in vain.'

It was a week later when my father, who had been skinning a rabbit, suddenly stood up and raced to the front of the cave where he stood very still, signalling us to be quiet.

'What do you hear, Gorrane?' said Lady Ellen, quite agitated.

'I could be wrong,' he said. 'But I thought I heard my brother's bird call. I am certain.'

Lady Ellen took in a deep breath. 'Could he have returned, could it even be possible?'

My father asked us to hush again as he listened carefully.

Once again, she asked, 'Do you hear soldiers?'

'No, my lady, not soldiers – but something tells me it is one of our own. Yes, I think it might be my own brother. That's the call we had for each other when we were young.'

I strained to listen but heard nothing. My father stepped cautiously onto the ledge and lay down on the ground so that he would not be seen immediately. And then I heard a long trilling call from him to which there was a distinct reply.

My father rushed back in and took Lady Ellen by the shoulders. 'My lady, I bid you not to step out for this may be a trap, so wait till you see me with your own eyes. Don't reveal yourself at the entrance. Don't let my son out until you see me with your own eyes.'

She nodded silently and grabbed my hand and we moved quickly into the darker recesses of the cave where we sat and waited. A few hours later, when we had given up all hope I heard a sound. It was my father at the entrance and behind him came his brother. I ran to my uncle and wrapped my arms around his legs. He had always been good to me, and with a cry of joy he lifted me up and threw me into the air and caught me and did that several times over until I was giddy.

'Your husband, my lord O'Sullivan, has sent word.' My father was looking at his brother.

Lady Ellen was calm. 'What has befallen him?'

My uncle immediately put me down on the ground and, remembering his place, knelt to the floor in front of her. 'My Lady Ellen, your husband reached the sanctuary of the O'Rourkes' in Leitrim, and he is safe. We were just thirty-five who survived. My lady, I have been entrusted to fetch you, to take you over the mountain to a safe harbour near Ardea, where a Spanish galleon is expected any day – at the behest of my lord, your husband. Our allies in Spain await your safe arrival. You and the child are to be away, with no time to lose.'

'But there were over a thousand who followed him out of this fastness in Glengarriff! And you say only thirty-five are with the O'Rourkes? Lord have mercy on the poor souls. And now you tell me I am to leave too? Where and how are we to travel? I have a child, how will we survive?' she said, holding Dermot to her breast.

'We have word that the ship will arrive soon, and you will be rowed out under the cover of darkness to board it. I have three men and two horses waiting above at Rossnagreena to escort us to a kinsman's boolie by the coast. I am to take you there immediately; we must make our way over the Caha mountain and down past Gortnabinny before dark.'

'And what of my faithful guardian? What is to become of your brother Gorrane and his child?'

'My lady, the passage is just for you and the infant. My lord sends Gorrane this bag of coins and prays that his foster brother will return home to Eyeries if and when it be safe. But the men and horses await, my lady, and it will take us an hour or more to reach them, for the climb is steep and the ground soft. We should leave right away.'

She took a tiny gold cross from around Dermot's neck and put it over mine and then kissed my father's hand. 'God be with you and your child.'

In a matter of minutes, they were gone and my father and myself found ourselves left on our own, with no purpose. He collapsed, sliding down along the rocky wall, his head in his hand. I wasn't sure if the sudden, unexpected departure was a relief to him or whether he was fearful, having been abandoned with no warning. I was full of questions that I could not ask so I lay down on the bracken and waited for him to tell me in his own time. I touched the velvet cord around my neck and rubbed my fingers over the small gold cross and wished my mother could have seen it.

He spoke as much to himself as to me, his tone gentle and consoling. 'Don't think badly of my lord O'Sullivan. I did what was asked of me – I swore allegiance many summers ago and I kept my word. What would we do in Spain, in a foreign land? It is in Beara that we belong, this is where we were born, and this is where we will die.' He shook the small bag of coins. 'We'll leave tomorrow, find our way home and make the best of what's left of Eyeries.'

From the deepest part of the cave he brought out all the stores of food to which he had been adding every day, never daring to dream that we might be able to leave someday. 'Eat up, my son, anything and as much as you want, for we will not be able to take more than what I can carry on my shoulders.' So, we sat opposite each other and laid into the food like beasts come out of hibernation. We laid down on the sheepskins that Lady Ellen had used and with bellies full we slept fitfully, waiting for a new dawn.

It was my father's guttural cry that woke me. Two men were at his throat and his legs kicked and flayed as they held him in a chokehold.

'We hear your brother was here and the lady has made her escape. To Spain no less.'

'They left you a bag of coins for your troubles, we see.'

'And what have we here? A drinking horn with enough silver to buy a horse or two.' With that the plaited leather lanyard was slashed and the horn ripped away from my father's side.

My father kicked out with all his strength and sent one of the men crashing into the wall near me. Then staggering to his hands and knees, he reached out to snatch the horn back. 'You cursed villains – that'll be the last thing you'll be taking off me.'

They laughed at him. 'And you can be true to your last word.'

With that, a raised axe severed my father's arm from his shoulder entirely and he swooned to the ground. They picked up the horn, pocketed the bag of coins and debated if they should spare me.

My father looked at me as his life drained away into a bloody pool. 'Bring my horn back for me, lad, that was your mother's.'

The two men were backing out towards the gorse door, now lying ripped away from the entrance. I ran towards them and as I lunged to grab the horn, I felt the cold metal come down between my shoulders. I staggered back towards my father but even as I died, I found myself rising up and shaking off my earthly remains. I followed them, oblivious of my strange new state, only wanting to do as my father had asked.

I watched as they argued over the coins before hiding the horn in the hollow of an oak tree in the meadow, afraid that they might be robbed of it themselves. Their evil must have followed them for I kept watch for days that turned to years, but they never did return, and the horn has remained in the tree that is now ancient, a silent guardian in the Big Meadow.

So there you have it, you know all of my wretched story now, from beginning to end, you know why I am still here wandering the forest with An Cearc, stalking the valleys and lingering here at the entrance to the narrow cleft. It seems an eternity has passed while I have waited to bring the horn back, to do my father's bidding as he lay dying. Of course, it's only bones that remain now, just a few of our bones, his and mine in a pile together, where I crawled to him and perished close by his side.

I could not utter a sound then, all those years ago, but now I am able to shout it out to you, I can tell you aloud that my wait is over – I have a friend who will carry it to me, do what I no longer can, bring back my father's silver horn. For I am merely an old soul – but Sully, he is a boy, every bit the boy I used to be.

CHAPTER FIFTEEN

Marlo had decided to hold off the news about Sully until a good few of the regulars were on the bus to save him from repeating his explanations. He also knew that once Mags had the story, he could leave it to her to give everyone the full scoop, each in their own turn as they boarded, embellishing it with details plucked from her imagination. So that Monday morning when he drove past Ellen's Rock, heading to Glengarriff without stopping at Kitty's gate, three of the regulars shouted out in unison, but not before Mags clutched her seat, a hundred yards from the house. 'You'd be wanting to start slowing down now. My breakfast could be on your dashboard like, if you brake suddenly at the child's gate.'

Her words were drowned out by Fionn and Connie who both whistled sharply to get Marlo's attention. Even the Hare Krishna stopped humming and opened his eyes.

But it was Bernard who stood up and leaned towards him. 'Hang on here now, Marlo boy, have you forgotten our young champ?'

Marlo looked over his shoulder. 'Sully won't be on the bus any more.'

There was consternation.

'I knew the social services would poke their nose in. They've taken him away, haven't they?'

'Shocking state of affairs if they did. I'd go straight to my TD.'

'No politician would want to be seen helping the likes of her, you know, his mother.'

'There's talk of the elections around the corner, they'll all be jumpy, like.'

'She could refuse her vote if they don't help.'

'Are ye thick? They wouldn't care about one vote.'

'That happened to a child in Adrigole, d'you not remember, Fionn? Taken away with hardly any notice.'

'Is he not well?' asked Bernard very loudly, trying to drown out all the other voices.

Marlo looked at him in the rear-view mirror and shook his head. By the time he pulled up by the Eccles Hotel to pick up Daragh Keohane, Marlo realised that he would have to give them a proper explanation with plenty of detail. As Daragh loaded his gear into the hold, Marlo stood up and they fell silent. He nearly wanted to laugh. If only Kitty could see the anxiety writ across their faces.

'Now relax, everyone, Sully hasn't been taken away and he isn't sick and nothing bad has happened. He's just being minded at home from now on.'

'Jesus, was the bus not good enough?'

'What kind of an eejit question is that? How could the bus ever have been good enough?'

'Yes, the child needs to go to school, not be minded on the bus.'

'Or at home.'

'Sure, don't we all know that?'

They hushed when Marlo spoke again. "Look, that's for his mother to decide and what she has decided is he's going to be minded and schooled at home. Our Mossie's Assumpta is going to be teaching him.'

Mags nodded ahead sagely. 'Oh yes, she was a teacher in her time. Was forced to give up work like so many of us when we had our children. The young ones today wouldn't believe the half of it – a real disgrace the way we were treated, turfed out of good jobs that we loved and shooed back to the hearth.'

Daragh slapped the side of the bus as he boarded and immediately pointed to the empty seat. 'Where's the young fella?'

All the voices rose up in unison and Marlo sat down, putting the bus into gear. *Here we go again, I'd best leave them at it.*

As he rounded the corner at Derrycreha, he thought about the weekend gone past. On the Friday when he had dropped

240

Sully off, Kitty seemed quite nervous. 'I know this is the right thing for him, Marlo, I know he couldn't be on that bus for ever. But it seems a huge step – you didn't already tell the regulars, did you?'

'I didn't, not until you're sure yourself. Look, don't overthink it, Kitty, just take it a day at a time.'

'Yes, that's what I've been telling myself. Assumpta will be here tomorrow afternoon she said, and then most of Sunday.' She watched as Sully picked up the cat who had wandered up to them. 'I really hope he likes her.'

Marlo turned to the boy. 'You'll be good to her, won't you, Sully – don't forget Assumpta said the tractor could be yours when you're big enough. Plus, she'll be much better at the lessons than your mam.'

Kitty smiled, nudging him on his shoulder. 'Oh, for God's sake, Marlo, don't be turning him against me already!'

He looked on as she knelt down on the gravel to coax the smaller cat out from under the fuchsia hedge. 'Do you fancy a drive out towards Gougane Barra tomorrow? We could be back before Assumpta arrives. It's to be cold but dry.'

'Oh no, Marlo, I need to give the house a really good clean in the morning before she comes. My mam will turn in her grave if Assumpta found a speck of dust.' She rolled her eyes. 'She literally would.'

He laughed. 'Don't forget to hoover behind the dresser.'

'Already did. While I was waiting for you both to arrive.'

So Gougane Barra had been put on hold and instead he had spent Saturday morning giving Dolores a hand repairing fencing along the river at her grazing by Pooleen Wood. He was shocked at the extent of the damage. 'Jesus, it must have been some flood that came down, Dolores.'

'I know, boy. It hadn't stopped raining all night but, still and all, that's some wreck the river made. But listen, my three heifers were in the field across on high ground, so I won't complain to no one.'

Marlo had unloaded the stakes and had dropped them off in intervals along one side of the field. 'It's pure mush, Dolores. These stakes are not going to hold steady for long, I reckon.'

She put both her hands on her hips. 'Yes, I think we best wind the sheep wire between the trees as well, it will take some of the pressure off the stakes. Here, be a good lad now and get us the bag of staples from the trailer. I thought I had it – but I don't. Me brain's been fried like, these last days.'

They worked together, holding and hammering the fencing posts, keeping them in line with the trees. Marlo got the feeling that Dolores was not quite herself – there was none of her usual banter and he saw her wince a couple of times as she lifted the heavy stakes.

'Are you in pain, Dolores?'

'Sure, it's nothing new, me back's been at me as usual.'

Marlo must have looked sceptical because she sighed. 'Sure, I may as well tell ye like, seeing as ye have a mother and a sister. It's a bit of women's problems, ye know.'

Marlo wasn't sure whether she wanted to divulge anything more, so he hammered away, the nails held in his mouth giving him an excuse to remain quiet.

She set a roll of sheep wire down on the ground beside him. 'They've asked me to go down to the Mercy in Cork for a couple of tests. Dr Feeley said he'd just like to be sure to be sure. A waste of time like! It's the animals I'm worried about not myself.'

He took the nails out of his mouth. 'For feck's sake, Dolores, I'll worry about the animals, and you get sorted at the hospital. Batty Mor will give a hand if I asked. He owes you after the incident with the digger. As do the Crowleys.'

'I don't want to be collecting my debts too soon, boy. And not all at once like.'

'Is that a nugget of wisdom you're throwing at me for free, Dolores?'

'Ye better believe it. In any case, Marlo boy, it's only for two days. It's all routine, nothing dramatic according to Dr Feeley. Now I'll know exactly how my heifers feel, I said to him. Ye know, when strangers go poking around in my nether regions. But he didn't laugh, which has me worried, like.'

'You can come up with me in the bus, Dolores, and I'll collect you when you're ready the next day.'

'Much obliged. I'll let ye know when I have the appointment letter.'

He nodded. 'Sure. It's no bother at all.'

'I wonder how Assumpta's getting on?'

Marlo laughed. 'Kitty was up to ninety, I can tell you that. I'm going to stay away this weekend. I don't want to intrude. It might look like I was checking up – on both of them.'

'Kitty was up to ninety? Come here, let me tell ye, Assumpta called to me after dinner last night. I thought she was there to ask me about my appointment with Dr Feeley but no, I think she was plain fecking nervous. Blathering on about how to teach the alphabet and spellings tests and numbers and telling me about copy books for handwriting and such. I shut her up fair quick, gave her a hot whiskey and told her to have an early night before I sent her off.

'I'm still surprised that she even volunteered.'

'She knows it's what Mossie would have wanted her to do, to be of help like he had. Lord have mercy on his soul, he was a good man and took his duty as Kitty's godfather very seriously. She means to honour his memory. Plus, she's staring loneliness in the face and, as she told me herself, it's an ugly sight.'

'Are you ever lonely Dolores?' *No, no, no! I can't take back that stupid question, can I?*

She kicked a few stones with her boots before she spoke. 'Every minute of every day, Marlo boy, every minute of every day. But I wouldn't exchange it for being any man's wife. It's a pity now I didn't have children because of that. I would've

243

been a good mother, ye know. A very good one, for sure.'

'I'm sorry, Dolores, I was out of order there.'

'Ahh now, boy, yer allowed to ask. Anybody that could coax a blind calf into thinking it's a dog is allowed to ask stupid questions.'

'I shouldn't have. I mean, I know what happened. I mean, with the priest. All those years ago. Jesus, I'm making it worse, aren't I?'

'Listen, boy, I learned never to be ashamed of my circumstances. Shame leads to secrets, the source of every unhappiness. Better to wear your story on the outside like an armour.' She slapped him on his back. 'Now don't feel bad – I got that off my chest too. So, have you any plans?'

'Well, I'm working tomorrow at the Headley-Stokes', it's only two weeks before their big party.'

'No, you eejit. I meant, what are your plans for Kitty? The whole valley's wondering when you are going to pop the question.'

'You've got to be taking the piss.'

'No.'

'You serious? The whole valley is waiting?'

'Yes.'

Marlo put down the hammer and started laughing. 'Like I'm the light entertainment? Why am I even surprised?'

'You haven't answered my question, boy.'

He held his thumb and forefinger a hair's-breadth from each other. 'I'm this close, Dolores, I'm this close. I just need to be sure she feels the same.'

'Ask and you shall receive sayeth the Lord.'

'Jesus, Dolores. What if she says no?'

'She'd be a fool.

'Mary said the same.' *But for all the wrong reasons.*

'Your sister Mary?'

'Yeah. Enda Crowley the fecker landed in Croydon and didn't

waste telling his Aunt Philomena who told my mam at bingo.'

'It's a small world.'

'I see you really want this to happen.'

'I'm ready to order me hat, like.'

'Why is everyone so anxious for us, for me?'

'Listen to me, boy, you know all the people who pointed a finger at her and cast her aside? All of them will feel so much better, their own consciences. I mean, if her story has a happy end. They won't have to bear the burden of having judged her, if they can be happy for her now. It's a good news story, you eejit – if only you'd cop on yourself.'

'Let me get my head around this, Dolores. You telling me that all the people who scorned her and Sully – I'm going to be their latter-day Redeemer?'

'Yes.'

'Jesus!'

'Yes, you'll need him. I can see that.'

Marlo started laughing. 'This has to be the craziest place in the whole world.'

'It's just Beara you know, it's just Beara.'

That was Saturday. Yesterday, when he arrived in Bocarnagh, Tiggy was clearing away Sunday brunch as he walked into the kitchen.

'Ah, Marlo! You just missed a very nice quiche, Kitty's spinach and ham no less, she'd put chunks of Milleen in it.'

Edward blew a chef's kiss towards the leftovers. 'And a lovely salad to go with it too.'

'Will you join us for coffee, Marlo? I'm going to brew a fresh pot right now. These lovely aromatic beans arrived on Friday, sent all the way from Kenya. Old friends of ours, we haven't seen them for years, but they send us coffee and we write them long letters telling them we miss them.'

Marlo pulled up a chair. 'Sounds like a fair exchange. I know

Mam loves if I write letters, she keeps them and reads them over again. But Mary, she's more modern, she prefers the phone.'

Tiggy floated around the kitchen, tidying away things, burying her nose briefly in a jug filled with pink roses, humming to herself as the coffee brewed.

'Edward sir, we might make a list of the jobs left before the family arrive. I don't want to leave anything to the very end, in case the weather turns. I'll put in a few hours today and will be available all of next Saturday and Sunday.'

'I was thinking the very same, Marlo. The children and grand-children arrive on Wednesday week. The rest of the guests on the following weekend, but of course they will stay at Casey's.'

Tiggy brought the coffee to the table and sat down. 'Put this on top of your list, Marlo, I want you please to check the radiators in all the rooms and bleed them, especially in the bedrooms. Kitty will sort the hot water-bottles during the week, we might need to buy new ones. Also, I'd like some wood stacked up inside the house please. On either side of both the stoves.'

'Boys love doing that – leave it to them, Tiggy.'

Tiggy smiled. 'I'd nearly forgotten! It makes our young grandsons think they're superheroes. There is a lot of walking back and forth, but it keeps them occupied for a little while each day. I told Kitty that she could bring Sully here for a play if she wanted, three of our grandsons are about the same age. We have two young teenagers as well, both girls, and then our eldest grandson Ben.'

Edward stirred his coffee. 'I'm looking forward to a full house; it's been a few years since we had all of them home together at the same time.'

'I'll clean out all the gutters today and sort the clothesline as well. Kitty said it was leaning heavily to one side. Would you like me to paint the gate to the estate, Edward sir?'

'If you have the time, yes, why don't you do that? And let me see, I need a hand bringing a few bottles up from the cellar.

I'm sure Tiggy will add to the list as she thinks of things. I'll take my coffee to the study – there's a good bit of unopened post to deal with.'

Tiggy laughed. 'There's never anything exciting in the post, Edward, just more bills.'

Marlo watched him leave. 'Are the sketches for the Garnish Island sculpture finalised?'

Tiggy became thoughtful. 'Hmm. I'm not quite sure. I've made suggestions, but Edward seems to be chopping and changing it around a good bit. Plus, he hasn't settled on a size, which is a major problem.'

'Oh, I thought he was nearly there.'

'The creative mind is a funny thing.' She put her cup down and sighed softly. 'He's just a little wired – he had a dream the other day that we wouldn't make it to our fiftieth anniversary. It threw him a bit.'

'That's hardly a dream, Tiggy ma'am. That's a nightmare and they're never ever to be believed.'

She looked at him, delighted. 'Marlo, that's pure genius. I'm actually going to tell Edward that. I'll be back in a minute.' With that she headed off, skirting the *Beara Belle*, her fingers trailing the rim of the ceramic yawl, flitting like an apparition across the expansive room. As he watched her through the open door of the kitchen and then past the sheet glass walls, he marvelled at how the waterside home still took his breath away each time he drove in.

When she came back, she looked a little tearful. Marlo looked away discreetly and then felt that he had to say something. 'Is everything OK, Tiggy ma'am?'

She dabbed her eyes. 'Oh, we just had a bit of a moment together, Marlo. Sometimes I wonder whether this fiftieth anniversary party was a good idea in the first place. When it's your twenty-fifth you are joyous, you're confident that you're only at the halfway mark. With the fiftieth – you don't quite know whether to be happy or fearful. I think that's what's bothering Edward.'

Marlo was quite shocked. 'I always thought you both were optimists.'

'You lose a little bit of it, it sort of fades away when you realise you no longer have that lifetime together left, the one you counted on always having.'

'Sounds like life boils down to sadness then.'

'But I forbid you to be put off, not before you've been as happy as us.' As Marlo washed his cup at the sink and placed it on the draining rack, she walked up to him and clutched his arm firmly. 'Be warned that Edward and I are such unashamed optimists for you.'

Marlo gave her a wide smile. 'Thank you, you both have been so good to me. But I better head off now, Tiggy ma'am, to check these rads. Did you say there was something that you wanted me to get down from the attic?'

'Oh yes,' said Tiggy. 'There's a box full of board games and puzzles – you'll find them on the left-hand side as you go up the ladder. And, Marlo, I would like the barbecue to be cleaned out too. Kitty and I have decided to have a hog roast on the day.'

'Oh, that should be great fun.'

'Dolores is going to supply the suckling pig and rod it for us.'

'No better woman.'

'And the butcher said he'd get us a small spit in advance.'

'John Bosco won't let you down. I'll sort out collecting it from him, Tiggy ma'am, when he has it.'

'Thank you, Marlo. If it rains, we'll place the spit just inside the shed door. Hopefully it won't absolutely lash!'

The rest of the morning at the Headley-Stokes' went by quickly and he went in to tell Tiggy he was done. 'I'll be off now, if there's anything else between now and next week, just let Kitty know. She'll tell Assumpta to pass the word on to me.'

'I'll do that, Marlo. Anything planned for the rest of the day?'

'I thought I'd drop in at Kitty's.'

'Two strong, smart women – it could go either way, you know.'

He nodded. 'I think Assumpta's on a mission.'

'She should be allowed to accomplish it then. They both need this to work, so they will. Leave them to it, Marlo.'

So he took Tiggy's advice and the weekend passed without seeing Kitty, and now Monday had arrived and here he was, back on the bus driving the regulars. He had glanced towards the empty seat at the front several times – it was strange to think that Sully would no longer be on the bus, his small nose pressed to the window, only the rhythm of his swinging legs giving away his mood for that moment.

When they arrived in Cork, Mags gave him a funny look as she got off. 'So, I won't have to take the lad to the toilet any more. It seems awful strange, Marlo. Would you be lonely now going back on your own?'

'It's in his best interest so I'm happy really.'

'I'll see about doing a collection for him, a goodbye present from all of us regulars. We could buy him something nice – a good set of paints and brushes even. I'll talk to the others tomorrow.'

Marlo left Cork city, on the return leg, with three passengers who kept him occupied nearly all the way. Two young Mormons, in ill-fitting black suits with the narrowest of lapels and skinny black ties sat right behind him, asking probing questions about each village and town that they passed, one of them scribbling into a diary, while the other regurgitated what Marlo had said, slowly and precisely, in case anything was missed in the note taking. In the rear-view mirror, he could see the third passenger, a girl with a nose ring, chewing on gum vigorously, occasionally blowing huge pink bubbles that she sucked back skilfully. Both her wrists were tattooed in a barbed wire design and when she had handed him her fare, she had pulled her sleeve up and turned her wrist out to reveal a heart ensnared.

'Most people want to see the whole thing but are shy asking.'

When the Mormons got off at Skibbereen, handing him a bible as they stepped of the bus, she sauntered up to the front seat and sat down. 'Always feel sorry for the poor buggers,' she said. 'They're all over London, boys from Utah on their mission years, but people run at the sight of them.'

'Home for a while?'

'Yeah. What happened to the nice old man who drove this bus? You are new, aren't you?'

'He died suddenly. Had a heart attack.'

'The best ones go quickest.'

With that she stayed quiet till they got to Ballylickey.

'Thanks,' she said as she stepped off, her dirty duffle bag in tow.

'Can I ask you something?'

She raised her eyebrows.

Are you vegetarian?'

'Yes. Weird question, though.'

She rolled her eyes at the friendly honk as he drove off. He laughed. *I'm blaming you, Assumpta.*

As he drove into Glengarriff he remembered to stop off to buy some sausages from John Bosco.

'Throw in a few rashers as well, will you, JB,' he said. 'Crow loves his bacon.'

'All those animals know a soft touch when they see one. How's the bullock doing?' the butcher asked, as he weighed out the order. 'Come here to me, ladies, this man here's got himself a blind calf for a pet, d'you know that?' he said, looking at the women in the queue behind Marlo.

'I'd a blind lamb once, a pet I thought,' said one woman. 'But Daddy slaughtered him while I was at school and Mammy roasted a leg at Easter – I never cried so hard like.'

'And here's you planning to buy a pound of lamb cutlets – you didn't cry nearly hard enough!'

'Lord have mercy on her, but Mammy would have given me a right clather if I'd fussed about what she put on the table.'

As the two women hung onto each other's arms laughing, Marlo made his escape. 'I'll see you on the pitch Wednesday, John Bosco.'

His lobbed the plastic bags into the bus and then walked down to the phone booth outside the Garda station. Mary should be home by now he thought as he heard the phone ring. Mrs Kelly had a bad cough and she made sure that Marlo knew it was very bad. In fact, there was so much coughing that he held the phone away from his ears and waited, till she herself went quiet, wondering if he was still at the end of the line.

He took the opportunity before she started again. 'Mrs Kelly, you seem in a bad way.'

'Yes, Mary's going to take me to the surgery tomorrow, if I don't get better. I'll fetch her now and she can have a look at me again before she goes back.'

'Jesus, Mrs Kelly's got some cough,' said Mary. 'Did you hear her?'

'Of course I did. I'm not deaf, Mary.'

'Oh, don't get smart on me, Marlo. I'm just afraid she'll pass it on to Mam. Ray called in a few minutes ago, so I won't stay long. Mam's trying to get him to gossip about everybody who's died this past week.'

'Can't be half as interesting if they're dead.'

'God forgive me, but some of the stories – you'd be shocked!'

'So have you both decided where you're going on your holidays next week?'

'Oh, he has my heart broken, Marlo.'

'Christ, that was quick.'

'He suddenly has five funerals to arrange so he's not going to be taking as many days off after all. The young lad he has can't cope entirely on his own. He's very good at makeup but not much else. We've just five days instead of two weeks, isn't that so disappointing?'

'The dead can be so inconsiderate, yes.'

She paused and he knew he had annoyed her unnecessarily.

'Why d'you even ring, Marlo?'

'Mary, stop, I was only messing – go on now and tell me what are you planning with the five days in that case?'

'We were thinking of going to Blackpool and then Ray has this notion of taking the ferry across to Cork. What d'you think of us coming to Glengarriff? He has Blackpool sorted already – we are going to take the train up. He's being an absolute gent with separate bedrooms and everything.'

He laughed. 'Well, no fear of you getting pregnant then!'

She was quiet for so long that Marlo felt a rush of blood to his brain. 'You're not pregnant, are you, Mary?' He could hear her breathing. 'For God's sake say something, Mary. You're not pregnant, are you? It's bloody dangerous at your age, you know. I fecking hope he hasn't made you pregnant.'

'He did once.'

'What are you on about? You've only just started going out with him.'

'I had you, didn't I?'

'What's that got to do with him?'

She began to cry.

'Mary, stop with the tears.'

She sniffed loudly and took a deep breath. 'Ray's your father, Marlo.'

It was his turn to go completely silent.

'Don't be angry with me, Marlo,' she said, repeating herself again and again. 'You won't be, if you just let me tell you – just let me tell you what happened.'

He slowly slumped down the side of the phone booth. 'I can't even begin to get my head around what you're telling me, Mary.

I mean, I thought my father was a mystery but this – this is something else altogether. Does he know?'

'No'

'Jesus!'

'I couldn't tell him. I couldn't tell him because I couldn't bear to tell Mam.'

'Mary, you listen to me now. You need to start at the beginning or I'm not going to listen to any more of your half-truths and full lies. I'm fecking going to hang up now if you don't start at the beginning and finish where I want you to.'

'Yes, OK I will. But I never intended for you to find out this way, Marlo, I swear.'

'But I have.'

'Life came to a standstill for us the day Daddy was killed in that accident. Mam shut herself in her room howling, crying for hours, and when she did step out she never said a word, not to the line manager from the factory or to the policemen who came to tell us there would be a post-mortem. No, she just sat with her hands on her lap, her eyes closed with the rosary beads going decade after decade round and round, as our neighbours fussed around and tried to console us. She held my hand all right when I sat beside her but that was all. I wanted to shake her, to ask her if she had no feelings, we had both adored him after all. Then for the next few days the talk was not about Daddy, just his pension, the emergency pay and workplace compensation and where we were going to live and how we'd survive and whether we were going to return to Ireland. Not much talk about my father, the loving, kind man he was, no it was all about money.

'The man from the union came and that's all they spoke about, money and more money. I was sick of it. I had just turned fifteen, Marlo, and I didn't know it then as I do now, that Mam held it together that week only for my sake. She was determined that we wouldn't have to return to Ireland or to be left penniless or God forbid both.'

Mary stifled a big sob. 'They were so good to us, you know, Raymond's parents, when Daddy was brought back, a week later nearly, from the coroner's to their funeral home. They came themselves to collect us and walked us down the High Street into their front reception, where the lilies that Mam had asked for were waiting. They insisted on some tea first and sat quietly, allowing us to take hold of ourselves before letting us see him. I still remember Ray watching us through the window as we were shepherded in. It was he who brought the tea, leaving it down for his mother to pour. Then they showed us into the room where he was laid out . . . he looked alive, Marlo! I felt sick, d'you know what I mean? I was too scared to look at him again, and when Mam put her hand over his and wrapped her rosary around his rigid fingers, I thought she was going to ask me to help – oh, Marlo, I really couldn't bear the thought of touching him and I ran out.

'Raymond's mother was going to come after me but I think Mam stopped her. I heard her say to his parents – let her be, she needs time. It was only a little anteroom, Marlo, and oh Lord, I could feel the vomit rise up, so I pushed open a door that was ajar and found myself in a sluice room. I vomited into the huge sink in the corner and I was crying so much that when I felt arms go around me, I leaned back into them thinking it was Ray's mother consoling me. But no, it was him, Ray, holding me, telling me to cry as much as I wanted.

'I clung to him, shaking uncontrollably for a while and then – oh, Marlo, Lord forgive me, I don't even know how it happened – one minute he was hugging me, trying to console me and the next minute he wiped my face and we kissed – don't ask me what got into me, into both of us.'

A sob choked her as Marlo listened in disbelief.

'I've been so ashamed, ever since that day, so ashamed – Daddy in the coffin and me and Ray in the sluice room . . . oh, I've regretted it so much! Oh no, Marlo, I didn't mean that the way it came out, no I didn't. I didn't regret it, I didn't regret having you, Marlo. But can you see what I mean? Oh, God forgive me, I don't know, I can't even explain what went through our heads that day, two eejit teenagers. You see now why I could never tell Mam who your father was. How could I? Daddy was gone and I would have lost Mam as well.'

Mary burst out crying again. 'Are you there, Marlo, are you listening to me? I don't blame him, you know, I don't blame Ray, there was two of us in it, I don't know why we did it. Will you say something now? Will you please say something?'

All the while he had been sitting on his haunches, listening to her distressed monologue, Marlo thought of how every expectation of who his father might have been had been reduced to a monumental embarrassment, an unshareable story, not remotely nice, a hurried one-off encounter surrounded by embalming fluids.

'What can I say, Mary? I don't know what to say. Why didn't you tell him about me?'

'Don't you see, Marlo, if I had told him, I'd have to tell Mam, his parents – the absolute shame of it. But I was never ashamed of you, I loved you from the moment you were placed in my arms. I only wish I hadn't had to share you with Mam. But I was rightly punished for I had to step back, right back, and be just your sister in the eyes of everybody else, yours too.'

She blew her nose loudly. 'He wasn't a complete stranger, you know, Marlo; he wasn't just any boy. The week before Daddy died, he had come across the room to ask me to dance at the hop in the church hall and I thought he might have fancied me. But months later when Mam and I returned to Croydon after I had had you, I never wanted to see him or look him in the eye again. And I think he felt the same, we were so ashamed – the years passed and it was like those few minutes had never happened. Can you understand, Marlo? Sometimes you do things that you can't explain, even to yourself.'

She was sniffling constantly and then like as if she had completely forgotten the bombshell she had dropped on him, she carried on. 'Now it's like we're starting again as strangers, which is what we are, well, we were – till a few months ago. Did I tell you how it happened, Marlo? Ray came into the surgery for a consult, his back was at him, and you know how Dr Khan is – they got chatting and I had to go in and remind him that there were other patients waiting. Ray was behind the counter paying and he had the pen hovering over the cheque book for so long I thought he'd had a stroke. Then he blurted it out. I don't know still why he asked me out and heaven knows why I said I'd go but I did say yes, didn't I? And he's such a nice kind man. I think you'll like him. Will you say something now, Marlo? He wants to spend two days in Blackpool and then come to Ireland. He has it in his head, I don't know why. I mean, would you like if we came to Glengarriff?'

She waited for a long minute. 'Are you ever going to say anything – are you listening, Marlo? Oh Lord, I can hear Mrs Kelly coming. You're going to have to say something, Marlo, and if you aren't going to say anything now, ring me again when you are ready.'

A knock on the pane of glass made Marlo jump. It was John Bosco peering in. 'You OK there, boi?'

Marlo stood up and put the phone back on the hook. 'Yeah, yeah, JB, just my sister was having such a long rant about this, that and the other, an exhausting tale so I had to sit down to listen.' He stepped out of the phone booth and ran his fingers through his hair. 'Thanks, I'm fine, you know yourself how it can be.'

'Oh, you got the double dose, did you? From your mam and sister?'

'Two-in-one for sure. The combination is nearly going to drive me mental.'

'Well, come in with me for a drink like, sure there's nothing like a pint of the creamy stuff to soothe the soul.'

Casey's was quiet as a Monday in autumn would be and Marlo had hardly brought the pints to the table when John Bosco asked him about Sully. 'D'you know how they got on?'

Marlo stared at his pint. 'I let them at it over the weekend, but I'll call in to her after this pint. I didn't want to be nosy. Kitty sent word that he wouldn't be on the bus today, so I assume everything went OK over the weekend.'

John Bosco nodded. 'Good call. They need to work it out between themselves like, and when I say they, I mean the two women. The little lad will be no problem at all. I was hoping to get some time with him before I left, d'you know, as my remaining four weeks will fly by. Would you believe it now, boy, my mam wants me to bring Sully to our house. It's almost like Assumpta has given the whole valley the green light. Ridiculous, isn't it, they were all waiting to see who'd take the first step. And now my mam doesn't want to be outdone by Assumpta, not with her own grandson. She can't bear the notion that someone else might know her grandchild better than her. Oh no, that wouldn't do. I didn't have the heart to tell my mam that Kitty might not jump at the offer of sudden friendship, not after the way they treated her.'

'I would have said that too till recently, JB – but look how she agreed to let Assumpta help. She only has her son's best interests at heart ,you know. She won't say no to your mam – now, she may not jump at it, but she'll come around, I'm quite certain.'

'I could never understand my mam's attitude. She is the child's grandmother, after all. I tell you, boi, when I held him in my arms the day he was born, all I could think of was – this is my brother's flesh and blood.'

Flesh and blood! I was made flesh and blood in a funeral parlour.

Marlo drank deeply from his pint.

John Bosco carried on. 'And d'you know who's the happiest? My fecking father. He told me he was going to give the boy a lamb for a pet, would you believe it? Five years later he's going to give the child a lamb. Seriously, my mam had him on such a short leash these last five years and now he's beside himself, with sheer relief mainly. Sully can have his pick anyway – there's forty of them ewes in lamb in the grazing above the house. The ram had a field day.'

Marlo shrugged. 'Reconciling is a difficult act; I'd grab any solution if it was me. A little lamb seems the most Christian of offerings. Symbolic, d'you know.'

'You're in some mood, boi. I'll get us a next round,' said JB, and when he came back with the pints, he leaned on the table. 'To tell you the truth, I'm glad that I'm gone to Australia in a few weeks. It'll be baptism by fire for them, negotiating with Kitty, without me their convenient middleman. Oh, I'll make sure to ask her to be kind to my mam and da. The rest – they'll just have to figure it out on their fecking own. It will be strange being on the beach for Christmas. I can't wait to see herself, you know. Just can't wait.'

'You're both definitely coming back, though.'

'Yeah, why the doubt like? Don't be at me now – you're sounding like my mam! She fears I'll abandon Beara for Melbourne, that I'll be seduced by the weather. But my soul would shrivel away anywhere else. I couldn't stay away so you can count down to next Christmas. We'll be back.'

A while later, Marlo left Casey's and he hesitated for a good while by the phone booth. It was only when he saw Batty Mor in the distance that he stepped in and quickly put the coins in.

Mrs Kelly sounded peeved. 'You want to talk to her again? Well, she was out of sorts after the last time you called, didn't pay any attention to my coughing, she didn't. Her Ray just left – I heard them on the landing, I'll go fetch her now.'

Mary sounded breathless like as if she had run across the hall-way. 'Oh, thanks be to God you called me back, Marlo. I've been praying every minute since I spoke to you. I'm sorry, Marlo, so sorry. Will you forgive me? But you know I still can't say this to mam, I couldn't. I just couldn't. It was hard enough telling you. I know it was a wicked thing to do with Daddy not even in the ground. It was a wicked thing I did to you then, not telling you. It was a wicked thing I did to Ray. But look, I've told you now and my heart is much lighter for it. Are you going to say something, Marlo?'

'Christ's sake, Mary if you ever just stopped talking I would.'

She sniffed. 'I'll let you have your go at me, I deserve it.'

'I'm hardly going to do that, am I? What is the point anyway?'

'Would you mind if we, Ray and meself, came to Beara? I told him I would ask you and let him know in the morning.'

'Are you going to tell him, Mary?'

She started crying. 'Oh, Marlo, I just couldn't. Can't you see he would never forgive me!'

'I think he would. There was two of you in it as you said yourself.'

'I'm only just getting to know him, Marlo. I will, in my own time. I promise you.'

'Honestly, Mary, I couldn't live with a lie that huge, especially if he's going to mean something to you now.'

'I will, but not just yet. Ray has it in his head to meet you.'

'To meet your brat of a younger brother?'

'That's very cruel.'

He bit his lip. 'Yes, I suppose it was.' He sighed. 'So what day are you planning on taking the ferry?'

Her relief was palpable as they hung up a few minutes later but his brain was wrecked with the knowledge that Ray and Mary would be with him at the weekend. He drove to Kitty's house, his thoughts assaulting him in every direction.

She was delighted to see him. 'We missed you the last two days. Would you look and see who's here, Sully? It's Marlo.'

'Ah, Sully! I've a message for you, champ, from all the regulars on the bus – they send you their very best, everybody misses you and it's only day one.'

Sully looked at him briefly, his legs kicking, and turned his attention back to the television.

'Sorry, Marlo. Priorities, you know.'

Marlo laughed. 'He has them right. Nothing like a bit of television to remove you from reality.'

'Has something happened, Marlo?'

He debated whether to tell her and held off for a while. 'I was helping Dolores with fencing, and we got chatting. She told me that instead of being ashamed she wore her life story like a piece of armour, you know on the outside. Interesting approach, don't you think?'

'Yeah, I'm listening. Go ahead, Marlo, to wherever this is leading.'

'Mary and Ray are coming to Glengarriff.'

'Oh! Aren't you happy about that?'

'I suppose I am.'

'You don't sound the least bit enthusiastic, if you are. D'you think it's serious between them?'

'All signs point in that direction,' he said.

She smiled. 'He could be your stepfather, you mean?'

He looked at her for a long minute.

'Did I say the wrong thing?'

'Jesus, no, Kitty.' With that, it tumbled out, every last detail that Mary had revealed to him.

She sat there without a word and then took his hand across the kitchen table. 'Can you imagine what it was like for Mary, holding all that back, for all these years? It's a contradiction in itself, but helplessness is the most powerful of emotions, it can batter you senseless. I do feel for her, I really do.'

'I'm not exactly feeling terribly charitable towards Mary at this very moment. I was tired of curved balls and then a boomerang arrives.'

She raised an eyebrow. 'What's that supposed to mean?'

'I was looking for the truth and it came right back to slap me in the face.'

'Listen to me, Marlo, ask yourself what exactly you are feeling. You've no reason to be anything other than shocked, shocked that she had to go through all of that just to keep you.'

He looked at her. 'You mean, I'm making this about myself.'

'No, what I'm saying is, anger just makes you feel you might have control, but you can't actually change a thing. Marlo, it's going to be sink or swim.'

'I'm not allowed to wallow for a while?'

'You might drown, you see, and that would be a shame.' She got up and checked on the casserole in the oven and then called out to Sully to wash his hands. 'You'll stay for a bite?'

He nodded and watched as she readied Sully's lunch for the next day. *She has the measure of me. Christ, I love her so much.* He gripped the table to steady himself.

She cut the ham sandwich she'd made into quarters and wrapped it in cling film. 'That's Sully sorted; it'll save Assumpta the trouble. I've a mushroom pie for her and some soup.'

He suddenly remembered why he had driven to Kitty's in the first place. 'How did you get on with Assumpta?'

'Wasn't as difficult as I thought it would be. We skirted around each other at first on Saturday but by the afternoon she was telling me stories about my father and Mossie that I'd never heard before. And I never knew that she and my mother were related by marriage. So, it was grand really and Sully seems to like her. I saw her just observing him, you know; she wasn't all over him from day one which was good. Clever of her, really. And yesterday went off well too.'

The casserole was delicious, and they ate reminiscing about their childhoods and school friends. As he left, she gave him a hug. 'I think it's lovely Ray wants to meet you. He obviously likes Mary very much; must know how much you mean to her.'

The week flew by quickly and Marlo suddenly found himself drawn into housekeeping mode. He swept up the yard, raked away fallen leaves and gave the whole cottage a good hoover and wipe down. Spiders were the bane of Mary's life, and he didn't need the drama that would follow. Looking around the cottage he was struck at how sparse his home was and he decided, quite impulsively, to remedy the situation. He stopped off at Murnane's in Bantry and took his time picking new bed linen, towels and some cushions for the second-hand sofa that he had bought when he first arrived. He splurged on an electric blanket for the spare bed-room, remembering that Mary absolutely hated being cold, and at the last minute he added a blue-checked tablecloth for the kitchen table as well as door mats for inside the front and back doors. On Thursday, while waiting by the newsagents in Cork for two return passengers, he bought a mixed bouquet of flowers and stuck them in a milk jug and placed it on the kitchen table. *Look at me arranging flowers.* Is this what happens when your parents visit you for the first time? He repeated that to himself. *My parents.*

On Friday, Mags got onto the bus and waited till they left Bantry, till all the regulars had been collected, before taking out a gift-wrapped box. 'This is for the little lad from all of us.'

Nancy leaned forward in her seat. 'Tell him that we miss him, we really do.'

There was a burst of applause for Sully and Nuala burst into a few bars of 'He's a Jolly Good Fellow' as Mags pushed the gift under the seat that Sully normally sat at. Marlo breathed in deeply and thought of Mossie and how much he would have loved that moment.

That afternoon on the return he had a full load of visitors from Boston heading to Castletownbere – an extended family, two brothers and a sister, with their wives and husband and ten children between them, home for their father's eightieth birthday celebrations. They were in a raucous mood and sang near-ly all the way, stopping only to gasp at seascapes made slightly ethereal in the afternoon's soft rain. Hungry Hill's ribs of stone made them go completely silent and Marlo slowed down as he approached Adrigole, so they could see the iconic mountain in all its glory with the Mare's Tail rushing down, the wind whipping up the frothy white waterfall, swishing it from side to side.

He drove back home to Glengarriff in a thick fog that had descended out of the blue and resisted the temptation to stop at Kitty's. He had his eye on the clock in Assumpta's kitchen as he walked in with the cash box.

'There's a good bit in it, Assumpta, I had a full busload going back to Castletownbere today.'

She put the kettle on. 'Ah, I was wondering why you were running late. I've only just got back myself.'

'Oh, was Kitty working late?'

'No, she asked me to stay on and we had dinner together. Don't look at me like that, Marlo. I'm allowed to change my mind, amn't I?'

Marlo laughed. 'You are, and you have to tell me more but not this evening, Assumpta. My sister is coming this evening with her friend, you know, Ray.'

'Lord, where did the week go! Yes, Kitty reminded me that they were coming this evening all right. Raymond McCarthy, the name rang a bell the minute you first mentioned it. I was thinking about it all week and put two and two together only this afternoon. I think my father knew his grandfather, a coffin maker from Dunmanway. Funerals run in their veins, so your Mary's Ray – he didn't lick it off the floor.'

As he walked out of the door, she called after him. 'You might want to wear more than that sweatshirt before you go to collect them. Don't be making a show of your sister, like.'

'I've the tux rented,' he called out, grinning and giving her a thumbs up as she watched him from the window at her kitchen sink.

Half an hour later he was parked and waiting in the car park at Casey's, thinking about what Assumpta had said. All these months he'd been driving through, stopping and collecting passengers at Dunmanway and he never would have guessed he had relations there. He closed his eyes, leaned back and said it aloud. 'My father's people, my flesh and blood.' He jumped at a sharp honk as Eamon O'Reilly swept into the car park, turning his bus around in a dramatic circle.

He watched Mary standing in the bus chatting to Eamon before getting down, and Ray shaking the driver's hand before stepping off himself. His heart was beating fast as he got out of the car. *Hold your tongue now, boy, and don't ruin it for everyone.*

He found himself giving Mary a big hug and she held onto him for a long time, her face against his chest. He extricated himself gently. 'Would you ever let me go now, Mary?'

Ray held out his hand, a warm smile across his face. 'She hasn't spoken of anybody but you.'

Marlo shook his hand. 'I don't want to hear what she's told you about me and you mustn't believe any of it anyway.'

Ray laughed as he loaded their bags into the car and pulling the boot down, he walked around it. 'A Mk2, a very nice car you have, Marlo, very nice.'

Mary sat in the back seat and tapped Marlo on his shoulder. 'Ray loves his motors. He's been telling me about this car that he's going to get. Go on, tell him about it, Ray.'

Ray started laughing. 'Mary, it's a hearse I was talking about. I wouldn't be bragging about a hearse!'

'But why not? You did say it was the best hearse that money could buy.'

Ray shook his head, smiling, but Mary had moved on before he could say anything else. 'Come here now, that fellow Eamon O'Reilly, was very good to us on the bus. He pointed out all the sights on the way.'

'We aren't here for long enough this time,' said Ray. 'Not long enough to see it all. It's just Glengarriff this trip. I might have a few cousins left in Dunmanway, you know, the ones that never took the boat, but that's for another time.'

'That O'Reilly fellow knew nearly everybody in Croydon.'

'He's only back a few years, Mary, from living there. Said he was fed up with being abused for being Irish, so he left it all behind and started over again here. It was Mossie who suggested it to him and now I do the morning run and he does the evening – we work well together, even swap over sometimes if needed.'

On the way home, Marlo pointed out the entrance to the forest car park and then a mile or so later, stopped at Pooleen. They got down and walked up to the waterfall.

'It's a good day to see it, Mary, most days it's just a trickle and it's nothing special, but sometimes it's like today.'

Ray and Mary hung onto the fencing and followed Marlo up a rocky slope where they stood, looking down in wonder at a tiny gorge through which water thundered before flowing into a very large pool that had two small islands. The water was crystal clear and even from where they stood each stone and pebble could be seen clearly.

'I can see why you insisted we stop here, Marlo. It's some sight.'

'The shape of the pool changes constantly, Ray. Every time it rains, the force of the water shifts those pebble islands, making them smaller or bigger or sometimes leaving no islands at all. I come here with Kitty and Sully often. He loves playing on the island; we could spend a whole day here, you know.'

'It is so strange to see this place with my own eyes,' Mary continued. 'Daddy told me he learned to swim here. I remember him talking about an underground river. Marlo, you must show me the school they both went to.'

'That's at Youngfields, you could just walk across from the cottage.'

When they got to the house, Mary walked around curiously.

'Isn't it just as Mam described, Marlo? I must tell her you have it so nice, she'll be happy.' Then she collapsed into the armchair. 'Oh Lord, Marlo, make me a coffee, will you. I'm absolutely exhausted with the travel.'

Ray laughed. 'Speak for yourself, Mary, I think it's time for a drink.'

'I've a couple of cans in the fridge and some whiskey as well. Or d'you want to go down to Casey's?'

Mary was horrified. 'Oh no, I couldn't today, Marlo.'

Ray looked a little disappointed, but Mary wasn't for turning. 'Why don't you both go ahead? I'm just going to put my feet up and read my *Ireland's Own*. I picked it up at the airport and haven't had a chance to look at it as yet.'

'Oh no,' said Ray. 'Mary, I'm not going without you and anyway I'm sure you and Marlo have a lot to catch up on.'

'We do for sure.'

Mary went red and Marlo felt guilty. 'I'll light that fire now, Mary. I had it all set before I came to pick you up. We can eat whenever you want. Kitty gave me some dinner for us for this evening. I didn't want to subject you to my own cooking.'

'Did she know we were coming so?'

'Of course she did – around here everyone knows everything about everybody.'

'Where is the promised coffee?' she countered, rolling her eyes.

Marlo headed off to the kitchen and he could hear them chat.

'What do you think of him, Ray? Didn't I tell you he would be so nice?'

Marlo couldn't hear Ray's reply. *Maybe he had nodded a yes.*

He called out to Ray. 'How about yourself, Ray. Will I pour you a whiskey or will I get you a can?'

'Whiskey will do fine and I'll have it neat please.'

They sat down over their drinks and Mary filled him in with what was happening in Croydon. Mam and Mrs Kelly had become obsessed with the bingo. 'It's worse than when you left, Marlo. She is convinced she's going to win the big one and Mrs Kelly is no better – would you believe she keeps her biro, the one she uses at bingo, at her altar! I saw it the other day when I was in checking if her cough was any better. "What's the biro doing at the altar, Mrs Kelly?" I asked. "It's being blessed by Our Lady," she said. And when I told Mam about it, she promptly did the same. They're wasting their pensions away, the two of them.'

Ray laughed heartily. 'Mary, in all my years I never put anyone in a coffin that took their pension with them.'

'Oh, you just want her to like you, so you encourage her. Really, Ray, you do.'

'But it's the truth, Mary, there's no pockets in a shroud.'

'She could spend it on herself so. Bingo is just as good as frittering it away at the bookies.'

'But you enjoyed that day at the races.'

'I just wanted to wear a hat.'

'Marlo, you should have seen the hat. It turned heads, it did.'

'Go away out of that. I borrowed it, Marlo. Pauline two doors away was just after coming back from her daughter's wedding and she said it would look nice on me.'

They were like an old married couple and as Marlo listened he realised that he was actually happy, happy to see Mary's face lit up as never before. He had never seen her blush and as he watched her gently teasing Ray in return, it struck him that this in front of him was far more than the elusive longing he had been chasing. He hadn't just found out who his father was, but here they were, in his house, both his parents together.

I'm swimming, Kitty, and loving it.

He stood up. 'I need to go and put Stevie in the shed. I won't be too long.'

Ray laughed. 'We haven't heard the famous singing yet.'

'It won't be long. D'you both want to come out and see him?'

'I'm too tired but Ray's ready, I see.'

'There is a spare pair of boots by the back door when you want to come out, Ray. I'll just grab his feed in the meanwhile.' Marlo stepped out and called out to Stevie. The bullock let out a roar of delight and Marlo could hear Ray clapping as he stepped out and walked towards the field.

'That would wake the dead that would.'

'That's my problem, Ray. He's always so happy to see me, the poor creature. I can't stop him, he just loves the company.'

'Isn't that what life is all about in the end, it's nice to have company. I mean, look at us, Mary and me, it's so nice to have found each other.'

'Yes, she's spoken a lot about you over the phone.'

'You probably wonder why I waited so long. It took me a long time to pluck up the courage to ask her out. To be honest, for years I thought I was going to be alone. I mean, I was shocked when she agreed. I know I took my own time, but she agreed straightaway. She told me on the flight over to Cork that it was Dr Khan who told her not to change her mind. He told her his loneliest patients had every ailment possible and he didn't want her to end up like that.'

'Do you have brothers and sisters, Ray?'

'No, my mother couldn't have any more children after she had me.'

'It must have been hard for you to lose both of them at the same time.'

'I was probably just as old as you, Marlo, when they died. It was a priest, a good kind man, and many of my Irish neighbours checking up on me nearly every day that pulled me through. And you know what's strange, Marlo, I actually found solace in my work, giving people the sort of funerals for their loved ones that I would have wanted for my own parents. That's what kept me going. It was easy to cry a little every day, to let myself go for just a short minute or two at every funeral. People admired my empathy. I mean, I did tell them that I was remembering my own parents, but nobody would believe it. And the more I continued to cry at other people's funerals, the more they came to me. I can hardly cope with the business now. I have a young lad, and he's very good. But I think, you know, he's probably way too interested in makeup to be normal. But I like him, he's honest and he brings the dead alive.'

They were leaning over the fence now and Stevie had arched his neck for Marlo. Crow had flown up and was sitting waiting on the half door of the cowshed.

Ray cleared his throat. 'I know this might come a bit out of the blue, Marlo, especially since we've only just met. But I know how much you mean to Mary and how much your opinion matters.'

'Ray, her way was the only way when I was growing up and we still fight like cat and dog!'

'Oh, it does matter. I knew that fairly quickly.'

Marlo looked at Ray. All he could see was a very nice man who obviously loved Mary.

'I know that Mary doesn't have a father and if she had, I'd be asking him, but instead I wanted to tell you that I plan to ask Mary to marry me.'

This is getting utterly ridiculous. My father's asking me if he can marry my mother.

Marlo put his hand out. 'I am absolutely delighted for you both, she'll make you very happy, Ray. I just know she will.'

'Of course, I've asked Agnes before we left, and your mam was delighted. I just felt I needed to tell you as well, which is why I wanted to come to Glengarriff.'

Later on, when they had said goodnight, Mary paused at the bottom of the stairs. 'Ray, go on ahead, I'll be up in a minute.'

And she came back into the kitchen and gave Marlo a big hug.

'Thank you for being so kind to him, Marlo. What d'you think, he's nice, isn't he? Do you like him?'

'I'm relieved he isn't a complete bollocks.'

Mary's face fell. Marlo laughed as he grabbed her by the shoulders and looked into her face. 'Jesus, can't you see I was just messing? Mary, I never thought I'd say it this soon, but I really am happy for you and d'you know what, Mary, I'll say this as well – I'm very happy for myself too.'

When he woke up on Saturday morning, he was surprised he had slept so soundly. His head was roiled when he put it down on the pillow.

Mary was downstairs already making breakfast. 'There you are, Marlo.'

'You're up early.'

'I think it was that crow of yours that woke us up. Does he do that every morning?'

'Yes. Unfortunately he doesn't know the days of the week so he's here early on weekends as well. Did you give him anything, Mary?'

'Well, I did what you've been telling us. I put out some buttered bread on the windowsill.'

'You buttered the bread?'

'Don't you give him bacon and eggs, so what's wrong with buttering bread?'

He laughed. 'Did you sleep well, Mary?'

'I did, surprisingly well.'

'Is Ray up?'

'He's in the shower.'

'What've you planned for the day?'

'Mam asked me to call in to a few people and I will. I suppose I better start with Assumpta. There are two old school friends of hers that she wanted me to say hello to. D'you know Nan Murphy? And Dolores?'

'Oh yes, I know them both. Dolores is a good friend.'

'Perfect so.'

'Mary, I'm going to go for a run in the woods. We've a match coming up and John Bosco is after the whole team to get the fitness up. I'll let Assumpta know that you're going to call in. I normally take her dogs with me when I go for a run. Hers is the house at the bottom of the hill, the first one on the right.'

He collected the dogs and headed to the car park in the forest. The dogs headed off a few steps ahead of him, their noses to the ground, scampering between various scents that they got interested in and then abandoned in turn. They splashed in and out of the river undeterred by the current or the cold.

Marlo was surprised how quickly he had got fit over the last few weeks and he was glad John Bosco had insisted it was the only way they would win their next few matches. The footpath was quite slippery, treacherous with wet leaves, and he kept his head down, watching every step. It had rained overnight, and the river rushed past on its way to the sea. He could hear voices ahead as he approached the Big Meadow and when he turned the corner, he was delighted to see Kitty and John Bosco. Sully, who was just about to start climbing the big oak, stopped to pet the dogs who had run straight up to him.

John Bosco gave him a big wave. 'Look what we have here!'

'Following team instructions. Remember, you threatened to leave me on the bench if I didn't get fit.'

Kitty laughed. 'I'm very impressed, Marlo.'

John Bosco slapped Marlo on his back. 'I wanted to take the little fellow for a swim in the West Lodge but he kept putting the swimming gear back into the drawers. Kitty said we'd best stick to the usual walk here in the Big Meadow.'

'How's it going with Mary and Ray?' Kitty asked.

'He seems a really nice guy, Kitty. I'm glad for her, I really am. She'd love to meet you but they're only here till Sunday night.'

'Well, d'you want to bring them over? To my place?'

'I'll let you know. They want to do a few visits – my mam has given Mary instructions. And they want to go to Garnish Island.' He was watching Sully climb the big oak tree and sit in the crook of three huge trunks. 'You've got really high today, haven't you, champ? I haven't seen you climb that high before.'

'He keeps my blood pressure up.'

Sully was looking into a huge hollow in the tree.

'Watch it, champ! Don't fall into the hole and disappear now.'

'Look at him! He's at it again, putting things into that backpack. The last time he was up that tree he came home with every kind of insect in his hair and clothes plus bits and pieces of everything that you could think of.'

The three of them laughed and chatted for a while.

'I won't be home tomorrow morning, Marlo. Tiggy and I are planning a big cook and freeze for the guests, and I told her I was happy to come in for half a day on Sunday. She said I could bring Sully along, which is handy.'

'Yeah, I'm going to be there too. Suits me as Ray and Mary will head to Garnish in the morning. I think Edward needs a hand with a few bits and pieces and I have yet to paint the gate.'

He whistled for the dogs and waved to Sully as he headed off, but the child was busy zipping up his backpack and didn't look up.

It was late afternoon when they came back from their visits and Mary was full of news.

'Assumpta was very nice, Marlo, she even made Ray hot chocolate. We had soup and sandwiches after as well and she couldn't stop talking about her school days and about Mam and Mossie. She walked with us to Dolores. Jesus, how does she live in that very pink house?'

Ray winked at Marlo and then ducked as Mary tried to swat his shoulder. She carried on regardless. 'We went to Nan Murphy's after that and met Batty Mor on the road outside

Nan's house. Can you imagine, all of them that went to that little school that doesn't look like it could hold more than two dozen children. And today they all still live beside each other, isn't that just so wonderful? To know that your neighbours are the same ones that you went to school with forty or fifty years ago, all still living around you.'

Marlo looked out of the kitchen window. 'Would you like a walk up to Barley Lake? We still have plenty of daylight and it's really very beautiful.'

They walked the half mile up the mountain road that deteriorated steadily with every few feet in elevation. Mary was shocked. 'Dear God in Heaven, do they actually expect people to come up this road. The state of it!'

'Yes, but the council patch it up for the summer, Mary. Just watch your step now that we are at the top. It's hard to get out of this soup if you fall in.' They followed Marlo as he stepped from stone to stone. Water oozed out of the peat with every move they made, and they were out of breath by the time they crossed the boggy patch and clambered up onto a high rock. The spectacular vista of the placid lake below them, ringed by high mountains, was well worth the effort.

Ray pointed to the rocks. 'Must have been gouged out by a glacier.'

'Exactly, and there's no water sports allowed here because this is our water supply.'

'I had a drink of it this morning – the nicest tasting water I've ever had, didn't I say that to you, Ray?'

Mary was turning around on the rock slowly, taking in the panorama. She looked across the valley and pointed to a ridge in the distance. 'I just saw a car disappear straight into that mountain!'

'That's the first of the Turner tunnels, Mary – they were dug to give people famine relief. Many, many dozens died there, too weak to dig. I'll drive you up there. It's an absolutely

273

magnificent view. You can see the cottage, the lake, all of Bantry Bay and beyond. It's terrible the way the Sitka plantations have scarred the landscape though. Edward says it's an absolute ecological disaster.'

'What would that Englishman know?' said Mary. 'Daddy once took me and Mam on a tour of Parliament. The oak beams came from Cork and Limerick, did you know that?'

'Yes, I actually wrote about it for the *Montana Courier*.'

'How's that going for you?'

'Very well actually, Ray. They've asked me to do a longer piece for their Christmas annual. I'm going to use some of my photographs as well.'

'Where do you find the time to write?'

'Well, I'm done with the bus by late afternoon. I do have time.'

'He's going to write a book, you know, Ray. That's what he wants to do.'

'Mary, would you ever stop.'

'She's told me about that already. It's a wonderful thing. I love reading.'

'And what kind of books would you read?'

'Travel really. I wasn't able to travel, so I did it through books.'

Mary poked him in the ribs. 'We've started travelling, now haven't we, Ray?'

Ray smiled and put his arms around her, and she blushed. Marlo's heart was filled with such an unexpected sense of joy. He'd never seen Mary so happy, and it had all happened so quickly.

Just like it happened for me.

She must have read his mind, because she looked at him. 'So when are we going to see this Kitty?'

'I thought we might call in in the evening tomorrow, after you've come back from Garnish?'

They had started walking back down to the house, stopping every few hundred yards to admire the view again. As they walked around the last bend, he pointed out the various neighbours to them.

'That's Dolores there, the pink house you've already seen, directly above her is old Donal and across there, above the forestry on the other side of that mountain, is where the Crowleys live and then the Dutch are across the river – they're crazy about Stevie.'

'Are they very foreign like?'

'Why would you say something like that, Mary?'

'It was just a question, you know, have they taken into our ways?'

'I wonder if your English neighbours ask the same in Croydon.'

Mary was annoyed. 'You drive me mad sometimes.'

Ray was walking ahead, and he called out over his shoulders. 'He's just doing what little brothers do, Mary.'

Marlo saw her lower lip was trembling and he quietly squeezed her hand. They had a long road ahead, both of them.

Sunday turned out to be the perfect day for Garnish Island. After breakfast, Mary headed out to get ready and when Ray was sure that she was in the shower, he pulled out a little box from the inner pocket of his coat and opened it. It was a beautiful opal ring with a cluster of small blue sapphires around it.

'It was my mother's. D'you think she'd like it?'

'Ray, I hope you have the smelling salts in the other pocket because Mary is going to faint with delight. Of course she will. She'll love it.'

'She won't say no, will she?'

Marlo looked at him shocked. 'Why would she? What makes you think that?'

'Well, she's not young – I mean, I'm not young either. What I mean is, you know she's been alone for a long time and quite set in her ways. She might just prefer to carry on as we are. D'you know what I mean?'

'Ray, you won't know until you've asked her.' *Did I just say that?* Marlo smiled and shook Ray's hand. 'Ray, she's not going to say no and I wish you both the very best for the years ahead.'

'You're a good lad, Marlo, exactly like she said you were.'

An hour later, he dropped them off at the Blue Pool in Glengarriff to take the ferry across to the island. He shouted a reminder as he waved them off. 'Wait for me in Casey's when you come back.'

Driving down to Bocarnagh, all he could think of was the look of happy excitement on Ray's face.

At the Headley-Stokes', Kitty and Tiggy were busy in the kitchen. The worktop counters were full of chopped vegetables and trays of cooked food. Kitty was weighing out flour while Tiggy had the eggbeater going.

'Ah, Marlo, the coffee is brewing.'

'I am going to go ahead to paint the gates, Tiggy ma'am. I'll get the coffee after.'

He was putting on the final coat when there was a honk behind him. It was Dolores heading down to the house with the suckling pig that JB had slaughtered for her in the trailer. He stood aside to let her through.

'I'll be down there myself in a short while, I'm nearly done here with painting. Would you tell Kitty to get the coffee going again, Dolores?'

When he was done, he walked back to the house and met Edward coming off the jetty with Sully in tow.

'Hello, champ, did you have a good look about and was there any boat that you fancied particularly?'

Edward patted Sully on the head. 'We had a tour of the boathouse and he was a very good boy. We're going in now because I want to show him that boxful of puzzles that you took down for us the other day. I think that will keep him occupied for a good while. Come along now, little fellow, your mother might have something for you to eat first. But what's in the backpack, d'you want to take it off?'

Marlo laughed. 'That's Sully's famous backpack and he never goes anywhere without it. Isn't that right, Sully?' Marlo gave him a big wink and headed to the shed.

When he got back to the kitchen, Dolores was still chatting. 'I reckon you'll get some good crackling as long as you keep basting it well. Let me know if you need anything more before the big day but I must head off now. I've to be in Coomerkane in ten minutes, I told the O'Sullivan Bawns I'd be there by twelve to pay for the grazing I rent off them. I've seven cows there and I think your Stevie's mother is in calf again but, if she should have another blind one, by God, you know who I won't be telling.' She was looking directly at Marlo and everyone laughed as she left.

Tiggy called out to her. 'Dolores, come back – you've forgotten the money for the suckling pig.'

'Look at me, going off without the main business.'

'You sure you won't have some coffee before you go, just to keep you ticking till you get home?'

'I might do that at the O'Sullivans', once I get to Coomerkane. It smells really good here, Kitty. The visitors are going to be spoilt with a great old time.'

'Would you like to take some food with you, Dolores? Kitty can box up some of the carbonara for you.'

Dolores put her palms up and smiled as she walked out. 'None of that fancy stuff for me – I need my meat, mash and two veg to keep going with the work I do.'

'D'you need a hand reversing the trailer?'

'I'd do that with me eyes closed, Marlo boy.' She drove off with little fuss.

Tiggy took off her apron. 'Kitty, I've a few phone calls to make. I promise I'm not abandoning you; I'll be back.'

Kitty checked the ovens before turning to Marlo. 'I have coffee going here, Marlo, if you'd like some. I need to portion up this bolognaise and label the boxes for the freezer. Did you see Sully as you were coming in? I sent him to take off his wellies at the door. I was going to give him some soup before he headed to Edward's study. They were going to do puzzles apparently.'

'No, I didn't actually, I went straight to the shed to leave the paintbrushes.'

She walked to the kitchen door and gave a shout out. 'Sully, have you taken off your wellies and will you please come in now.'

He watched her for a few minutes as she bent over the counter, the tip of her tongue touching her lips as she carefully wrote out the labels.

'You're making me nervous, Marlo, watching me like that. Why don't you help yourself to some coffee.'

It's now or never, boy.

He walked up to her. 'You couldn't be as nervous as I am, Kitty.'

She looked up at him, smiling. 'And what could be making you nervous, Marlo? Not me surely?'

'Jesus, of course it's you. I mean, what I mean is – Kitty, will you marry me?'

She put her pen down. 'Of course I will marry you, you nervous eejit.'

He put his arms around her, and his heart was nearly ready to burst as they kissed. There was a cough at the other end of the kitchen. It was Tiggy. 'I think I've come at the wrong time but maybe it's the right time. I'm so delighted, so very delighted.'

'Kitty's just agreed to marry me.'

Tiggy clapped and called out to Edward. 'Would you come in here please, Edward, these two have some wonderful news for us.'

The phone was ringing, and they could hear Edward pick it up.

Tiggy rolled her eyes. 'We absolutely have to open a bottle of bubbly, but let's wait for Edward to come in first.'

Edward looked distracted as he walked in. 'Where's young Sully?'

'I sent him out to take his wellies off, when you came back from the boathouse. I wanted to give him some soup before you showed him the puzzles.'

'I just had a most peculiar phone call from Dolores to say that when she got to Coomerkane, his backpack was in her trailer.'

'He was here. I only sent him out to take off his wellies – he has to be around.'

Marlo saw the look of panic in her eyes. 'Let me go and check in case he walked back to the boathouse.'

'I'll check the toilets,' said Tiggy. 'Maybe he's just in there washing his hands.'

Edward had already hurried out and Marlo saw him turn left and head for the shoreline.

Kitty was standing frozen holding onto the kitchen counter. Marlo shook her by the shoulder.

'Kitty, check Edward's study, Sully might already be there playing with those puzzles.'

They fanned out looking for the little boy, calling out to him, but he was nowhere to be seen. Edward had come running back. 'He isn't in the shed or anywhere around The Lump. Tiggy, I want you to search down the walking trail. Marlo, give me a hand hitching the outboard motor on to the dinghy. I'll skirt around the shore and leave you to search the grounds. Kitty, look, we'll find him, he can't be far. But I want you to ring the Guards right away. The more hands we have the better.'

Kitty was trembling uncontrollably and Marlo was loth to leave her to make the call. They could hear Tiggy calling the child's name and as he followed Edward he looked back. 'Make that phone call, Kitty. Let's not lose time.'

She nodded and went into the house. By the time Edward

279

headed off in the dinghy, Kitty had run up the long driveway right to the freshly painted gate. She was crying as she walked back to the house, calling for Sully continuously.

'I may as well be dead, Marlo, if anything has happened to him. Marlo, where could he be? He's never done something like this. And why would he put his backpack in the sheep trailer?'

Tiggy appeared from the trail head behind The Lump. She was out of breath and distraught.

Marlo was filled with a rising sense of dread. 'Kitty, I don't think he is in Bocarnagh. I think we need to get in the car. I think he's gone to Coomerkane. He must have snuck into the trailer when Dolores told us she was going to Coomerkane – you had sent him to take off his wellies, so he was already at the door. There is no other reason his backpack would be found in the trailer. Tiggy ma'am, will you keep looking and stay here till the Guards come? Kitty and I will search in Coomerkane.'

Tiggy nodded. 'Yes, do what you have to. Edward and I will continue searching here.'

All the way in the car, Marlo held Kitty's hand as tightly as he could. It wouldn't stop trembling.

'What if he's fallen into the water in Bocarnagh? Maybe we should have checked the shed again and the boathouse too?'

'Edward and Tiggy are doing just that. Kitty, he wouldn't have wandered off on his own, not in Bocarnagh he wouldn't. He doesn't know it well enough.'

She was shaking now, her arms wrapped around herself as she wept. Marlo's mouth was dry as they pulled up at the O'Sullivans' farm.

Dolores was standing waiting. One look at Kitty and she realised what had happened. 'Sweet Jesus, ye think he might be here? See, I haven't a notion how this got in my trailer. I pulled up here, went in to pay Mrs O'Sullivan and when I came back, I just wanted to make sure the trailer door was shut. That's when the backpack got my eye. Right, let's get searching. Let me tell the O'Sullivans as well.'

They started calling out to Sully. Kitty ran down the laneway towards the grazing. 'He might be with the cows.'

Marlo called her back. 'Kitty, wait, something tells me he might have headed for the cliffs. I think I know exactly where he is. I have a feeling he's headed up to that cave we were at.'

She looked like her legs would give way under her. 'Marlo, he could be badly hurt if he's fallen trying to climb there. My poor child!'

'Let's not think the worst, Kitty. Come on, let's start looking.'

Dolores followed right behind. 'The O'Sullivans said they would start looking along the lakeshore – he might have seen the ducks swimming there. Why are we heading towards the cliffs? Has the little fellow been here before?'

'He's been here once with Kitty and me. I scrambled up one of those ledges and just poked my nose into a tiny cave up at that cleft, but he stayed well below with his mother. We said we'd bring him some other day. I just have a hunch he might have decided to see it for himself.'

They arrived at the bottom of the cliff and the three of them stood looking up, scanning the bare stone walls. There was no sight of the child.

Kitty called out to him. 'Please, Sully, please come back, please come back.'

Marlo had his eyes shaded, looking up as the sun bounced off the cliffs, blinding him as he did so. Dolores and Kitty set off on either side walking along the bottom off the cliff.

Dolores called out to them both. 'OK, I'm going to follow this stream here – he might have been attracted by the water.'

Marlo looked up once again, squinting, and his heart raced faster. He was quite certain he saw something moving; the curtain of ivy that covered the cleft seemed to sway slightly. Then suddenly they all heard a shout and then they heard it again.

Kitty ran back and grabbed Marlo's arm. 'Oh my God, Marlo, it's him and he just called out to me! Marlo, he spoke!'

Sully had emerged from behind the ivy, his little arm raised as he waved at them slowly. 'Mam!'

'Wait right there, Sully, don't move now, champ. I'll come up to you, so don't move.'

The boy stood on the ledge and waited as Marlo scrambled up, with Kitty right behind him.

Dolores called out to say she was running back to call the O'Sullivans for help.

Marlo got to the boy in a few minutes and when he was within touching distance he let Kitty go past and onto the narrow ledge. She scooped up her son in her arms and collapsed against the wall of the cliff.

She held him tight and wept. 'I thought I had lost you. I thought I had lost you, Sully.' He hugged her back and kicked his little legs as he clutched a little gold cross firmly in his hands.

CHAPTER SIXTEEN

Cloichin's Story, November 1986

My story comes to an end, for I have now what I waited for all eternity. The boy Sully brought my father's silver horn to me, from the hollow in the oak, just as I had asked. He placed it beside our remains, our bones which are now turned nearly to dust. It wasn't long before we heard voices calling us, but as he ran back towards the entrance of the cave, I held his hand, held him back and pressed my gold cross into his palms. Wait, I said to him, wait till they are closer, it is safer that way, they'll come for you. We stood by the ledge, looking down towards the forest and the world beyond.

I can hear both our mothers calling out to us, but my own mother's voice is the sweetest. She calls me by my name and when I turn to look back, I see my baby sister, her little fingers reaching out for mine, she remembers me still! An Cearc gets impatient beside me, shaking his glossy mane as he prances; he knows it's time. And yes, there is my father! I can hear his call, he is the cuckoo in winter – he calls me, asks me to return and so I will.

Now it is the boy Sully's turn to tell you my story. He will say my name, he will tell you that I too was once Sully, Sullivan McSwiney.

HISTORICAL NOTE

The Long March of O'Sullivan Beare

After the Battle of Kinsale in January 1602, Donal Cam O'Sullivan Beare, renowned as the last great Irish Chieftain of West Cork and South Kerry, found himself besieged in Beara by Elizabethan forces. In June 1602, he lost his stronghold at Dunboy Castle, and a few days later many of his followers and kinsfolk were massacred on Dursey Island by English troops.

In the aftermath of that defeat, O'Sullivan Beare and his remaining people withdrew to the impenetrable fastness of Glengarriff Forest where they managed to remain hidden in the cover provided by the dense oak woods. They relied entirely on their herd of cattle and sheep, the 'creaght', to keep them fed and, as winter approached, this dependence was even more pronounced.

On 31 December 1602, the English army, led by General Sir Charles Wilmot, located the hidden creaght and slaughtered every animal. The fields ran with rivers of blood and to this day that townland is called Derrynafulla – oak field of blood.

O'Sullivan Beare knew that his people were faced with almost certain starvation and within hours of losing the creaght, he had given orders for all his soldiers and able-bodied followers to leave the forest, to flee north to Leitrim where he knew the O'Rourkes would give him sanctuary.

Knowing they wouldn't survive the journey, he left behind his wife Lady Ellen and their infant son Dermot in Glengarriff, in safekeeping with a trusted kinsman. Not much is known about the man who was entrusted with O'Sullivan Beare's family or how he helped them survive, though legend insists his name was Gorrane McSwiney.

Some 1300 men women and children, including 400 soldiers, set off on an epic march fighting their way through over three hundred miles (500km) of treacherous country,

ACKNOWLEDGEMENTS

This story about families, friends and communities could not have been written without the help of my family, neighbours, close friends and the supportive communities that I belong to.

To my wonderful neighbours in Beara: Mary and Micheal O'Sullivan and Donal Deasey - I'm so grateful for all the help and invaluable advice over many years as I researched and wrote the novel. Gesine Pelke-Bastian, Ida Corry and Ethel Crowley thank you for reading the draft and reassuring me when I needed it most. A big thank you to Kate and Marnie from Bantry Book Shop who sourced books, encouraging me at every step. Love and thanks to my dear friend and mentor Sue Booth Forbes. I continue to bask in the belief that Rosemarie Hudson has shown in my writing. Thank you Sue Cook for your careful read of the manuscript and making the editing process so painless.

I would like to thank Felicity Hayes-McCoy and Eimhin Liddy for their help with my many Irish language queries. The scaffold of my story was built on the work of many historians of Early Modern Ireland. Thank you Micheal G Hall and Jim O'Neill for generously sharing your research and expert knowledge about the history of the period of the Nine Year's War.

My neighbour Breda Mchale was my guide in all matters to do with the afterlife and the journey of souls, while Paula Fahy held my hand from start to finish. I am forever indebted to you both my dearest friends.

My family - my darling Prakash and my three precious children Sagari, Rohan and Maya and my mother Bollu, thank you for indulging my whims and always enabling my writing.

About HopeRoad Publishing

HopeRoad was founded in 2010 by Rosemarie Hudson, a publisher who's spent her life encouraging exciting new talent, mentoring and publishing new authors and bringing them to wider attention. Often hailed as a 'trailblazer', she's always promoted the best writing from and about Africa, Asia and the Caribbean. And it's thanks to her HopeRoad is known as the indie which loves to share untold stories around themes of identity, cultural stereotyping, disability and injustice.

Rosemarie was joined in her venture by Pete Ayrton, founder of the hugely respected independent publisher Serpent's Tail. Pete heads up HopeRoad's imprint, Small Axes, which republishes out of print post-colonial classics – books which shaped cultural shifts at the time they were first in print, and remain as relevant today.

HopeRoad recently joined forces with Peepal Tree Press. Working together they will make a significant contribution to the diversity of independent publishing in the UK, giving voice to the underrepresented. Both share a long-term commitment to literary values that is not dictated by fashion, as well as a compatible ethos, backlists and complementary publishing identities.

By reading, buying or borrowing this book you're helping to support authors at a time when their ideas are needed more than ever.

Keep up to date with what's new through our newsletter at https://www.hoperoadpublishing.com/about, discover all HopeRoad and Small Axes titles at https://www.hoperoadpublishing.com/, and join the debate on social media at @hoperoadpublishing and @hoperoadpublish